PERFECT STRANGERS

J.T. GEISSINGER

This is a work of fiction. Names, characters, organizations, places, events, and incidents are either products of the author's imagination or are used fictitiously.

Published by J.T. Geissinger, Inc.

www.jtgeissinger.com

ISBN-13: 978-1-7338243-4-7

ISBN-10: 1-7338243-4-0

Cover design by Letitia Hasser

Printed in the United States of America

For Jay, my perfect stranger.

PART I

The world breaks everyone and afterward many are strong at the broken places. But those that will not break it kills.

~ Ernest Hemingway

1

The blonde is naked on her back on the mattress with her knees drawn up and her pale thighs parted, her hands clenched to fists in the sheets. Fully dressed and unmoving at the side of the bed, the man stands gazing down at her. At her nude body, young and lithe, taut with anticipation, offered for his inspection like a display of ripe fruit.

The man leans over and plants one hand on the bed beside the blonde's head.

The other hand he wraps around her throat.

"…getting along so far? How do you like the apartment?"

The gravelly voice in my ear is my literary agent, Estelle, whom I've known for years. She smokes two packs of Virginia Slims a day and has the same towering beehive hairdo she's worn since the sixties, though it's gunmetal gray now instead of shoe polish black. Not five feet tall in heels, all mouth and moxie, she's a tiny spitfire in vintage Chanel who'll bite off your head just as easily as she'll grant you a smile.

Most people find her terrifying, but I've got a soft spot for abrasive women.

I know only too well the kind of hits you have to take from life before you grow hard.

"The city is just as beautiful as you promised it would be, Estelle. And your apartment is"—The blonde arches as the man kisses her hard, hungrily, his hand sliding down from her throat to a full, pink-tipped breast—"amazing. The location is perfect."

How perfect? Top floor of an elegant ten-story building in a swanky residential area, one floor above and directly across a shaded courtyard from an attractive couple about to have sex.

They haven't bothered to close the curtains to their bedroom. Which means that from where I'm standing in Estelle's living room, I've got an unobstructed view.

Maybe that's part of it? The wicked thrill that they could be being watched by any of the neighbors?

Or maybe that's the whole point.

Estelle says, "That's great, doll! I'm so happy you like it." There's a loaded pause, then: "Hopefully the change of scenery will be inspiring."

Oh, it's inspiring all right, just not in the way she means.

The man pins the blonde's wrists in his hands and moves his hungry mouth from her breast to her belly, then between her legs. Tipping her head back on her pillow and closing her eyes, she moans.

It gives me chills, that moan, floating across the courtyard on the balmy afternoon air. I can't recall the last time I might have made a sound so guttural with pleasure. If ever.

Evidently her partner has quite the talented tongue.

I haven't been able to see his face, not clearly, only a glimpse in profile, and now not at all as it's buried between a pair of nubile thighs, and I'm seized by curiosity. What does this exhibitionist look like? Is he handsome? Homely? Plain as a slice of white bread? What kind of man could convince a woman to writhe around so wantonly in clear view of several dozen potential witnesses?

Or was this *her* idea? I mean, she's young and beautiful. That's a combination that can make a person do tremendously stupid things.

I should know. The list of dumb shit I did under the influence of my misspent youth is depressingly long.

But *this*. Well. Let's just say this particular behavior wasn't in my repertoire at that age.

I shouldn't judge. They're not harming anyone. I'm probably just jealous.

No—I'm *definitely* jealous. God, listen to her! That scream could wake the dead!

I turn from the window as the blonde climaxes at the top of her lungs and head into the kitchen in search of booze.

A fondness for bourbon is one of many things Estelle and I have in common, and I'm grateful to find one side of the pantry in her kitchen fully stocked with liquor. There's a wine fridge, too, but the sugar gives me headaches, so I bypass the collection of fine Burgundies and crack open a bottle of Kentucky's finest. I take a swig straight from the bottle, not bothering with a glass.

If I'm going to be spending the next three months listening to the orgasmic shrieks of my neighbors, I'll need serious backup.

Estelle says, "The number for the property manager is on the refrigerator, doll. Don't you dare hesitate to call him if the air conditioner goes out. I know you hate to be a bother to anyone, but that unit is unreliable. And it's bound to be about a thousand degrees there this summer. Global warming, you know."

I take another swig as I listen to her chatter on.

"Are you jetlagged? I've got some herbal stuff for that in the medicine cabinet in the master. Of course you know you're welcome to anything in the liquor cabinets. The little market on the corner has a divine selection of cheeses, and there's a farmers' market every Tuesday and Thursday through September on rue Desnouettes, one block over from the flat."

She already told me all this before I left New York, but

Estelle is nothing if not thorough. Another orgasmic wail from beyond the living room windows has me chugging more bourbon and wondering if I'll have to check into a hotel to avoid all the noise.

"Now, listen," says Estelle, turning serious. "I meant it when I told you to take it easy and just relax. Get some rest, eat some good food, take a lot of long walks. Try not to think."

What she really means is *Try not to remember.*

Try to stop blaming yourself.

Try to let the past go.

As if.

If letting the past go were as easy as simply deciding to do it, I wouldn't be here in the first place, thousands of miles from home. But the thing people don't realize is that the past is a living, breathing entity that exists apart from our wishes or best intentions. It's not gone, and it's certainly not invisible. Its fingerprints are smeared all over every moment of the present, its weight drags on every second of the future, its consequences echo down every hallway of our lives.

We can no more rid ourselves of the past than we could stop the earth from spinning.

But I have to seem like I'm making an effort because nobody likes a nihilist. You can only stay depressed for so long before people lose patience and start rolling their eyes behind your back.

"Definitely," I say with fake cheer. "No thinking will be attempted."

Estelle sounds satisfied. "Good. And if you happen to get struck by the muse—"

"You'll be the first to know."

As another delirious scream bounces off the living room walls, I close my eyes and bang my head gently against the pantry door.

Two hours later, I've showered off the travel grime, installed myself at a table in a charming sidewalk café near the apartment, and am drinking an overpriced espresso as I curse every decision that brought me here.

The trees are alive with birdsong. The sweet scent of cherry blossoms perfumes the air. The sky above is an endless fairy-tale blue, dotted with cottony clouds so perfect they look painted on a movie set.

It's June in Paris and romantic to the point of ridiculousness.

I feel ridiculous, anyway, a woman accompanied only by ghosts while throngs of young lovers holding hands stroll past on the shaded avenue and make tender eyes at each other over crisp white linen tablecloths to my left and right.

City of Love. What had I been thinking, coming here?

I feel attacked by all the love around me. Personally victimized, as if love itself were mocking my pain, stabbing gleefully at me with poison-tipped knives.

The perils of an overactive imagination. If I hadn't become a writer, I'd be in a padded cell somewhere, clawing at the walls.

When my mobile rings, I answer quickly, grateful for the distraction. "Hello?"

"Hey, kiddo! How's it hangin'?"

It's my girlfriend, Kelly, her tone a touch overbright. I have the sneaking suspicion I'll be getting a lot of these cheerful calls from people I know over the next few days as I settle in. They're all so anxious for me to move on it makes *me* anxious.

But I suppose two years has passed at a different speed for them than it has for me. The laws of time and physics are disfigured by grief, warping around it so a single moment can be lived over and over, forever.

I tell Kelly, "If by 'it' you mean my boobs as one unit, the answer is, sadly, low."

"Psh. You've got the best tits of anyone I know."

"Thank you for that vote of confidence, but you work at an assisted living facility. Most of the boobs you've seen lost their elasticity during the Carter administration."

"Everything's relative, babe. Look on the bright side: if you were naked and had to bend over to sign something, you wouldn't have to tuck your boob into your armpit to keep it out of the way."

I think of the nubile blonde, whose breasts were so firm there was no visible effect by gravity, even while lying on her back, and say drily, "Something to celebrate, for sure."

"What time is it in Paris? Are you ahead of me or behind?"

"I'm ahead by six hours. How do you not remember that? You've been here a dozen times!"

Kelly sighs. "I can't remember anything anymore. Mike keeps telling me I've got a brain like a sieve."

"You don't have a brain like a sieve, Kell. You've got four kids and you work full time and your husband thinks housework is something only someone with a pair of ovaries is qualified to do. Quit beating yourself up."

In response, Kelly says something that I don't catch.

"What? I'm sorry, I didn't hear what you were saying."

I'm too preoccupied staring at the Adonis who just took the table across from mine.

A quick rundown for posterity. Or skip the list and form a mental picture of a stallion in his prime galloping in slow motion across a beach as his silky mane streams out like a flag and his glossy coat glistens under the sun, and you'll get the general idea.

He's got tousled brown hair that brushes broad shoulders, a cleft chin that would impress Superman, and a graceful way of moving his limbs, despite his formidable size. Dressed in an untucked white button-down shirt and a pair of faded jeans, he sports a week-old growth of beard on his angular jaw, a leather cuff around one wrist, and exudes an air of animal magnetism so strong I can feel it from where I'm sitting.

Evidently so can everyone else, judging by the ripple of awareness his presence sends through the diners. Heads turn in his direction as if pulled by strings.

But the stunning stranger is oblivious to all the attention he's drawing. All the furtive glances, both male and female.

No doubt he's used to it. He's prime rib, as Kelly would say. Check out all the sizzle on that steak.

Truly, he's devastating.

If you knew me, you'd know that's not a word I use lightly.

And my, oh *my*, what incredible eyes. Bluer than the cloudless heavens above and ringed by a thicket of black lashes, they're potent. Piercing. Penetrating. And some other sexually suggestive words I can't recall at the moment because the horrible realization that I've been caught staring at him has stalled my brain.

He's staring right back.

"I was asking if you've been over to Café Blanc yet," hollers Kelly, as if I've developed a hearing problem since we said hello. "Be sure you tell Henri I sent you or he'll charge you double—he's a friggin' cheat!"

She says that last part with affection. There's nothing she enjoys more than the enduring friendships she forms when someone unsuccessfully tries to swindle her.

Thinking her a hapless American tourist on her first visit to Paris during college, the café owner inflated the price of her meal. The ensuing argument has become something of a local legend. When I introduced myself to the hostess as a friend of Kelly's, she asked if Kelly still keeps Henri's left testicle in a jar on her kitchen counter.

I replied with a straight face that she keeps it in her fridge.

"I'm actually at Café Blanc as we speak," I tell her, holding the stranger's gaze.

"Awesome! It's fantastic, right?"

The stranger's blistering gaze drops to my mouth. A muscle in his jaw flexes. He moistens his full lips.

Holy...was that a hot flash or did someone just light a fire under my chair?

Whatever it was, it's new. For years my body has felt nothing but a boneyard chill. Flustered, I say faintly, "It's...gorgeous."

"What?" Kelly thunders. "Babe, I can hardly hear you! Speak up!"

"I said it's gorgeous!"

A waiter with no chin and a nose like a toucan's bill materializes at my tableside, frowning at the phone in my hand. He speaks in French, gesturing sharply at the phone.

I don't understand the language, but I get his gist: *You're being rude. How American of you. Perhaps next you'd like to shit on the Eiffel Tower?*

I frown at him, wishing there really was a testicle jar because I'd be adding a few more to it. "Gotta go, Kell. I'll call you back later, okay?"

She's still shouting on the other end when I hang up.

The waiter drops the check on the table then looks at me pointedly. He wants me to clear out so he can give my table to one of the lovely couples waiting in line at the door.

I was about to leave, but jerks bring out the stubborn Sicilian in my blood. I offer him a smile so sharp it could cut steel. "Another espresso, please. And a dessert menu."

"Dessert? You haven't ordered a main course yet."

His English is heavily accented. His brow is cocked. His lip is curled.

Before now, I've never met a person who could sneer with his entire body.

I say, "Are you always so observant or is this a special occasion?"

With a huff and a flare of his enormous nostrils, he spins off.

That's when I hear the chuckle.

What annoys me is that I know exactly from whom it's coming. I don't even have to glance over to know that the blue-eyed stallion witnessed my little drama with the waiter and found it amusing.

So I don't look over. I'm not interested in being a comedy show for the hottie who's got half the restaurant in thrall.

I know it's a strange sort of prejudice, but I've always secretly thought that a man's ethics exist in reverse proportion to his good looks. You just can't trust a guy who can have his choice of any woman within shouting distance. That kind of power will corrupt even the saintliest soul.

Ignoring everything but the warmth of the sun on my face, I tilt my head back and close my eyes.

A moment later, a deep voice says, "May I?"

Startled, I look up. The blue-eyed stranger stands beside my table looking down at me, his hand resting on the back of the chair opposite mine. I can tell from his confident stance that he assumes my consent is forthcoming, which won't do.

I refuse to be a foregone conclusion.

"No. I'm waiting for someone."

Ignoring my answer, he sits.

Entitled jerk.

We recommence staring at each other, this time up close.

Despite my discrimination against his pretty face and his bad manners, I have to admit he's incredibly attractive. Whatever DNA produces a jaw that square, he should clone it and gift it to my chinless waiter.

Gazing at me intently, he says, "I'd love to draw you."

Don't you just hate it when a man opens his mouth and ruins everything?

I suppose it shouldn't be a shock that this guy hasn't had to develop better opening lines than that cheeser he just laid on me. He's probably had women throwing themselves at his feet since birth. Plus, beauty like his is rarely paired with equivalent intellect. But still, I have to force myself not to roll my eyes.

"Just out of curiosity, does that work?"

His dark brows draw down over his blue gaze. "Does what work?"

His English is perfect. He doesn't have an accent, French or otherwise. He must be here on vacation from the Land of the Beautiful People Who Don't Understand the Word *No* Because They've Never Heard It.

"That line. 'I'd love to draw you.' Do women really fall for that?"

Blue Eyes cocks his head, examining me. "You think I'm propositioning you."

He says it as a statement, not a question. A statement underscored by a hint of laughter.

Cue my instant, scorching humiliation.

This guy isn't trying to pick me up. His stares weren't those of a man sexually attracted to a woman. He was merely curious, looking at me so alone and etched with grief as I am, sticking out like an unruly and unwanted weed in this garden of roses.

Aiming for nonchalant, I wave my hand dismissively. "My mistake. Sorry."

"Don't be. I *am* propositioning you."

I start to blink and can't stop. Now the humiliation is gone, but I'm confused and blinking like a crazed owl.

As I direct my attention to the tablecloth and my hand resting there, trembling slightly, Blue Eyes continues in a conversational tone, as if he hasn't completely crossed my wires.

"To sit for a portrait, I mean. You've got an incredible face. And your eyes, they're…"

He trails off, searching for a word, then says quietly, "Haunted."

My invisible shields slam down and envelop me, protecting my heart from the anguish welling up inside my chest. I've spent a long time developing my shields, and until I look up again they've never failed me.

But when our gazes meet this time, I'm unprepared for the force of it.

I stepped on a live wire once. I was eight years old. A utility pole had been damaged in a storm and came down in our backyard. I ran outside to investigate before my father's warning shout could stop me, and the power of the voltage that surged through my body when my bare foot touched the wire threw me halfway across the yard.

Looking into this stranger's beautiful blue eyes feels exactly like that.

"I'm James."

His voice has turned husky. There's a new tension in his body, as if he's restraining himself from reaching out and touching me.

Or maybe that's my imagination, which excels in running wild.

"Olivia," I manage.

In the silence that follows, the sounds of the café seem unbearably loud. Silverware clatters against plates. Chattering voices become nerve-scraping shrieks. The flush on my cheeks spreads down my neck, and my pulse goes haywire.

I've never been looked at like this by a man, with such raw, unapologetic intensity.

I feel naked.

I feel *seen.*

When the waiter appears beside me, I nearly jump out of my skin.

"Madame." Dripping condescension, he holds out the dessert menu and offers me a mocking bow.

"I've changed my mind. I'll just take care of the check and be on my way, thanks." I yank my handbag off the arm of my chair and dig through it for my wallet.

"You said you were waiting for someone," James reminds me.

"I lied."

James leans back in his chair and considers me, his intense gaze unwavering. The waiter looks back and forth between us, arching an eyebrow, then says something in French to James, who shakes his head.

I get the feeling they know each other, that James is a regular, and decide I'm never coming back.

I toss a few bills onto the small black plastic tray that holds my check and stand, bumping the table and knocking over a glass in my haste, trying unsuccessfully not to notice how the three young women at a nearby table are looking me up and down and whispering to each other behind their hands.

Those catty giggles. Those snide, mocking smiles.

One day they'll be like me, hurtling toward forty with stretch marks and wrinkles and a new compassion for others that only the decay of your own body and the weight of all your crushed dreams will bring, but for now they're beautiful and smug, certain of their superiority to the awkward tourist lurching away in terror from the first real feeling she's felt in ages.

I don't look back on my way out, but I feel James's burning gaze follow me all the way to the door.

Somehow, this time I know it isn't my imagination.

2

Estelle's apartment is the love child of Buckingham Palace and a nineteenth-century Moroccan bordello.

A neoclassical breakfront displays commemorative bone china plates from the 80's royal wedding of Charles and Diana. Tufted red velvet sofas are strewn with purple silk pillows. Gold tassels draw back burgundy brocade drapes from soaring windows, the master bathroom is a riot of inlaid indigo-and-green mosaics, and imposing gilt-framed oils of grim ancestors and hunting parties on horseback garnish the living room walls. The ceilings bristle with a hodgepodge of lighting fixtures varying from ornate crystal chandeliers to carved bronze lanterns inset with colored glass.

The decorator was clearly schizophrenic, but by some miracle all the clashing elements come together to make the place feel homey.

I'm not surprised that I like its eccentricity. The older I get, the more rational weirdness seems.

I'm yawning and stretching my legs under the Egyptian cotton sheets of Estelle's massive four-poster bed when I hear the moan. It drifts in through the window, which is cracked open to the courtyard outside.

I freeze, listening.

The moan comes again, louder this time. I flip the sheets over my face and sigh deeply as the moans continue to increase in volume and length. A quick check of my watch confirms it's not yet six a.m.

I can't be human at this hour without half a pot of coffee and something to eat with enough sugar that could induce a diabetic coma, and those two across the way are going at it like rabbits. Who has that kind of energy?

"Gotta be drugs," I say to the empty room as the blonde nears orgasm. Hopefully the leaded glass windows will survive her ear-piercing screams.

Abruptly, I'm angry. Who the hell do these people think they are, disturbing my first night's sleep in what Estelle promised would be a "soothing" and "healing" space? That racket is definitely *not* soothing or healing, I'll tell you what!

For me, anyway. By the sound of it, the blonde is being healed from the inside out by some pretty spectacular dick.

Flinging off the sheets, I glare at the ceiling. I'm contemplating whether to throw open the windows and shout obscenities at them or leave a strongly-worded letter taped to their door, when I realize that my brain is the only part of my body annoyed by my neighbor's frisky antics.

The rest of me is aroused.

Within seconds, I'm engaged in a mental argument with myself and another voice that's Kelly's, because she knows all my darkest secrets and is always showing up unannounced in my head.

Go ahead, girl. Rub one out. You deserve it.

Please. I'm not going to masturbate to the sound of my neighbors getting it on.

Why the hell not? They're sexy as all get-out!

Because it's pervy, that's why not. And they're not sexy, they're showoffs.

Uh-huh. That's why your lady garden just burst into flames, because they're not *sexy.*

"Lady garden?" What are you, ninety? And I can't help it if my vagina has a mind of her own! That doesn't mean I have to listen to her!

Right. You're not listening. Then I wonder why your hand's between your legs?

I groan, banishing the conversation from my head as I squeeze my thighs together and try very hard not to enjoy the sensation of my fingers rubbing back and forth over the damp seam of my pajama bottoms.

Try—and fail spectacularly.

Truth be told, I'm shocked to discover I still have any erotic feelings at all. It's been years since the slightest flicker of heat has touched my loins, even more years before that that I tried to pleasure myself. I had what I consider a solid sex life with my husband, though we weren't adventurous by any stretch of the imagination. And though in the last dying embers of our marriage the sex disappeared altogether, I never turned to self-pleasure because I never had the urge.

My libido died along with everything else that mattered.

Except for yesterday, when a stranger's searing blue gaze lit me up like a Christmas tree and sent shockwaves of heat pulsing straight through my core.

"I'm James," he said, with a tone like he was already thrusting inside me.

A series of masculine grunts from across the courtyard has my fingers slipping inside my cotton pajamas and past my panties. I'm already soaked. I bite my lip and squeeze my eyes shut like a guilty child caught with her hand in the cookie jar.

A superheated, long neglected cookie jar, whose cookies are quickly crumbling to bits.

"James," I whisper, picturing him on top of me.

He was a big man. Much bigger than my husband or the few lovers I had before him. I usually go for men with trim builds who look good in expensive suits. Your typical Wall Street type, a clean cut WASP with manicured nails who'd give himself a hernia if he tried to lift me.

James the rugged blue-eyed stallion could probably hoist me overhead with his pinky.

What would it be like to lie beneath a man that size? To feel all those muscles bunching as he flexed his hips, to feel the slide of his rough hands over my skin, to feel his hot breath in my ear as he grunted in animal pleasure the way the man across the courtyard is grunting?

Probably delicious.

My fingers move faster as my imagination takes the reins. I sketch a scene in shorthand with myself and James in starring roles.

Her thighs clamp around his strong hips. Her hair spreads out in dark waves over the pillow. She writhes beneath him, crying out as he fucks her with short, hard strokes, her breasts bouncing with every thrust. He's braced above her, his arms corded, his skin slicked with sweat, dominant and focused, fully in control.

Suddenly, he rises to his knees. He flips her over. With one arm around her waist, he hikes her bottom in the air and drives into her from behind.

As pleasure obliterates every thought from her mind, she buries her face into the pillow and screams.

He fists a hand into her hair, slaps her ass, and makes a noise like the growl of a wolf.

I come violently with a sound that's part gasp of shock and part yelp, my entire body stiffening, my back bowing up from the bed. My eyes fly open as contractions rack me, over and over, jerking my body and the whole bed, too.

Then I collapse against the mattress and dissolve into weak, disbelieving laughter.

I just brought myself to orgasm to the soundtrack of the exhibitionists getting it on.

I'm a pervert.

Kelly would be so proud.

As great as my impromptu little porno was, it did contain one glaring flaw: if a man ever slapped me on the ass, I'd whirl around and punch him in the face.

I mean, I think I would. I'm pretty sure. I've never had anyone attempt it, but ass slapping during sex strikes me as borderline abusive. Or just silly, I can't decide which. In any case, I seriously doubt I'll ever be forced to choose because my chances of a future sexual encounter with a man who'd be into that sort of thing can be classified as slim to none.

No alpha wolf ass slappers need apply, thank you very much.

Interesting that you're fantasizing about it, then, notes the Kelly that lives inside my head while calmly filing her nails.

To which I answer, "Shut up," and rise from bed, avoiding my reflection in the bathroom mirror as I head to the shower.

It's too early in the morning to see what a voyeur with haunted eyes and conflicted feelings about rough sex looks like.

Later that afternoon, I'm sitting at the huge roll top desk in Estelle's stuffed-with-first-edition-classics library staring at a lined yellow pad of paper, pen poised in hand, filled to the gills with every bit of the fear, conceit, and existential anguish every writer feels when faced with a blank page, when the doorbell rings.

"Thank God!" I shout, wilting with relief. I throw the pen down and heave a sigh.

It's moments like these that affirm to me the existence and

merciful nature of a supreme being. I'd been sitting in the same spot, staring at the same blank page, for going on an hour.

I was just about to crack open the bourbon again.

Springing from the chair as if launched, I hustle through the apartment to the front door, which I throw open with an overabundance of exuberance. It slams against the wall. To the small elderly man standing there, I boom with a theatrical flourish of my hands, "Hello! How may I help you?"

For a moment, he's a deer in headlights, his eyes wide and unblinking. The black beret tilted at a rakish angle on his bald head seems to quiver in fear.

Poor man. I really shouldn't be allowed to interact with the rest of the human race.

But then he recovers, straightening his bowtie and offering me a tentative smile. "Er…bonjour, mademoiselle."

Mademoiselle, not madame. I am in love with him.

"Bonjour." So grateful for the interruption and the polite flattery, I beam at him like a maniac. "*Joues-tu au tennis*?"

He blinks once, slowly. "No, mademoiselle. I do not play tennis."

"Oh shit. Sorry. I don't actually speak French. That's all I remember from the one class I took in high school a hundred years ago. I thought I was saying, 'Isn't it a beautiful day?'"

"I give you points for the effort." He pauses. "What would you have done if I'd answered back in French?"

I casually lift a shoulder. "Probably tried out some Italian on you. But hopefully you don't speak it because all I know are the curses my grandmother used to shout at my brothers when they came home drunk."

His smile deepens. "Ah yes. The Italians. *Très passionnant*. I once had an Italian mistress named Sophia who stabbed me six times in the neck with a fountain pen when she caught me looking at another woman."

I arch my brows. "Seems like a bit of an overreaction."

"The other woman was her sister."

When I don't say anything, he adds, "With whom I was also having an affair."

I make a face at him. "I hope you won't take this the wrong way since we only just met, but now I'm thinking you deserved it."

"Oh, indeed I did," he says with zero remorse. "I also deserved it when my wife set my car on fire when she found out about Sophia and her sister." He exhales a wistful sigh. "I really loved that car."

Men.

Normally, I'd judge his character as sadly flawed based on this anecdote, but he's just given me a wonderful idea for a plot for a novel, so instead I cut him some slack and smile. "It sounds like you've lived an interesting life, monsieur..."

"Edmond Chevalier. The building manager, at your service." Sweeping off his beret, he bows. When he straightens, he's smiling. The beret he claps back onto his bald head. "And oui, I have lived a very interesting life. Ah, the stories I could tell you, mademoiselle, they would curl your hair!"

I'm totally getting this talkative old geezer drunk and pilfering every plot idea I can.

Estelle's been patient, but I'm afraid if I don't come up with a new story by the end of the summer, she'll give up on me altogether. Edmond here could be just the inspiration I need.

Trying not to wring my hands and cackle like some crazed comic book villain , I say, "I'd *love* to hear your stories. Won't you come in?"

"Thank you for the kind invitation, but I'm on my way to lunch. I only stopped by to introduce myself and invite you to the cocktail party this evening in the grand salon. Estelle was most insistent that I make you feel welcome and introduce you to the other neighbors so you'd feel right at home. And I know they're all very eager to meet *you*. A writer in our midst! How exciting!"

As my stomach sinks, he claps, hopping a little in glee.

It would be adorable except I'm too busy planning my imminent bout of infectious colitis to notice.

I don't do parties. Especially parties where I'm trotted around like the prize hog. People tend to think authors are magical unicorn creatures who lead interesting and glamorous lives, when really we're a bunch of awkward nail-biting introverts who'd rather have our eyes put out with hot pokers than be forced into conversations with total strangers, which for an introvert is about as fun as bathing a cat.

Then there's the inevitable, "Have I read anything of yours?" to which I always pray *God, let's hope not.*

I live in terror of the person who's read my work and would like to offer a helpful critique.

"I'm so sorry, Edmond, but I don't think I'll be able to—"

"Seven o'clock sharp, my dear!" He waves a hand briskly back and forth, as if erasing my refusal from existence. "*Don't* be late. You won't want to miss the introduction from our artist-in-residence to his new collection, a few pieces of which will be on display. He's incredibly talented, just *incredibly* talented. The party is in honor of him, in case I didn't mention it."

I can already tell Edmond will be banging on my door at 7:05 if I don't show up.

I suppose I could hide in a closet and pretend to be out, but I don't want it getting back to Estelle that I'm being rude and antisocial. Especially since she so generously offered me her apartment for free for months and is sincerely trying to help me get my shit together.

So I resign myself to enduring a hideous evening filled with painful silences as I struggle to make polite conversation with people who don't have the kind of anxiety that compels them want to take a dive off the nearest tall building at the prospect of socializing.

But if anyone asks me if I'm married or have children, blood will be shed.

With the enthusiasm of a convict facing a firing squad, I say, "All right, Edmond. I'll be there."

"Excellent! And I'll introduce you to James as soon as you arrive. I'm sure the two of you will have much to talk about, being creative types as you are."

"James?"

"Yes. The artist." Edmond chuckles. "Handsome devil. Popular with the ladies. He's the most eligible bachelor in Paris. Reminds me of myself at his age."

Edmond doffs his beret and bids me adieu, then goes on his way down the corridor, whistling. I stare after him with a strange feeling of foreboding forming in my gut.

It can't be. It's a coincidence. There must be a million handsome artists in Paris named James. It's not the blue-eyed stallion from the café.

But when I walk into the grand salon that evening, I'm reminded again exactly how much fate loves to prove me wrong.

3

He's even more handsome than I remember.

It's probably the combined effect of candlelight and the hazy glow of sex hormones being produced en masse by the cluster of simpering females surrounding him, but the man is positively stunning.

Standing beside a grand piano in a corner of the elegant salon, James is all in black. Black dress shirt open at the collar, black slacks, black leather shoes that I can tell from where I'm standing cost more than the gross domestic product of Guam.

Conversing with his admirers, he appears neither happy nor at ease. In fact, he looks like a cornered wolf.

Interesting.

Then he glances up, catches me watching him, and falls still.

I'd look away, but I'm frozen. Pinned in place. Turned to stone by that same jolt of electricity that crackled through me at the café when he looked into my eyes.

No, not stone.

Molten lava.

Heat rises in a wave from my chest to my neck, then engulfs

my face. I stand there, ears burning, heart pounding, until the connection becomes unbearable, and I tear my gaze away.

The relief is instant.

I vow to myself I'll never look his way again.

"Ah, there you are! Welcome, my dear, welcome!"

A beaming Edmond appears beside me and proceeds to kiss my hand. Then he bends his head close and speaks in a conspiratorial whisper. "You look *très magnifique* in that gown. Half the men in this room are probably in love with you already."

The gown in question is the only dress I brought with me, a body-skimming number in sapphire blue chiffon that manages the miracle of complementing both my complexion and my figure. I brought it on impulse, thinking maybe I'd wear it to the opera or such, but as the rest of my clothing consists of jeans, T-shirts, and comfortable shoes, I figured this was as good an occasion as any.

"Thank you. I thought I'd be overdressed, but I can see I was wrong."

The salon is filled with people who obviously attend the fashion week couture shows. I've never seen such glamour in my life. You'd think we were about to receive the Queen of England. Even Edmond is dressed to the nines in an exquisite navy suit with a robin's-egg blue silk tie and matching pocket square. His patent leather loafers are so shiny they're blinding me.

"That's the guest of honor over there by the piano, but he's surrounded at the moment so let me introduce you around. Come."

Edmond takes my elbow and leads me forward into the crowd. I feel like a cow being led to slaughter.

As luck would have it, the first person I'm introduced to is the nubile blonde with the firm tits and lungs like Pavarotti's. Even clothed and upright, she's instantly recognizable as the screamer across the way from Estelle's.

"Mademoiselle Gigi, please meet mademoiselle Olivia." Edmond adds proudly, "Olivia is a writer."

I murmur an alarmed hello as Gigi throws her arms wide and lunges at me, lips pursed. She grabs me by the shoulders and gives me a hearty kiss on both cheeks, then holds me at arms' length, grinning like a lunatic.

Her breasts are even more impressive up close.

"Bonsoir, Olivia!" she shouts. "I am so pleased to meet you!"

It's drugs. It's got to be.

She turns her head and hollers over her shoulder, "Gaspard! *Venez ici*!"

A man in conversation with a few others halfway across the room turns and looks our way. He's tall and slim, dressed in a lovely dark suit, and walks with a slight hitch in his gait that I can only assume is due to his chapped, dehydrated, and overworked penis.

It's Gigi's partner. The cause of all her caterwauling.

The grunter.

Smiling in a friendly way, Gaspard stops in front of me and extends his hand. He says something incomprehensible because it's in French.

I take his outstretched hand and try not to feel like I'm in one of those terrible sitcoms, the ones with the canned laugh tracks starring the kind of bumbling idiot who would be in jail in real life.

"*Bonsoir*, Gaspard. Nice to meet you." *I know how you sound when you come.*

Either Gaspard doesn't speak English or he's the type of Frenchman who does but wouldn't admit it on pain of death, because he answers back in French, still smiling his pleasant smile while openly ogling my cleavage.

"I'm sorry, I don't speak French."

In response, Edmond, Gigi, and Gaspard launch into an animated conversation in—you guessed it—French.

Gaspard still has not released my hand.

"Lovely to meet you both," I tell Gigi, extracting my hand from Gaspard's clammy grip and edging away, "and now I'm going to get a drink."

I turn and make a beeline for the bar set up on the opposite side of the room, hoping Edmond isn't scurrying along behind me because I might be forced to kick out at him like a frightened horse.

Not even five minutes in and I'm already panicking.

"Bourbon," I tell the bartender when I arrive, breathless from my short sprint.

I really should start exercising, but unfortunately I only enjoy physical activities that can be done lying down.

The bartender is a young woman with beautiful skin and an elegant neck who doesn't bat an eyelash when I down the bourbon she's poured me in one go and demand another. She might be the only person in this room I could like.

Then beside me appears a tall form dressed all in black, and I wonder what I did in a previous life to make God hate me so much.

"I'll have whatever the lady's having," says James to the bartender, tilting his head my way.

Not sure if she's got any extra mental breakdowns lying around, but knock yourself out.

She pours him his drink, then turns her attention to a couple who've just walked up, leaving James and me standing there in silence facing the wall with our drinks in our hands.

He smells delicious.

I hadn't noticed that at the café. Most likely because all my other senses were too scrambled from looking at him to function properly. But now I've got his scent in my nose, and it's just as delicious as the rest of him. The only sensible thing to do is chug the rest of my bourbon, which will sear his smell right out of my nostrils, so I do.

"Hello," he says after a while, not looking at me.

I debate on a dozen different responses—including bolting from the room—before settling on a reasonably calm sounding, "Hi."

I couldn't even manage the two syllables that would be required for *hello*. This person is not healthy for me to be around.

But I'm a grownup who's been through much tougher shit than standing beside an attractive man, so after a quick mental pep talk, I speak to Mr. Delicious again.

"So apparently you really are an artist."

A hint of laughter warms his voice. "Apparently."

"I hear you're very talented."

He turns his head and looks at me. It feels like standing in the sun.

"Are you a fan of the arts?"

"No. Well, yes. I mean, sort of. It depends. Some arts more than others. Cinema. Music. Literature. Those I like. But I don't know anything about *art* art. Like you do. Drawing and painting and such."

He's silent for a moment, probably wondering just how far advanced my brain cancer is. Then he says, "You don't like me."

I finish the rest of my bourbon and set the glass carefully down on the bar. "I didn't say that."

"You didn't have to. That full body cringe of yours is doing the job pretty well."

"That's not dislike."

It's out before I can retract it, hanging there as dangerous and raw as an open wound.

"No?" says James quietly. "What is it, then?"

Shit. "I…don't enjoy parties."

"Hmm. So your obvious discomfort now and at the café yesterday has nothing to do with me."

He sounds unconvinced. I really hate it when people are too

observant. And by "people" I mean men. Why is he just standing there, looking at me?

Seeing me?

I say drily, "You are inconveniently perceptive."

"I can pretend to be stupid if it will get you to look at me."

I think about it, aware that I've made myself a vow to never again look his way, and also aware of the growing urge to do so. With his lovely smell in my nose and the rich timbre of his voice in my ears, my resolve is quickly crumbling. But I can't give in without setting some boundaries.

"I'll look at you if you promise not to ask to draw me or say anything weird about my eyes."

"Deal," he says promptly.

That was too easy. "And maybe try to dial down that stare of yours a few thousand notches."

"*Stare*? I don't have a stare."

"You definitely do."

His voice drops an octave. "If I do, it's only because you're such a pleasure to look at."

"Ha! Flattery will get you nowhere, Romeo. I'm immune."

I had to go with sarcasm so he didn't notice the little shiver that went through me at his words, how all the hairs on my arms stood on end.

I'm in danger here. Serious, imminent danger of being charmed senseless by a handsome artist who arouses in me the dueling urges to run away screaming or strip naked and fling myself onto his torso and cling there like a crab.

My mind takes the opportunity to present me with a Technicolor memory of the fantasy I conjured up of him while masturbating. The fantasy of him fucking me like a champ and slapping my ass.

"Bartender! Another bourbon, please!"

She returns and fills my glass again without giving me a

reproachful look that I've ordered three drinks in as many minutes, bless her.

When she drifts away, James and I lapse into silence again, but this time he's staring at my profile, and I'm wishing I had something to fan myself with.

When I don't turn to look at him, he gently chides, "C'mon. You can do it. I promise I don't bite."

"Sure. That's what all biters say."

"Really? You know many biters?"

"Oh yeah. I'm kind of a biter magnet, to be honest."

"How interesting. Do you work at a kennel?"

"Worse." *In publishing, where the piranha are only outnumbered by the sharks.*

"If I guess your job right, will you look at me?"

"You'll never guess. But go ahead."

"You're a writer."

I whip my head around so quickly to stare at him I'm surprised my neck doesn't break.

"There you are," he says, smiling into my eyes.

Jesus, yes, here I am, all ten thousand degrees of me. My veins have begun conducting fire. "How did you know I'm a writer?"

"I heard Edmond introduce you to Gigi."

"Heard? You were across the room. Talking with other people."

"Yes, but I was paying attention to you, looking like you'd wandered into the seventh circle of hell, wearing this dress that nearly gave me a heart attack."

Speaking of heart attacks, I'm having one. I can't think of anything to say, so I simply stare into the endless blue depths of his eyes and hope he can't see the smoke rising up in curls from my skin.

After a long, blistering moment, he murmurs, "Tell me I'm

not the only one standing here feeling like I just stuck my finger into an electrical outlet."

I say faintly, "I have no idea what you're talking about."

He exhales slowly, his jaw working, his gaze locked onto mine with such force he could pick me up and pin me against the wall with it.

"If you want me to leave you alone, I will. I don't want to bother you—"

"You're not bothering me," I blurt. "You're *bothering* me."

When he moistens his lips, I almost collapse. Thankfully, Edmond arrives to rescue me.

"My dear! You've met James! Wonderful, *wonderful*!"

I don't know why he's so excited about it, but he's practically levitating at the discovery that James and I are already acquainted. Perhaps he senses all my invisible fault lines and assumes the blue-eyed stallion who is so "popular with the ladies" will help shore them up.

I'm telling you, single women of a certain age make people jumpy.

"Yes, we've met," says James. "In fact, this isn't the first time."

"Oh?" Edmond's ears perk up. He looks back and forth between us with open curiosity while James continues to gaze steadily at me, a faint smile playing around his lips.

Time to finish my drink.

"Yes. I saw her at Café Blanc yesterday and asked permission to draw her portrait."

Edmond's gasp is low and thrilled. He turns to me with his hands clasped to his chest, as if in prayer. "Oh, you must sit for him, my dear. You *must*. James is an incredible artist. Just *incredible*. It's quite an honor to be asked to sit for him. *Quite* an honor, to be sure."

His habit of repeating himself with more emphasis the second time is really starting to grate on my nerves. But I suppose I'm guilty of that with my crushingly awkward admission that James wasn't bothering me, he was *bothering* me, so I really don't have a leg to stand on.

I offer Edmond a pinched smile. "I'm sure he can find a much more interesting subject than me."

"No," Edmond replies solemnly. "You're perfect. It's in the eyes. They're very arresting, if I may say so. Almost..." His gaze turns pensive as he looks at my face.

If he says "haunted" I'll strangle him with his necktie.

I turn to James. "You didn't ask permission."

He lifts his brows.

Maybe my tone was a bit too tart. "What I meant is that you said you'd love to draw me. You didn't ask if you could."

"Is that why you ran away? Because I didn't ask?"

He knows full well why I ran away. It's written all over his face. In the knowing heat in his eyes. In the way he's moistening his full lips again and *good God why does he keep doing that?*

Sweat breaks out along my hairline. My heart beats uncomfortably fast. I have the painful sensation of being a peeled grape, stripped of my skin, everything raw and achingly tender. Even the air hurts as I breathe it into my lungs.

But I refuse to be like those women clustered around him at the piano. The school of desperate minnows vying for his attention and longing for his smile.

I say, "The thought of someone immortalizing my likeness for generations of people to stare at long after I'm dead is about as attractive to me as contracting the Ebola virus."

He says, "I'm guessing you're not a big fan of selfies, then."

"I'd rather be shot than post a picture of myself on the internet."

"That flair for exaggeration must serve you well as a writer."

"I'm not exaggerating."

"Like you weren't lying yesterday when you told me you were waiting for someone?"

His tone is neutral, but he's pushing me. Challenging me. Scaling that wall I keep trying to build between us to keep him at a safe distance. Why is he doing that when he could have, with a snap of his fingers, any one of a dozen willing women in the room?

We stare at each other, unsmiling. My heartbeat pulses in the palms of my hands.

It's Edmond who finally breaks the tension. "Perhaps you'd like to see his work before you decide if you want to sit for him?"

I've already decided I won't sit for him, but this seems like a good opportunity to escape the tractor beam of James's gaze, so I allow myself to be led across the room by the elbow by Edmond, who wouldn't keep doing that if he knew how much it makes me want to trip him.

Then we're standing in front of a row of easels lined up against the windows of the salon, and I temporarily lose the ability to breathe.

Edmond was right: James is incredibly talented.

The six portraits I'm looking at are done in pen and ink with such meticulous and lifelike detail they appear to be photographs instead of drawings. Each is of a woman from the shoulders up. The subjects are all facing forward. The backgrounds are left blank, which emphasizes the startlingly realistic quality of the faces and also adds an eerie three-dimensional quality.

And my God, their eyes.

I've never seen human misery so perfectly depicted.

What's that cliché? A picture is worth a thousand words? Well, it's inaccurate. I could write a million words and never come close to capturing the emotion I'm seeing here. The suffering I'm seeing. The black, bottomless pain.

In a hushed voice, Edmond says, "The collection is titled *Perspectives of Grief.*"

Like a key fitting into a lock, I understand why James is

drawn to me. And why he would be moved to create these particular drawings of these particular people, their anguish so raw I can almost reach out and touch it.

Birds of a feather flock together, as my mother used to say. Water seeks its own level, and like attracts like.

Death has touched him, too.

I turn and look at him, standing where I left him at the bar. He's looking back at me, of course.

His gaze is snapping white heat. Shimmering intensity. Velvet blue darkness.

I know we'll be lovers the same way I knew as a young girl that someday I'd put pen to paper and write stories for others to read. The same way I knew my marriage would collapse under the weight of guilt, shame, and sorrow. The same way I knew, sitting on the cold front pew in St. Monica's church gazing at my daughter's small white casket, that I would never be whole again.

Our bones have a wisdom that our hearts will always follow, regardless of the roads down which our rational minds think we should head.

"Edmond."

"Oui?"

"Please tell James I'd love to sit for a portrait."

I turn and make my way from the room.

4

I spend that night as I've spent countless others, lying on my back in bed staring at the ceiling until the sun comes up.

The tranquility of the morning is shattered by an orgasmic wail from Gigi, but this time her lusty screams don't disturb me. It could be meeting her that has taken the edge off my irritation at the noise, but it could also be gratitude.

If it weren't for her and Gaspard getting it on so loudly, I wouldn't have enjoyed the first orgasm I've had in years.

Today I don't find the sound of their lovemaking arousing, either. It's simply another morning sound, like a garbage truck rumbling down an alleyway or a rooster crowing at the dawn. It's background noise, meaningless and pleasant.

I'm too preoccupied with thoughts of James to be moved by anything else.

The memory of the way he licks his lips is torture. How can a mannerism so small be so seductive? I could write a thesis on the shape of his mouth alone.

I wait until I hear my neighbors' shared climax before I rise from bed. Then I spend a few hours unpacking my bags, doing laundry, and getting organized. It's just after ten o'clock when the knock comes on the front door.

I open it to find a young man holding a vase of snowy white tulips.

"Olivia Rossi?"

"That's me."

He hands me the bouquet, then leaves without asking for a signature. Apparently he thinks I have a trustworthy face.

I bring the flowers into the kitchen, where I set them on the counter and remove the card.

"When you're ready," it reads, followed by a phone number.

He didn't sign his name.

He didn't have to.

With my heart in my throat, I dial James's number. He picks up on the first ring.

"You got the flowers."

His voice is low and pleased. He's happy I called so quickly. But how did he know it was me?

"Flowers? No, I've just been sitting here for the past twelve hours randomly dialing phone numbers. I can't believe I finally tried the right combination."

"Imagine the odds," he says, playing along. "Your dialing finger must be cramping."

"You have no idea. It's crooked as a fish hook. I might have to visit the emergency room. By the way, who is this?"

His chuckle sends a shiver of pleasure straight through me. "When am I going to see you, funny lady?"

"I could text you a selfie. Would that do?"

"I thought you'd rather be shot than take a selfie."

"No, you weren't paying attention. I said I'd rather be shot than post a selfie on the internet."

His voice drops. "I paid attention to everything."

In the short silence that follows, I hear my blood rushing through my veins. "So I take it Edmond gave you my message."

He makes a soft sound that I interpret as amusement at my awkward segue. "He did. He also gave me your apartment number."

Hence the flower delivery. "I have a feeling he would've also given you a key if you'd asked for it. The man thinks you walk on water."

"I'll be sure to ask him for one."

When I pause, swallowing, James says, "That was a joke. I promise."

"Hmm. Like you promised you weren't a biter?"

Another drop in his tone, and now he's all husky sex line operator. "I'm not a biter. I'm a nibbler. There's a big difference."

I break out in a cold sweat. *Steady, Olivia. Take a deep breath.*

After it becomes obvious I'm not going to respond, James prompts, "Are you not saying anything because I'm bothering you, or because I'm *bothering* you?"

I exhale in a noisy rush. "Honestly? I don't know if a woman has ever been more bothered by a man in the whole of human history."

He unleashes that devastating chuckle again, the bastard. "I'll take that as a compliment. When am I going to see you?"

I note he doesn't ask, "When can you sit for your portrait?" because we both know when I told Edmond I'd sit for a portrait, that wasn't what I was agreeing to at all.

I say quietly, "I haven't done this in a long time."

"Talked on the phone?"

"Taken a lover."

His exhalation is slow and rough. I imagine him gripping the phone so hard he puts a crack in it.

After a while, I ask, "Are you still there?"

"Just recovering the power of speech. Please hold."

I smile, gratified I affect him as much as he affects me. "Not to be presumptuous, but it does seem like the feeling is—"

"Mutual. Yes. Jesus. Are you always this direct?"

"Life's too short to mince words. But since we're on the subject, I should tell you I'm going to need some time. I can't just…"

"Hop into bed with me on the first date."

"Bingo."

"You want to get to know me better first."

I think about that. What is it, exactly, that I want? I'm here for three months, then I'll go back to real life in the States. This can only be a temporary thing, a brief affair with a beautiful stranger to be remembered fondly when I'm sitting in my rocking chair on the front porch of the old folks' home.

So why waste any time?

I'm hardly a virgin. We're both adults, we're both single, and we both know what we want. Aside from a nod to "morality," what's the point of delay?

Anticipation, whispers my brain.

The point of delay is to build desire.

I take a moment to marvel at this thirsty new version of myself. Perhaps it's the influence of my exhibitionist neighbors, but whatever it is, I'm going with it.

"I hope you won't take this the wrong way, but…no. I don't need to get to know you better first. Everything I need to know is what happens to me when I look into your eyes."

He waits, his silence bristling with heat.

"I'm not in Paris for long. If this gets personal, if we get too close and share all our sad stories, it will be much harder when I leave. I'd rather keep things light." I close my eyes, ashamed by how mercenary that sounded. "Forgive me if that's crass or insulting. It's just the way I feel."

"So you only want me for my body," he says in a throaty, teasing drawl. "Well, I *never.*"

I whisper, "It is a pretty good body."

He sounds insulted. "Pretty good? Oh, stop, you'll spoil me."

"Okay, fine, egomaniac, it's an *amazing* body. Satisfied?"

He sniffs. "No."

Smiling, still with my eyes closed, I say, "It's hands down the best body I've ever seen, and that's saying a lot since I haven't even seen you naked."

Yet.

"What about the face?"

"Oh my God! You're totally fishing for compliments!"

"It's a small price to pay for using me for my many charms, don't you think?"

I start to laugh and can't stop. "Okay, fine. Your face. Your face is…well, it's pretty good, too."

"I'm going to hang up on you."

"No, you're not."

It's his turn to laugh. "You're right. I'm not. Now give me another compliment before my ego deflates and I go off and cry in a corner."

"Fine. Are you ready?"

"I'm ready."

I picture his face, all those perfect angles and lines. "Your face is the most beautiful thing I've ever seen."

Astonishingly, I actually mean it.

"Go on…"

I shake my head, trying not to laugh. Adopting a theatrical breathy voice, I say, "And your eyes…your eyes are like two limpid pools. Your voice is the honey-smoke croon of a blues singer, setting all my nerves aflutter. And your lips—oh! Your lips are like strawberry wine!"

He mutters, "Oh, for fuck's sake."

My tone turns practical. "Hey, you started it."

"You must've grown up with very annoying siblings."

I start to make a joke about how annoying my older brothers actually were, but stop myself.

My hesitation isn't lost on James. "Right. We're not getting personal."

I make a face. "Is that weird? Will it get too awkward and weird if we can't talk to each other?"

"I'm sure we'll find plenty of things to talk about."

Heat has crept back into his voice. It causes a vivid flashback of my fantasy of him thrusting into me from behind as I'm on my knees, my face buried in a pillow.

"You're quiet again."

I fan my face with my hand. "Just trying to manage this hot flash. It's a doozy."

"I'll give you a minute."

In his pause, I hear stifled laughter. Then he comes back on the line, all business. "All right, let's agree on terms."

"That sounds depressingly practical."

"It is practical, but it doesn't have to be depressing. This way, we both know what to expect. It will cut down on the weirdness."

"Okay. I'm listening."

"You mentioned you're not in Paris for long. When do you leave?"

"The first day of fall. September twenty-third."

"I'm marking it on my calendar. What do you have planned while you're here? Visiting with friends? Sightseeing?"

"You sound like a customs officer. Do you want to stamp my Visa?"

"I want to know what your schedule looks like, smartass."

I can tell by the abrupt following pause that he didn't mean to call me that. I find it oddly endearing that he did.

I say, "Normally I'd object to a man calling me names before we've even had our first date, but considering the timetable we're working with, I'll let it slide. Also, it's apropos: I am a smartass. And I like that you're comfortable enough with me to call me out on it."

"Still. It was rude. I apologize."

He sounds satisfyingly contrite. "Apology accepted. When you're not demanding compliments or ignoring people's wishes that you not sit at their bistro table, you have very charming manners, you know that? Thank you for the flowers, by the way. White tulips were a classy touch. Sophisticated, but not trying too hard. If you'd sent red roses, I would've been forced to downgrade my opinion of you."

"What's wrong with red roses? Aren't they romantic?"

"Only to people lacking imagination. Real romantics never go for the cliché because passion is so utterly individual."

After a moment, he groans softly. "You're adorable. Three months won't be long enough."

"Sorry, big guy. You already marked it on your calendar."

I say it lightly, careful not to let the tremor in my hands leak into my voice. Even over the phone, his desire is palpable.

I've been around long enough to know that things like this aren't made to last. This kind of instant, thermonuclear attraction inevitably flames out as quickly as it appears, leaving broken hearts and bewilderment in its wake. It could never withstand the day-to-day drudgery of marriage, child-rearing, and real life.

But in our case—with our real lives thousands of miles apart—it's perfect.

We'll be perfect.

Perfect strangers, unencumbered by all the bullshit that poisons desire.

"Speaking of calendars," says James, "what's on yours for tonight?"

"You're taking me to dinner. Just not Café Blanc, please."

"Not up for more verbal sparring with Jean-Luc? You seemed to handle yourself well."

"Condescending waiters make me feel stabby. That reminds me: did you know Edmond was once stabbed in the neck with a fountain pen by one of his mistresses?"

"Oh yeah. He loves to tell that story. Has he told you the one about the beautiful Asian woman he fell in love with who turned out to be a man?"

I gasp, thrilled at the drama of it. "No! Tell me right now how it ends!"

James chuckles. "I see you haven't yet met his current wife."

"Wow. Really?"

"Really. They've been married nearly twenty years and have never spent a night apart."

I take a moment to reorient this new information in my brain. "That's possibly the most romantic thing I've ever heard. Do you think they'd let me interview them about it?"

"You mean as the basis for a book?"

"Not a biography, per se, but maybe just as inspiration for a story."

"I think Edmond would pay you a gigantic sum of money if you wanted to create a fictional character based on his life."

I think of the obvious delight with which Edmond shared the story of the passionate Italian and her sister. "You know, I think you're right."

He gently teases, "Not everyone would rather contract the Ebola virus than be immortalized."

Wow, he really was *paying attention to everything.*

"So this dinner you're taking me to," I say, smiling. "Make it somewhere casual, please, because all I brought with me are jeans and T-shirts."

His tone goes rough. "Which you make look spectacular, by the way. When you walked away from the table at the café, I thought I'd fall off the chair. Your ass should be put on display in the Louvre."

That makes me laugh out loud. "Now who's the one exaggerating?"

"I'm not exaggerating."

"I know what my butt looks like, Romeo."

"You don't know what it looks like to a man."

I don't have a smart comeback to that. The hunger in his voice leaves me momentarily speechless, though I know for a fact there were dozens of far perkier asses than mine in attendance at the café.

"Okay. I'll play your game. What does it look like to a man?"

"Before I tell you—and I will tell you, this is just a side note—I want to mention that not even three minutes ago you ragged on me for fishing for compliments. And now you want me to describe your derriere."

"This is completely different."

"How so?"

"For starters, you're gorgeous. *Everyone* stares at you, even men."

"Thank you, but I don't see the difference."

"Okay, I'm not trying to be coy now, this isn't like when someone tells a supermodel she's beautiful and she goes all bashful and says something outrageously false like, 'Oh, I'm just an average girl. I'm totally plain without all this makeup.' I have no illusions about my looks. I've got a great head of hair, my teeth are good, my figure is generally in proportion, but—"

"I think you're stunning," James interrupts. "I haven't been able to stop thinking about you since the first time I saw you. In fact, I've never been as attracted to a woman before."

I allow that to wash over me for a moment. I let the sheer pleasure of those words to settle over my shoulders and wake up a sleeping swarm of butterflies in my stomach who flit ecstatically all around.

Here's the thing: if he'd said, "You're stunning," as a statement of fact, I could refute it with facts, like the list I was about to give him of all my physical shortcomings.

But you can't argue with "*I* think you're stunning," because then it's a matter of personal taste.

After a rough throat clearing, I offer a weak protest. Because maybe I am fishing for compliments, just a little bit.

"I'm almost old."

He shoots back with an irritated, "The finest bottle of wine is almost old. And by the way, that age bullshit is an American thing. In Europe, women are considered sexy at all ages. For that matter, in all shapes and sizes, too. Beauty and desirability have nothing to do with the number on your birth certificate or scale. The United States of Advertising has made everybody insecure about their looks."

It's very possible I'm going to swoon like I'm a heroine in a bodice ripper. Instead I reply, "The United States of Advertising. I like that."

"I like it, too. Anne Lamott coined the phrase in her book, *Bird by Bird*."

My shock is so great, I have to restrain myself from falling face first onto the floor. "*You've read Anne Lamott*?"

He says drily, "Try not to sound so surprised. I'm quite capable of reading a book."

"But *that* book—I mean, the woman is practically my idol. I *love* her work."

"Me too. In fact, there are a lot of books I love." His tone grows warmer. "Looks like we found something we can talk about when we're busy not getting personal."

The swooning threatens to encroach again. This man is terrible for my blood pressure.

"First things first," I say, struggling to remain cool. "We were supposed to be talking terms. Oh, and you were supposed to tell me what my ass looks like to a man."

James chuckles. “Over dinner. I’ll pick you up at eight.”

“Okay. See you then.”

“And Olivia?”

“Yes?”

His voice turns husky. “Be ready to tell me everything you want me to do to you in bed.”

The line goes dead in my hand.

5

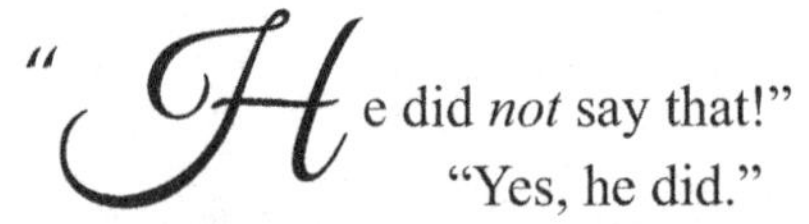

"He did *not* say that!"

"Yes, he did."

"Holy shit. I would've dropped dead on the spot."

"Trust me, I came close."

I'm pacing back and forth in the kitchen of the apartment, trying to burn off some of the adrenaline that has my hands shaking and my heart thumping like mad. I've been on the phone with Kelly for half an hour already, filling her in on everything that happened since I hung up on her at the café.

James is due to arrive in ten minutes. My antiperspirant has failed, my mouth has stopped producing saliva, and I *really* need a bourbon, but I'm afraid one will become two, then three, and then I'll be out of my wits.

And I desperately need my wits about me right now.

The few that haven't already been paralyzed by James's parting sentence.

"So what're you gonna *do*?" says Kelly, sounding almost as panicked as I am.

I laugh a little in disbelief. "I guess I'm going to make him a list."

I have to yank the phone away from my ear to save my hearing from Kelly's piercing shriek. Then she comes back on, groaning.

"I'm so jealous of you right now. *So. Jealous*. The last time Mike asked me what I wanted in bed was back when we were first dating." She stops to think for a moment. "No, that's wrong. He didn't ask me what I wanted—he asked me if I'd let him do butt sex."

I grimace. "Thanks for that. Now I'll have to picture the two of you having butt sex every time I see him."

"I said no, dummy! That hole is exit only. So what's gonna be on your list?"

"*Not* butt sex. I'm with you on that one."

"Oral?"

"Yes, of course."

We're both quiet for a moment. Then Kelly says, "Well, I'm all out of ideas."

"I know, right? I can't tell the man I really enjoy the missionary position, that's just sad!"

"We're pathetic."

"How did we not get any better ideas after buddy-reading *Fifty Shades*? That was practically a sex manual."

"That was just fantasy, babe. Nobody does that stuff in real life."

"Of course they do. There are millions of couples who enjoy bondage and spanking and stuff."

Kelly snorts. "Do you know any of them?"

"No, but that doesn't mean they don't exist. I don't know any koalas, either, but they're out there in droves, living their fuzzy little lives in the branches of eucalyptus trees."

"I feel like we're getting derailed. Back to this sexy-time list. What about dirty talk?"

That stumps me for a moment. "Huh. I don't know, I've never had a dirty talker."

"Me, neither, but it sounds kinda fun, right?"

I crinkle my nose, thinking about it. "Or it could be the stupidest thing in the world. I saw a porno one time and the guy kept repeating to the girl, 'Come for me, come for me,' and I was like, nagging a woman into orgasm has never worked in the history of sex, pal."

Kelly scoffs. "When did you see a porno?"

I adopt a tone of withering disdain. "Excuse me, but I'm a grown woman. I have watched a pornographic film."

"Sure you have. What was it called?"

"I can't believe you don't believe me!"

"You're a fiction writer. You make things up for a living. And you exaggerate more than anyone else I know."

I mutter to myself, "Why am I even friends with this person?"

"Moving on. What about sex in a public place?"

"Like where?"

"A restroom?"

"Gross."

"The back seat of a car?"

"I'm not that flexible. Something would cramp and unattractive flailing would ensue."

"A park?"

I consider it, trying to picture the scene. James and I are on a bench—a secluded one, under a tree—and I'm on his lap. I'm wearing an overcoat that's hiding my legs, which are straddled on either side of his hips as I ride him, getting closer and closer to orgasm, my head thrown back and my fingers clenched into his hair as he ravishes my breasts with his hot, hungry mouth…

When an old man walking a poodle dodders past and shouts, "I'm calling the police!"

"I don't want to get arrested for public indecency, thank you."

Kelly heaves a sigh. "I'm gonna get on Google and see if I can find any good ideas. I'll text you if I have anything."

"You sure you want to do that? Google can be a scary place. I once searched on 'natural headache remedy' and became convinced within five minutes that I had an infestation of parasitic fleas feasting on my brain. If you start looking up ideas for sex you might wind up on some site with graphic pictures of gangrene of the genitalia."

Kelly makes a soft sound of condolence. "It must be scary inside that head of yours."

"You have no idea. I wish I could clone myself so I'd have someone who understood."

The doorbell rings, and I freeze. "Oh shit."

"What's wrong?"

"He's early!"

Kelly hoots. "All right, let's get this party started, sister! *Rawr*!"

"Please stop making tiger noises. I'm having a breakdown here."

"You'll be fine."

"I'm scared."

"You're not scared," says Kelly firmly. "You're nervous. Two different things. And remember…"

"What?"

Her voice gentles. "You can survive anything, babe. A date with a hot guy is nothing compared to what you've been through."

My throat gets tight. I have to blow out a hard breath before I can speak again. "Have I told you lately that I love you?"

"I love you, too. Now go break off a piece of that man candy and have yourself a good time. And call me *first thing* in the morning. I want to hear *every* dirty detail."

As the doorbell rings again, I say, "Copy that, Sarge. Talk to you tomorrow."

We hang up and I head to the front door, grabbing my purse from a chair and stuffing my cell phone into the back pocket of my jeans. Then I stand in front of the door with my hand on the knob, gathering my courage.

I pull open the door and there he is, all tall, dark, and gorgeous six-foot-plus of alpha male. A lion on the hunt in the Serengeti wouldn't look half as majestic.

Or hungry.

We stand there staring at each other in crackling silence until he says, "Your face is red."

"And my palms are sweaty. How are you?"

"Feeling like a champagne cork right after that wire thing on top is removed."

"About to blow, huh?"

Eyes flashing, he looks me up and down. "Have you ever snorted heroin?"

"Nope."

"I haven't, either, but I bet this is what it feels like."

"I know. This isn't normal. I'm glad it's not only me, though, because that would be sad."

His cheeks crease as he smiles. He's wearing jeans and an untucked white dress shirt, like the first time I saw him at the café. He's unnaturally good-looking. It's intimidating, to be honest. The guy has a face that should be on the cover of magazines, and here I am…not looking like that.

I say, "I think you need to tell me what my ass looks like to a man now, because I'm having trouble wrapping my head around how pretty you are." I make a motion with my hand indicating the two of us. "Is it glorious enough to bridge the gap?"

Blue eyes burning, he says roughly, "It is definitely fucking glorious. It's perfect, in fact. Do you know why women's asses are sometimes compared to fruit?"

"*Fruit*?"

"Yeah. An apple. A peach. Like that."

"I think we're reading different books."

He ignores me. "It's because when a man sees a perfect, round, ripe ass—like yours—his mouth waters and all he can think about is sinking his teeth into it."

I purse my lips, examining his expression, finally deciding this right here is enough for me to go on for the next fifty or sixty years. We don't even have to kiss or have sex or anything —the way he's looking at me is so deeply satisfying an orgasm wouldn't even be close.

Okay, that's an exaggeration, but you know what I mean.

He holds up a finger. "Also? Your breasts—"

"Wait, let me guess. My breasts are like cantaloupes."

"I was going to say honeydew melons."

After a moment, I say, "You know, if anyone had told me I'd so thoroughly enjoy a man comparing my body parts to various fruits and melons, I'd have told them they were crazy."

Nodding, he says somberly, "You're a modern woman, after all."

"Exactly. I consider myself a feminist. I have a college degree. Several, in fact. Yet here I am, wallowing in how fantastic it feels to hear you call my boobs cantaloupes."

"Honeydew melons."

"Right. Sorry. Where was I?"

"You're a feminist with an advanced education."

I nod. "Exactly."

"You don't need a man to be complete."

"Yes! You understand what I'm saying!"

"And you definitely don't need a man bossing you around."

"No. No way, Jose."

James takes a step closer, crossing the threshold and gazing unblinking down into my eyes. His voice throaty, he says, "Except in bed."

Every nerve in my body jumps into full, screaming alert. My heart slams against my breastbone. He's so close I feel the heat radiating from his body, the same heat that engulfs me in a wave and rocks me back onto my heels, leaving me burning with lust.

I exhale a quiet, unsteady breath. "Wow."

"I know. Imagine what it'll feel like when we kiss." Looking at my mouth, he moistens his lips.

"I'm starting to wonder if that might be a bad idea. Have you heard of those people who randomly explode into flames?"

"Spontaneous human combustion," he says, still staring at my mouth.

"Yes. I'm the type of person that could happen to."

Slowly, James leans forward and lowers his head. He runs the tip of his nose along my jaw, then whispers into my ear, "I'll have to be careful, then, won't I?"

Never in the history of rhetorical questions has one been so scorching hot.

He straightens, smiling—obviously recognizing I'm fighting to maintain consciousness—and takes my hand.

"Let's go get dinner. We'll eat, we'll drink, we'll talk. Then we'll come back and sit on your sofa and I'll practice being careful with you until you're completely satisfied."

Oh, that devilish smirk. I knew I was in trouble.

I say lightly, "Okay, but I have to warn you: I'm very hard to please."

He lifts my hand to his mouth and brushes his lips across my knuckles. "Good. I love a challenge."

I'm so distracted by all the possibilities that I forget to lock the door as we leave.

6

He takes me to a lovely restaurant overlooking the Seine. It's quiet, candlelit, and cozy, the view of the river breathtaking as it sparkles under the glow of the rising moon. Like the rest of Paris, it's a spot perfectly designed for romance.

I feel sorry for anyone who dares to be single in this city.

We're seated in a corner of the room by an immaculate maître d'. He and James exchange a few words in French, then the waiter disappears. We're left gazing at each other across the table as the elegant notes of a jazz trio wafts over from another room.

James says, "Are you all right?"

"Yes."

No. I'm wound so tight I could snap.

He takes a moment to examine my expression. "Let's try that again. And this time tell me the truth."

I flatten my clammy hands on the linen tablecloth on either side of my plate. I draw a breath, let it out, then say, "I originally thought not jumping into bed with you right away would enhance things—you know, heighten desire and whatnot—but now I'm thinking I underestimated the effect you have on my nervous system."

When he simply sits there, waiting for me to continue, I admit sheepishly, "I could be in danger of passing out."

His eyes burn, but he keeps his tone light. "If you fall face first into your entrée, I promise to rescue you."

"You won't let me aspirate my bouillabaisse or choke on my coq au vin?"

His lips twitch as he tries to suppress a smile. "No, I won't. And if you require CPR to dislodge a chicken bone that might fly down your throat when your face hits the plate, I'm your man."

I smile a little. It's much easier to do this when we're being silly. "But are you *certified* in CPR? I don't want anyone with such bulky muscles as yours bashing away at my sternum like it's a bongo drum. You could crack something."

His smile breaks through in all its dazzling glory. "I think we've already established that I'm going to be careful with you."

When I swallow hard, he chuckles. Then, eyes twinkling, he reaches across the table, squeezes my hand, and lets me off the hook by changing the subject.

"I hope you don't mind that I ordered us cocktails. I know you're a modern woman, but a gentleman does like to make some things easier for a lady."

His hand is big, warm, and rough—exactly how I imagined it would be when I masturbated to the thought of him.

It's a good thing I recently had a complete physical that showed I was in perfect health, because otherwise I'd be convinced this feeling I'm experiencing is either a stroke or some obscure variety of seizure where you appear normal on the outside, but inside every muscle has clenched to stone.

"As long as you don't go overboard and try to order my dinner for me," I manage to say. "There's a fine line between being gentlemanly and being domineering."

His gaze holding mine and his tone serious, James replies, "That's a line I love to walk."

Stroke. Seizure. Acute aortic catastrophe. Through it all, somehow my lungs continue to work. "Now you're deliberately baiting me."

"It's just nerves. You've been through worse."

The way he says it—and the similarity to what Kelly said earlier on the phone—startles me. It's as if he already knows me, as if he knows everything there is to know about me, where all my deepest scars and wounds are hidden, where every black hole of anguish lies.

My mind starts to whir.

Did Estelle tell Edmond why I came to Paris? Did Edmond then tell James about me? Does he know?

A waiter arrives with two bourbons in cut crystal glasses and sets them on the table in front of us. I release James's hand. The waiter begins to speak in English, but I'm tuned out, listening instead to my churning thoughts.

What if he looked me up online? There were articles in the paper. He knows I'm a writer, all he'd need to do is type in my name—

"Olivia?"

I jerk back into the present to find James and the waiter looking at me. Waiting for an answer to a question I missed.

"I'm sorry, what were you asking?"

Patiently, the waiter repeats the evening's specials. I feel the weight of James's stare, but I don't look at him.

"The scallops sound lovely, thank you."

"Anything to start?"

I realize I must've missed that part of his speech, too. "Um, whatever you suggest."

He beams. "The foie gras is incredible."

"Anything but that."

He blinks at my disgusted tone, then offers, “Perhaps the phyllo-wrapped brie with fig preserves?”

“Yes. Perfect. Thank you.”

James orders filet mignon and a green salad, the waiter departs, and then we’re left alone with my blossoming anxiety.

James takes me in for a while in silence. “I’ve said something wrong.”

Crap. If he’s going to be this damn observant all the time, this will never work.

“No, not wrong. Just…” I glance up to find him staring at me with his signature intensity, all smoldering masculinity and hungry eyes. “I was wondering if you spoke to Edmond about me.”

He leans back in his chair. Without breaking our gazes, he says evenly, “Yes. I asked him to tell me everything he knew about you.”

My heart does a painful flip beneath my breastbone. “And what did he say?”

“That you were a friend of Estelle’s, staying in her unit. A writer on holiday from America.”

I study him. *Is he holding something back?* “What else?”

“That you seemed very bright and charming, but you had the saddest eyes of anyone he’d ever met.”

Our locked gazes feel like a physical connection, fingers interlaced and squeezing, a live wire conducting heat and electricity between us across empty space.

I say, “The next person who tells me I have sad eyes is going to get a fork stuck into one of his own.”

“I know,” comes the soft response. “You don’t want to talk about anything personal, and I’ll respect that. But you did ask.”

His tone is both gentle and intimate, as if we’re already lovers. The sheer tenderness of it makes a lump form in my throat. I haven’t had tenderness from a man in forever. I haven’t had this kind of undivided attention in forever, either, and the worst thing about it is…I don't deserve it.

I don't deserve to be sitting here living and breathing when the only reason I had to live is six feet underground.

I'm horrified to discover my eyes are watering.

Desperate to escape his searing eyes, I tear my gaze from his and stand. "Excuse me for a moment, please. I need to use the ladies' room."

Without waiting for an answer, I turn from the table and walk at a breakneck pace across the restaurant to the double doors near the foyer we passed on the way in.

I burst into the restroom and collapse against the opposite wall as the door closes behind me. I stand there trembling, wondering how the hell he makes me feel stripped so raw when all I've felt the past two years is entombed.

He melted me with his first look. His first searching, *seeing* look.

I drop my face into my hands and groan.

This was a stupid idea. I'm obviously not ready for this. It's naïve to think emotions won't get involved if I can't even sit at a table with him without bolting in a panic.

It's not like this is the first time it's happened, either. Every time I talk to the man, I end up running away. If I slept with him I'd probably unravel completely!

I picture myself curled naked in a sobbing ball on his bed as he looks on helplessly, wondering which mental institution to call first.

"Olivia."

I look up and emit a peep of terror. James stands across from me inside the ladies' room door, materialized as soundlessly as a ghost.

I open my mouth to stammer some mortified excuse for why I'm acting like such a lunatic, but before I can speak, James closes the distance between us and gathers me into his arms.

All my distress instantly quiets. I descend straight from the frantic chaos of my head to the real and grounding presence of his body.

Oh Lord. Oh holy…

If I thought I were melted before by his eyes, his big, warm, solid frame against mine proves to be an entirely different form of liquefication. Parts of me I didn't even know I had are thawing and beginning to burn.

"Just breathe," he says quietly, his mouth close to my ear. "Just feel me and breathe."

Seven more beautiful words have never been spoken.

The way I sag against him in relief, it's as if a spell has been cast. I wind my arms around his shoulders, bury my face into his neck, and inhale a breath scented of his skin. When I let it out, I'm almost groggy with desire.

Against my breasts, his heart hammers as madly as mine does.

He presses his cheek against mine. He twines a hand into my hair, cradling my head in his palm. He curves around me, protecting me from—what? My own fear, I suppose. My imagination. My past and all its baggage.

Myself.

Someone pushes open the door and proceeds toward the stalls as if we're invisible. She uses the toilet, washes her hands, and leaves without a word, as if two lovers entwined in the entry of a restroom is completely unremarkable, a thing so commonplace it doesn't even merit a look.

Maybe it is. It's Paris, after all. Entwined lovers are as common a sight as street lamps.

"Better?" James whispers, his rough jaw tickling my cheek.

"So much better," I whisper back, burrowing closer to him. "Do you have a side gig taming wild animals, by chance? Because if not, you'd be really good at it."

His chuckle is a low rumbling vibration against my face. It's ridiculous how much I like the sound. I want to record it and play it back when I'm stressed out, let it soothe me like the hypnotic chanting of a thousand gathered Buddhist monks.

Yeah, I tried group chanting with monks. I've tried everything. Grief sends people in desperate search of any kind of relief.

"When I was a kid, I wanted to be a veterinarian," says James, withdrawing slightly to smile down into my eyes. "Does that count?"

"So you're an animal lover along with everything else. Great."

"Why do you sound disappointed?"

"I'm trying to find a fatal flaw for insurance."

"Insurance? Against what?"

I open my mouth but stop myself before blurting, *Against falling in love with you.* Instead I give him a mysterious smile.

"I forgot," he says, examining my face. "We're not getting personal."

"Although you made an oopsie a second ago by telling me you wanted to be a vet as a kid."

"We better talk terms over dinner so I don't put my foot in my mouth again. I need to know what the ground rules are." His gaze drops to my mouth.

When he just keeps staring at my lips, I start to get self-conscious. "Don't tell me you're thinking about fruit-to-body-part comparisons right now."

He says gruffly, "I'm thinking about how much I want to kiss you, and how much I also don't want the first time we kiss to be ten steps away from a toilet."

That sends a little thrill straight through me. I love how he says what's on his mind without any attempt to hide it or dress it up.

This man is very good for my ego. Very good, indeed.

Smiling and much calmer than before, I flatten my hands

over his hard pecs. "Hold that thought until we get through dinner. If I don't get something to eat soon, you won't be able to kiss me at all because I'll be hauled away to jail for gnawing on all the furniture."

His eyes warm and his smile indulgent, James brushes his thumb over my lower lip. "And here I thought *I* was the reason you were feeling light headed."

I grin at him. "Nope. Hypoglycemia is the culprit, my friend."

We both conveniently ignore the fact that I told him not even ten minutes ago about his effect on my nervous system.

He turns and leads me by the hand out of the restroom, holding it tight even after we're sitting down at the table and have started on our drinks.

7

We end up closing the place down.

We eat, drink, laugh, and talk until we're the last ones in the restaurant and the wait staff are clustered near the kitchen doors, collectively glowering in our direction.

Not that I care. I'm having the best time I've had in years. I never want the night to end.

I say, "Ugh, I can't *believe* you like Hemingway! He's so unbearably macho."

I'm rolling my eyes but smiling as I lick from my spoon the last morsel of a delicious chocolate mousse we shared. James ordered no less than four different desserts, because I couldn't decide on just one.

"And I can't believe you're such a literary snob," James shoots back. "Macho or not, the man was a genius. Look at his legacy. Look at his body of work—"

"Genius? Please. He was a bully and a braggart and wrote some of the worst fake biblical prose ever to hit the market. 'I am thee and thou art me…' What bullshit. Combine his love of three word sentences with a pathological aversion to adverbs and the man is insufferable. I can't believe he's still being taught in schools."

"Do you object more to his writing style or to his personal character? Because you have to separate the artist from his work. Otherwise we'd have to burn every Picasso. Now *that* was an arrogant asshole."

I nod in agreement. "A womanizer, too. Like Hemingway."

James shrugs. "Many famous and successful men are. Imagine having beautiful women constantly wanting to sleep with you—"

"I'm straight, but thanks," I interrupt drily.

"—literally throwing themselves at you day and night. A man would have to be a saint to resist that kind of temptation."

"Funny, that's exactly what I thought about you the first time I saw you. Every woman in the café had a spontaneous orgasm when you walked in."

He scoffs. "You're exaggerating again."

"If I am, it's only a teeny bit. Even some of the *men* looked at you like they wanted to lick you from head to toe."

When his expression sours, I laugh. "C'mon, James, don't be modest. You must know how gorgeous you are."

He pauses for a moment, staring at me in a strange, weighted silence. Then he drops his gaze to his empty bourbon glass and says darkly, "Only on the outside."

A tremor of recognition passes through me. It's the same feeling I had when I looked at his portraits. The animal sense of awareness of one's own tribe.

Birds of a feather flock together. Though we're still not much more than strangers, I know intuitively that he and I are alike.

Suffering is the great equalizer of humankind.

I recall him standing there surrounded by admiring women at the party, looking miserable and alone, and how oblivious he was to all the stares he received walking into the café, and realize with a jolt that this is a man for whom most other people have ceased to exist.

The happy ones, anyway. The normal ones who still have light in their eyes.

It's only people like me he can see or connect with. People submerged in their own darkness, the way he's submerged in his.

I say urgently, "Whatever bad thing happened to you, it hasn't made you less beautiful. There's beauty in darkness, too. It just takes a different kind of vision to see it."

When he lifts his head and looks at me, the anguish in his eyes pierces my heart. His lips part. For a moment we simply stare at each other, our surroundings forgotten.

Then he reaches around the table, grasps me by the arms, and drags me onto his lap.

He kisses me with a fierce desperation that takes my breath away. With one arm wrapped around my back and a hand gripped around my jaw, he eats me with kisses, his mouth hard and demanding, until I'm shaking and making soft noises of need low in my throat.

He breaks away, breathing roughly, and mutters, "*Fuck.*"

My fingers are clenched in the front of his shirt. My armpits are damp, my nipples are hard, and there's a throbbing ache between my legs. I'm dizzy and panting, my taste buds and nose full of him, my skin in flames.

Without opening my eyes, I whisper, "More. Please, *more*."

He doesn't hesitate. His mouth slides back over mine. Gentler this time, slower, but somehow even hungrier. He takes my head in both hands and makes fists in my hair, holding me still for his tongue to probe deeply as he takes what he wants and gives me what I need, his erection big and stiff against my bottom.

This time when he breaks away, he's softly groaning.

And I'm about to explode with desire.

Someone clears his throat. "Ahem. *Excusez-moi.*"

My lids drift open. Standing beside our table is our waiter, smiling politely. He says something in French, pats the leather billfold he's holding, places it at the edge of the table, and leaves.

I say breathlessly, "I think that's our cue."

James gazes at me, his face inches from mine, his eyes hazy and hot. He adjusts my body on top of his, using a belt loop in my jeans to pull me closer and a little lower, so I'm leaning back in his arms, my face tilted up toward his. I'm a purring kitten curled up in his lap.

He says in a guttural voice, "I'm not ready yet," and takes my mouth again.

These kisses of his…they're demanding and possessive. They're hungry and deep. They're the kisses of a man who wants more of a woman—who wants everything—and isn't going to stop until he gets it.

I cling to him and tremble, knowing I'm going to give it to him. Knowing deep in my bones that whatever it is James demands of me, I'm going to give it, no questions asked.

He moans into my mouth. I arch into him, growing more desperate by the second, digging my fingers into his arms, then sliding my hands up around his strong shoulders so I can dig my fingers into his hair. All that thick, silky hair. And his neck—God, even his neck is beautiful, strong and hot, his pulse pounding wildly under my palm.

We slowly melt into each other, our lips fused, our bodies on fire, until I can't tell where I end and he begins. He squeezes my ass and flexes his hips, breathing hard through his nose as he presses his erection against me and drinks deep from my mouth.

If he pinched one of my nipples right now, I'd climax.

Another throat clearing, this one louder.

Breaking our kiss, James turns his head and glares at the waiter as if he's going to kill him with his bare hands. He says something low and sharp that makes the waiter's eyes widen and has him taking a step back. Then the waiter recovers his composure, sticks his nose in the air, and whirls around and leaves.

Reeling, I watch him stalk away. "I hope he's not off to call the police."

James presses a kiss against my jaw, another—firm and quick—against my mouth. "If people could get arrested for kissing in public in this country, the police wouldn't have time to do anything else."

He takes me with him as he rises, sets me on my feet—steadying me when I wobble—and pulls his wallet out of the back pocket of his jeans. He throws a wad of cash on top of the billfold, then grabs my hand.

I barely have time to pluck my handbag from the back of my chair before I'm following James at a half run toward the front door of the restaurant, pulled along helplessly in his wake like a swimmer caught in a riptide, headed out into dangerous waters as the shoreline swiftly recedes.

Outside on the street, he hails a taxi with a whistle and bundles me inside. As soon as the door is shut and he's instructed the driver where to go, we're on each other again, frantic and grasping, as horny and hurried as two teenagers on a curfew, wild for each other, oblivious to everything else.

With a suddenness that's shattering, he breaks away.

For a moment I'm so surprised, I can't speak. When I do, my voice is a rasp. "What's wrong? Are you okay?"

Collapsing back into the seat on his side of the cab, he holds his arm out between us like a barrier. I'm not sure who he's protecting, me or himself.

"Wait. *Wait.*" He swallows, gulping air and sweating, his hand shaking along with the rest of him. "We haven't talked about—the rules—the terms you wanted—we didn't go over any of that."

I'm so bewildered I just stare at him as the city passes by the windows in flashes of light and color. “You want to talk about that right *now*?”

“I need to know…before we…I need to know what’s off limits. What’s allowed. What might drive you away—”

“Drive me away?” I repeat, growing more and more confused.

He just stares at me, his eyes wild, his chest heaving up and down. He appears as if he’s restraining himself from lunging at me.

His look of raw need is electrifying.

Whatever’s behind this hesitation, I understand instinctively that he won’t go any further with me unless I articulate what I want and don’t want from this situation.

From *him*.

“Okay. Here it is: don’t ask what happened to make my eyes sad. Don’t ask Edmond any more questions about me, either. No personal questions. No pressure. No strings. In fact, let’s not even exchange last names. Let’s just enjoy this while it lasts before I have to leave.”

He glances at my mouth, moistens his lips, then meets my gaze again. “That’s it?”

“I’m sorry, but that’s what I need to feel comfortable. If you’re not good with that, I completely understand.”

“I’m good with it.” He drags a hand through his hair, exhaling, and drops his arm to his side. “And you never have to apologize to me for being honest. It’s what I want.”

I stare at him for a moment before saying, “You seem relieved. What were you expecting I was going to say?”

His laugh is soft and husky. He shakes his head. “Nothing, it’s just…I haven’t had a woman…I haven’t been with someone in a while…a long time, actually…”

I arch my brows, watching him struggle to find words. Words I can’t believe I’m really hearing.

A man as desirable as he is hasn’t been with a woman in *a*

long time?

Terror seizes me.

There are only a few reasons why a man like him would go without sex for a long time, and none of them are good. Especially the one I'm thinking of.

He catches the look on my face. "What?"

"Um…wow, this is awkward."

"Just spit it out."

"Do you…are you…contagious?"

He blinks. "Excuse me?"

Heat rises up my neck. My ears begin to burn. "I'm so sorry if this is indelicate, but we're adults, and I guess we just need to get this conversation out of the way."

He looks at me in obvious confusion. I square my shoulders and take a deep breath.

"Do you have an STD?"

In the front of the cab, the driver snorts.

Deep furrows appear in James's brow. "That's the first thing you come up with when I tell you I haven't been with anyone in a while? That I'm *diseased*?"

"Not the first thing, just the worst, because that's how my brain works. I wasn't sure if you were trying to find a way to tell me I'd have to buy a special latex body suit to wear or get some powerful antibiotics or something."

When James simply sits there staring at me in wordless dismay, the cab driver says in heavily-accented English over his shoulder, "You're right to ask. AIDS cases *are* on the rise."

I turn and give him the stink eye. "Thank you for that enlightening kernel of unsolicited information. You're a gem. Now go back to minding your own business, please."

He shrugs, turning away.

I look back and find James still staring at me. I say, "So it's a no on the STDs, then."

"It's an unequivocal no. You?"

"Also no."

After a moment of awkward silence, he sighs heavily. All the electrifying need from a few moments ago drains out of him. Now he simply looks tired.

"I just…I can't do small talk anymore. I can't do fake. I don't have the energy it takes to flirt and pretend to be interested in all the shallow, superficial shit I have to wade through before I actually get to know someone. Before I can tell if she's worth my time. Because that's…"

After a tense moment, he goes on more quietly, his voice almost lost under the sound of the tires moving over the road.

"It's like you said, Olivia. Life's too short to mince words. Our existence is measured in minutes. Seconds. Heartbeats. Time is the most valuable commodity we have, because it can never be replenished. Once it's gone…it's gone forever. And so are we."

A powerful wave of emotion sweeps over me. That headsmack of recognition again, kicking me between the eyes.

I'm such a fool. He hasn't been with anyone for the same reason I haven't: desire is the first thing that grief kills, before it kills everything else.

I think of those portraits of his, all those lovingly detailed renderings of human anguish, and want to curl into a ball and cry.

Whatever happened to him, whatever toll life has forced him to pay, and has inspired his morbid obsession with immortalizing the faces of people grieving, and has drawn him straight into my arms like a moth to a flame, it's just as terrible as what I've been through.

I exhale an unsteady breath and say in a tight voice, "I'm an asshole."

He knows exactly what I mean. Shaking his head, he reaches for me. "No."

"Yes. Oh God, I'm so sorry. I should've known you didn't have an STD."

"You couldn't have known. It was a legitimate question. And stop apologizing, goddammit."

He tucks me under his shoulder and winds his arms around me. I curl both my legs over his. Into his neck, I whisper, "Oh, James, I feel like such an idiot."

"Why?"

"Because I sometimes forget that other people have had bad things happen to them, too. I forget I'm not the only one walking around with a hole in my chest where a heart used to be. I had no idea how self-centered I'd become…or how isolated. How I'd spend almost every waking moment feeling as if I'd been stranded on an alien planet and there was nothing left for me to do but take scientific notes about the hostile native life forms while I waited around to die."

A sound breaks from his chest. A chuckle of amusement or a gentle snort of disbelief, I don't know which. Then I feel his lips press against my hair and hear his sigh.

"God, you talk in long sentences. Hemingway wouldn't approve."

I nudge him with my elbow. "Shut up."

"Make me."

When I lift my head, he's smiling. The heat is creeping back into his eyes.

"By the way," he murmurs, pressing a soft kiss to my mouth, "that was a *very* personal speech you just delivered. You little rule breaker, you."

I tuck my head into the crook between his neck and shoulder and close my eyes. "Last one. Scout's honor."

"You were a Girl Scout?"

I gently tease, "Hello, personal question."

"Shit. You're right. Strike that."

Smiling, feeling safe in his arms, I say, "I *was* in the Girl Scouts…until they threw me out."

When I'm silent too long, he says, "That's evil. You can't just dangle that out there and not expect a follow up question!"

"Let your imagination run wild."

He growls, "Oh, I'll let something run wild all right, but it won't be my imagination."

He grasps my jaw in his hand and crushes his mouth to mine.

8

It turns out to be convenient that I didn't lock the apartment door on the way out, because it means I don't have to stop kissing James to dig through my handbag for keys on the way in.

I simply turn the knob and we go right back at it.

We fall through the door, kissing madly. I drop my handbag on the floor. James kicks the door shut behind us, then pushes me against the wall and pins me there, his chest flush with mine. He clasps both my wrists in one of his big hands and holds my arms behind my back as he kisses me hard in the unlit entryway, his free hand firmly gripping my face.

It's hot. It's insanely hot, dominant, and passionate, just this side of rough.

When we stop to gasp for air, I start laughing.

"Oh my God, this is just like in the movies!"

"Only better," he says in a husky tone, blue eyes glowing with lust. "Because it's real."

"It can't possibly get better than this," I say, panting. "Maybe we should stop at kissing, because this is absolutely *epic*—"

I yelp in shock when he swiftly bends and throws me over his shoulder.

The man throws me over his shoulder! Wait until I tell Kelly about *this*!

"We're not stopping," he growls, striding into the living room as I swing from his shoulder like something he caught in a trap in the forest and is bringing home to eat.

Laughter threatens to break from my mouth again, so I bite my lip to stop it. I feel crazed, possessed by the weirdest mix of glee and terror, like the feeling you get when you're at the tippy top of a high, dangerous roller coaster, just about to crest over the edge and go zooming recklessly down.

James tosses me onto my back on the living room sofa. I bounce, once, then stare up at him wide-eyed as my heart threatens to burst inside my chest.

I've had panic attacks less severe than this.

He gazes at me with unwavering intensity as his fingers fly over the buttons of his shirt. "You look scared."

"Shitless," I admit, shaking. "You better hurry up and take off your clothes before I suffer some kind of serious health crisis and you have to call an ambulance."

His shirt parts under his fingers. He shrugs out of it and lets it drop to the floor.

And I simply stare up at him with my mouth open.

Maybe God doesn't hate me so much after all, because if he, she, or it did, I'd never have been given something as incredible as this.

He's.

Fucking.

Perfect.

Chiseled, sculpted, carved, hewn…you name it, he's all the adjectives there are for hard, masculine beauty. His chest is a masterpiece. His abs could make angels weep. This guy makes Michelangelo's *David* look like something a first-semester art student at a community college glued together out of old newspapers and cat turds.

It's only a nanosecond after that thought hits that it's followed by another, far worse: *I have to get naked in front of this walking piece of art.*

My sudden terror isn't lost on James. "All the blood just drained from your face."

I say, "Oh, don't mind me, I'm just down here dealing with some major body image issues brought out in full force by how *ridiculously* ripped you are. Please tell me that eight pack is cleverly contoured makeup."

He kneels over me, plants his hands on the cushion on either side of my head, and smiles. "You know it isn't."

Is my gulp audible? I bet it's audible. I bet he can even hear all my cells screaming at the top of their petrified little lungs. "Spoiler alert: my body doesn't look like that."

He leans down to nuzzle my neck. "Good thing, too, because I'm not into guys."

He inhales deeply against my throat. Goosebumps erupt over every inch of my skin.

"You know what I mean. Compared to you, I'm sort of… gelatinous. Jiggly. Like Jell-O."

He lifts his head, gazes deep into my eyes, takes one of my hands and presses it against the monster straining for release under the zipper of his jeans, and murmurs, "I *love* Jell-O. Can't you tell?"

Before I can sigh dreamily and slide off the sofa to lie in a bedazzled heap on the floor, he settles his pelvis between my spread thighs and lowers his upper body against mine, balancing on his elbows above me. Then he kisses me again, a deep, slow kiss that has me squirming underneath him within seconds.

I need to remember to send Estelle a thank you note for buying such a large and comfortable sofa.

James chuckles against my mouth. "Is all this wriggling an escape attempt or am I doing something right?"

"You're fishing for compliments again. That's a bad habit of yours, Romeo."

His lips brush against mine, whisper soft. His voice comes very low. "It's not about compliments. It's about feedback. I want to make you feel good. I want to know what you like."

Heat detonates throughout my body, leaving me tongue tied and sweating. The heat wave is followed by panic, because I don't have any idea what I'm going to put on the list he demanded of all the things I want him to do to me in bed.

Though they're two of my favorite things, cuddling and foot massage are probably not what he has in mind.

I say meekly, "Oh, okay. Um…this is very nice."

One of his brows climbs. "Nice? Hmm."

The *hmm* sounds vaguely threatening, but I don't have time to dwell on it. I'm too preoccupied trying not to die at the electric touch of his tongue against my bare stomach.

He pushes my T-shirt up so my bra is exposed and bends his head to my belly, licking and kissing a slow path from the bottom of my bra to the top button of my jeans. I lie frozen, panting, staring glassy-eyed at the ceiling, convinced his tongue is equipped with tiny electrodes due to the pulsing currents of electricity shooting straight down between my legs.

When he sinks his teeth into my flesh, I jump, gasping.

"Too hard?" His voice is muffled by my skin. He kisses where he nipped, his mouth gentle.

"N—no. Just wasn't ready for it. Ignore me. Busy dying. Proceed."

He rewards my breathless blathering with an indulgent chuckle and a firm squeeze of his big hands around my waist. He flicks open the button on my jeans with his thumb, then eases the zipper down, nuzzling his nose deep into my panties.

When he gently bites me there, too, I moan.

"That sounds encouraging," he whispers. "Let's see if I can get you to do it again."

He tugs on the waistband of my jeans, sliding them past my hips to the middle of my thighs. Then he pulls down my panties and stares at me, exposed and trembling.

His eyes burning black with desire, he licks the pad of his thumb, slips it between my legs, and presses down on the engorged bud of my clitoris.

I suck in a breath, closing my eyes. When he lazily strokes his thumb up and down, I give him the moan he wanted, this one louder than before.

"Tell me what you want, Olivia."

"I want…" *To not have to talk about what I want.*

"Be brave. Talk to me."

His voice is soft and hypnotic. His thumb is wreaking havoc on my body. It's probably the combination of the two that makes me blurt, "I want your mouth."

He makes a pleased hum. "Good. Where?"

"You're killing me," I say, panting, my eyes squeezed shut. My hips start to flex in time with the up and down strokes of his thumb.

He teases, "You're a writer. Use a few of all those big words you must know."

When he slides his thumb inside me, I groan, arching.

"Although I love that sound, it's not a word. If you don't talk, I'm going to stop."

Through gritted teeth, I say, "Bossy!"

He chuckles. "You haven't seen bossy yet, beautiful, but you will. Here, I'll start a sentence for you. 'James, I want you to put your mouth…'"

When I bite my lip and stay silent, he removes his hand. I groan again, this time in protest, and open my eyes.

He's kneeling over me, staring down with bedroom eyes and a sultry smile. He lifts a hand to my face and slowly presses his thumb past my lips and into my mouth so I taste myself.

Then he kisses me, deeply, until I'm making desperate noises and pawing at him, at all those muscles of his and his warm, smooth skin. I grab his ass and grind my pelvis against his erection.

He moves his cheek against mine and whispers next to my ear, "Do you want my mouth on your pussy, Olivia?"

Dear sweet Jesus in heaven, I'm dying. This is it. I'm dying right here and now.

"Yes."

"Say it."

Now *that* was bossy. His tone is low, rough, and unmistakably dominant, and sends a thrill straight through me. It pulls the words right from my lips.

"I want your mouth on my pussy."

It's barely audible, but it does the trick. In one swift move, he slides down my body and puts his face between my legs.

I realize the benefits of frank sexual communication the moment I feel his hot, wet tongue stroke over my clit.

I cry out, my back bowing from the sofa. He slides his hands under my ass and grips it as he sucks and licks me, making little grunts of masculine satisfaction that are almost unbearably sexy. My jeans aren't low enough on my legs to allow me to open my thighs wider, but that small restriction seems unbearably sexy, too.

In fact, the only thing that doesn't seem sexy at the moment is that I'm too aware of my hands. They're clenched next to my hips. Am I supposed to put them into his hair? Fling my arms out to either side? Play with my boobs?

Obviously, I haven't had sex since the dark ages.

"James," I say breathlessly.

He lifts his head, licking his lips.

God, so fucking hot. "Since we're being so verbally expressive, is this a good time to tell you I'm feeling awkward about my hands?"

"What's wrong with your hands, sweetheart?" Still looking at me, he presses a gentle kiss on my throbbing clit.

"I don't know what to do with them."

A dent forms in his cheek. He's trying not to laugh at me. Then he sits up and whips off his belt. "I know what to do with them."

The thrilling dominance is back in his voice.

I could really, really get used to that.

He gathers my wrists together and quickly wraps his belt around them, slipping the buckle under one of the loops to keep it secure. Then he raises my arms over my head, resting my bound wrists on the arm of the sofa.

Looking deep into my eyes, he commands, "Don't move from this position, or I'll spank your ass until it's red."

I can't decide which one I'm more: outraged or turned the fuck on.

I say hotly, "You will *not* spank me!"

He smiles. "Oh, yes, I will."

"James! I'm a grown woman!"

"You are. A sexy, beautiful grown woman with an ass like a ripe peach that's going to get spanked for disobedience if you move your arms."

"I don't like spanking!"

He pauses to examine my expression. "That's something you've tried before?"

I twist my lips, loath to admit I haven't. "I mean…not exactly."

He's still examining me with slightly narrowed eyes. "Is that a yes or a no?"

After a moment, I admit grudgingly. "It's a no."

"So you just object to it in theory, then."

"Of course I object to it in theory! What kind of person enjoys pain?"

"Masochists."

"Ugh, semantics! You know what I mean!"

Another pause as he gauges my expression, then he demands, "Tell me what really bothers you about it."

I blow out a hard breath, annoyed that he can read me so easily. "Fine. Aside from the pain aspect—which I'm *not* into, for the record—it seems…belittling."

"Okay. I hear you."

I'm surprised by that. Now it's my turn to examine his expression. Never in the history of my experience with men has one said, "I hear you." For the men I've known, acknowledging a woman's feelings is like asking for directions: it simply isn't done.

"Oh. Well…thank you."

"If I promised it wouldn't be painful, but it definitely *would* be a huge turn on for us both, would you consider it?"

That exasperates me. "How on earth can slapping my bare ass with your bare hand *not* be painful for me?"

The dominant tone makes a reappearance. "Because I know what I'm doing, that's how."

All the breath leaves my lungs in a wheezing sound like a punctured tire leaking air. When I've recovered, I say, "Can I think about it?"

"Of course. And while you're thinking about it, I'm going to make you come."

Down between my legs he goes, the wonderful, wonderful man.

Except he's not wonderful, he's diabolical—all I can think about is not moving my arms. And what will happen if I do.

Exactly as he intended.

He strokes his tongue up and down and around, pausing to slide a finger inside me. Then he goes back to the stroking and the sucking as I close my eyes and rock helplessly against his face.

My nipples ache. I can't catch my breath. My awareness narrows to that tiny bundle of nerves between my legs that's throbbing under his tongue and the sensation of his thick finger pumping slowly in and out of me.

He reaches up with his free hand and tweaks my hard nipple, right through my bra. I jerk, groaning.

"You like that?" he murmurs, his lips moving against my sex.

"Yes. Both. Do both, please."

He knows what I mean, despite my being speech impaired at the moment. Slipping his finger out of me, he reaches up with both hands, scoops my breasts out of my bra, and strokes his thumbs over my rigid nipples. When I whine in pleasure, he pinches them.

"Yes. Yes, *that.*"

"Anything you want, sweetheart," he whispers, lowering his head to suckle my clit again as he continues to pinch and stroke my nipples.

Oh God, it's good. It's incredible. My entire body tingles. Tingles and pulses and shakes. A wave of intense heat radiates out from my core. I'm sure I'll set the sofa on fire. Then his teeth scrape over my clit and I almost lose consciousness.

Straining up toward his mouth, I beg, "*Yes, please, don't stop, please don't stop, oh God, I'm so close—*"

It isn't until James freezes that I realize something is wrong. When I open my eyes and glance down at him, I discover what it is.

My fingers are clenched in his hair. Which means I lowered my arms.

Which means I disobeyed him.

Which—judging by his sly smile—was the exact outcome he was hoping for.

9

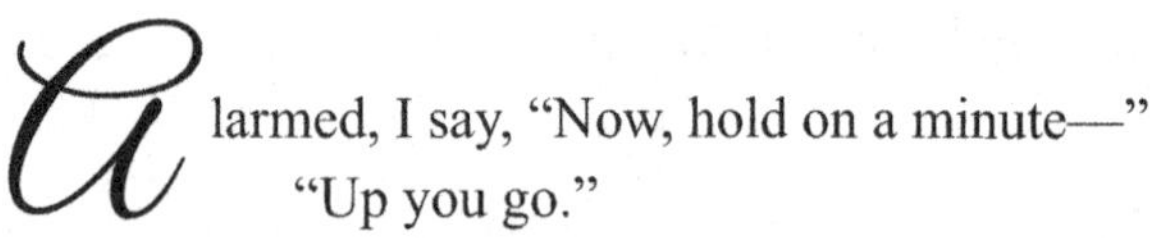

Alarmed, I say, "Now, hold on a minute—"

"Up you go."

He stands, pulls me up by my arms, then sits and pulls me face down onto the sofa, my belly over his lap, bare ass in the air. Pressing one hand flat between my shoulder blades and using the other to squeeze an exposed butt cheek, he ignores my frightened bleating and says, "I'm not going to hurt you. I will. Not. Hurt. You. Do you understand?"

I struggle to look at him over my shoulder, but can't rise because of that big hand pinning me down. "You're already hurting me!"

"How?"

I cast around frantically for a word, then decide on, "Psychically!"

"I'm hurting your *psyche*," he says sarcastically. "Really."

He begins to slowly massage my butt, running his hand back and forth over my cheeks and squeezing, gently stroking down between my parted thighs.

I fall still and take a moment to uncross my eyes before answering. "Um…yes."

He whispers, "Liar," and gently pinches my labia.

My heart pounds so hard I can't catch my breath. "James…"

"Yes, Olivia?" Calm. Solicitous. He's completely in control, and he knows it.

"I…I…" As he slowly rubs his fingers back and forth through my wetness, I bury my face into the sofa cushion and squeeze shut my eyes. I whisper, "That actually kind of feels good."

Laughter warms his voice. "Kind of?"

His fingers slip down farther and begin to stroke my clitoris. Lazily, gently. He's in no hurry to get to the slapping part of the festivities, and neither am I.

His erection is a hard bulge against my hip, but he makes no indication that he's concerned with anything other than calming me down and winding me up.

Of their own will, my hips begin to move in time with his fingers.

He pushes my hair off my face and whispers hotly, "You're so beautiful. You make me so hard. Your beautiful ass and pussy make my dick so fucking hard, and so does your trust."

I'm gasping for air and trembling madly. I feel like I'm going out of my mind.

He gently tugs on my clit. I make a soft, incoherent moan of pleasure.

In his dark, dominant voice, James says, "I'm going to spank you now, Olivia. Six times to start, then I'll see how you're doing. Are you ready?"

Terror lights all my nerve endings on fire. "Not hard," I plead.

"Not hard, sweetheart," he promises. "Just breathe."

The second he takes his hand away from between my legs, I tense in anticipation of what's coming. My mind explodes with panic.

What the hell am I doing? This is ridiculous! You're thirty-

eight years old, Olivia, how can you possibly allow a man to take you over his lap and spank you like a misbehaving little—

CRACK!

The flat of James's hand makes contact with my bare ass with a sound that seems as loud as gunfire. I jerk, yelping, my eyes flying open and my body stiffening.

James croons, "Breathe," and smooths his hand over the stinging spot on my behind.

I'm quaking. In sheer terror or blistering arousal, I'm not sure which. Probably both. The sound was worse than the sting, neither of which compare to the fear I built up in my head over how bad it might be. I was expecting pain, but this is…well, it's not *not* pain, but it doesn't hurt my butt half as much as it hurts my ego to admit that I'm pretty sure I liked it.

The instant James feels the tension leave my body, he rains down five more stinging blows on my bare ass, alternating cheeks as I squeal and squirm.

Then he stops and smooths his hand around, stroking my burning skin and murmuring praises.

Between my legs, I'm soaked.

He commands, "Talk to me."

I try to stop panting long enough to speak. "I would if I… could form…any words…"

He reaches between my legs and gently explores my folds, rubbing his fingers back and forth over my swollen clit. "Oh fuck," he breathes. "You're so wet. You loved that, didn't you?"

Maybe it's the reverent tone of his voice. Or maybe it's the waves of pleasure his magical fingers are producing. Or maybe it's just that it's been so long since I've let go. Whatever the reason, the logical part of my brain blinks offline, leaving me feeling wild, uninhibited, and blindingly alive.

The words break from my chest in one long, breathless rush.

"Yes I loved it and I want you to spank me until I come and then I want you to fuck me until I come again and then I want to suck you off until *you* come and then I want to do it all over from the beginning."

As if from far away, I hear the low, animal growl that rumbles through his chest. Then he flips me over and pulls me upright, settling me between his spread thighs. He kisses me hard with one hand fisted in my hair and the other around my throat as I tremble and whimper with desire.

"That was the sexiest thing I've ever heard, but I'm not going to fuck you tonight," he says gruffly, breaking away from my mouth and breathing hard as he looks into my eyes. "You said you didn't want to jump right into bed with me, and I'm respecting that."

My eyes widen in horror. "Nooo, I didn't say that. Whoever said that was a stupid, stupid person."

"I don't have a condom anyway."

And I'm not on birth control, so it's a definite no-go.

I close my eyes and rest my head against his shoulder, hiding my face. A shudder of disappointment runs through me. The ravenous ache between my legs howls with need.

"But we're not done yet," he whispers, working at the belt around my wrists.

He unwraps it and flings it to the floor, then tugs on the hem of my T-shirt. I lift my arms overhead, and he drags the shirt off me and tosses it aside. He makes quick work of the hooks on my bra strap and tosses it aside, too, then pulls off my jeans and panties after I kick off my shoes.

Then I'm sitting nude in his lap, resting in the circle of his strong arms.

He begins to fondle me, my breasts and arms and hips, kissing me as he strokes and squeezes me in all my soft, secret places, sighing against my mouth when I arch back and part my thighs.

I'm in a thick, sweet stupor of pleasure.

I've never been petted like this. Certainly not by someone

who looks like he does, or by someone for whom the mere act of exploration and appreciation of my body seems so sacred. He's learning my curves with his hands, mapping the hills and valleys of my flesh with his avid, burning eyes. I've never seen a man look so enraptured. So spellbound and beguiled.

Simply put, it's intoxicating.

"I love the way you look at me," I whisper as he gazes, mesmerized, at his hand cupping my breast. Any self-consciousness I might have had about my body has evaporated by the awed way his eyes drink me in.

He lifts his gaze to mine. The intensity of emotion reflected in his eyes is stunning. For one heart-stopping moment, I can't breathe.

"And I love to look at you, beautiful Olivia," he whispers back, his voice hoarse. "It's a privilege I don't deserve, but one I'm so grateful for."

A lump forms in my throat. Something inside my chest tightens. I suddenly feel as if I'm going to cry.

He knows. I know he does, because he wraps me up in his arms and squeezes me tight, kissing my neck and shoulder and rocking me gently. I don't understand what's happening, why this should suddenly feel like…like so *much*.

But it does. Whatever's happening between us, it feels big.

It feels real.

And that feels terrifying.

When I inhale a hitching breath, he murmurs my name. It sounds like a prayer.

Then he's kissing me again, passionately, making low noises deep in his throat. I wrap my arms around his broad shoulders and lean against him, sucking in a breath through my nose when his clever fingers find the center of me.

He pulls a cushion off the back of the sofa and repositions it. "Lie back."

I recline, stretching out on the cushion and lifting my arms overhead so all of me is available to him.

Blue eyes burning, he murmurs, "Christ. Look at you."

I've never felt this pretty. Pretty and feminine and powerful, all because this beautiful man is worshipping me with his possessive hands and ravenous eyes.

He bends over me, cupping my breast and drawing one of my nipples into his hungry mouth. As he swirls his tongue around and around, stopping occasionally to suck, I sink my fingers into his hair and exhale a ragged breath, my heart beating like a hammer.

The hammering gets worse when James whispers against my skin, "I want to spank your pussy."

He lifts his head and stares at me, waiting for an answer.

Instead of words, I simply hold his gaze and part my thighs.

His eyelids flutter. He moistens his lips. The pulse in his neck is going wild.

I'm not sure which one of us is more excited, him or me.

"I promise I won't hurt you."

I whisper, "I know."

Somehow, I actually mean it.

He kisses me, softly, closing his eyes. When he opens them again, all the heat I saw from moments ago has hardened into something different.

Something darker…and far more dangerous.

Electricity crackles over my skin, pebbling my flesh into goosebumps. In the same moment that James lifts his hand, I stop breathing, my eyes widening and my heart exploding with small animal panic.

His arm flashes down. He slaps me smartly between my spread legs.

It sends a violent shockwave of pleasure jolting through me.

I moan, arching, my eyelids sliding shut and my thighs opening wider.

At my reaction, James inhales a hard breath. Then he lets loose a stream of the hottest, filthiest words I've ever heard, spoken through gritted teeth as he slaps me again. And again.

And again.

Delirious, I cry out, writhing in his lap like a wild thing, something released from its shackles. Any shame I might have expected to feel is absent. There's only the throbbing wet heat between my legs, the incomprehensible pleasure of his hard hand colliding with my tender flesh, and the hypnotic sound of his voice as he praises me and tells me everything he feels in the most shockingly obscene and thoroughly erotic language.

"*—so fucking beautiful, I can't wait to fuck this sweet cunt—*"

My climax hits in a series of violent contractions that leave me screaming.

"*—my hard cock pounding deep inside you—*"

"James! James!"

"*—come so deep inside this gorgeous wet pussy—*"

I sob, overcome with sensation, oblivious to anything but his voice and the convulsions wracking my body, knowing in a hidden dark corner of my brain that we've each unleashed something in the other. Something long suppressed or forgotten, some unnameable, powerful force that only time will reveal to be good or bad.

This casual summer fling has the potential to burn the whole city down and leave a path of smoking ruins in its wake.

Then it's over, and he's kissing me.

And I'm a crying, shaking mess in his lap.

"Hush. Sweetheart, you're okay. It's okay. Here, put your arms around me."

His words are so gentle now. So tender. The contrast shreds me up even more. He gathers me into his arms, cradles me against his chest, and starts to rock me, smoothing his hands over my hair and down my back.

"I'm s-sorry. I don't know why I'm c-crying." I hiccup, sniffling, my face buried in his neck.

He says warmly, "Because I'm a sex god. Obviously."

I start to laugh through my tears. "I could've been faking it, you egomaniac."

He tips my head up with a finger under my chin and looks deep into my eyes. Smoothing a thumb over my wet cheek, he murmurs, "Except you weren't faking it, sweetheart."

The way he keeps calling me sweetheart is screwing with my mind.

Or is it my heart?

"Talk to me," he says, brushing his lips over mine. "You're all up in your head. How do you feel?"

"I feel…" *Scared. Confused. Satisfied. Thirsty. Worn out. And I need to pee.* "Um…I feel good."

James surprises me by throwing back his head and laughing.

"What?" I ask, a little defensive.

"I think the only time you're unflinchingly honest with me is when I've got my hand between your legs is what. You want to try that again?"

I grouse, "Stop grinning at me like that. It's not exactly easy for me to talk about my feelings."

His smile dies. With the speed of two fingers snapping, he grows somber, staring at me with a furrow dug between his brows. "I know. I'm sorry. I didn't mean to make you feel bad."

I stare at him, helpless against his devastating combination of sweet sensitivity and raw masculinity. *How is this perfect man single?*

I drop my head against his chest and sigh. "Okay, here goes. For starters, I feel—physically—amazing. I mean, *wow*, James. You've reduced me to a smoking pile of ashes. That was incredibly intense."

When I pause, he says quietly, "I'm glad. Thank you for trusting me. It means a lot to me. You have no idea how special that is, and how much of a turn on it is for me to watch you fall apart under my hands."

I shake my head in disbelief. "Someone's feeding you lines through an earpiece, aren't they? You've got a team of script writers on call 24/7, and right now they're frantically scribbling the most outrageously romantic things they can think of and whispering them into your ear. Right?"

"Oh yes," he says seriously. "It costs a pretty penny, mind you, but it's totally worth it."

When I peek up at his face, he's biting his full lower lip and trying hard not to smile.

He's so handsome it hurts.

In the dim of the apartment, with only the moonglow and the city lights shining through the windows to light his face, he looks like something from a dream. Part myth and part man, a visiting angel sent in all his dark beauty to dazzle me with his charms.

The swell of emotion I felt earlier returns and begins to expand inside my chest. My heartbeat picks up a notch. I have the strangest sensation of weightlessness, as if gravity has vanished and I'm floating in outer space with nothing holding me down to the ground.

His gaze locks onto mine, and those blue, blue eyes of his… they do what they do best.

Burn.

"Tell me the rest," he demands in a rough tone, all teasing gone. "Tell me what you're feeling right this second."

My lips part. The words are whispered as I gaze into the endless depths of his eyes. "Every single thing I thought I'd never feel again."

His face contorts. He looks as if I've just stabbed him in the gut.

When he looks away, drawing a deep breath, I go cold with horror. *What the hell have I done?*

"It's my turn to apologize," I say stiffly, trying to sit up.

"That was over the top. We're not supposed to be getting person—"

"Stop."

He grabs my arms and holds me in place so I can't stand. We sit in silence for a moment as I listen to his irregular breathing and watch the erratic rise and fall of his chest. Then he swallows and slowly exhales, and I catch a glimpse of how hard he's trying to hold himself together.

"What we just did is about as personal as it gets, regardless of whether or not we exchange histories." A muscle flexes in his jaw. His voice turns gravelly. "I love that you said that. It was just...unexpected." His eyes close. "This whole thing is unexpected. I'm afraid I'm not handling it very well."

I'm drenched in shame. Burning with it. All my skin is peeling off, eaten away by the acid of humiliation.

I took something insanely sexy and fun and turned it into melodrama, and for that I'd like to punch myself in the face.

"I guess I'm not either," I say, my voice tight. "Maybe this was a bad idea."

He swings his head around and stares at me with that same gut-stabbed look. "No, it's not a bad idea," he says urgently, pulling me closer to his chest. "Please don't say that."

I crinkle my brow, utterly confused. "James, you're going to have to help me out here. You asked me to be totally honest with you. You asked me to tell you my feelings, and I did. Then you freaked out. Then I freaked out because you freaked out. And now…" I huff in frustration. "I honestly don't know *what's* happening now."

He rests his cheek against my forehead and quietly sighs, gathering me close against his body and tucking my head into the crook of his neck. "What's happening is that I'm a fucking idiot."

When it becomes obvious that's the only explanation I'll get, I say drily, "Oh good. That explains everything, thanks."

He lifts his head and slants me a heated look. "Someone's looking for her ass to get spanked."

I smile sweetly at him. "No, actually I'm looking for a neck brace, because these mood swings of yours are giving me a serious case of whiplash."

I'm about to add another smart remark along the lines of "Did you forget to take your medication?" when I realize that might be a legitimate question.

He could be medicated. He could be completely unhinged for all I know.

His eyes narrow. "If you're thinking I'm a serial killer or something, the answer is no."

I exhale a shaky breath. *How the hell can he read my mind?*

"I'm just fucked up, Olivia. It's nothing sinister. You're not in any danger from me. I'm just very fucked up, and I don't know how to be normal anymore, and I hope…I mean I want…" He blows out a hard breath, then mutters, "Fuck."

Watching him look so wretched and hearing how negatively he thinks about himself gives me a one-two combo punch of sadness and maternal instincts right in my solar plexus.

"Hey," I whisper, taking his face in my hands. His cheeks are hot. The stubble on his jaw tickles my palms. "Fucked up I get, okay? Fucked up I'm good with. Me and fucked up are best friends, if you want to know the truth. So don't feel bad about that. Please don't feel bad about anything.

"This is completely unexpected for me, too, but I think you're amazing. I feel amazing when I'm with you." I pause for a moment. "Actually I feel hysterical and on the verge of a mental breakdown or a massive heart attack most of the time I'm with you, but in a good way, if that makes sense. You make me feel…"

I have to stop to think of just the right word. It comes to me accompanied by a deep sense of astonishment.

"You make me feel *alive*."

In the low light, James's eyes shine like gems. His Adam's apple bobs when he swallows. Wrapped tightly around me, his arms shake. So does his voice when he says, "Same."

One word. One syllable. Yet it conveys his true emotions more clearly than if he'd gone on and on.

I imagine a tightrope stretched out in front of me, stretched high and taut over bottomless darkness, stretched so far into the distance I can't see the end. The air is silent and still but tense with anticipation, like a held breath. The only sound is the thundering roar of my heartbeat in my ears as I gaze in concentration at the slender length of cord awaiting my decision. Waiting to find out if I'll turn around and climb down from the high platform I'm standing on or step forward and give it the weight of my foot.

If I'm going to stop this thing with James, I should stop now. I should tell him it's too much, too soon, too dangerous a thing to play with. I should tell him to walk away.

Instead, I ease one bare foot off the platform of safety I'm standing on and step out onto the rope.

PART II

When you start to live outside yourself, it's all dangerous.
~ Ernest Hemingway

10

I come awake gradually, floating up into consciousness as if on a whisper-soft cloud. When I open my eyes, I'm lying on my back in bed, nude but covered with a sheet. It's early in the morning. Pearl gray light sifts through the curtains, brightening the edges of the room.

I'm alone.

I take a moment to simply breathe and marvel at this shiny new feeling of happiness.

James carried me to bed last night. Picked me up in his arms from the sofa and carried me into the bedroom as easily as if I were a child. He laid me down on the sheets, then curled up behind me, curving our bodies together and tightening his arm around my waist, nuzzling his nose into my hair. I fell asleep listening to the sound of his even breathing.

But now I'm awake, and there's a book on the pillow beside me, lying open with a yellow sticky note stuck to one of the pages.

I sit up, pick up the book, and look at the note. In neat handwriting, it reads, "How can you say this is the worst fake biblical prose? This is the *best* fake biblical prose *ever*."

The book is *For Whom the Bell Tolls*, by Hemingway. James must have retrieved it from Estelle's library.

The note is stuck directly under the line I ridiculed during dinner: "Now, feel. I am thee and thou art me and all of one is the other. And feel now. Thou hast no heart but mine."

My world must have tilted on its axis, because I have to admit, at the moment those words look pretty damn good.

Then I stop and wonder how long it must've taken James to find this particular book in Estelle's large and disorganized library. And, upon discovering it, how long it took him to hunt down that exact quote. Or did he know what page it was on by heart?

"Oh no," I say aloud, alarmed. "Is Hemingway *his favorite writer*?"

We're going to have to have a serious discussion about this. I don't know if I can continue to fool around with a man whose favorite author once famously said that the only real sports were mountain climbing, bull fighting, and car racing.

I mean, come on. Macho much?

Personally, I think he was overcompensating for some deep-seated feelings of inferiority, but that's just me.

Out of nowhere, a flash of inspiration hits. Fully formed, a scene in Technicolor arrives in my mind's eye. It's as clear as a picture, sudden as a slap, and accompanied by a burning rush of adrenaline.

I leap from bed and run naked into the library, where I throw myself down into the chair in front of the big roll top desk, snatch the pencil up from where I abandoned it in my last attempt to write, and begin to scribble furiously on the yellow lined legal pad of paper.

I don't stop until three hours later, when my right hand begins to cramp.

Drained and amazed, I lean back in the chair and flip back through the pages I've written.

It's rare that inspiration hits me like that, in one fell swoop, the characters, dialogue, and scene so detailed. Normally, writing is a grueling process, whole manuscripts completed page by painful page as I beat my natural self-doubt and laziness into submission. But this…

This is what writers call "flow," a unicorn state of total immersion where time loses all meaning and words pour out like water from a faucet with no more effort than it takes to blink.

The muffled sound of a phone ringing is what finally makes me rise from the chair.

I pad into the living room, the parquet cool and smooth under my bare feet. Finding my handbag on the floor of the foyer, I retrieve my cell phone from it and smile when I see the number on the screen.

"Girlfriend," I say after answering, "I hope you're sitting down, because what I'm about to tell you will pull the rug right out from under your feet."

Kelly shouts, "Oh my God! *Did you do sex with James?*"

She's always using verbs in unique ways like that: "do" sex instead of "have" sex. Her husband finds it irritating, but I think it's cute.

I say coyly, "I don't know…what's your definition of sex?"

"When the outie enters the innie! Duh!"

I roll my eyes, headed back to the bedroom to find something to wear. "Genitals aren't belly buttons, you weirdo, but by that definition, no. We didn't have sex."

She sounds confused. "Did anything of his enter anything of yours?"

"Yup."

A thrilled gasp, then: "Omigod, tell me quick." She pauses. "Unless there are toes involved. I don't want to hear anything about toe sex. That's just nasty."

Crinkling my nose, I say, "Toe sex? Is that even a thing?"

"Babe, you have *no* idea. Remember how I said I was gonna

Google sex stuff for you? Well, I did. And there's a whole *world* out there of kinkiness I had no idea existed. Did you know some people get off by having stinging insects crawl all over them? That would just make me shit myself, not come."

I can't help but start to laugh. "I told you to stay off Google, you nut!"

"And you were right. After some of the pictures I saw, I'm gonna need extensive psychotherapy."

I grab my robe off the hook on the back of the bathroom door and shrug into it, switching the phone from one ear to the other. When my stomach emits a loud rumble, I head into the kitchen to hunt for something to eat.

"I promise you there were no insects or toes involved, okay?"

"Okay. I'm sitting now, so go ahead and tell me what happened. And don't skip any of the juicy parts. I'm living vicariously through you over here."

I open the fridge and peer into it. "Well, for starters, he spanked my pussy until I came so hard I cried."

I hear a loud *thud* and wonder if Kelly fell out of her chair.

She shouts, "*Are you kidding me? Are you fucking kidding me right now*?"

"Hand to God, girlfriend."

"You went straight from not liking any positions other than the missionary to getting your coochie spanked? *And calling your coochie your pussy*? What the hell has this man *done* to you? One date and suddenly you're Rebecca De Mornay in *Risky Business*?"

I say drily, "Enough with the pearl clutching, grandma. May I point out, you just used the word 'fuck' not even ten seconds ago? So I'm not the only potty mouth in this conversation. And you're seriously dating yourself with that movie reference."

She says prissily, "Well, excuse me for not knowing any more recent movies about hookers."

I grab a can of soda, pop the top, and guzzle half of it in one go. "I can't even be Julia Roberts in *Pretty Woman*? Or what was that other movie, the one with Nicholas Cage where he's an alcoholic and that pretty blonde hooker falls in love with him?"

"*Leaving Las Vegas*!" Kelly hollers. "And why the hell are we talking about hookers?"

"Hey, you're the one who brought it up." I chug the rest of the can of soda, stifling a burp.

Some muttering and annoyed grumbling comes over the line, then Kelly says, "If you don't tell me in extreme detail what happened last night from start to finish, I'm firing you as my best friend."

She sounds serious, so after a short pause to gather my thoughts, I tell her everything.

When I'm done, thundering silence echoes over the phone.

"Hello?"

"Still here," Kelly says faintly.

"So? What do you think?"

"What do I think? What do I *think*? I think I would shove my own mother down a flight of stairs to spend ten minutes alone in a room with this stud of yours. Jiminy Cricket, Olivia. Talk about *intense*."

I close the fridge door and wander out of the kitchen into the living room, distracted from my hunger by memories of last night. Memories of James's beautiful face and all the emotion shining in his eyes. "I know," I say softly. "It's pretty surreal."

"Surreal is right!" She cackles, sounding on the verge of hysteria. "He never took off his pants! How is that even possible for a man? He's got a naked woman orgasming in his lap and he keeps his pants on? Talk about superhuman willpower! Mike rips off all his clothes and jumps me if I even *breathe* in his direction."

I muse over that for a moment. "Maybe his penis is pierced

and he knows I'd faint if I saw that, so he's trying to ease me into it one orgasm at a time."

Kelly snorts. "Well, you ride that fat pierced anaconda, sister, and make sure you take good notes when you do, because from now on, I'm gonna be *living* for my daily episodes of *Olivia Gets Her Coochie Spanked*, starring Handsome James the Dirty Talking Artist."

I dissolve into laughter. "You're deranged."

Her voice turns dry. "Twenty years of marriage to a man who thinks foreplay is standing at the edge of the bed and sticking his limp wang in my face when I'm about to fall asleep would make any woman deranged."

"Yikes."

"Yeah, don't get me started. But listen."

The change in her tone has me worried. "What?"

"Just…be careful. I know you set ground rules and you've both agreed it's not gonna get personal, but sex has a way of complicating things. I don't want to see you get hurt."

A faint warning bell goes off in the back of my mind, the same urgent alarm I heard last night when I was falling apart in James's arms. I push it aside.

"Don't worry. My eyes are wide open. I actually think this is going to be good for me. Clear out the cobwebs, so to speak. I woke up this morning and wrote five chapters of a new book."

Kelly's excited whoop is ear-piercing. "That's amazing!"

I grin. "I know. I'm feeling really good about it, too. It's much different from my usual work, but I think it could be some of my best."

"Holy shit, Olivia, I'm so happy for you! This is exactly why you went to Paris in the first place! Who knew all you needed was some legendary dick to get your brain kick-started?"

Her excitement is infectious, and I laugh again. "Technically, I haven't had his legendary dick yet, just a legendary orgasm."

"Jesus, think what will happen when you have intercourse

with this guy! You could end up writing the next great American novel. If you win the Pulitzer, you'll have to go on stage and give all the credit to your vacation hookup's lovely penis."

I picture myself in an evening gown on stage in a crowded amphitheater, accepting an award from a dapper gentleman in a tuxedo, then turning to the podium to give a heartfelt speech of gratitude to James's wonderfully inspiring genitals while the audience looks on with their mouths hanging open.

The imagery is interrupted when another call rings through. When I glance at the screen, I see that it's James.

"Kell, Mr. Legendary Dick is calling. Can I call you back?"

"I'll talk to you tomorrow. And don't forget—*take good notes*."

She ends the call, leaving me smiling. I click over to James.

"Hello?"

"You're smiling," he says, his tone warm.

I turn and look out the living room windows. "How did you know that? Are you looking at me through binoculars right now?"

"I can hear it in your voice."

"Oh. Really?"

"Yes, really. Did you know you look like an angel when you're asleep?"

Heat creeps into my cheeks. I wander over to the sofa and sit down, smoothing my hand over the spot on the middle cushion where James held me in his lap. "I don't believe anyone has made that observation before, no."

"Well, you do. A pornographic angel, if there is such a thing. I was worried I'd have to seek medical attention today because my dick stayed hard the entire night."

I whisper, "I noticed that."

After a beat, he whispers gruffly back, "You're so fucking beautiful. Your skin makes me want to cry."

I grin, blushing furiously. "I know that's a line from a song, Romeo."

"Damn. You caught me. My script writers are on break. Bonus points for effort, though?"

"You don't sound the least bit sorry, so no bonus points."

"Hmm. What if I told you I'm hard right now just from hearing your voice?"

"Less romantic, but more realistic. I'll give you one point."

His voice turns teasing. "Oh, it's *romance* you want, is it? And here I thought you were only after me for my body."

"Your *incredible* body, yes, I'm sorry to say that's all I'm interested in. By the way, I wanted to ask you about something."

"What?"

"That tattoo on your shoulder. It was too dark last night for me to read it. What does it say?"

His hesitation is a sudden crackle of tension over the line. "*Duris dura fraguntur.*"

It's Latin, I know that much. I also know by the change in his voice that I've stepped into dangerous territory, but I can't help but step farther. My curiosity is too strong. "What does it mean?"

He answers in a low voice. "Hard things are broken by hard things."

I think of the simple italic text tattooed onto the rounded muscle of his shoulder. Beneath it were two mysterious rows of short black lines, like a bar code.

An eerie uneasiness creeps over me, as if someone has stepped over my grave.

"Oh."

We sit in awkward silence, until he says, "I noticed you don't have any tattoos."

It's as elegant a segue as possible, considering the circumstances, so I go with it. "I'm not a big fan of needles."

His voice warms. "That's right. You said you're not into pain."

"Of any kind. I'm a big baby when it comes to physical pain. A hangnail can send me into a crying fit."

"So can an orgasm."

I know he's only teasing because his tone is strokingly soft, but still I'm embarrassed. My ears start to burn.

He guesses why I'm silent. "Don't be embarrassed. I hope to make you cry as often as possible from now until September."

Picturing myself weeping every time he touches me makes me nervous. Dropping my head into my hand, I groan. "I have a bad feeling I'm going to need a lot of tissues."

He chuckles. "We'll go to one of those big box stores, get stocked up."

"Judging by how wound up you get me, we'll have to stock up on smelling salts, too. I'm liable to collapse into a heap every time I see you."

"Do you think they carry defibrillators? Because I'll probably need one of those at some point. Sooner rather than later, considering what it did to my heart when I watched you come." His voice goes rough. "I can't wait to put my mouth on you again. I had dreams about how sweet you taste. When I woke up, my dick was throbbing."

His voice is so hot, I start to sweat. He's not the only one who might need a defibrillator.

I say faintly, "Things are starting to throb over here, too."

He makes that growling wolf noise that I find so weirdly thrilling. "Is your pussy getting wet, Olivia?"

He loves that word: pussy. I admit, it's never been a favorite of mine, but coming from his mouth, the way he says it with so much masculine need, it has recently gained in stature.

"Yes. When can I see you? I'd like to reciprocate for that incredible orgasm you gave me last night."

His sharp intake of breath tells me the need in my voice affects him the same way the need in his voice affects me.

"I have to go to Germany for a few days, but I'll be back on Friday. Dinner?"

"Definitely." I'm proud of myself for not asking what's in Germany, because this whole not-getting-personal thing was my idea, after all.

"Good. I'll pick you up at five."

"Seems a little early for dinner."

"There's somewhere I want to take you first."

"Ooh, a mystery. I like it."

"And Olivia?"

"Yes?"

"Wear a dress."

He hangs up, leaving me with shaky hands, a pulse going gangbusters, and my imagination running wild with every possible scenario of why he'd want me to wear a dress.

Another flash of inspiration has me sprinting back to the library and the yellow pad of lined legal paper.

I don't get up from the desk again until it's dark.

11

I spend the next three days in a state of suspended animation, cocooned in the apartment, writing in a blind, compulsive frenzy and ignoring the outside world. I'm consumed by the story and have a hard time tearing myself away from the page even to eat or sleep.

It's like I'm obsessed by the characters. Or, more accurately, that I've *become* them. I see what they see. I feel what they feel. When they're sad or happy or confused, I am, too. They've arrived in my brain so dimensional and complete, it's as if I've known them my entire life.

They seem more real to me than some people I'm related to.

None of this strikes me as strange, only fantastic. A spigot inside my head has turned on and started gushing. A locked door has swung open wide.

Finally, after more than two years, the thing that makes me *me* has returned.

With it has come a profound sense of relief.

I haven't allowed myself to consider what would happen if I'd permanently lost the ability to tell stories. The idea of a life without creativity is too terrifying, because I've seen firsthand what happens to artists when they can no longer create.

They shrivel up and die.

But now I'm feeling very much alive. Alive and on *fire.*

When the doorbell rings at five o'clock on Friday, I head toward the door with a grin splitting my face from ear to ear. The grin dies a death from shock when I open the door and see James standing there.

He's wearing a gorgeous black suit, expensive looking, probably custom made due to the way it hugs every contour of his big frame. His white dress shirt is open at the collar to more perfectly showcase the strong, tanned column of his throat. His silk pocket square is white, too, his smile is small and mysterious, and the hunger in his eyes is that of a feral wolf.

Looking him up and down, I say faintly, "Oh."

He glances down at himself. "What's wrong?"

"Nothing. I've just never met a man who could make a suit look so hot." I wave a hand in the air. "This is like...suit porn. If I took a picture of you and sent it to my girlfriend Kelly, her ovaries would explode."

He flattens his hand on the back of the door and pushes it open wider, steps close, then takes me into his arms. Bending his head down, he softly presses his lips to mine. "And what are your ovaries doing?"

Tightening my arms around his broad shoulders, I say breathlessly, "The cha-cha. But they just noticed that hard bulge in your trousers that's pressing against my hip, and now they're about to faint."

His grin comes on slow and wicked. "We can't have that. Let's give them something to stay awake for."

His mouth takes mine in a deep, passionate kiss.

Though we've only been apart for a few days, we both must have been starved for each other, because we stand there for uncounted minutes, our bodies and tongues entwined, until we're both breathing hard and I'm digging my fingers into his hair and sagging against him. I'm sure it's only the strength of his arms that's keeping me upright.

Then he breaks away, leaving me panting.

"Hi." His voice is low, rough, and warm with stifled laughter.

I open my eyes to find him grinning down at me, his gorgeous blue eyes half-lidded and twinkling with amusement.

I grouse, "Hi yourself. And stop laughing at me. It's not my fault you're so sexy."

He reaches down, grabs a handful of my ass, and squeezes. "I'm not the sexy one here, sweetheart. You look absolutely edible."

"I borrowed this from Gigi."

When he arches his brows, I say, "You said to wear a dress, but I only have that blue gown you already saw, and I didn't have time to go shopping because I got so caught up in work, so I called Edmond this afternoon and asked him for her number. I thought we might wear about the same size."

The dress Gigi loaned me is a sleeveless red silk wraparound with a plunging neckline that I had to pin together with a safety pin so my boobs don't fall out. Her gravity-defying cleavage probably holds the neckline in place without any assistance, but mine needs a little help.

Cupping the back of my head in one palm and my butt cheek in the other, James says, "There's no way she looks as good in it as you do. I want to rip it off your body with my teeth."

He kisses me again, hungrily, until I'm shaking. This time when he pulls away, I'm laughing.

"Oh my God. I'm dead. You've killed me."

Something sharp and dark flickers in the depths of his eyes. "Don't say that."

I was teasing, so the terse tone of his voice surprises me. "I was paying you a compliment, silly. I only meant that you're a great kisser."

A thundercloud settles over his mood. He pulls away, his shoulders stiff and his smile vanished. "You ready to go?"

"Sure," I say, confused. "As soon as you explain to me how I just upset you."

He opens his mouth to answer, but closes it again. Then he looks away, brows drawn down, and drags a hand through his hair. "I can't do that without getting personal. *Very* personal."

He swings his gaze back to mine and pins me in it. "I'll be honest with you if you want me to, but I'm telling you right now you don't want to hear it. Your rules. Your call."

War erupts inside me.

Of course I want to hear whatever it is that brought on such a change in his demeanor…but I also don't. It's obvious he doesn't want to tell me, that he thinks telling me will change something between us. I appreciate that he's giving me the choice, but for someone with an imagination like mine, ambiguity is dangerous.

Three months, Olivia. You're only in Paris for three months. Keep it light. Let it go.

James watches me, waiting.

I say, "I'm feeling really ambivalent about this."

He nods, his gaze searching mine. "I hear you."

I love it when he says that. So many arguments could be solved with that short phrase alone. "Maybe we could compromise?"

"Compromise how?"

"What if you just told me if what I said is somehow related to your work?"

His eyes widen. He repeats gruffly, "My *work*."

Why does he look so surprised? "Yes. Your art. Those portraits you drew, *Perspectives in Grief*. Death is kind of a thing for you. Right?"

A muscle in his jaw flexes over and over. He stares at me so hard I think he could ignite me with the heated intensity of his gaze. When it finally comes, his response is careful.

"Let's say it's…a touchy subject."

I study his expression, convinced he's telling me the truth, and also that he doesn't want me to push it any farther.

Watching him waiting so tensely for me to speak, I decide I don't want to, either.

I already know death has touched him somehow, the same way it's touched me. There's no need to exhume the graves.

"Okay."

His eyes are wary. "Okay?"

I nod. "We've already agreed we're not going to share our sad stories. I get that you don't want to talk about yours, because I definitely don't want to talk about mine. So…okay. From now on, if either of us doesn't want to get into the details of something, we'll just say, 'touchy subject.' It'll be our safe word. Safe phrase, technically. Deal?"

The thundercloud over his head evaporates with dizzying speed, leaving his shoulders relaxed and his eyes smiling. Pulling me close against his chest, he says in a throaty voice, "What do you know about safe words, sweetheart?"

The heat in his gaze tells me that *he* knows an awful lot. "I've…read about them. In books."

He murmurs, "Have you now?" and presses his face against my neck, gently biting the muscle above my collarbone. This time when he cups my ass, it's with both hands.

Then he kisses me until almost every thought is eradicated from my mind.

Every thought except the memory of how his eyes changed so quickly from light to dark when I said he killed me.

I have the sneaking suspicion that one's going to stick with me for a while.

~

"A book store?"

Standing beside me in the dappled shade of linden trees on a quiet, cobblestone avenue, James smiles and squeezes my hand. "Not just any book store. *The* book store. Shakespeare and Company is probably the most famous independent book store in the world."

I gaze at the quaint shop across the street with its green awning and matching trim, rustic yellow sign, and weather-beaten book stalls lining one side of the small plaza in front. It looks like a place time forgot.

"I'm embarrassed to admit I've never heard of it."

"That's all right. But I have to warn you, you'll fall in love with it as soon as we walk through the door."

He tugs on my hand and pulls me away from where the taxi dropped us, on the left bank of the Seine, a stone's throw away from Notre Dame. A small crowd of people mills in front of the store, browsing through the outdoor book stalls and chatting, sipping espressos from the café next door. The building the store is housed in appears centuries old, a tall stretch of pitted stone with crumbling corners and a white façade mellowed to ivory with age.

As soon as we pass through the glass-paned front door and a bell somewhere out of sight jingles merrily, I'm flooded with the most wonderful sense of connection, like I've been plugged into a socket and have started to hum with energy. I feel as if I've come home.

It's the smell.

Books—especially old books—have a smell all their own, a sweet and musky scent warmed by a hint of vanilla that floods the brain with good memories and good feelings. I stop in the entry and close my eyes, inhaling deeply.

I exhale and open my eyes, drinking in my surroundings.

The shop is crammed to the ceiling with shelves of books. Narrow passageways lead away from the entry to a nest of other rooms. A wooden staircase winds up to a second floor. Dusty chandeliers cast warm light over red velvet draperies and the occasional leather chair, their seats cracked and worn.

In a voice like you'd use in church, I say, "This is heaven."

Standing beside me, James chuckles. "Told you. C'mon, let's look around."

He nods to the lovely blonde behind the register, then leads me down a passageway. Stenciled on the soffit above us an inscription reads, "Be not inhospitable to strangers lest they be angels in disguise."

I trail my fingertips over spines as we pass shelf after shelf of books, until we turn a corner and stop in a quiet alcove. I glimpse a copy of Dostoevsky's *The Brothers Karamazov* shelved next to *War and Peace* by Tolstoy.

"The Russian section is my favorite," says James, coming to stand close behind me, his chest against my back. He grasps my upper arms and dips his nose into my hair, inhaling deeply the same way I did when I walked in and smelled all the delicious books.

"That's good news. For a minute there, I thought you were leading me straight to Hemingway."

I pluck *The Brothers Karamazov* off the shelf and open it, lifting the pages to my nose for a sniff. Sighing in pleasure, I look at a random line and read it aloud. "The mystery of human existence lies not in just staying alive, but in finding something to live for."

"Indeed," murmurs James into my ear. He slides his hand down my arm, over my hip, and between my legs.

I freeze. My heart takes off like a rocket. Through small gaps in the shelf in front of me, I see other people browsing in the front of the store.

I whisper, "James."

His strong fingers delve into the gap between my thighs, gently rubbing. "Hmm?"

"Someone will see us."

"Maybe."

He sounds nonchalant. Meanwhile, I'm starting to sweat. Is this why he asked me to wear a dress?

"I'm not sure we should—"

"Read me some more." He pinches his fingers together, making me gasp. Then he slides his hand down my thigh, slips it under the hem of my dress, and slides it back up again. He settles his warm palm between my legs. Now the only barrier between his hand and my naked flesh is my panties.

The way he cups my sex feels possessive.

"James—"

"*Read*," he commands, his voice low.

I look at the pages, but the words have started to blur. With shaking hands, I flip a few pages, then focus on a line. "L-love in action is a harsh and dreadful thing compared to love in dreams."

"Mmm. How eloquent. You see why I like the Russian section? It's so romantic." James slips his fingers under the elastic of my panties and glides them over my clitoris.

I jerk, sucking in a startled breath.

Into my ear he breathes, "Guess you like it, too. You're already wet."

My heart bangs so hard against my sternum it's painful. He winds his other arm around my waist and pins me against the wall of his body, then starts to move his fingers faster, stroking me until I'm breathless and throbbing.

"Read, Olivia."

Panting, feeling scared and desperate and insanely turned on, I stare at the book in my hands. Pages whir past as I flip forward, then back, almost dropping the book in the process. I find a page and read, my voice shaking.

"You will burn and you will burn out; you will be healed and come back again."

James kicks my feet apart wider, then sinks one finger deep inside me.

When I shudder and let out a soft cry, he whispers harshly into my ear, "Burn for me, sweetheart. Let me feel it."

His erection is a hard, insistent heat against my ass. If he bent me forward a little, he could yank aside my panties and fuck me from behind.

I'm out of my mind with the thought of it.

The possibility that he could make love to me here, in a public place, in partial view of the patrons at the front of the store or full view of anyone who wandered into the alcove, has me so hot—and terrified—I can barely think.

He uses my hair as a leash to pull my head back. Then he kisses me deeply as his thumb works my clitoris and his index finger slides in and out of me, over and over.

The book falls from my hands and clatters against the floor.

He winds me tighter and tighter, coiling me up into a super-heated ball of nerves. Powerful waves of heat lash me, scorching my skin and hardening my nipples to two aching points of need. I reach out blindly and brace myself against the shelf, clawing at the wall of Russians like I might start to climb.

James breaks away from my mouth. Breathing hard, in a guttural voice, he says, "I could fuck you here, sweetheart. I could take you right here. Do you want that?"

"No! Yes! Oh God…" I groan, frantic for release.

"Or I could get on my knees and push you up against the shelf and make you come with my mouth."

My moan is soft and pleading. I'm so wet I can feel it on my thighs. Incoherent, I rock against his hand.

"Or I could put you on your knees and make you suck me off. Would you like that, sweetheart? Having me fuck your mouth with my hard cock while you play with your wet pussy, on your knees in the Russian section?"

I picture it. My cheeks hollowed, his big hands gripping my head, his erection sliding in and out between my lips as I kneel in front of the open fly of his trousers, finger fucking myself while taking the entire thick, hard length of him deep down my throat as all the shelves of books look on.

A sob breaks from my chest.

James whispers hotly, "Oh, yes, you'd *love* that. My sweet, dirty, beautiful girl."

He tugs firmly on the swollen bud of my clitoris, and I come.

He swallows my gasp with a kiss, holding me tightly with that arm like an iron bar around my waist as I convulse and shudder through a violent orgasm. He plunges his finger deep inside me once more, setting off another series of hard contractions.

James turns his face to my ear and says through gritted teeth, "I need to feel your gorgeous cunt throb like this around my dick."

I'm lost. Lost to his voice, his taste, his filthy words. Lost to pleasure, to sensation, and to a sudden, overwhelming fear.

This isn't me.

This woman, so reckless and overtaken by desire, isn't anyone I recognize. She's wild and uninhibited and doesn't care who might see her jerking helplessly through her orgasm as a beautiful man in a beautiful suit holds her tight against his body and growls obscenities into her ear. She doesn't care what she looks like, arching in ecstasy as he works his hand between her spread legs. She doesn't care what anyone might think, seeing her so exposed.

The only thing she cares about is the man behind her and how he's brought her back to aching, blistering, terrifying life.

I lean against James's chest, throw my arms up and back around the mass of his shoulders, and tilt my head for his kiss.

Because fuck it.

I've already jumped off this high cliff I've been standing on since I met him. Might as well do it with my eyes open and my arms flung out wide.

At least I'll be smiling when I smash into a million pieces when I hit the ground.

12

James whispers sweet words against my lips that I don't hear because I'm floating somewhere out in space. It's only when he slips his hand from between my trembling thighs that I open my eyes and find myself back in the book store, in a hazy cloud of afterglow.

Through a gap in the shelf in front of me, I see the blonde cashier. She's looking right at me. Our gazes hold for a moment, then she turns away to help a customer.

I know she saw us.

I don't care.

James turns me toward him and kisses me softly, then whips out the silk pocket square from his suit jacket and swipes it between my legs, gently drying me. Then he stuffs the square of silk back into its place, adjusts the hem of my dress, and kisses me again, cupping my face in his hands.

Weaving slightly on my feet, I grasp his jacket's lapels and pronounce, "This is the best book store I've ever been to in my entire life."

He chuckles. "It's my favorite, too. Been coming here for years, since I first moved to Paris."

I bite my tongue not to ask *From where?* Instead, I manage the presence of mind to tease him. "If you tell me you bring all your girlfriends to the Russian section, I'll be forced to take off one of my shoes and stab you with a heel."

His expression turns serious. Rubbing his thumbs back and forth over my jawline and gazing into my eyes, he murmurs, "I've never brought anyone here, love. No one but you."

Love. My heart does this complicated thing where it seizes up and melts, all at the same time. Then I notice the hard pressure against my hip and suffer a twinge of guilt.

"What's wrong?" he asks sharply.

I blink, startled again by how easily he sees through me. "Did you take a course in mind reading? You're crazy good at it."

He hesitates a moment before answering. "I'm experienced with deciphering people's facial expressions."

I can tell we're in Touchy Subject area, but I'm not sure why. It makes total sense that an artist who creates portraits as detailed and full of emotion as his would obviously have a lot of experience reading the nuances of people's expressions, but he's acting like there's more to it than that.

You're the one who insisted on no personal questions, genius. Move on.

"I was just thinking that you've, ahem"—I glance down briefly toward his erection, trapped between us in his trousers—"taken care of me twice now, but I haven't taken care of you at all."

His blue eyes grow warm. "Delaying gratification is something I do well."

Another mysterious statement that I know will go unexplained.

The man is a sphinx.

"Let me show you around the rest of the shop," he says, offering his arm and smiling his sphinxlike smile.

I curl my fingers around the rock of his biceps and let him lead me out of the alcove and down another winding passageway toward the back of the store.

~

"So a famous book store, a famous library, and the former residence of one of the most famous writers in the world. You're giving me the grand tour."

"The grand *writer's* tour," corrects James, smiling at me. "Paris isn't known as the literary capital of the world for nothing."

I study him. Sitting across from me at a table in a restaurant on the second floor of the Eiffel Tower, he's elegance personified. He's powerfully magnetic, too, his raw masculinity straining the edges of his graceful manners and exquisite suit. The woman at the table next to us can't stop ogling him, despite her male companion's obvious irritation.

She's not the only one. I'm aware of several women and their heated stares turned James's way.

I suppose it's disrespectful to me how indiscreet they're being, but I can't blame them. His mere presence is commanding of attention. He could be passed out on the floor and it would still be impossible to look away.

"Thank you for doing all this." I toy with my fork, flattered by how much effort it must've taken him to plan and arrange this date. "If it weren't for you, I'd have stayed holed up in Estelle's apartment for the summer."

He doesn't reply. He simply watches me play with the cutlery, his gaze penetrating, until I get too self-conscious and fold my hands in my lap.

Finally, he says, "I'm bothering you again."

"You're bothering half the women in this restaurant."

"I don't care about them," comes the instant response. "I care about you."

The intensity in his eyes flusters me. I have to look away so I don't make a fool of myself and start reciting odes to his beauty. Very quietly, I say, "Same."

I hear his low inhalation. From the corner of my eye, I see his hand—resting on the arm of his chair—curl to a fist, then flex open.

Why that should make my pulse double, I don't know.

His voice low and controlled, he says, "You have no idea how beautiful you are, and how much I love knowing that color in your cheeks is because of me."

I reach up and touch my face. Sure enough, my cheeks are burning. "You're tough on my equilibrium," I admit sheepishly. "I'm not normally this affected by anything." My laugh is small and nervous. "Or anyone."

"Look at me."

When I do, I find him staring at me with blistering focus, his blue eyes clear and fierce.

He says, "Me neither."

There's a little heartbeat between my legs, pulsing in time with every hot surge of blood through my veins. I've never been this strongly attracted to a man before. The frightening thing is that it's not only a physical attraction. I'm drawn to everything about him, from the way his eyes change with his mood and the light to the obvious depth of his intelligence and sensitivity.

"Tell me," he commands, because of course he can read me like an open book.

I whisper, "You scare me."

He leans forward, his voice urgent. "You're afraid of me?"

I know he's asking if I think I'm in physical danger from him, which stops me for a moment. The assumption is so off base it seems uncharacteristic. He can usually gauge me so well. "No, not like that. Like…"

I take a breath for courage, glancing down at the tablecloth in search of a safe place to hide from his piercing eyes. "Like if I'm not careful, I could fall into you and drown."

After what feels like an eternity, James reaches across the table and grasps my wrist. Wary of his reaction and if I've admitted too much, I glance up at him from under my lashes.

The savage hunger on his face takes my breath away.

"Don't tempt me, Olivia. Don't make this a hypothetical. Because if I thought you were actually going to give me an inch of rope with this thing going on between us, I'd take it to the last goddamn mile. And believe me, that's not something you want."

My lips part, but no sound comes out. I'm too stunned by the combination of his expression and his words, spoken in a dangerous, terse monotone in stark contrast with all the heat and desire on his face.

"Bonsoir, monsieur *et* madame! *Bienvenue chez* Jules Verne."

I jump, startled by the sudden arrival of the waiter at our tableside.

His eyes shuttering and his expression wiped clean, James releases my wrist and leans back into his chair, crossing his legs. He casually adjusts a cufflink, then offers the waiter a disinterested smile.

He went from a boiling vat of molten lava to cool as a cucumber in one second flat.

It's incredibly unnerving. Not only because it seemed so effortless, but also because it seemed…practiced. Professional.

As if he learned it in school.

The waiter rambles on in French through what I have to assume is an introduction to the menu or the restaurant itself, which is named after the famous French novelist, poet, and playwright Jules Verne. Then he directs a question to James, who orders two bourbons and sends the waiter on his way.

With a shaking hand, I reach for my water glass. I gulp the

cool liquid, trying to buy some time to calm down. When I set the glass back onto the table, James says, "I should've asked if you have any spots in particular that you'd like to visit in Paris. I know the city well."

His tone is polite. Distant, even. I don't know if this is part of his breakneck mood change or if he's taking pity on me and letting me off the hook. I think if he tried to force me to respond directly to that mind-blowing speech he just gave, I'd bolt right out of the room in a panic.

I clear my throat and moisten my lips. Despite all that water I drank, my mouth is desert dry. "I didn't…I haven't really thought about it, to tell you the truth. I expected I'd be focused mainly on trying to write, not…" I trail off, picturing our passionate tryst in the book store. Heat creeps back into my cheeks. "Sightseeing."

"Sightseeing," he repeats, his voice husky.

Don't look at him. You'll burst into flames. "But I suppose now that I've got someone with experience to show me around, I should take advantage of it."

"Yes, I'm very experienced. And I'd very much enjoy showing you around."

That's a double entendre if I've ever heard one. Spoken in the same husky tone from moments before, his words carry a hidden meaning, a dark undercurrent of sensuality that tightens my stomach and makes me swallow hard around the sudden lump in my throat.

Or is my imagination playing tricks on me? Is he merely making conversation and I'm reading too much into innocent words?

Dammit, I hate having a brain that manufactures magical portals out of everyday cracks in a wall! Life would be so much easier if I were an accountant.

"That would be great," I say carefully, looking everywhere but at him.

I hear his low chuckle and know that I'm amusing him.

Then from somewhere inside his suit jacket comes a muted electronic *ding*. I glance over. Frowning, he reaches inside his jacket and pulls out a cell phone, small and black, the size of a credit card. It's the thinnest one I've ever seen. Must be a European model not available in the States.

He takes one look at the screen and his entire body stiffens.

"Everything okay?"

His gaze flashes up to meet mine. He stares at me for a fraction of a moment, a strange new hardness in his eyes, then he says curtly, "I'm sorry, but I have to go."

"Go? Where?" I look around the restaurant, as if searching for a plausible explanation for this sudden turn of events, but James is already standing.

When he doesn't answer, I know we're in Touchy Subject area again.

Feeling dismayed, I allow him to help me out of my chair. Then he ushers me through the restaurant with his hand flattened protectively on the small of my back, moving his gaze swiftly left and right as if visually sweeping the area for land mines as we head to the door.

When we're in the elevator heading down and he's standing stiff and silent beside me, I lose my patience with the cloak and dagger routine. "Are you going to tell me why you're so angry all of a sudden, or am I going to have to make up some story in my head that will probably be a thousand times worse than reality?"

"I'm not angry," he snaps, sounding angry.

I sigh and close my eyes. "Okie dokie, then."

A few seconds later, the elevator jolts to a stop.

I yelp in surprise, throwing a hand against the wall for balance. My eyes fly open. James turns away from the panel of buttons and looms over me, fire burning in his gaze as he backs me up against the elevator wall.

"It's work. I don't want to leave, but I have to."

I stare up at him with narrowed eyes and a crinkled nose. "Work? An emergency portrait session, is that it? Somebody decided on a whim on a Friday night that they desperately needed you to get their mug on paper before they went to bed?"

"No, smartass. That's not it."

He's big and bristling and obviously mad, but I'm not afraid of him and I'm not backing down. I know I'm the one who set up this whole no questions format, but that was before he started acting so suspicious.

"No? Okay. So your agent texted you to tell you he just lost a big sale? You have to run over to the gallery and beat him up or something?"

Through a clenched jaw, he says, "No."

Nose to nose, we glare at each other. The heat of his body burns me right through my dress. I'm as pissed off as he is, but holy shit do I want him to kiss me.

He can tell. He drops his gaze to my mouth. The heat between us ratchets up a few hundred degrees.

"I'm taking you home," he growls. "I'll come by later. It might be late. Don't wait up for me."

"Ha! You're taking a lot for granted there, Romeo! *Don't* come by later, I need my beauty sleep. You can try giving me a call tomorrow, but I'm not guaranteeing I'll answer, because I'm feeling a little weirded out by this whole scenario. The only reason *I* can think why you'd suddenly get called away in the middle of dinner on a Friday night and then start acting all sorts of freaked out and paranoid is because you're—"

I stop, the words turning to ash in my mouth.

I was about to say "in the witness protection program"—which I realize doesn't make a whole lot of sense, but I was on a roll there—but something far worse has presented itself as an option. A word even more terrifying than "fugitive" has leapt into my mind.

That word is "married."

I stare at him in horror.

When Edmond told me at the cocktail party that James was the most eligible bachelor in Paris, I took that to mean he was single. But considering Edmond's blasé attitude toward monogamy, it's possible he thinks all men are lifelong bachelors, no matter what legal commitments they've made.

James could have a wife holed up somewhere.

This is France, after all. In America the national pastime is baseball; here it's having a mistress or two.

James sighs heavily and closes his eyes. "You've got that look again like you think I'm a serial killer."

"Okay, lover boy, I'm going to ask you a question. And you *have* to tell me the truth."

He opens his eyes and stares at me, his expression wary.

"I promise this will be the last personal question I'll ever ask. I swear on the baby Jesus and all the saints and every single angel and cherub in heaven."

His brows draw together. "Are you very religious?"

I wave a hand dismissively in the air. "No, I'm just big on hyperbole. It's a bad habit. My editor is always yelling at me to tone it down. Anyway, here's my question. And you better look me *right in the eye* when you answer. Okay?"

Another heavy sigh. I could smack him.

I pronounce each word slowly and carefully. "Are you married?"

His eyes drill straight down into the blackest bottom of my soul. "No," he says, just as slowly and carefully. "I'm. *Not*. Married."

Folding my arms over my chest, I inspect his face. He appears to be telling the truth, but this is the same guy who pulled a credible Dr. Jekyll/Mr. Hyde impression when the waiter first arrived at our table.

An alarm sounds. James grabs me and kisses me. Hard.

When I turn my head and break the kiss, he commands gruffly, "Stay at the apartment until I come back."

Damn, he's bossy. I say sourly, "If you think you're the boss of me, pal, you've got another thing coming."

"Think."

I give him a side-eye. "Excuse me?"

"The correct phrase is, 'You've got another think coming,' not thing."

"No. That makes no sense."

"I'm telling you, that's what it is."

"Who's the writer here? Me or you? It's *thing*."

The elevator alarm sounds again, but this time it doesn't stop, it just keeps on blaring. Looking all sorts of frustrated and sexy and hot, James mutters an oath and turns to the panel of buttons, jabbing a finger against one of them. The elevator jerks into motion again, and we're headed down.

When the doors open moments later, he takes me by the arm and leads me out to the street, where he whistles for a cab. One immediately screeches to a stop at the curb, because even taxis are obliged to obey him.

"Why we don't just take the Metro, I'll never know," I grumble under my breath.

James swings open the door of the cab, quickly inserts me into the back seat, and leans in to glare at me. "Because you're safer in a cab, that's why."

That makes me blink. "Safer from what?"

He slams the door shut in my face.

Then he leans in the open front window to give the driver the address, tosses a handful of money at him, and turns and stalks away.

As the cab pulls away from the curb, I twist around in my seat and stare out the back window, watching the receding figure of James striding off into the warm Paris evening until he's swallowed by the crowd and disappears.

13

The first thing I do when I get back into the apartment is head straight over to the computer in Estelle's library and fire it up.

Into Google's search bar, I type "*You've got another thing coming*."

Google helpfully provides me with 798,000,000 results.

The first one is a video for the heavy metal band Judas Priest's song of the same name, which fills me with smugness. If a famous rock band recorded it as "thing" instead of "think," I'm obviously right.

My brief bout of smugness lasts until I scroll farther down the page and find an article in Merriam-Webster regarding usage of the phrase. When I click the link, I'm dismayed to learn that a debate still rages to this day about the correctness of word choice. Apparently "think" is the older usage, originating in nineteenth-century British English, and "thing" is more current—and more common—but frequently criticized by language purists as an incorrect bastardization.

In other words, James and I are both right…except he's *more* right than I am.

Hello, dented ego, my old friend.

Because I'm in need of a morale boost, I dig my cell phone out from my handbag on the desk and send Estelle a text.

Question for your superior literary brain: Which would you say is correct? "You've got another THING coming" or "You've got another THINK coming?"

While I wait for an answer, I wander into the kitchen. I kick off my heels, open the fridge, and stare into it for a while until I realize I'm not hungry. I haven't eaten since breakfast, but between the orgasm at the book store, James's sudden impersonation of Houdini at dinner, and the memory of how far up my lip curled when I told him he was wrong about think vs. thing, what I'm really craving is a drink to settle my nerves.

I pour myself a bourbon and am just about to tuck into it when my cell phone chimes. Estelle has answered.

DOES THIS MEAN YOU'RE WRITING AGAIN???

Not even five seconds later, my phone rings. I smile and hit the *Answer* button. "Hi, Estelle."

"Doll!" she shouts gleefully. "Tell me you have good news!"

I can't resist teasing her a little. "Gee, no pressure or anything. Couldn't I just be asking your opinion?"

She scoffs. "Puh. The only time you've ever asked my opinion on anything is when I took you to lunch at Le Bernardin for your thirtieth birthday and you couldn't decide between the sashimi and the caviar."

"That's not true! I distinctly remember asking your opinion on whether or not I should marry Chris."

There's a long pause, then Estelle says soberly, "No, doll, you didn't. You would've fired me as your agent if you had."

"What do you mean?" I ask, surprised.

There's another long pause, which is so unlike Estelle it gives me an uneasy feeling. The woman normally has no filter.

"What I mean is that Christopher isn't a good guy. And he certainly wasn't good for you."

That shocks me. Though Chris and I are divorced, I feel defensive of him. I'm upset and confused that she'd speak about him this way.

"Estelle, what are you talking about? We had our differences, like any couple, but we—"

"He abandoned you when you needed him most," she cuts in, her voice hard.

I remember how alone I felt, sitting on that cold pew in the church by myself. How gutted and alone.

My voice shaking with emotion, I say, "Everyone deals with grief in their own way."

Estelle's voice softens. "Yes, they do. But a father who doesn't show up to his own child's funeral—"

I snap, "He couldn't deal with it. That's not unusual. The grief counselor said—"

"—*or* his child's birth—"

"He wasn't able to get away from work in time! You know she came early!"

"—who left his wife *in a foreign country* on their honeymoon—"

"For God's sake, Estelle! He's a diplomat! A war broke out! He was needed! *I'm* the one who said it was fine for him to go!"

In the wake of my angry outburst, we both fall silent. Estelle sighs heavily. Then she says, "Anything he did was fine with you. All his silences, all his absences, all the ways he didn't meet your needs…all fine. Because you loved him.

"But he didn't deserve it. He didn't deserve *you*."

The hot prick of tears stings my eyes. My throat is so tight I can barely swallow a mouthful of bourbon, but I manage to choke it back. It burns a hollow path down to my stomach and sits there, angrily churning.

I speak through a clenched jaw. "Anyway. To answer your question, yes, I'm writing again. I'm writing quite a lot, actually.

And it's goddamn good. I'll send you what I have soon. I have to go now. Thanks, Estelle. Bye."

I click *End*, then throw the phone all the way across the room. It hits the wall with a clatter, splinters apart, then falls in pieces to the floor.

I leave it where it is and head out of the kitchen, swiping angrily at my watering eyes.

There's a Juliet balcony off the living room with a small deck, just large enough for one person to stand on. I push the curtains aside and open the French doors, then step out and lean against the curved railing.

The sky is sullen with dark clouds. The bass rumble of thunder echoes somewhere off in the distance. The air is humid and fragrant with the sharp smell of ozone, all signs of a coming summer storm.

When the first drops begin to fall, I turn my face to the sky and close my eyes, letting the rain mingle with my tears.

"A father who doesn't show up to his own child's funeral."

That one hurt the most. Of all the times Chris was absent, that time carved itself so deep into my heart the wounds are still as fresh as if they were slashed there yesterday.

My baby girl was gone, my soul was in ashes, and my man was nowhere to be found.

Everything crumbled after we lost her. We couldn't talk anymore. We could barely meet each other's eyes. The silences in the house would stretch on so long I'd sometimes wonder if we'd lost the ability to communicate. Group therapy was a horror, more painful than pouring acid on open cuts. All those stories of loss piled up on top of my own until I felt suffocated.

Marital counseling wasn't much better. There was no way to make sense of such a senseless thing, and no amount of talking was going to help or change it.

Then, finally, after Chris packed his bags and moved out, I went to individual therapy on my own in one last ditch attempt to find peace with the worst thing that had ever happened to me. Or at least some sort of meaning.

But there's no meaning to be found in violence. Murder is an end unto itself.

A moan jolts me out of the swamp of my memories. I open my eyes and look across the courtyard from where it came, at a window that was dark only moments before but now is illuminated.

Gigi and Gaspard are in their bedroom, doing what they do best.

I turn away and go inside, chugging the rest of the bourbon. Then I turn out all the lights and go to bed.

I wake up hours later knowing instinctively that something is wrong.

It's that mother's intuition. The heightened hearing. The sharper sense of smell. The finely-tuned antennae you never lose, even when your child has long since been ripped from your arms.

Heart pounding, I sit up in bed, my ears straining to hear any sound. I'm not sure if it *was* a sound that woke me, but I listen hard into the dark. My eyes slowly adjust until I can make out the edges of the dresser, the curved arm of the chair near the door.

And the tall figure of the man standing beside it.

I scream in terror, but he's on me before I can jump out of bed. He grabs me and pins me beneath his heavy body, flattening me against the mattress as I struggle wildly underneath him.

"Olivia," growls a rough voice into my ear. "It's me. Stop. It's only me."

I fall still, panting, realizing from one heartbeat to the next that it's James. It only takes another few seconds for the fury to hit.

"*What the fuck*!" I shout. "*You nearly scared me to death, asshole*!"

"I'm sorry."

"Sorry? You're *sorry*? How did you even get in here?" I continue to struggle, but he's not letting me go. If anything, his hands tighten even more around my wrists. He slides a leg over both of mine, stopping me from kicking him.

"You left the front door open. I knocked and rang the bell, but you didn't answer."

I was so distracted by the stupid thing vs. think argument when I came in that I can't remember if I locked it or not, but it doesn't surprise me that I left it open. I did the same thing the other night when he took me to dinner. The man always puts me out of sorts.

"So you thought it would be a good idea to just waltz in uninvited?"

"I told you I'd come."

"And I told you not to!"

I feel his hot breath on my neck when he whispers, "Tell me to leave and I will."

I lie there glaring at the ceiling and grinding my teeth until I get my breathing under control. Part of me wants to snap *Get the hell out*...but there's another part of me—a bigger part—that doesn't.

I haven't had a man in my bed in years. *Years*. Every neglected nerve in my body is shrieking.

And considering it's this particular man, who gets me so hot with a single look that my eyes cross, I'm inclined to let him stay and see where this is going.

I grit out, "You can stay, but you'd better make it up to me."

He releases my wrists, props himself up on his elbows, and

kisses me. It's a gentle kiss, a searching one, and seems apologetic. He knows I'm walking on the razor's edge of my temper.

He says, "I want to make it up to you, sweetheart, but you haven't given me your list yet."

Grr. "Fine. You want a list of what I like to do in bed? Here's the top five: sleep, read, watch TV, cuddle my boyfriend pillow while daydreaming about winning the Nobel Prize for literature, and sleep."

It takes me a moment to realize the slight shaking in James's chest is stifled laughter.

"You said sleep twice."

"That's because I really like to sleep!"

He kisses me softly in the sensitive spot under my earlobe, making me shiver. "I see. And what is a boyfriend pillow, exactly?"

Another kiss, lower on my neck, and I shiver again. "You'll laugh."

"I won't."

Kiss. Kiss. Nibble. Kiss. He works his way slowly down my neck to my collarbone, then dips the tip of his tongue into the hollow of my throat. He adjusts his weight on top of me, sliding his leg between mine.

He's so big and heavy. So warm and solid. So *strong.* And God, how I love it.

There's nothing that makes you feel more like a woman than lying under the powerful bulk of a man.

"It's…um…like a big comfy sleeping pillow about half the length of my body."

"Mmm." He slides a hand under me and squeezes my ass, drawing me closer against him and flexing his hips.

He's already hard for me. My pulse goes arrhythmic. I clutch his shoulders, sinking my fingers into the fine fabric of his suit.

Why is he still wearing his suit? Did he come straight here from wherever it was he went? "It's very supportive," I say, breathing harder. "I love my boyfriend pillow."

James lifts his head and locks eyes with me. His gaze is intense and heated. "Interesting."

"My pillow?"

"No, the fact that I'm insanely jealous of it."

Because I sleep with it or because I said I love it? My heart flutters, but I don't ask the question aloud.

I whisper, "If anything, it should be jealous of you. I've never given myself an orgasm while thinking of my boyfriend pillow."

James's eyes flare, drilling down into mine. "You made yourself come thinking of me?"

I can tell he's excited by the idea. His voice is raw and there's a new tension in his body, a telling change in the rhythm of his breathing.

I nod.

"When? Earlier tonight?"

Oh God. He wants all the dirty details. Why did I even open my mouth? I moisten my lips. James tracks the motion of my tongue with the eyes of a predator. "No. After I met you at the café."

His lips part. Astonished, he gazes down at me.

I grumble, "Don't judge me."

"I'm not judging you. Fuck, Olivia, I am *not* judging you." He laughs. "Especially considering I did the exact same thing."

I peer at him, unconvinced.

Seeing my narrow-eyed look, he laughs again. He kisses my neck and jaw, chuckling against my skin, his stubble tickling me. "It was this ripe peach that did it," he murmurs, squeezing my butt again. "You walked away from me and my dick got so fucking hard watching this ass sway that I had to go into the café's restroom and jerk myself off."

I shove at his chest. "That's a bald-faced lie!"

"No, sweetheart. It's the God's honest truth."

He kisses me, his mouth hard and demanding, his heart crashing against my breasts. Then he rolls off me, flicks on the lamp on the nightstand, and stands at the side of the bed looking down.

"Tell me what I did to you in your fantasy," he says in a low, urgent voice, shucking off his jacket and tossing it carelessly aside. "Tell me *exactly* what I did."

He whips off his shirt while I stare at him, feeling electrocuted.

And scared as shit.

I swallow and try not to hyperventilate as I watch him kick off his shoes, peel off his socks, unbuckle his belt, and rip off his trousers. If there's a speed record for undressing, he's about to break it.

Then he's standing there in all his glory wearing only a pair of black briefs. An enormous bulge distends the front.

The sight of his gorgeous body must be crossing all the wires in my brain, because I say, "You fucked me like you owned me, body and soul."

Without breaking eye contact with me, he palms his erection, squeezing it through his briefs then stroking his hand up and down the length. "Go on."

His voice is controlled but strain shows on his face. His muscles are all tensed, as if he's restraining himself from lunging.

Heat blooms over my skin, prickling all the tiny hairs on my body. A fine tremor runs through my stomach. I lie motionless on my back, watching this aroused, beautiful man fight himself not to pounce on me, and feel more powerful than I have in my life.

"You were on top of me. Fucking me. Hard."

His jaw muscles flex. He slides his hand under the elastic waistband of his briefs and grasps his jutting erection. Even surrounded by his big hand, it looks huge.

My voice comes out breathy. "You fucked me like that until I was about to come, then you flipped me over and put me on my knees and fucked me from behind."

He begins to stroke his bare cock, running his hand up and down the shaft, thick and veined. All the veins in his arms are standing out, too, and so is one in his neck that's throbbing.

"Then you spanked me, over and over as you fucked me, until I came, screaming into the pillow."

He says sharply, "You said you'd never been spanked before."

"I hadn't."

"But you fantasized about me doing it?"

"Yes."

His eyelids drift lower. His hand moves faster. He stands still, stroking himself, watching me, his chest moving erratically up and down.

The cotton T-shirt I wore to bed rubs against my hard nipples with every inhalation I take. I'm aware of a heaviness between my legs, a tingle quickly turning into an ache.

James commands, "Sit up," and my heartbeat goes haywire.

I follow his instruction, folding my legs underneath me and waiting for his next command as I struggle to keep my breathing even.

With his free hand, he motions me forward. I crawl to the edge of the bed, then fold my legs underneath me again, looking up at him, my entire body trembling.

He says softly, "On your hands and knees."

I exhale in a gust. Then I do as I'm told, acutely aware of every inch of skin on my body. My nerves are singing. My blood pounds through my veins.

Still stroking his erection, James moves closer to the edge of the bed until his cock is inches away from my face.

I can't look away from it. My vision narrows to a tunnel, at the end of which is a huge, beautiful dick, standing proudly erect with a small bead of moisture welling at the slit in the crown.

James grasps my jaw in his free hand and forces me to look up at him.

His eyes are dark and wild.

He says gruffly, "You're going to suck my cock and play with your pussy while I spank your ass, sweetheart. Are you ready?"

A thrill like terror blasts through me. But it's not terror, it's elation, the shock of how much I want this scorching through me like nuclear wind.

Quaking, I whisper, "I'm ready."

My dark commander rewards me with a dangerous smile.

14

Eyes burning, James waits for me without speaking another word. He doesn't move, either, he simply remains patiently unmoving as I take a ragged breath and drop my gaze to his cock gripped in his fist.

I shift my weight forward on my hands and tentatively lick the bead of moisture glistening on the tip.

All the muscles in his stomach contract. Curled around my jaw, his fingers twitch.

I take that as a positive sign and slide the engorged head between my lips.

He sucks in a quiet breath.

I close my eyes and take more of him, loving how hot and tight he feels against my tongue, loving his faint taste of salt and musk. Drawing back to furl my tongue around the head, I linger there for a moment, sucking, enjoying myself, feeling the vein on the underside of his shaft pulse against my tongue.

His hand slides down my jaw to my throat, and he gently squeezes.

Why do I like that? Why should that small gesture of dominance make me clench and shudder? Why should it make me moan?

In his dominant voice, he says, "Get your fingers in your panties and take that cock all the way down your throat."

Balancing on one hand, I shove the other hand between my legs, fumbling with my damp panties, pushing them aside. As soon as my fingers glide over my throbbing clit, I relax my throat and slide my lips as far down his shaft as they'll go.

He groans, then curses, his hand hot around my throat. Tightening.

I withdraw slowly, opening my eyes to look up at him when I suck on the crown. His eyes are hazy and he's breathing hard, licking his lips as he watches me.

He reaches down and fondles my breasts through my shirt, first one then the other, rolling my hard nipples between his fingers, pinching them, squeezing their fullness with a rough, needy grip. I start a rhythm, my hips rocking against my hand as I take him deep down my throat and out again, my heart hammering like mad.

"I'm gonna spank you," he pants. "Don't come."

Don't come? What does he mean don't *come? Isn't that the whole—*

CRACK!

I jump, sucking in a hard breath through my nose. When he spanks me again, I whine at the sting and work my fingers faster between my legs. I'm so wet I can hear the sound it makes in the room, even above the gentle drumming of the rain. I suck harder on his cock, greedily swallowing as much of it as I can.

"Christ, Olivia. You're so fucking beautiful. Jesus Christ."

Every other word is punctuated by a pant. He leans over and slaps my ass again, six times in hard, quick succession. My orgasm approaches like a cresting wave. Naturally, he knows.

"That orgasm belongs to me. It belongs to my cock, not your fingers. Don't you dare come before I'm inside you."

Or what? You'll spank me?

I'm delirious. I must be. The only reason I don't laugh is because I've got a twelve-inch steel pipe rammed down my throat, but I feel as high as an untethered kite, pinwheeling recklessly through the sky, tumbling into a bright, dangerous nothingness.

Then suddenly his cock is gone and I'm flat on my back, blinking in surprise as James looms over me.

"I'm not trying to punish you by not letting you come," he says raggedly. "It's just that if we delay as long as we can, it increases the pleasure. It's called edging."

Edging smedging! Let's ride this baby all the way home! Lying under him, I'm sweating and shaking, unable to speak.

"Okay?"

I groan in protest, closing my eyes.

He kisses me on the neck, whispering, "Tell me what you want. If you really need to come right now, tell me. You know I'll take care of you."

I open my eyes and gaze up at him. He's staring down at me with intense focus, his dark hair falling onto his forehead, his face shadowed and beautiful and filled with concern.

Something inside my chest unlocks. A heavy door squeaks open on rusted hinges, letting light flood in.

"Okay," I say, my voice almost inaudible. "Let's do the edging thing. I trust you."

He falls completely still. He doesn't even seem to be drawing a breath. But underneath all the stillness and perfect control something massive is churning and burning, blazing out from the dark, searching depths of his eyes.

"You trust me?"

"Yes."

He says my name in a reverent whisper, lifting a hand to tenderly brush a lock of hair off my cheek and tuck it behind my ear.

I say, "Don't get all weird on me now, lover boy. I haven't had sex since Duran Duran was topping the charts. Let's do this."

He shakes his head, laughing softly. "Were you even alive in the 1980s?"

"Yes."

"So you were having sex as an infant?"

"No. Gross. Will you please put your mouth on me now?"

"Sure." He drops his head and kisses me softly on my throat.

"Not there."

Lifting his head, he sends me a lazy and knowing smile. "No? Where, then?"

"Between my legs."

He cocks his head and arches his brows, as if he has no idea what I'm talking about.

"On my pussy."

He whispers mockingly, "Oohhh, *there*."

"Yes, please. Now, please. Unless you want to spank me there instead, because I love that."

Looking down at me, his smile fades. He examines me, his intensity growing by the second, until he says in a low, terse voice, "It's a good thing you're not here long. Otherwise, I'd make you mine."

His words thrill me and so does the passion in his eyes. But the passion is tempered by that darkness that wells up at unexpected moments, the darkness that should frighten me but instead makes me want to dive in deep and lose myself in it.

"You say that like being yours would be a bad thing."

"It wouldn't be good, Olivia. Not for you."

"Why not?"

After a tense hesitation, he murmurs, "Touchy subject."

Outside, thunder rumbles. A crack of white lightning briefly illuminates the room. I push aside the eerie and irrational feeling that nature herself is warning me away from him and frame his chiseled jaw in my hands.

Gazing deep into his beautiful blue eyes, I say, "You can't see yourself like I can, James. Any woman would be lucky to belong to a man like you. You'll find the right one someday. And whoever she is, I hope I never meet her, because I'll be so envious I'll want to punch her right in the face."

He inhales, nostrils flaring. His eyes narrow to slits.

Then, with startling ferocity, he crushes his mouth to mine.

He kisses me so hungrily I'm instantly breathless. My heart pounds violently, so hard it feels as if it's beating outside my chest. In the next instant he's gone, rearing back on his knees to shove my thin T-shirt up my chest and over my face and arms. He gathers it around my wrists and ties the ends together, yanking the knot closed hard.

Gripping my forearms, he presses my wrists against the mattress above my head and stares down at me. His eyes are glassy and burning, like he's running a fever.

"Don't come until I say you can."

His voice is deadly soft. It sends a zing of exhilaration skittering across my nerve endings.

I like him like this, on the outer edge of his control. I like knowing this weird intensity of desire and need is mutual, that he wishes he could manage it but can't, not really, not enough for us to stay safe.

It's clear to me that neither of us believes in safety. Not anymore. Not after what life has put us through.

We're bound by the awful truth that safety is an illusion.

It's also the thing that, in this moment, sets us both free.

He tears off my panties. Literally tears them, ripping through the lacy material with ease and yanking the shreds out from under me. Then he shoves his face between my thighs and starts to greedily suck on my clit, reaching up to roughly squeeze my breasts in his big hot hands.

I love it. I love it so much I arch and shudder and reward him with a guttural moan that turns into the shape of his name.

He pinches my nipples and works his tongue between my legs, driving me higher and higher until I'm pleading with him for release. But he doesn't give it to me. Instead, he turns his head to my thigh and bites me there, his teeth sinking into my tender flesh with a sting that brands my heart.

"Not yet, beautiful," he warns, his voice hard. "Not without me inside you."

I rock my hips, groaning, turning my head restlessly from side to side. "Fuck me, then. Hurry. Please."

That animal noise rumbles through his chest. The one that tells me he loves my reaction, my words, my unapologetic need for what he's giving me. The mattress dips as he steps onto the floor. I hear him rummage through his clothing, then I hear the rip of foil and know he came prepared this time.

The mattress dips again. James says, "Open your eyes."

He hovers above me, his hands planted on either side of my head. I glance down and see his erect cock, sheathed in a condom, bobbing heavily between my spread thighs.

It's thick and long, much bigger than I've had before, but I'm no virginal bride. I know he'll fit me just right.

I watch in fascination as he fists his cock in his hand and nudges it against my soaked folds. He slides it up and down until the crown is glistening.

"Look at me."

When I meet his dark gaze, he growls, "You're mine until September. Say it."

I say breathlessly, "Yes. I'm yours until September. I'm all yours."

With one abrupt flex of his hips, he shoves the entire length of his thick cock deep inside me.

Crying out, I arch from the mattress. He props himself up on one elbow, fists his hand into my hair, and reaches underneath me with his other hand to grab my ass in a possessive grip.

Into my ear, he commands, "Wrap your legs around my waist."

I do, trembling all over. He exhales, slowly withdraws until only the crown of his cock remains inside me, then thrusts again.

He smothers my moan with a kiss, deep and demanding. Then he thrusts again and again, driving hard into my aching wetness.

It's not gentle. This isn't lovemaking. This is fucking, raw and animal and beautiful in it's urgency.

A single hard contraction inside me makes me break away from his mouth and beg. "James, oh God, James, please, I need to come, *please let me come…*"

Breathing hard, he slows the motion of his hips until it's the smallest movement, then he falls still. In a firm voice, he says, "No."

He bends his head to my breast and draws my hard nipple into the hot, wet heat of his mouth.

Delirious, I writhe beneath him. My skin is on fire. All my muscles are clenched. I rock my hips, grinding my clit against his pelvis and chasing the burn building in my core. I feel a rush of exhilaration when his dick twitches in response.

He puts his mouth next to my ear. "Such a bad girl. My beautiful, bad girl. If you don't stop moving your hips right now, I'll pull out and spank your ass until it's so sore you won't be able to sit for a week."

I sob in frustration.

I know this edging thing is a game I agreed to play, but holy fuck am I regretting it.

Falling still, I lie beneath him, panting and trembling, my skin slicked with sweat. He bends his head to my breasts again, lavishing the other nipple with attention, nipping at it and flicking it with his tongue.

I need so badly to move my hips. Instead I bite my lower lip, hard, and remain motionless as James goes back and forth between my throbbing nipples, sucking and gently biting, testing my flesh with his teeth to see what makes me moan, what makes me gasp.

When I'm about to break down and cry, James whispers, "Perfect. You're perfect. I love you like this, trying so hard to be good for me even though you have to come so bad."

"So so bad," I babble, "so so *so* bad."

James says something I can't understand.

Either I really am delirious and my brain is too enflamed to comprehend the words, or he's speaking in a language I don't recognize, something that sounds exotic and masculine, all snarling fricatives with an edge to it like a purr.

For whatever reason, it's the thing that finally makes me break.

I start to buck my hips, frantically fucking myself on the hard length of the beautiful cock buried inside me.

James curses, and that I understand.

"I'm coming! I'm coming! I can't stop oh God James I can't stop—"

He thrusts into me and snarls, "Give it to me."

"Oh fuck oh fuck—"

"Yes, love, *give me every fucking thing you've got.*"

Convulsing and crying out, I thrash underneath him as he fucks me. My orgasm rips through my body with such force it feels like a detonation. Clench and release, clench and release, wave after wave after wave of pleasure crashes over me. Helpless, I give myself over to it as James drives into me, grunting, his mouth latching onto where the pulse throbs in my throat. Holding my wrists and sucking hard on my neck, he thrusts with powerful strokes, ravaging me.

Owning me.

He briefly falls still, then lets out a husky moan. His entire body jerks. He rears up on his hands, throws his head back, and shouts.

Then he starts to flex his pelvis again, fucking me straight through his orgasm.

I clench my thighs tightly around his waist and hold on for the ride, trying to ignore Kelly's warning voice inside my head telling me to be careful.

It's far, far too late for that.

15

Sometime near dawn, the rain tapers off. I lie drowsing in the warm sanctuary of my lover's arms, listening to his heart thump slowly and steadily against my cheek, feeling the wonderful soreness in my body, the tender spots where he used his teeth on my skin and sank his strong fingers deep into my flesh as he took me.

He's marked me. In more ways than one.

I'm trying not to think about it.

James murmurs, "You're awake."

"So are you, apparently."

"I never went to sleep."

I tilt my head back and look up at him. He gazes down at me with soft eyes and an even softer smile. His dark hair is mussed and he badly needs a shave, but he's so gorgeous he takes my breath away.

He bends his head and presses a tender kiss to my lips, then adjusts my body against his, pulling me closer so I'm snug against his side. His shoulder supports my neck. Our legs twine together under the rumpled sheets. He rests his cheek on my forehead and toys with my hair with one hand, while the other glides gently up and down my bare back.

He traces the bumps of my spine with his fingertips, slowly and reverently, as if he's memorizing the shape of each one.

It feels so right, lying here with him like this. So intimate and right.

A well of raw emotion makes me hide my face in his neck and squeeze my eyes shut. I draw a breath and fight the feelings back. *Get your shit together. This isn't personal. This is sex. This is fantasy land. It's nothing more than a summer fling.*

"I know," James murmurs, his lips moving against my hair. "I'm struggling with it, too."

I'm so startled by his uncanny perception that for a moment all I can do is lie there in shock. When I've recovered, I say too loudly, "That is so *weird*. You *have* to stop doing that!"

"I can't help it."

"You could not say anything!"

"I'd still notice."

"Maybe, but I wouldn't feel like you've hacked straight into my medulla oblongata!"

He chuckles, giving me a squeeze. "You mean your cerebrum."

I scowl at his chin. "What?"

"The cerebrum performs higher intellectual functions like processing speech and emotion. The medulla oblongata handles involuntary bodily functions like sneezing or vomiting."

I mutter, "I'm about to show you a few involuntary bodily functions right now, I'll tell you what."

He squeezes me again, trying to smother his laughter because he knows I'm pissed.

"Stop being smarter than me. It's annoying."

He adopts a serious tone. "Sorry. I forgot about your advanced degrees."

"Exactly."

"It's probably an insult to your proud feminism, too."

"Dude, you have *no* idea."

He pauses. "Did you just call me 'dude?'"

"I grew up in San Diego. If you're not properly programmed with surfer slang by your senior year in high school, they don't let you graduate."

The moment it's out, I realize my mistake. I close my eyes and rest my head against his shoulder, hoping he won't notice what I've done.

But I've forgotten whom I'm dealing with. The man is a savant. He notices everything.

"A California beach girl," he says, nuzzling his nose into my hair. "Does this mean you know how to surf?"

I debate whether or not to call Touchy Subject, but decide the cat's already out of the bag on this one. Might as well go with it. "I tried to surf as a teenager, but it turns out staying indoors lost in books for an entire childhood doesn't make a person particularly athletic."

"You couldn't get up on the board?"

"I wish it were that simple. Not only could I not stand up, I nearly drowned."

He replies with complete confidence, "I could teach you how to surf. I have excellent water skills."

"*Water skills*? You say that like you took a course or something."

"An advanced course, yes. Water competency is fundamental."

It's a good thing I don't use Botox, because I scrunch up my forehead so hard in response to that bizarre statement that I would've cracked my face.

After a time, James says, "Go ahead. Ask me."

His tone is indulgent. He doesn't sound worried. "What about Touchy Subject land?"

"I'll waive it this time. But I get one free pass in return."

"I just gave you a free pass when I said where I grew up!"

"Yes, but that was by accident. I want one *on purpose*."

I look up at him and study his face. "You are a profoundly strange person."

He smiles. "Right back atcha, hot stuff. Do we have a deal?"

Defeated, I sigh. "Okay. Deal."

"Good. So you'll want to know about the water competency, then."

"Yes."

"Were you thinking I'm secretly a Navy SEAL, something along those lines?"

I consider it. "Not really, but now that you mention it, you do seem as if you could've had some formal military training."

He gazes down at me with arched brows. "Really? How so?"

"You're very…alpha."

He bursts out laughing. "*Alpha*?"

I say sourly, "As opposed to beta, yes."

"Is this how all feminists think of men? In terms of Greek letters?"

I roll my eyes at that. "Not alpha like the Greek letter, alpha like the wolf. The leader of the pack. The strongest one who protects all the others."

His laughter slowly dies until he's staring at me with his signature intensity and blistering focus.

I say, "I can see the gears turning."

"I'm only giving you one free pass."

"I'm not asking, I'm just saying."

"What exactly are you saying?"

"Doesn't matter. Back to the water competency question. Spill."

James gazes at me. The silence grows until it becomes unbearable. My mind crackles with a million different theories, each more implausible than the last, everything from him once being a movie stuntman to a water boarding expert, interrogating enemy combatants in a filthy Guantanamo Bay prison cell.

When he finally answers, his tone is matter-of-fact. "Growing up, I was the lifeguard at our community pool."

My disappointment is crushing. "Oh."

Seeing how crestfallen I am at hearing his simple explanation, he starts to laugh again, only this time he can't stop.

I pound a fist on his chest. "Shut up, you jerk!"

He drags me on top of his body and laughs and laughs, his head tipped back into the pillow and his eyes closed, arms tight around me so I can't escape, even as I squirm and struggle.

"You should've seen your face!" He hoots. The entire bed shakes with his laughter. "You looked like someone just told you Christmas was cancelled!"

"Ha ha," I say drily. "Laugh it up, lover boy, because the next time you fall asleep and you're gently snoring, I'm going to sneak into your apartment and drop a worm into your open mouth. You won't be laughing then."

James abruptly stops laughing and looks at me. "Worms get a bad rap. They're highly nutritious and actually don't taste so bad, once you get used to the texture."

I stare at him with my mouth hanging open until he dissolves into gales of laughter once more.

I sigh in disgust, rest my head on his broad chest, and wait for him to get it out of his system.

"God, you're so fucking adorable." He peppers kisses all over the top of my head.

Glaring at the dresser across the room, I say, "Glad you find me so amusing. Maybe I've got a future in stand up comedy."

He takes my face in his hands and kisses me deeply, his tongue searching my mouth. When he pulls away and speaks, his voice has gone husky and his eyes have grown hot. "Yes, I find you amusing. Amusing and addicting and fascinating and so goddamn sexy I could spend an entire lifetime with you and never get my fill."

Shaken by the intensity and unexpected pleasure of his words, by the rule-breaking honesty of them—and especially by the mention of 'an entire lifetime'—I have trouble drawing a full breath. In a small, strangled voice, I say, "You're not so bad yourself."

That earns me a smile. He whispers, "You know, for such a badass brilliant writer, you get awfully tongue-tied when someone gives you a compliment."

"Writing is different than speaking. It's much harder to be coherent out loud than it is on paper."

He gazes at me thoughtfully, stroking his thumbs over my cheeks. "Write it down for me, then."

"What do you mean?"

"I mean instead of a smartass response to what I said, write down what you really felt."

I stare at him, alarmed, my eyes growing wide. "But…we're not getting personal."

His blue eyes lock onto mine with the force of a gravitational field. He says gruffly, "You're too smart to believe that."

"James—"

He flips me over and rolls on top of me, so quickly I let out a startled peep. Then, with his fingertips gripping my scalp and his eyes blazing blue fire, he says, "You said you didn't want me to ask you any personal questions, and I'm trying to respect that. I'm trying to respect that, for whatever reason, you don't want me to get close."

My heart bangs around wildly inside my chest. "The reason is that I'm leaving the country at the end of the summer."

"No, it's not," comes the hard and fast response. "The real reason is because you're afraid."

"You're conveniently forgetting your cryptic statement about how it wouldn't be good for me to belong to you. And your sudden, unexplained disappearance during dinner, and how you said you're fucked up. And let's not forget about your abnormal obsession with death. Is all that supposed to make me feel secure about opening up?"

"I never said I was obsessed with death," he says, teeth gritted.

My reply is icy. "Tell the truth now, James."

"Just because my latest collection features portraits of people grieving doesn't mean—"

"What did you see when you first spotted me at the café?"

His breathing rough and his nostrils flared, he stares down at me in silence.

"I know exactly what you saw," I say quietly, looking him in the eye. "And it wasn't all butterflies and rainbows."

"I saw a beautiful woman I wanted to get to know."

"Bullshit. You saw a woman walking around in her own personal graveyard. The same way, I suspect, you're walking around yours."

The expression on his face is indescribable. It's part anger, part frustration, and part horrified surprise.

Because I nailed it. I nailed that damn nail right on the head.

Just as fast as he rolled on top of me, he rolls off. Staring at the floor, he sits on the edge of the mattress and drags a hand through his hair. Unsettled, I sit up, draw my knees to my chest, and pull the sheets over my breasts, watching him.

After a while, he says, "Do you want me to go?"

"I want you to be honest with me."

His tone is flat. "You really don't."

Heat creeps up my neck. I stay quiet for a moment to get my anger under control, then say, "That was condescending and not appreciated."

He turns his head and stares at me over his shoulder. His eyes are as flat as his voice. "Did you ever see the movie *The Matrix*?"

"What the hell does that have to do with this conversation?"

"Just answer the question."

The heat in my neck spreads up to my ears, where it settles, throbbing. "Fine. Yes, I saw it. And?"

"When Morpheus approaches Neo and offers him two pills—a red one that will reveal the truth that the world he knows is an illusion, or a blue one that will allow him to stay blissfully ignorant and return to his old life—which pill would you choose, knowing what comes after?"

I glance at the tattoo on his shoulder, the strange Latin phrase and the rows of thin black lines, and a cold wind slices through me. My mouth goes dry.

James says with hard finality, "You'd choose the blue pill."

"Is that supposed to be some kind of allegory for you being a red pill?"

"No. It's supposed to reveal how much reality you're willing to deal with. Because the truth is that sometimes ignorance is a far wiser choice. Wiser and safer for everyone concerned."

He stands and starts to get dressed.

Filled with ambivalence and a sharp, unnamed fear, I watch him pull on his briefs and trousers, socks and shirt. He buckles his belt with quick efficiency, slips his feet into his expensive black loafers, and retrieves his rumpled suit jacket from where he discarded it to the floor.

Then he stands gazing down at me in bed, his eyes dark.

"Those rules you made for us were smart. No questions, no strings…it really is better that way. Better for you, mostly, but also for me, because if I didn't have that framework to operate within, I would've already decided that I was going to give you a red pill, consequences be damned."

He turns and makes his way across the room. At the doorway, he pauses and glances back at me. "If you want to see me again, Olivia, you know how to reach me. And if you don't, I understand. If I don't hear from you within two days, I'll take that as my answer."

He turns and walks out.

~

"Shut the front door! What on God's green acre was the man talking about?"

"I don't know, Kelly, but it freaked me the fuck out."

I pace back the other way in front of the large desk in Estelle's library, the phone's receiver clenched in a death grip in my hand. My cell is still in pieces on the kitchen floor, so I had to use a landline.

Though it's almost midnight in New York, I'm so discombobulated by what happened with James that I couldn't wait to call Kelly until it was morning there.

"So what're you gonna do, babe?"

I blow out a hard breath. "Do you think Mike might be able to look into him? Just to find out if I'm dealing with a psychopath or not?"

There's a shrug in her voice. "Don't see why not. I'll ask him right now." She covers the phone with her hand. I hear muffled shouting, a brief silence, then more muffled shouting. Then she comes back on the line. "He'll take care of it. Just email me your stud's name and whatever other info you've got."

"Oh shit."

"What?"

"I don't know his last name."

Kelly snorts. "Slut."

"I can get it from the building manager."

"He lives in the same apartment building?"

"Yeah."

"Then why don't you just go break into his place and have a nice look-see around?"

I stop pacing. "Please tell me you're joking."

She says matter-of-factly, "Make sure you look in his medicine cabinet. Everyone's juicy secrets are in their medicine cabinets, and you don't need a password to get in like you would with a computer."

"So that's how you found out I was on anti-depressants."

"Oh, hon, that was no state secret. You went from walking around like a zombie to walking around like...well, like a medicated zombie."

Good to know I was so transparent. "Getting back to James. Mike won't get in trouble for looking into him, will he? Because if it's going to be any kind of risk, I don't want him to do it."

"Don't worry about that. Mike's got the clearance. Just get me your boy toy's full name and you'll have the real 4-1-1 by the end of the day."

A long yawn comes over the line, making me feel guilty. "I'll let you get back to bed, Kell. I'm sorry for bothering you so late."

"Don't be. This shit is gold. I can't wait to see what Mike digs up on your stud." Her voice brightens. "Hey, do you think he's in the witness protection program?"

Great minds think alike. "Doubtful. Would you be putting on art shows all over Paris if you were in the witness protection program?"

"Hmm. Good point. But honestly, even if he was, would you really want to give up that beautiful twelve-inch dick?"

I say seriously, "I regret telling you anything about that."

"Ha! As if! You painted such a vivid picture of his junk, I can see the damn thing like it's been branded onto my brain!" She sobers. "But we should talk about outcomes."

"Why does that sound ominous?"

"So, for instance, what if it turns out that he's a member of the mob?"

"What do you mean, 'what if?' I run very far away is what if!"

She sounds doubtful. "Really? You'd walk away from a man who goes down on you before he even says hello just because he's involved with the mob?"

"*Just because*? Who am I talking to right now? What've you done with my best friend?"

"So the mob is a hard no."

"Of course it's a hard no! Kelly!" I rap the receiver several times on the top of the desk. "I can't be hearing you right!"

Her tone is casual. "I mean, nobody's perfect. And a big dick makes up for a lot."

I make a face at the phone. "How much wine did you have with dinner?"

She ignores me. "What if he's a spy?"

I sigh, looking at the ceiling and shaking my head. "Same answer as if he's in the mob."

"An escapee from a mental institution?"

"Okay, this conversation has reached terminal velocity of silliness. Time for you to go to bed." But that one unsettles me, just a bit.

"Ugh, you're ruining all my fun. Fine, I'm off to bed. Technically, I'm already in bed, but I'm off to sleep. Not that I'll be *able* to sleep because of that story about your orgasmic little liaison in the Russian section of the bookstore, but whatever. I'll have nice dreams."

I told her everything that happened with James since we last spoke. It's not as if I had a choice: she outright demanded the details as soon as she picked up the phone.

I don't think she was joking when she said she'd be living vicariously through me. Mike seems to have slacked off in the sex department of late.

Kelly and I say our goodbyes and hang up, then I return to the kitchen and get Edmond's number from the note Estelle left on the fridge. I start dialing, but stop after taking a look at the clock.

It's six in the morning.

Then I get the brilliant idea to look at the wall of mailboxes in the mail room on the first floor. The building's ten stories tall, and, from what Estelle said, there are four apartments on each floor. So there should be only forty mailboxes.

Each marked with a name.

There could be more than one James who lives in the building, but I'll just have to give Kelly those names, too. Determined, I head into the bedroom to get dressed, then take the elevator downstairs.

Fifteen minutes later, I send Kelly an email composed of only two words.

James Blackwood.

Within minutes, she emails back.

Sounds like a movie star.

"Or an alias," I mutter, staring at the screen.

I can't shake the odd feeling that I've heard that name somewhere before.

16

I try to write, but my muse is in a snit and refuses to show up. So I spend a few hours cleaning the apartment, trying as best I can to keep busy and keep thoughts of James from invading my head.

I'm more successful at one than the other.

After the apartment is spotless, I occupy myself with a trip to the corner store. I come home with enough cheese to last several lifetimes and a poufy baguette so large it could double as a futon. I have to wrestle it through the front door.

Finally, I give up, go into the master bedroom, and flop onto the bed, where I spend hours spacing out and staring at the ceiling, occasionally thinking about my work in progress but mostly about James.

I must doze off, because when the house phone on the nightstand rings sometime later, I jerk upright in a panic. Disoriented, I look around.

The light has changed. The afternoon sun paints glowing golden streaks along the walls. For a moment I don't recognize where I am, but the insistent ringing of the phone finally tugs me back into reality.

"Hello?"

"Babe, it's me."

Yawning, I rub a fist into my eye. I gave Kelly the house number on our last call, because it might be several days until I can get my cell fixed or buy a new one if the old one's too far gone. "Hey."

"You sound like you were sleeping."

The somberness of her tone makes me pause for a beat. "And you sound like you have bad news."

"I do."

My stomach tightens. My pulse starts to pound. I swing my legs over the edge of the bed and grip the phone tighter. "Oh God. James is in the mob, isn't he?"

Kelly sighs, and it sounds sad. "No, babe. He's not in the mob. Nothing like that."

"He's married." *If she says, yes, I'll kill him with my bare hands.*

"No."

When she stays silent too long, I break. "Jesus, Kelly, what the hell is it? I'm dying over here!"

"Let me start with the good stuff. Your boyfriend's got great credit. He pays his taxes on time. He's clean as far as the law is concerned: no felonies, criminal history, outstanding warrants, blah, blah, blah."

I'm breathless with impatience. "Yes? *And*?"

She clears her throat. "He grew up in San Francisco. Got a scholarship to the Art Institute in Chicago, then continued his education at the National School of Fine Arts in Paris."

So he's an American, like me. Why are my hands shaking? "What else?"

"Do you want to know how much he's got in his bank account? Because I was surprised how loaded he is, considering the whole starving artist stereotype—"

"Kelly! No, I don't want to know how much money he has! I want to know whatever it is you're stalling to get to!"

After a beat, she answers. "He's got ALS."

I frown, searching my memory for any clues about what ALS is, but come up empty. "I have no idea what that means."

"Amyotrophic Lateral Sclerosis. Lou Gehrig's disease."

I can tell by the tone in her voice that it's bad, but I don't know exactly how bad until she adds, "You know, the thing the astrophysicist Stephen Hawking died of."

I picture the shrunken and twisted figure of a man in a motorized wheelchair. A man completely paralyzed, who cannot speak, move, or do anything independently. A man trapped in a useless body, but with the full capacity of his brilliant brain.

A man entombed in his own flesh.

I gasp in horror, then clap my hand over my mouth.

"I'm sorry, babe. I know that's a lot. Especially after...after everything you've already been through."

"Are you sure?" I whisper.

"Unfortunately, yes. When Mike didn't find anything in James's credit or criminal records, he decided to look into his medical history in case he had herpes or something worse he might be trying to hide from you. He was diagnosed last year. Apparently, he's been involved in several clinical trials."

Oh sweet Jesus, that's why he had to go to Germany. "What's the prognosis for this disease? Is the progression slow? Is there a cure?"

Kelly's voice grows quiet, but her words kick me right in the gut. "There's no cure. It's always terminal. Most people die within three to four years of being diagnosed."

It makes sense now. It all makes perfect, awful sense.

James's elusiveness. His melancholy. How he said he doesn't have time for small talk, and that sometimes ignorance is the wiser choice. His strange intensity. His portraits of people in pain.

His obsession with death.

It all meshes seamlessly like the pieces of a puzzle fitting together, until I can see the complete picture revealed in its awful truth:

James is dying.

I think I might throw up.

My voice shaking, I plead, "What do I do?"

Kelly's answer is instant and firm. "Break it off."

"*What*? God, I can't be that ruthless!"

"He already gave you an out. You wouldn't have to explain yourself. Just don't call him again. Walk away and save yourself a lot of heartbreak." Her voice gentles. "Haven't you already had enough?"

That idea feels completely wrong. I shake my head, insisting, "No, I need to talk to him about this."

"You *can't* talk to him about it, babe! What would you say? 'I had my friend in the FBI take a peek at your *entire life history* because I thought you might be a psycho?' How do you think he'd feel about that? Violated much?"

I stand and start to pace the length of the room, chewing on my thumbnail and trying to think, but my thoughts are so scattered it's impossible.

It was wrong of me to ask Mike to look into James. No matter my reasons, it was wrong, and I can see that now. I've violated his privacy. If I wasn't cool with the way things were between us—with the no-questions policy that *I* set up—I should've said so, not gone behind his back to get answers.

Answers to questions I had no right asking in the first place. Simply because we're having sex doesn't mean I deserve to know all his secrets.

He doesn't owe me that.

He doesn't owe me anything at all.

I collapse into an overstuffed armchair near the window and

rest my head back, closing my eyes. "Yes, he'll probably feel violated, but I have to tell him anyway."

"You don't *have* to do anything."

"It's the right thing to do, Kell. I won't mention the FBI because that makes the whole thing sound ten times worse. I'll just say I ran a background check on him because I'm a single woman trying to protect herself. Women do that with new men they're dating all the time."

Kelly's tone is dry. "Sure. Great idea. Except if the man has half a brain, he'll know you can't just dial up someone's legally protected medical history on the internet to find out they're in clinical trials."

"I could be a hacker."

She snorts. "You, a *hacker*? You're barely computer literate! You don't even use a computer to write your manuscripts!"

"He doesn't know that!"

"If he's seen the bio on your website, he does."

I groan. The bio. That stupid bio my publisher insisted had to be included on my author website, along with a picture of me sitting at my desk at home…writing longhand on a yellow legal pad like someone's secretary from the fifties.

It's cool to go old school, the caption under the photo reads, because I am a gigantic idiot.

"It's possible he's seen that," I admit grudgingly. "He told me he asked the building manager here about me. I don't know how much information he got, but it wouldn't take a genius to figure out who I am and look me up."

"So there you go."

I think for a moment, chewing the inside of my mouth. "Maybe I'll say I hired a private detective. They could probably access medical files, right?"

"Illegally, in theory, yes. But that would cost you *beaucoup* bucks. In the many thousands. Do you really want to tell the guy who's been spanking all your lady parts like they're naughty kids that you blew the equivalent of a mortgage payment to hire some unethical gumshoe to dig into his private dirt?"

"*Gumshoe*? We're in a forties noir movie now?"

"Don't say anything to James about what you know," replies Kelly, ignoring my interruption. "It's the smartest move and the best one for you. You're not responsible for his problems, so don't grab them on."

I know 'grab' means 'take,' but I'm too busy feeling offended to think her word choice is cute. "I'm not taking on anyone's problems. I'm just talking about being honest."

Kelly's voice goes soft. "I know you, babe. You're a caretaker and a huge softie. There's nothing more irresistible to you than a lost cause. Remember that time you rescued all those feral kittens from the freeway underpass?"

"They were sick! If I didn't rescue them, they would've died!"

"Instead, they lived—all *eight* of them—in your gorgeous house, tearing up the furniture and pissing on the carpet because you couldn't bear to take them to the animal shelter, until Chris forced you to put them up for adoption. And let's not forget the ostrich incident."

Ah yes. The infamous ostrich incident.

A circus came into town once when my daughter was a newborn. I refused to go, because I can't bear to see majestic animals like lions and elephants enslaved for human entertainment. But somehow one of the ostriches escaped...and wound up in my backyard.

I smuggled it into the garage and fed it bird seed and lettuce for a week, trying to figure out how and where to release it into the wild, until Chris came home from a business trip and found the thing contentedly nesting in a bed of his clothes that I'd made for it in a corner.

Startled, the ostrich charged. Chris claimed it tried to kill him, but I think he was exaggerating. In any case, he called animal control and they took the ostrich away.

Weeks later, I was still cleaning up feathers and piles of poop.

Kelly says, "My point is that James isn't a stray who needs rescuing. And—forgive me—you're in no shape to be taking care of anyone but yourself."

We both know I haven't exactly been excelling at that, either.

"Okay. I have to go now. My mental breakdown is calling."

Kelly pauses before speaking again. "Don't joke about that."

My sigh is big and deep. "Oh, Kell, if I haven't had one yet, I think I'm safe."

"You never know. Fate has a dark sense of humor."

"Great. Thanks for the pep talk."

"I love you, you know."

I have to take a few breaths to clear the frog from my throat. "I know. I love you, too. You're a good friend. Thanks for looking out for me."

"That's what friends are for, dummy. I'm gonna hang up now before our hormones snap into sync and we start sobbing. I'll call you tomorrow."

"Talk to you then."

After I return the receiver to its cradle, I sit with my hand on the phone and stare out the window for a long time, trying to decide what to do.

I'm still sitting in the same position when the phone rings again. But this time when I pick up, it isn't Kelly. It's someone I haven't spoken to in almost a year, who shouldn't have this number, or even know I'm in Paris.

It's my ex-husband, Chris.

17

The first thing out of his mouth after I say hello is an abrupt and irritated, "What the hell are you doing in Paris?"

His voice is exactly the same upper-crusty New England voice it's always been. The kind that suggests polo ponies and private social clubs and vacation "cottages" on Martha's Vineyard. The slightly nasal Kennedy twang that comes across as rich and entitled, even when it's cursing.

After a shocked pause, I answer evenly, "Why, hello there, Chris. So nice to hear you haven't lost your charm and good humor since we last spoke."

He bypasses my sarcasm and goes right back to barking questions. "Why didn't you tell me you were going out of the country?"

"Gee, let's see. It could be because we're not married anymore. Or because we haven't communicated since the divorce was finalized. Or because, I don't know, it's none of your business?"

"You're my wife," comes the hard response. "Everything you do is my business."

I remove the receiver from my ear and stare at it in confusion for several seconds. *Maybe this is a dream. Did I have bourbon earlier? Am I face down on the bed right now, asleep and blissfully snoring?*

"Not to put too fine a point on it," I say after coming back on the line, "but as I recall, you signed the same paperwork I did. I'm very much no longer your wife."

"Marriage is for life, no matter what the fucking paperwork says."

My eyes bulge to the point that I fear they might pop right out of their sockets. I'm in too much disbelief over what I'm hearing to muster any outrage. Instead, I start to laugh.

"I'm sorry, sir, but you've obviously dialed the wrong number. The person you're speaking to is single, and has been for a long time, and thinks you should seek immediate psychiatric intervention for this delusional episode you're experiencing. And by the way, how did you get this number?"

"When I couldn't reach you at the house, I called Estelle. I knew she'd know where you were." He adds in a clipped aside, "That old bat always knows where you are."

Why is he angry? Why is he acting so strange? What the hell is going on?

"Christopher?"

"What?"

"Why are you calling me?"

His silence is long and tense. I know exactly what he's doing during it: pacing back and forth with one hand propped on his hip while scowling at the floor. He's in his penthouse in Manhattan or in some swanky hotel room in the emirates on a high floor with a good view and thousand-thread-count Egyptian cotton sheets.

His dark blond hair is perfect. His crisp blue dress shirt is rolled up his forearms. Though he's been working non-stop for more than a dozen hours and is exhausted, he looks like an ad for

Brooks Brothers. There's a half-empty bowl of peppermints somewhere in the room.

No matter what time zone he's in or if it's day or night, his laptop is open and a 24-hour news channel plays in the background on TV.

He says, "I needed to make sure you were safe."

His voice is low and rough, and scares the holy living fuck out of me.

There's an edge to it I've never heard before, a worried and emotional edge he never allowed himself to show during our marriage. Not even at the hospital. Not even at the morgue. He was always perfectly in control, perfectly calm, perfectly…

Cold.

And now, suddenly, he's not.

I stand, then sit back down again because my heart is beating so fast I'm dizzy. "What's happened?"

He says tightly, "Nothing's happened. I'm just checking in on you."

"That is a giant steaming pile of ostrich shit, my friend, and we both know it. Is it…is there news about…"

He knows what I'm asking without me having to ask it. "No. The case is still open. No new leads."

All the breath leaves my lungs in a huge rush. I close my eyes and flop back onto the mattress, settling a hand over my pounding heart. "What, then? I know you're not giving me a random social call after an entire year for no good reason."

"I just…I've just been thinking."

My eyes fly open. "Thinking?"

"About us."

Now not only are my eyes wide open, so is my mouth. Is it my imagination, or is his tone *longing*? "There is no us, Chris. There hasn't been in a long time. Even before…" I swallow, then go on. "I don't know what's going on with you that's motivating this phone call, but—"

"What's going on with me," he cuts in loudly, "is that I need to know you're safe. That was all I ever wanted: to keep you safe."

We breathe at each other for a while, until I say, "And how did that work out for you?"

He snaps, "Don't be a bitch."

Anger finally rears its ugly head, scorching through me like a hot and bitter wind. I push myself up, stand, and resist the urge to punch a hole in the wall.

Chris must sense my fury, because he turns contrite. "I'm sorry. Please don't hang up. I'm sorry I said that, Livvie, it's just…you can't understand what it's been like for me…"

He exhales a ragged breath. Then his voice comes in a miserable whisper. "You're not the only one who lost her."

My face crumples.

I can feel it, scrunching up like it does before I'm about to ugly cry and it gets all red and squishy. It's not only the mention of our daughter, but the entire bizarre and unexpected conversation itself, including the way he said his old nickname for me. The soft and pleading way he said it, like he's drowning and he needs me to throw him a life preserver.

How conveniently he forgot that I was once drowning, too, and the only thing he did was turn his back and walk away as I went under.

"Whatever this is, Chris, it's coming too late. Don't bother with apologies now. I'm sorry to hear that you're having a rough time, because I wish you well, honestly I do, but the only thing this phone call is doing is ripping the scabs off old wounds that I'm still trying to heal."

After a moment, he says haltingly, "I…if I could only tell you…I know I made a lot of mistakes—"

"Stop."

My tone must be convincingly severe, because he falls silent.

"Please don't call me again unless you have news from the police. You've got my email. Use that."

"You hate me, don't you?"

I draw a hitching breath and answer in a high, tight voice. "You gave me the greatest gift I've ever been given. And even though Emmie's no longer here, I'm grateful for every second we had her. I'm grateful for every memory, good and bad. So no, I don't hate you. I could never hate you, Chris. I'm just not strong enough yet to deal with whatever this is."

I hang up the phone and promptly burst into tears.

Then I decide the only appropriate way for a woman to handle discovering that her new lover has a terminal illness on the same day she gets a phone call from her estranged ex telling her that they're still married and he's filled with regrets is to get stark raving drunk.

And so, without further ado, I set out to make that happen.

The first rule of deliberately inducing intoxication is that it should always take place at home.

Many people make the mistake of going out to a bar or restaurant to get bombed, but not only is that a bad idea for obvious safety reasons, it's expensive, too.

My father was so frugal he'd use the same laundry dryer sheet for a dozen loads. He grew up desperately poor and was always convinced every penny he made would be his last. I'm proud to say that I inherited several of his tightwad tendencies, though it was often a source of friction in my marriage because Chris was born with the proverbial silver spoon in his mouth.

His parents bought him a Porsche for his sixteenth birthday. When he promptly wrecked it, they blamed the car and bought him an Aston Martin instead.

Imagine how nuts it drove him when I rinsed out Ziploc plastic baggies so they could be used again.

The second rule of deliberate intoxication is hydration. One must drink at least eight ounces of water for every alcoholic drink consumed. One of the worst parts of a hangover is the dehydration, so it's important to suck back the agua while you're busy getting snockered. Your head will thank you in the morning.

And the final rule—the one that can never be broken—is that you can't deliberately get drunk alone.

You can *accidentally* get drunk alone, but if you're doing it on purpose, you really need to have another person around. Otherwise, it's just you and your chronic alcohol problem, and that's no fun at all.

As my acquaintances in Paris are limited to Gigi, Gaspard, Edmond, and James—one half of the reason for my deliberate intoxication project and therefore disqualified— it takes me all of five seconds to decide who I'd like most to get shitfaced with and pick up the phone to call.

"Edmond," I chirp brightly when he answers, "would you and your wife like to come over for cocktails this evening?"

He sounds excited by the prospect. "Ah, *mais oui*!" After a moment, he adds tentatively, "Who is this?"

"Olivia." When the silence stretches too long, I start to feel a little desperate. "Estelle's friend? The writer from America?"

Edmond exclaims, "My apologies, mademoiselle! You sound so much happier on the phone!"

I regret this choice already.

"Sorry for the short notice, but I just realized I bought all this bread and cheese today that I can't possibly eat alone, and I've got enough wine up here to get an army drunk." Or one writer teetering on the edge of insanity. "How soon do you think you can come?"

He says a French word that sounds zoomy and enthusiastic, which I take to mean *now*.

"Great! I'll leave the door open, just let yourselves in."

"What shall we bring? We can't arrive empty-handed."

"Nothing. Just your wonderful selves. I'm *so* looking forward to seeing you and meeting your lovely wife." *And getting cross-eyed drunk within the hour.*

Flattered by my gushing, Edmond makes a cooing, grandfatherly noise. "Ah, mademoiselle, you are such a delight! If it wasn't for those sad eyes of yours—"

"See you soon!"

I hang up the phone, knowing it's going to be a long night.

In the morning, I don't remember much.

Edmond's brunette wife was beautiful and elegant, I can remember that. Also tall: she towered over him. I recall that she had very long legs I spent too much time staring at, marveling how they were the legs of a person who was born male, because I'd never seen legs as gorgeous on anyone born female.

I know we all had drinks—many, many drinks—and ate too much cheese and laughed a lot, but I couldn't tell you what we talked about. It's all a blur.

The thing I'm really trying to figure out is why there's a man sitting in the armchair across from my bed, glowering at me from under lowered brows.

"James," I say, my voice thick. "What are you doing?"

"Making sure you didn't die of alcohol poisoning."

He seems as if he's barely controlling his temper. His tone is low and clipped, and his words are spoken through thinned lips. He's gripping the arms of the chair as if he's going to rip them off at any moment.

I'm lying on my side in bed, atop the covers, wearing the same clothes I had on last night. Outside, birds are chirping. The sun is up. I don't know what time I passed out, but it's a new day.

A new day in which I'm hungover and James is still dying.

Filled with guilt about how I know that, I push myself up to a sitting position and look at him. "I need to tell you something."

He arches his brows. "You're not going to ask how I got in your apartment? Or how I knew you were drunk?"

I frown, trying to focus through my brain's haze. "Did I leave the door open again?"

"I saw Edmond and Marcheline in the elevator last night. They said they'd just left your place after a nice visit. They were both staggering and reeked of booze. Edmond mentioned that you seemed even more sad that usual."

Fucking Edmond. I exhale and run a hand over my face.

"He said you cried at one point."

Horrified, I gape at James. "I *cried*?"

"You cried," he repeats, his gaze locked on mine, "over me."

I look away, pinching my lips together in shame. I don't remember crying, but that doesn't mean it didn't happen. I also don't know if I said something to them about *why* I might be crying over James.

About what I'd found out.

Shit.

"I tend to get overly emotional when I've had too much to drink." I wait, tensed, my stomach churning, to see how he'll respond to that. If I told Edmond and Marcheline his private medical situation, I'll never forgive myself.

Very softly, James says my name. I glance over to find him leaning forward, his forearms balanced on his spread thighs, his fingers threaded together, and his eyes blazing hellfire blue.

He says, "I want so fucking badly to take you over my knee right now and spank you. And not in the good way."

A tremor runs through me. I whisper, "Why?"

"Because it's me you should've talked to about whatever made you cry. It's me you should've turned to if you were that upset about our conversation. But mostly because you're too smart, and frankly too old, to decide to tie one on and make yourself sick as a way to deal with your emotions."

He's right, of course, but that doesn't mean I'm not going to be pissed about it. "Ouch."

He knows which part of what he said angers me and shakes his head in frustration. "I'm not saying you're old, for Christ's sake. I'm saying that's a teenage move."

I'm relieved about one thing: judging by how he said "whatever made you cry," I must not have gotten detailed with an explanation to Edmond and Marcheline last night.

"Maybe. But it was my move, and I'm owning it." When I can't stand the intensity of his gaze anymore, I glance down and pick at the bed covers.

"And it wasn't only about you. I got a call yesterday that knocked me off kilter." My laugh is small and bitter. "Knocked me off kilter and brought back a lot of old, painful memories. I guess I should've gone jogging or taken a long walk to work it out—or journaled, like my two dozen therapists suggested—but honestly sometimes the only way I know how to cope with pain that huge is to drown it."

Fighting tears, I draw a long breath. My voice comes out choked. "I guess you were right about me and the blue pill."

There's a brief pause, then James is out of his chair and closing the space between us.

He takes us down to the bed, rolling to his back and pulling me on top of his body so I'm lying on him with my arms wrapped around his shoulders and his wrapped around my back.

I rest my cheek on his broad chest and struggle not to cry.

He doesn't say anything for a long time. He just holds me, giving me the occasional squeeze and a kiss on top of my head. When I'm fairly sure I've got my emotions under control and my breathing has gone back to normal, he whispers, "So how do I compare to the boyfriend pillow?"

I huff out a small laugh. Even when he's mad at me, he's still angling for compliments. "Meh. You'll do."

His chuckle stirs my hair. "I know something it can't do for you."

The suggestive tone of his voice makes me look up. James is smiling down at me with a devilish twinkle in his eye.

His moods change even faster than mine do, and that's saying something. "Like what?"

He traces his fingertip along the line of my jaw. "First you have to tell me what you decided about us."

Feeling how solid and strong he is underneath me, how his body can comfortably support my weight, how damn *healthy* he looks and feels, it's impossible to believe he could be sick. I don't want to believe it.

I want him to be well. I want him to live a long, happy life and die an old man surrounded by family.

Realizing how fiercely I want both of those things, I understand the true value of what I'm being given.

When I told Chris on the phone that I was grateful for every moment we had our daughter, for every beautiful memory we made, that was the truth. Even knowing as I do now that we'd only have a few years with her, I'd still do it all over again.

It wasn't how long we had that mattered. It was the strength of love we shared as a family. It was all the joy and indescribable pleasure that being a mother brought to my life.

A joy that hasn't been diminished by the agony that came after.

Maybe I am a red pill girl after all.

Looking into James's beautiful blue eyes, I say softly, "I've decided that meeting you is a gift, and it will always be a gift, no matter how long we have together. So what I promised still stands: I'm yours until September. If you still want me."

He swallows. Eyes burning, he says in a husky voice, "You know I still want you." He rolls me to my back and kisses me, deeply, his big hands cradling my head. His voice drops to the barest whisper. "I'll always want you. That's the problem."

I feel a tightness in my chest, like a vise clamping down on my heart.

God help me, but I already know that when September comes, I won't want to leave.

18

He kisses me again, more hungrily this time, sliding his hand underneath me to squeeze my ass, then groans.

"Christ, this peach."

I decide to be light and flirtatious instead of weepy and morose at the thought of leaving him in a few months…and what will come after. There will be plenty of time for weepy and morose later, when I'm alone. I say coyly, "Don't bruise the merchandise, please. The peach is *muy delicato*."

He nips my lower lip and squeezes my ass harder. "Yes," he breathes, "it sure fucking is. And now it's time to pink it up with my handprints."

His words thrill me, as do his eyes, which are darkening the way they do when he's starting to lose himself to desire.

I don't have time to dwell on it, though, because he stands, lifts me up, and tosses me over his shoulder, as easily as if I were as light as a feather.

Which, it should be noted, I definitely am not.

My hair hanging down and my eyes level with his magnificent ass—clad in a pair of tight jeans that showcase it to perfection—I pretend to be offended.

"In case you haven't noticed, sir, I'm not a sack of potatoes."

Swaggering through the bedroom toward the master bathroom with one big hand squeezed around the back of my thigh, James says, "I don't get the reference."

"Because you carry them over your shoulder."

He scoffs. "Who does? I've never once seen anyone carrying around a sack of potatoes like that."

That makes me laugh. "Me, neither, now that you mention it. I must've read it somewhere."

James stops beside the bathtub, flips me upright, and sets me on my feet. He says, "If you'd read Hemingway enough, you'd know that real men don't carry around sacks of vegetables on their shoulders."

He strips off my shirt, tosses it aside, and unhooks my bra. It also gets tossed. Then he pulls me against him and fastens his wonderful mouth around one of my nipples.

I gasp, digging my fingers into his shoulders and arching against him. Dear God, the man is good with his tongue.

"Oh yes. I forgot. Real men are too busy scaling mountains or waving red capes at confused bulls who were just standing around minding their own business before they got thrown into a ring with some idiot in a clown costume."

James's chuckle is muffled against my skin. Breaking away from my breast for a moment, he impatiently tugs down the zipper of my jeans, pulls the jeans over my hips, and yanks them down my thighs. I kick out of them, and he pushes them away, kneeling in front of me.

He grabs my ass and shoves his face between my legs, closing his eyes and inhaling deeply against my panties.

I picture Kelly's face if she were seeing this right now—popped out eyes and a gaping mouth—and suppress a giggle.

James looks up at me, arching an eyebrow. "Something funny?"

"You're very…" This calls for a big word, but I can't think of one. "Primitive."

"*Primitive*?" he repeats, as if I've insulted his intelligence.

"I mean it in a good way. Like a macho, Hemingway-ish way." Bashfully, I add, "I like it. You make me feel feminine."

His smile comes on slow and dangerous. "Me, Tarzan," he says, gazing up at me, his voice low and rough. "You, Jane."

Then, very deliberately, still staring into my eyes, he bites me between the legs.

I suck in a hard breath, though it doesn't hurt. It's just the sheer masculine sexuality of it, the dominance, the way it says *this is mine and I want to eat it*.

Before I have a chance to unpretzel my brain, James swivels me around so I'm facing the glass shower door. Still on his knees, he sinks his teeth into my ass.

Again, not hard enough to hurt. But again, oh so sexy.

He hooks his thumbs under the elastic of my panties and slides them down my legs, smoothing his hands over my bare flesh until he reaches my ankles. His warm breath fans over my bare bottom. I shiver with anticipation, my heart starting to pound.

I step out of my panties as James moves his mouth to the other side of my behind and bites. Then he commands, "Put your hands against the shower door."

It's his dominant voice.

My pulse skyrockets. Heat blooms over my skin. I do as I'm told, leaning forward to flatten my hands against the glass, which makes my back arch and my bottom stick out at an angle. When I hear James's low oath of pleasure, blood rushes to my cheeks. I'm suddenly breathless.

"I wish you knew what this does to me," he whispers harshly, squeezing big handfuls of my bottom. "Seeing you like this.

Presenting yourself. Trusting me. I wish I could tell you how much I fucking love it."

Sliding a hand between my thighs, he opens his mouth over my flesh, sucking and nipping first one cheek, then the other. He slips a finger between my folds and finds the bud of my clitoris, already wet and swollen.

His moan is the barest whisper of breath against my skin. "And this. So sweet and soft. My sweet Olivia. Always so ready for me."

I'm panting, canting my ass out and rocking against his fingers like the greedy little strumpet I am. He's made a sex kitten out of me. I might as well be purring.

The slap is a shock. Accompanied by a dangerous, low noise rumbling through James's chest, it comes without warning and makes me yelp in surprise.

James rises. He stands at my side, grips my hip in his right hand, and slides his left hand around the front of me, between my legs. Gently pinching my labia, he slaps my ass again.

I gasp and sag against him, my palms still flattened against the shower door.

"Give me your mouth."

I do as I'm told, tilting my head back for his kiss. As his tongue invades my mouth, he spanks me again and again, squeezing his fingers together around my aching pussy. Every collision of his hand against my bare flesh sends a stinging shockwave of pleasure through me until I can stand it no longer and beg.

"Please," I whisper, opening my eyes to gaze up at him through a fog of heat. "Please."

He knows what I'm asking, but his eyes are ablaze and his breathing is as ragged as mine. I can tell he's enjoying this far too much to let it be over so soon. He's not ready to give me the release I crave just yet.

"Get in the shower and turn on the water."

He steps away from me, pulls his T-shirt over his head, and waits for me to follow his command with eyes that are like living fire.

Shaking, I open the shower door and step inside. The first blast of water is icy, making me flinch, but it quickly turns warm, then hot. James kicks off his shoes and strips off the rest of his clothing, then joins me in the shower, closing the door behind him.

He kisses me hard and deep, his arms so tight around me it's borderline painful. The embrace feels desperate. That I can guess why makes a lump form in my throat.

We're on borrowed time. Even if I wasn't leaving in September, there's another clock loudly ticking—a far more doleful clock—though he doesn't know I know that, which makes it all the more difficult to bear.

A lie of omission is still a lie. The impulse that made me want to confess as soon as I saw him sitting in the chair beside my bed is growing, beating like a trapped hummingbird inside the cage of my chest.

I break away from his mouth and look up into his eyes. "I have to say something," I blurt, heart hammering. "I need to tell you what I've—"

"No." His head shake is vehement, and so is his voice. "If we're going to do this, we're going to abide by your rules. No questions. No strings. You were right: it's the only way it'll work."

Dismayed, I stare at him. "But James—"

"Until September comes and you walk out of my life forever, we're going to spend every day as if it's our last. No regrets. No looking back or forward. Just being in the moment. Making every minute count. Making memories we both can treasure after we go back to our real lives."

His calm and conviction are devastating. Here's a man who

knows he's dying, and has decided to live what life he has left to the fullest. Without self pity. Without fear.

His courage moves me like nothing has in years.

Hot steam swirls around my face, and I hope it helps hide the tears gathering in my eyes. "Okay," I say, trying to keep my voice even. "If that's what you want, then okay."

"That's what I want. And this, too."

He turns me toward the spray, pins me against his wet chest with one arm, then takes my hand and pulls it behind me and between our bodies, curling it around his erection. Into my ear he whispers, "Stroke me."

He releases his hand from mine and moves it between my legs.

The spray of water is hot and stinging against my sensitive breasts. When James glides his fingers back and forth over my clitoris, lazily rubbing, my nipples harden and start to ache. He flexes his pelvis into my hand. I squeeze his shaft, then slide my hand up to the crown and squeeze there, too.

When I slide my hand back to the base, he flexes his hips again, pumping into my grip. Tugging on my swollen clit, he hisses into my ear, "Feel how hard you make me? Feel how rock hard I am for you, sweetheart?"

He is. In my hand, his erection feels like a steel pipe sheathed in silk. I make an incoherent noise and stroke the length of his rigid shaft again, stopping on the downstroke to fondle his tight balls. That makes him suck in a hard breath.

He knocks my hand away, positions himself at my entrance, and thrusts inside me.

Groaning, I let my head fall back against his shoulder. He bites me on the neck and starts to pump into me, steadying my with one hand gripped around my hip and an arm clamped around my ribcage. Hot water pulses against my nipples, streaming down my body to funnel between my thighs.

"You're so big," I whisper, loving how he stretches me open with every thrust. Loving the way he fills me.

He responds by pulling the shower head off the wall and directing the hot, stinging spray right between my spread thighs.

When I moan and writhe against him, he slides his other hand up and squeezes my breast. "Imagine that's my mouth," he says in a guttural voice, holding the shower head inches from my flesh. "Imagine I'm fucking you and licking your pussy at the same time."

The noise I make is one I've never made before, an animal sound, low and carnal, sharp with need. The water streams against my sex, making an exquisite sort of torture as James continues to fuck me from behind with long, deep strokes.

"Would you like that, sweetheart? A hard cock buried deep in your cunt and a wet mouth between your legs, sucking on that sweet little clit?"

Picturing two of him making love to me at the same time, I whimper, clenching around his cock.

His voice hardens. "You like that idea."

"Only if it's you," I say breathlessly. "Nobody else but you."

He slows the motion of his hips. Breathing raggedly at my ear, he says, "You wouldn't want a threesome with me and another man?"

I don't have to think twice before vehemently shaking my head.

James's voice drops another octave. "Good. Because I'd never share you."

I've pleased him with my answer, but it wasn't my intention. I was only telling the truth. Letting another person into this moment would cheapen it. Besides, no one else could ever do for me what he does.

No other man could so easily and completely make me fall apart.

He shoves the shower head back into its wall holder, grabs

my jaw, forces my head up, and kisses me with an almost frightening hunger, his mouth unyielding as it plunders mine.

Then he releases my jaw and begins to rhythmically slap me between my legs.

He fucks me from behind and slaps my pussy, kissing me hard, holding me tight, until I'm moaning into his mouth, desperate for release. Then he stops and cups my throbbing sex, his fingers reverently exploring the place where we're joined.

If it weren't for his arm around me, I'd slide bonelessly to the ground.

Panting and shaking, steam billowing all around me, I say his name. It's a plea, and he knows it. This time he's willing to give me what I need.

"How do you want it? Cock or mouth?"

"Like this. Inside me. But my knees aren't working anymore."

"They don't have to."

He slides out of my body and turns me around. His face is intent. His eyes are blazing. He commands, "Wrap your legs around my waist," and picks me up.

When he pushes my back against the shower wall and grips my bottom in both his hands, I understand that he's going to fuck me *standing up*.

He kisses me, his mouth hot against mine. "Help me in," he pants, bracing his legs apart.

I wrap an arm around the mass of his shoulders and reach between us with my free hand. Then I guide him into where he belongs, until he's seated fully inside me, his slick chest pressed against mine so tight I feel every pounding beat of his heart.

He starts to fuck me again, his thrusts as hard as his eyes are soft.

Water sprays everywhere. All over our bodies, the ceiling, the tiled walls. Steam curls and billows. The sounds of my helpless moans and his harsh breathing echo around us until I'm dizzy, until I'm so close to orgasm my focus narrows to the brilliant white burn inside me, coiling tighter and tighter, poised to snap.

When I finally do, it's with a scream and a series of violent, full-body jerks. But James doesn't stagger. His arms stay strong and his balance holds steady as he continues to relentlessly drive into me through my convulsions until I'm spent.

Then he pulls out, kisses me hard, and groans deeply into my mouth. He releases himself into the swirling steam and hot water, all the while managing to support my weight without faltering. His arms aren't even shaking. He's as solid as a redwood's trunk.

Through the tangled and pleasure-soaked haze of my mind, a single, crystal clear thought emerges:

How can a dying man be so strong?

19

After the shower, James towels us both off and leads me back to bed. He rolls me to my side and pulls me tight against his warm body, drawing his legs up behind mine and curving protectively around my spine. His chest is broad and solid against my back. His lips softly brush the nape of my neck.

He whispers, "Go back to sleep."

Exhausted, I promptly do.

I dream of war.

I'm running through a bombed-out city at night, past the silent, hulking ruins of buildings, their shattered windows staring at me like thousands of dead eyes. The sky billows with thick black smoke that burns and chokes my lungs. Erratic bursts of automatic gunfire echo far off in the distance. The road I'm on is an endless stretch of cracked black asphalt littered with rubble and bodies. I stumble over them as I run, sobbing, the soles of my bare feet bloodied and raw.

I pass a band of soldiers headed in the opposite direction. Their uniforms are torn. Their faces are smudged with dirt and caked with blood. All are injured in various degrees, limping or bleeding from horrible wounds, faces twisted in pain or blank with exhaustion. They ignore me, all but one, who speaks to me as he stumbles past.

"Turn back," he rasps, glancing over his shoulder at the direction I'm headed. "You'll die if you keep going that way."

He staggers on.

I ignore his warning because I'm headed toward the light.

It's safety, the softly glowing white light just beyond a rise in the road ahead. It's a sanctuary. I can feel it.

So I keep running, lungs burning, the wails of crying children and church bells ringing in my ears.

At the top of the rise, I jerk to a stop. Weak and panting, I stare at the man standing in the middle of the road. He's surrounded by a glowing orb of white light. It seems to be emanating *from* him, suffusing his skin and shining out from the depths of his beautiful blue eyes.

"Hello, sweetheart," says James, smiling. "I'm so glad you found me. You're safe now. You're home."

I sob in relief and fall to my knees…which is when I notice the gun in his hand.

Lifting his arm, he points the gun directly at me.

He's still smiling when he pulls the trigger.

I jolt upright in bed, blind with terror, my heart thundering. Judging by the light, it's midday.

I'm alone.

Shaking, I press a hand over my pounding heart. The dream felt so real. I can still smell the smoke and see the dead bodies. Though it's been years since I believed in God, I make the sign of the cross over my chest.

Then I flop onto my back and lie there until I can breathe again. Until the deafening *crack* of a gunshot fades to silence in my ears.

The windows are open. A breeze whispers through the curtains, filling their folds in gentle waves. The lazy breeze ruffles the edges of the piece of yellow lined paper held down by a fountain pen on the nightstand next to the bed.

I reach over, pick the paper up, and read.

Write down what you feel. Everything you feel—about Paris, about life, about me—from now until September. Then leave it when you go, so I'm not alone with my memories. Leave me your memories, too, so I'll know it all really happened once you're gone. So I'll know you weren't just a beautiful dream.

The paper trembles in my hands, but the tremor isn't caused by my nightmare or the breeze from the windows.

I press James's letter against my chest and close my eyes, then simply sit for a moment in silence, allowing the emotions to pass through me like a sudden squall at sea, a frothy rage you fear might capsize you but that eventually calms to sunny skies and tranquil waters.

One of the few therapists I had who helped me in any real way once told me that people make the mistake of thinking that experiencing an emotion means you have to do something about it. In fact, you don't have to do anything with your emotions at all. You can simply acknowledge them as they arrive—oh, look, that old bitch Envy is back again—then go about your business.

It's the clinging to emotion that causes suffering, she said. A wiser choice is to let it go and breathe.

"Just feel me. Just feel me and breathe."

Remembering James's words to me when I fled in a panic into the bathroom at the restaurant, I feel better. His note has made me feel better, too, though constricted through the chest.

At least the hangover has had the good manners to vanish.

I rise, dress, and head into the library, the urge to write as strong as any addiction. I pick up the pen, take up where I left off on the yellow pad, and write until that pad is filled. Then I start on a new one.

I don't stop until I hear birds chirping. When I look around, I realize with astonishment that I've written straight through the death of one day and into the golden, sweet-scented birth of another.

After a break for a sandwich and a nap, I'm back at the desk, oblivious to the world. When the light begins to turn from yellow to violet and my hand cramps so badly my handwriting is illegible, I set down the pen and push up from my chair, mentally worn out but with an eagle soaring inside my chest.

There's nothing like the high I get from disappearing into my imagination.

Without bothering with edits or clean up of any kind, I scan all the pages I've written into the computer and email them to Estelle.

When she emails back with no other comment than a question mark, I check what I've sent. Then I scan all the pages again —this time the right side up.

I pour myself a bourbon and fall asleep face down on the kitchen table.

A minute or a year later, the house phone rings. It rings and rings until I can lift my big fat head, which somehow has gained a thousand pounds since I closed my eyes.

"Hello?"

"Doll. It's Estelle."

"You read the pages?"

"I read the pages."

Her tone is oddly neutral. When she says nothing else, I

eyeball my glass of bourbon, sitting where I left it on the table. There's an inch of amber liquid left. I glance at the windows, noting it's now night. *What the hell. At least I won't be day drinking.* I down the rest of the bourbon in the glass, then cross to the liquor cabinet because I have a feeling that by the end of this conversation, I'll need the bottle.

"I'm not getting any younger over here. Just tell me what you think."

"I would, except I can't find the right words."

She's not being sarcastic, that much I know. Her voice is thoughtful and more than a little surprised.

"Let me help you out: the manuscript is incredible."

Her tone turns dry. "Don't break your arm patting yourself on the back, Miss Thing."

"Except I'm right. Aren't I?" I don't have to ask. I already know this book is the best thing I've ever written.

Instead of agreeing with me, Estelle makes a sound of annoyance. "I can't sell this, Olivia."

Twisting the cap off the bourbon, I pour myself a healthy measure. "Seems strange, considering that's your job, and you're the best in the business."

"You *know* what I'm saying, doll."

"I'm afraid you'll have to spell it out for me. I've been writing non-stop for a bazillion years. My brain is ground beef at the moment."

Estelle sighs. Over the line comes the sound of rustling paper. I know she's got my printed manuscript in front of her, and I imagine her at her desk in her big corner office with its view of Central Park, a lipstick-stained Virginia Slims cigarette smoldering in an ashtray at her elbow though smoking in the building has been outlawed for years.

"Olivia, you went to *Columbia*. You have a *master's* degree in English *literature*."

"English and comparative literature," I correct, annoyed by

her unnecessary emphasis on every other word. "With a minor in creative writing."

She ignores me. "You've won many, many prestigious literary awards."

"Not the Pulitzer. Or the Nobel."

She ignores me again, because now I'm being ridiculous. "Your peers are the most highly regarded contemporary American writers."

"What about Hemingway? How would you say I compare to him?"

I'm not sure if her silence is because I've stumped her, or if she's trying to decide if I'm drunk.

"Do you really want an answer to that?"

"Yes. I'm in a masochistic sort of mood."

"All right, then." Her chair squeaks. I hear her draw on her cigarette, then exhale. "You're much more verbose than Hemingway."

I remember James telling me how Hemingway wouldn't approve of how I talked in such long sentences and make a face.

"And your style is much more feminine than his."

"Feminine? So my vagina is showing, is that what you're saying?"

She sounds cross. "Oh, stop it, you know very well what I'm saying. A brick wall is more feminine than Hemingway, for God's sake. May I continue, or would you prefer to sit there and feel sorry for yourself?"

I grumble something about going ahead and swallow another swig of bourbon.

"The thing you have most in common with Papa Hemingway is the themes in your work."

My ears perk, and I sit straighter in my chair. This is something no one's ever told me before. "Such as?"

"The futility of war. The beauty of love. The sacredness of

life. The struggle we all share to find meaning in a violent, hostile world that wants to kill us."

That flattens me, but Estelle is still talking.

"Which is why you can appreciate my complete shock when I found, on the *first page* of your new manuscript, a voyeuristic account of a couple engaging in cunnilingus."

I smile. "Oh. That."

"Yes, *that*. Since when do you write erotica?"

"It's not erotica. It's a story about two strangers falling in love."

She snorts. "Falling in love and screwing like rabbits. Have you counted the number of sex scenes in what you've sent me so far? By the end of the book, the poor hero's penis will be worn down to a nub!"

I deadpan, "That's actually how he dies. The heroine fucks his dick off and he bleeds to death. The end."

Her sigh is loud, but I can tell she's not angry or even particularly frustrated with me. Otherwise, she'd be shouting. "Maybe —and I'm only saying *maybe*—I can send it around and see if we get any bites."

"Yes!" I shout, jumping from my chair and pumping a fist in the air. "Estelle, you're the best!"

"I wasn't finished."

The flat tone of her voice deflates me like a popped balloon. "Why does that sound bad?"

"Because I'll only do it under the condition that you use a pen name for this book."

I scrunch up my nose. "Why do I need a pen name? Even if it *is* erotica, it's *literary* erotica. Many highly regarded novelists have written erotica. Collette, John Updike, Phillip Roth—"

"No need to provide me with a list," Estelle crisply interrupts. "I'm well aware of the history of the genre. My point is that *your* readership consists primarily of educated, married women of higher-than-average intelligence who expect a certain type of novel from you…one that doesn't include sixty-seven instances of the word 'pussy' in the first half."

I muse, "Gee, I wonder who all those *one hundred fifty million people* are who devoured *Fifty Shades of Grey* and its sequels?"

After a moment, Estelle says, "I don't know, doll, but if we're lucky, we'll find out."

My smile stretches my face so wide it hurts. "Estelle, you're the best."

She mutters, "Either that or nuts." Then, in a normal tone: "Think of a pseudonym you want to use and I'll send it off to make the rounds. Do you have a working title yet?"

I haven't until this moment, but it comes to me in a flash. "*Until September*."

She makes a sound of approval. "Perfect. I'll get back to you as soon as I have any feedback. And Olivia?"

"Yeah?"

Her tone is warm. "You're right. The manuscript *is* incredible."

Without another word, she hangs up.

I decide this calls for a celebration. Only I haven't forgotten my recent hangover, and I'm in no mood to create another, so I can't just sit around the house and drink bourbon all night.

I should go out. Into the world.

Where people are.

When that thought frightens me, I decide to call James to see if he's available.

His line rings and rings, but he doesn't pick up. He doesn't have voicemail, either, which I try not to think is strange, but low-key do. Who doesn't have voicemail?

My mind instantly provides me with a list:

- Prisoners
- The Amish

- Dogs (though cats probably do)
- House plants
- Anarchists
- The six native stone age tribes of the Andaman and Nicobar islands

"Enough!" I say loudly to the empty kitchen. "Go out and buy yourself dinner." I'm in Paris, after all. One doesn't have the opportunity to dine in Paris every day.

Except if you live here, but you know what I mean.

I shower, get dressed, and head out to wander the streets and decide on one of the charming sidewalk cafés inhabiting every corner of the city. Within a block of the apartment building, I've discovered a gem of a place with blue awnings and a pair of white miniature poodles dozing in a wicker basket outside the front door.

Feeling adventurous, I order champagne with my escargot and detest both. I have roasted lamb shanks with rosemary and potatoes *daphinois* for my main course, accompanied by an old fashioned and a side order of guilt about the baby lamb. Dessert is something so sweet it almost puts me into a coma. Then, stuffed and satisfied, I head back to the apartment with the idea of getting a few more pages down before bed.

That plan is shot when I open the front door and find James and my ex-husband standing in my living room, glaring at each other in bristling silence as if they're about to draw their guns.

20

I'm so shocked to see them that I simply stand frozen in the doorway for a moment, staring.

The weirdest thing? Neither one turns to look at me.

I made plenty of noise opening the door, but I might as well be invisible for the lack of attention I get. James and Chris don't break eye contact as they face off in silence on either side of the coffee table.

Chris is in a gorgeous bespoke gray suit, white dress shirt open at the collar, no tie. James is casual in head-to-toe black: a fitted crew neck T-shirt that showcases the astounding architecture of his upper body and a pair of jeans with combat boots. He's wearing the leather cuff around his left wrist again, the one he had on the first time I saw him at the café, and an expression I can only describe as eerie.

Where Chris is all crackling tension and red-faced fury, his hands fisted and the muscles in his jaw twitching like mad, James appears relaxed. All the lines of his body are loose. His breathing is even. He seems quite calm…until you look at his eyes.

They're as flat and unblinking as a cobra's.

I've never seen a man look so lethal.

A scene from my dream flashes into my mind's eye, the part where James is calmly smiling right before he pulls the trigger on his gun and shoots me. All the little hairs on the back of my neck stand on end.

I say loudly, "What's going on here?"

James remains motionless and completely focused on Chris when he speaks. His voice is a cool monotone. "Your husband didn't appreciate it when I knocked on your door."

"*Ex*-husband." I step into the foyer but leave the door open behind me. My nerves are so frazzled, I'm shaking all over. My voice shakes, too, when I say, "Who wasn't invited and so is about to leave."

Chris slashes his furious gaze to mine. "Are you fucking him?"

I can tell James doesn't like Chris's disrespectful way of speaking to me by the way his hands flex slowly open, as if itching to curl around Chris's neck. But otherwise he retains his strange stillness and unblinking intensity, gazing at Chris with the cold, calculated confidence of a predator who knows his next meal is only one lightning-fast strike away.

I drop my handbag on the floor and edge closer to them, feeling my pulse in every part of my body. I decide to sidestep Chris's question because a) it's none of his business and b) if I say yes, I have the distinct feeling that later I'll be scrubbing a pool of blood off the carpet.

Instead, I ask a question of my own. "Why are you here?"

"I told you on the phone," Chris snaps, eyes blazing. "I needed to know you were safe." He turns his blistering gaze back to James. "And now I have my answer."

James looks Chris up and down. The faintest hint of a smile plays at the corners of his mouth. "I think we both know she's safer with me than with you."

He says the words with something that sounds suspiciously

like satisfaction, as if there's a back story here I'm unaware of. An old bet that has been won.

Suddenly, I'm convinced of the impossible:

Chris and James have met before.

Looking back and forth between them with a growing sense of unreality, I demand, "One of you better tell me what the hell is going on. And I mean right *now*."

Still with his faint, smug smile, James says to Chris, "Go ahead. Tell her."

Chris is practically vibrating with rage. That he wants to kill James is patently obvious, but so much about this situation is a mystery that I'm having a hard time making sense of it at all.

Finally, Chris whirls away and starts to pace the length of the living room floor. One hand on his hip, scowling at the carpet, like I've seen him do a million times before.

"I didn't like the way our call ended," he says, not looking at James or me. "I wanted to talk to you in person, so I booked the next available flight out of Oman."

He booked the next available flight. The man who hasn't felt the need to speak to me in more than a year, who didn't feel the need to speak to me during a good portion of our marriage, booked the next available flight from Western Asia to Paris because he didn't like the way our call ended.

The out-of-the-blue, yet-to-be-explained phone call.

I watch him continue to pace, my sense of unreality taking a hard right turn toward fear.

I know James is now looking at me, because I can feel it. I feel his hot stare on my skin exactly as if it were a touch.

Screw this. Screw this entire weird scenario. I'm calling these assholes out.

I demand, "How do you two know each other?" and instantly feel James's gaze intensify.

Chris pulls up short. Swallowing, he looks at James, then back at me. "We don't."

I glance at James. His expression is as inscrutable as a cat's. His voice is tranquil. "We've never met."

My intuition tells me both of them are lying.

Or is that my imagination, sculpting dragons out of passing clouds?

Either way, my mouth is dry and my palms are sweaty, and I find myself backing up a step in growing alarm, aware that I've left the door open and fighting the urge to turn and run through it. To where, I don't know, but the irrational urge to flee is overpowering.

Very softly, James says my name. When I glance at him, he simply shakes his head *no*.

He's reading my mind again. He knows I was about to bolt.

That doesn't make me feel any better.

I exhale in an enormous gust. Then, my patience—never saintly in the first place—breaks. I holler at the top of my lungs, "*What the fuck is going on*?"

Chris says tightly, "Jesus, Livvie, calm down."

Hearing Chris call me my nickname, James shoots him a poisonous glare. Then his eyes focus back on mine, and they're burning. He says, "I knocked on your door. He opened it. When I asked for you, he said you were his wife and demanded to know how I knew you. Apparently my answer didn't satisfy him."

"What was your answer?"

The faint smile again. "Go fuck yourself."

I glance at Chris, who's staring at James in livid silence. That makes no sense. Chris was never the jealous type before. "How did you get in my apartment?" I know for sure my door was locked, because I made sure to check it when I left.

Chris says, "I told the building manager I was your husband and that I was here to surprise you for your birthday. He let me in."

I make a mental note to yell at Edmond later.

James says, "It's your birthday?"

I send Chris a hard stare. "No. But my *ex*-husband thinks that anything is a fair means to whatever end he's pursuing."

He stares back at me, his eyes wild. In a throbbing voice, he says, "The one and only end I've ever pursued since the day we met is keeping you out of harms' way, Olivia. You'll never know all the sacrifices I made to ensure your safety."

Before I can process how stunned I am by those words, James chides softly, "Maybe you should tell her. See what she thinks of the choices you made."

Chris turns on him and roars, "*Fuck you, you sanctimonious prick! One more word out of you and I'll tear out your fucking heart with my bare hands*!"

James replies evenly, "Pipe down before you get hurt, frat boy. You country club types are always big bleeders."

The old fashioned. It must be the old fashioned I had with dinner that's messing with my head. I can't be hearing what I'm hearing and intuiting what I'm intuiting, if that's even a real goddamn word.

Here are the facts: James is an artist. He's sensitive. He's also dying of ALS. Somehow also freakishly strong despite it, but still, *dying*. This is an act he's putting on in front of Chris, a macho, Hemingway-esque, I'm-a-scary-bullfighter act. The kind of posturing men—and apes—do in front of their competitors.

Right?

Right.

That settled, I turn my attention to Chris, reigning in my temper with an enormous effort of will. "We'll have lunch tomorrow. We can talk then. Now, please leave."

When he hesitates, his gaze darting back and forth between me and James, I say, "Christopher."

He looks at me.

"It wasn't a request."

To his credit, James doesn't smirk. He simply stands in

silence, observing. He's still calm and in control, but he's watching Chris carefully, and I know he's ready to take him down if he even so much as scowls in my direction.

I also know he could.

Though Chris is athletic and in great shape, his build is slim. He's inches shorter and at least forty pounds lighter than James. He's Mikhail Baryshnikov to James's Muhammad Ali. It would be no contest…especially with the added cherry on top of James's scary serial killer vibe.

Right now, he'd make a serial killer faint in fright.

Touchy Subject Land be damned, we're going to have a nice, long talk as soon as my ex-husband is out of here.

Chris huffs out a frustrated breath and drags both hands through his hair. "Fine. I'll come by at noon and pick you—"

"I'll meet you at Café Blanc," I interrupt, because I don't know what this is, but it definitely isn't a date. "Google it. Don't get a table in Jean-Luc's section."

"Livvie—"

"For once in your life, Christopher, please *listen to me*."

I say it through clenched teeth while a carousel of images plays in my head of all the times he dismissed me to do whatever the hell he wanted. All the times I asked him for something, only to be ignored.

Things like: love me. Hold me. Don't leave me to survive this nightmare all alone.

Chris holds my gaze for a beat. I'm astonished to see tears shining in his eyes. For a moment his throat works and he seems as if he's about to say something, but then he nods curtly and strides out of the apartment.

He doesn't look back.

The first thing I do after he's gone is retrieve the bottle of bourbon from the kitchen table and pour myself a drink. I gulp it down as James goes to the front door and closes it. He returns to the kitchen and stands across from me, his hands resting on the back of a chair.

He says calmly, "So that was your ex-husband. Interesting guy."

I wag a finger at him. "Oh no. *I'm* starting. And you're gonna talk. Sit."

When he arches his brows, I point at the chair in front of him and pretend he's a misbehaving dog. "*Sit.*"

Amused, he says, "And you say I'm bossy." But he lowers himself into the chair without further comment, then watches as I shoot the rest of my drink.

"James."

"Yes?"

"If I ask you a few questions about what just happened, will you tell me the truth?"

"Yes."

I search his face, but it's open and guileless. All the weird murderous energy from when Chris was here has vanished. I remember how quickly he changed gears at the restaurant—molten lava to cool cucumber—and wonder what else he can turn on and off in the blink of an eye.

"Had you ever met Chris before?"

"No."

He didn't hesitate, but he also didn't say, "Of course not!" or "Where the hell would I have met your ex-husband?" Just a simple *no* and that's it. Which of course isn't good enough.

Exasperated, I say, "Don't you even think it's weird that I'm asking?"

"You're upset. The two of you have a contentious relationship. It's not strange that you'd be shaken to find us both in your apartment when you came home."

Narrowing my eyes, I ask, "How do you know we have a contentious relationship?"

His voice softens, as do his eyes. "Aside from what was

said…your body language. Your face. Don't forget, I'm very attuned to you."

Oh. Yeah. That.

I drop into the chair across from him and study him in minute detail. I can't shake the feeling that I'm missing something, but I take another tack.

"Okay, so here's an observation. I'm just going to put it out there, and I'd like to get your feedback." I wait until he nods to go on. "You were very…how do I put this? You seemed dangerous when you were interacting with him. Like you could've literally killed him."

"He's an asshole," he says without heat. "A condescending, arrogant, narcissistic asshole who thinks his shit doesn't stink. That kind of person always brings out the worst in me."

When I simply stare at him, waiting for more, he says, "But you're right: I *could* have literally killed him. I'm a fourth degree black belt in Krav Maga."

"What is that?"

"A fighting system developed by the Israeli military that focuses on real world combat situations. It's similar to other martial arts: judo, karate, and the like." He smiles. "Only more badass."

"Uh-huh." I blink for a moment, picturing him grappling around barefoot on a mat on the floor with another guy in one of those belted cotton dude-kimono situations, trying to crack open each others' heads. "And you practice this…"

"Krav Maga," he supplies into my pause.

"Right. You practice it regularly?"

He nods.

"And I'm guessing a black belt is the most advanced?"

"Yes. And within the black belt level are five degrees, each more advanced than the last. One more and I'll be considered a master."

So that's why he's so freakishly strong. He's the Caucasian Bruce Lee.

He sees my smile. "What's funny?"

"Are your fists registered as lethal weapons?"

He snaps into one of those karate chop poses with his hands flat and his arms bent at an angle in front of his chest. Accompanied by a high-pitched, theatrical "Hi*yah*!" it makes me laugh.

"Better." He reaches across the table and takes my hands, giving them a reassuring squeeze. "Now it's my turn to ask a question: are you okay?"

I know he means because of the unexpected appearance of Chris. "To be completely honest…" I take a deep breath. "No. Seeing him brings back a lot of bad memories. A lot of..."

"Ghosts," murmurs James, gazing at me.

He knows. He obviously knows. Whether Edmond told him or he looked me up himself, James knows about what happened to my family.

Emotion tries to claw its way up my throat, but I fight it back, refusing to give in to it. Holding his gaze, I say, "Don't feel sorry for me. I don't want your pity."

His response is instant. "I could never pity you. You're one of the strongest people I've ever met."

"You barely know me."

"I know you." He pauses for a beat. When he speaks again his voice is lower. "Better than your husband ever did."

That statement causes such a riot of conflicting feelings, I'm tempted to call up my therapist of long ago who recommended breathing exercises for dealing with strong emotions and tell her she's an idiot. Withdrawing my hands from his, I sit back in my chair and simply look at him.

He waits patiently in silence, his expression unreadable, until the sound of a guttural moan floating from across the courtyard makes him quirk a brow.

When it comes again, he says, "Is that...?"

"Yes, it is. Welcome to my world."

The moans increase in volume. James says, "Who?"

"Oh, you haven't seen the resident exhibitionists doing their thing?"

"No. I live on the other side of the building, facing the boulevard."

"It's Gaspard and Gigi."

As if on cue, Gigi wails and Gaspard grunts. I make spokesmodel hands toward the windows. "*Voilà.* Morning and evening performances every day of the week, no reservations necessary, admission is free."

"You can see them?"

"From the bedroom and living room windows, I can practically count all their teeth."

James studies me with interest. "You've watched them."

He says it as a statement, not a question, in response to which my cheeks grow hot. "Yes."

His eyes sharpen, and his voice drops an octave. "You liked watching them."

Another statement. Maybe he does know me.

Maybe he knows me quite well.

I have to moisten my lips before I answer, because my heartbeat is going haywire and my mouth is suddenly dry. "Yes."

Before I have time to feel embarrassed about my admission, James stands. He takes my hand and pulls me to my feet, then leads me out of the kitchen and into the living room. He stops a few feet away from the windows, off to one side so we're hidden behind the heavy velvet drapery but have a clear view to the outside and the lighted apartment across the way.

Gigi is naked on her hands and knees on her bed, head thrown back, bare breasts bouncing as Gaspard drives into her from behind, his hands gripped around her slender hips.

Pulling me in front of him, James wraps his arms around my body so my own arms are pinned at my sides. Then he lowers his mouth to my ear and whispers hotly, "You want me to fuck you while we watch them fuck, don't you, sweetheart?"

There's no need for my answer this time, because we both already know what it is.

21

James strips me with swift, silent efficiency, tossing my clothes onto a nearby armchair. He stops to briefly consider the chair—a big purple velvet number with a high, rolled back and carved wooden legs—then drags it over to where I'm standing naked. It must weigh a hundred pounds, but you'd never know by the easy way he handles the thing. He faces it toward the windows.

Then he whips off the decorative gold silk tassel from the drapery, positions me so my belly rests against the curved upper part of the back of the chair, and pulls my arms behind my back.

He binds my wrists with the cord of silk.

My heartbeat jumps into overdrive. "James—"

"No talking," he growls in his dominant voice. From the seat of the chair he retrieves my panties, which he balls up and stuffs into my mouth. "I'll be doing the talking, sweetheart. You just listen and watch."

My helpless groan is muffled by the panties. It's warm in the room, but my skin prickles with goosebumps. I'm already shaking with anticipation. My nipples are hard. My breathing is erratic.

And my mind is going a million miles per hour trying to process all the unanswered questions I have about the man who's now kneeling between my spread legs.

When I feel James's hot mouth latch onto my clitoris, I suck in a breath. The pleasure is intense. He grabs my ass in both hands and makes a meal out of me, sucking and licking until my thighs shake.

Across the way, Gaspard turns Gigi onto her back. He hooks her ankles over his shoulders and reaches down to caress her firm breasts.

James slides a thick finger inside me. We both groan at the same time.

"This sweet pussy will be the death of me," he whispers, then goes right back to sucking, sliding his finger in and out as my hips begin to match his rhythm, rocking back and forth against his face.

I stand with my ass canted out, my hands tied behind my back, and my belly resting against the chair as James eats me and Gaspard thrusts hard into Gigi.

My low, helpless moan brings James to his feet. He stands behind me. I hear a rip of foil, his ragged breathing, then he shoves his hard sheathed cock into my aching wetness and wraps a big hand around my throat.

He doesn't even bother to get undressed.

I feel the rough fabric of his jeans against my bare bottom, the cool metal of the open zipper scraping my skin, the hem of his T-shirt brushing the small of my back, and find it so overwhelmingly erotic that he's fully dressed and I'm naked—helpless and vulnerable, *bound*—that I moan again, shuddering.

James's free hand cups my breast. He pinches my taut nipple between his fingers, does it harder when I arch into his palm.

"You like it a little rough, don't you, love?" whispers James, thrusting faster into me. "You like me to tie you up and spank your ass and your beautiful pussy. You love it when I fuck you deep and hard."

Close to orgasm, I whimper. I go up on my toes, tilting my pelvis back so he can find the deepest center of me and take it, own it, make it his.

"Oh yes," he breathes, tightening his hand around my throat. "You love it. You fucking love it all."

You, I want to say, *I love it all because it's you who's giving it to me*. But I can't speak a word around the wad of cotton stuffed into my mouth.

I'm thankful for the enforced silence. I don't trust myself at the moment. I fear I wouldn't have control over what dark truths would fly out of my mouth.

Across the courtyard, Gigi screams as she comes, arching up from the mattress as Gaspard bends over her, folding her nearly in half, his ass muscles clenched. He thrusts into her again and again, making a noise like an animal.

When James reaches down and pinches my engorged clit, I come, too. Instantly, violently, my entire body stiffening.

Behind me, he stills, holding me as I convulse.

"Oh fuck, that feels so amazing." He groans, pulling on my nipple, causing another cascade of contractions to rock me. "Milk that cock, sweetheart. Milk my cock with your gorgeous greedy cunt."

I sob, not understanding how I can like them so much, all his filthy, beautiful words. How I can adore being manhandled, no matter how carefully. How much I can enjoy abandoning my inhibitions under the spell of his voice and our crazy, carnal desire for each other, the likes of which I've never known.

He was right: I love it all. I *need* it all.

And that scares me straight down to the darkest corners of my soul where my deepest longings lie in secret, hiding.

Panting, I collapse against the chair. James removes his hand from my throat and sinks it into my hair, gently pulling my head back. He leans over me so his broad chest is pressed against my back.

Whispering into my ear, he begins to fuck me with short, perfect strokes, telling me how beautiful I am, how good I make him feel, how much he loves my trust. His words spin a dizzy web around me until I'm spinning, lost in a haze of pleasure, lost under the magic we make together, two perfect strangers who've found something rare.

We've unearthed a treasure most people dig for their entire lives and never find.

But, like most buried treasure, this one comes with a curse. There's a price to be paid for discoveries such as these. Nothing this valuable is free.

Please don't die. I don't want you to die. Please, James. Please.

I make a noise of desperation. My lover is still whispering into my ear, his voice thick, his breath coming in pants. I turn my head and glance at him. His eyes are closed, and there's a furrow carved between his dark brows.

He's not paying any attention to Gaspard and Gigi. All his attention is on me. On us. On this creature of bliss and insanity we create every time we touch.

He shudders, groaning. Standing more upright, he palms both my breasts and increases the speed of his thrusts. He pinches and rolls my nipples between his fingers as his heavy balls slap against my soaked folds, the sound lewd and impossibly hot.

I watch through the windows as Gaspard flips Gigi onto her stomach. He shoves his erection into the tight pink bud of her ass and holds her down as she bucks and wails.

But her wails are those of pleasure, not pain. She's spreading her legs wider for him, pushing back to take him deeper. He closes his eyes and turns his face to the ceiling, his mouth slack, fucking into her most tender space with an expression that's one of almost religious fervor.

James says my name. It's a fractured sound. Desperate. He's going over the edge and taking me with him.

Gaspard shouts.

Gigi screams.

And the warm Paris night breathes in the sounds of four lovers' passion.

When I wake in the morning and discover I'm alone—again—the disappointment is so crushing that for a moment I'm unable to breathe.

"Don't be a fool," I scold myself, gazing out the bedroom windows into another brilliant, beautiful summer morning. "You're too old for illusions."

Too old for hope. Too jaded for dreams. Too long in the tooth to be dumb enough to pin my heart to a shooting star.

I drop my head to my drawn-up knees and angrily promise myself that if I cry, I'll cut off all my hair with rusty scissors.

A few moments later, the front door opens. James calls out, "I've got coffee and croissants!"

Joy explodes inside me, as bright and burning as a swallowed sun. I topple to my side and bury my face in the pillow.

This is bad. This is so bad.

What's worse is that I *know* it's going to end in tragedy, but my stupid, stubborn heart refuses to get the memo.

Heavy footsteps cross the apartment and stop short at the bedroom door. "Don't tell me you've replaced me with another boyfriend pillow."

I lift my head and regard him, standing in the doorway like some Greek god bearing Starbucks. Instead of blurting the pathetic starry-eyed sonnet my brain has composed in the ten-second interval between now and when he came in, I say tartly, "Maybe I have. Mr. Pillow here is extremely charming."

Blue eyes twinkling, James purses his lips. "Hmm. I can see these feather-stuffed friends of yours are going to be an ongoing problem. Why don't you go back to sleep so I can round them all up and toss them out the window?"

Rolling to my back, I stretch, noting with no small satisfaction how James's gaze avidly follows every move of my naked body. "Are you jealous of an inanimate object?"

He smiles. Somewhere up in heaven a choir of angels break into song. "I'm jealous of anything that touches you that isn't my hands."

Dropping my fake indifference, I stretch out my arms and wiggle my fingers at him. "Speaking of your hands, I want them. Come here."

"So demanding," he murmurs indulgently.

"I'm always demanding before I've had my morning coffee. Crabby, too. Better hurry up and get your butt over here before I throw a tantrum."

His smile turns smoldering. He sets the bag of croissants and the cups of coffee on the dresser. Then he launches himself across the room and jumps onto the bed, landing right on top of me.

"Oof!"

Peppering kisses all over my face and neck, James chuckles. "Oof yourself. I was careful not to smash you."

He didn't smash me, but that doesn't mean I'm going to admit it. "You weigh a ton! I can't breathe!"

He lifts his head and smiles down at me. "You can't breathe because of how much I weigh, or because I'm lying on top of you in all my incredible manliness?"

I stop pretending to struggle to get out from underneath him and just stare at him, shaking my head. "It's not your muscles that weigh too much. It's your ego. You might be the most conceited man I've ever met."

"Might be?" he teases. "I'll take it."

We grin at each other for a while, until something inside my chest goes all melty, and I have to look away so he doesn't see it.

James bends his head and whispers into my ear, "You should know by now you can't hide from me, sweetheart."

I close my eyes and sigh. "God, that's so annoying."

He chuckles, nuzzling his nose into my hair. "You love it."

There's that word again: *love*. It keeps popping up during random cracks in conversations, like some persistent weed.

He must feel the tremor go through me at the thought of that scary four-letter word, because when he raises his head and looks at me, his expression has lost its lightness. It's Intensity James gazing down at me now, all sharp edges and laser like eyes.

I beg, "Please don't say anything. I just woke up. I haven't had my coffee. I'm in no mental condition to deal."

"Deal with what? No, don't look at the wall. Look at me."

Chewing my lip, I focus on the cleft in his chin. It's a much safer spot than the black hole of his eyes, which will suck the truth right out of me.

He waits for me to speak with his hands framing my face and his body taut with anticipation. When I take too long to answer, he prompts softly, "Deal with *what*, Olivia?"

Oh, fuck it. If I lie to him, he'll know, so there really isn't any point in trying.

I say, "This," then take his hand and press it to my chest, right above my pounding heart.

I thought I'd seen his blue eyes burn before, but in them now entire planets are on fire.

He presses down against my sternum, spreading his fingers wide so his big hand spans nearly the breadth of my chest. "This is how you feel about me?"

Beneath his palm, my heart is a wild animal.

Reaching up to sink my hands into the thick silken mess of his dark hair, I whisper, "That's a grain of sand in a universe made of beaches how I feel about you."

Then I kiss him, because someday not too far in the future, he'll be gone, and I won't ever have the pleasure of kissing a man as beautiful as he is again.

He kisses me back ravenously, making urgent noises low in his throat. When we break apart, we're both panting.

He slides his hand down the length of my body and under me, gripping my ass. When I grind my hips against his pelvis, he curses under his breath. "I'm getting on a plane in an hour. I've got a car waiting downstairs."

Germany again? So soon? He doesn't elaborate, and though I want to ask, I can't. But I'm distracted soon enough by his next statement.

"But we're going to talk about this when I get back."

His tone is dark. I can't decide if it's a promise or a warning, and that irks me. "Last I heard, we were being in the moment. No questions, no strings, no regrets. Any of that ringing a bell?"

His lips quirk. "You think I'd forget a single thing I said to you, smartass?"

"So you're just breaking the rules on the fly, then?"

He gazes at me for a beat with that same unnerving stillness that comes over him sometimes, that quicksilver change that brings to mind a predator stalking its prey.

As if making a confession of murder, he says softly, "You have no idea the kind of rules I'm breaking here, Olivia. But if you asked me to, I'd break every rule there is. I'd smash every one of them to pieces."

As we stare at each other, I have that same sensation of stepping out onto a tightrope balanced high over a black abyss...only now a cold wind has picked up and the rope is swinging.

Of a few things I'm certain.

One: we're talking about different sets of rules.

Two: I'm falling fast and hard for a man who's a complete enigma.

And three: the fact that he's dying might not be the only big secret James Blackwood is keeping.

22

Café Blanc is crowded with the same annoying assortment of lovers making googly eyes at each other as it was the last time I ate here, on my first day in Paris. I'm irritated at myself for suggesting the place for my lunch with Chris, but it's too late to change my mind. We're already here.

"You look beautiful."

Sitting across from me on the charming outdoor patio in the shade of a striped umbrella, Chris is somber and tense. He's trying to look calm. Anyone else observing us would think he is, but I know this man too well. Behind his sunglasses, his eyes are darting. His thumb beats a fast, staccato rhythm against his knee.

"Thank you." Unused to such compliments from him and unsettled by his energy, I'm not sure how to proceed. Self-consciously, I touch my hair. "I went to the hairdresser before I left. Apparently something called 'balayage' is the new thing."

Jaw clenched, Chris gives my hair a cursory look. "It suits you." His voice gains an edge. "You look happy."

Here we go. "Take off the damn sunglasses, Christopher," I say softly, "and talk to me."

Aggravated, he whips off his aviators and tosses them onto

the white linen tablecloth, muttering an oath. This display of irritation and jittery nerves is so out of character for him. The press didn't dub him "The Iceberg That Sank the Titanic" for nothing.

He drags a hand through his hair. All that dark blond hair, thick and shiny, the rich hue of a jar of fresh honey held up to the sun. He's always been that kind of Calvin Klein model good-looking. The all-American golden boy with a spotless pedigree that can be traced way, way back to his purebred British ancestors arriving on the Mayflower to wipe out the indigenous populations with their smallpox-infested blankets.

Poison comes in so many sneaky forms, but pretty is the sneakiest.

He says curtly, "You need to get back to New York as soon as possible."

Leaning back in the chic café chair, I fold my hands over my stomach and consider him.

I loved this man once. Truly. *Deeply*. I would have literally died for him. I would've sacrificed my life to keep him safe. But at the moment, I'd like to drive my thumbs into his eye sockets.

"And you need to tell me what the hell is going on."

He slams a fist on the tabletop, making the silverware jump. He snaps, "For fuck's *sake*, Olivia, this isn't a game. This is *serious*. You know I wouldn't be here if it wasn't!"

He stares at me, seething. Several diners send alarmed glances in our direction. From the corner of my eye, I see my arch enemy, the waiter Jean-Luc, smirking at us from a nearby table.

Holding Chris's furious gaze, I say evenly, "The days of you barking orders and me obeying them are long gone. You want me to jump for you now? I'm not asking 'How high?' I'm saying 'Show me the money, bitch' and negotiating price."

Chris's mouth opens, then closes. He's not used to this version of me.

Neither am I, honestly, but I'm about at the end of my rope with the men in my life and all their drama.

Chris snaps his fingers. A waiter materializes instantly at our table. "Oui, monsieur?"

"Blanton's, neat. Make it a double."

The waiter bows before scurrying away, because Chris has that effect on people.

I say, "Things must be dire if you're having a double bourbon at noon."

Leaning his forearms on the table, he runs his tongue along his teeth. He stares at the tablecloth for a moment, gathering himself, then glances up at me. In a low voice, he says, "Dire doesn't begin to cover it."

Knowing he'll spit it out eventually if I keep quiet, I wait, watching him, the muscles in my shoulders and neck pulled tight.

"I can't keep you safe in Europe, Livvie."

My brows shoot up. "Bypassing what a weird statement that is for a second, you say it like you *were* keeping me safe in the States."

He stares at me, all glaring eyes and a hard jaw. "I had twenty-four-hour surveillance on you in New York. So yeah, I was keeping you safe there."

My jaw drops. Horrified, I gape at him. "You…you were having me watched? You were *spying* on me?"

His tone stays even. "No. I was protecting you. The surveillance was a security detail."

Angry and confused, I sputter, "P-protecting me? From what?"

I watch him sift through a thousand possible replies before he settles on one. "Blowback."

When he doesn't add more, I spread my hands open, like *What the hell*?

He buys more time before answering because the waiter

returns with his drink, setting it down in front of him with a flourish then asking if we'd like to order our entrees. I banish him with an aggravated wave of my hand.

When we're alone again, Chris picks up the glass of bourbon and downs it in one go. Setting the empty glass carefully down, he licks his lips, then meets my eyes.

"My job is high profile. You know that."

"Congratulations on being the United States Ambassador to the UN," I snap. "You're the big cheese. Yay. What does that have to do with anything?"

He responds through gritted teeth. "High profile means high security risk."

I wait, but once again he fails to provide an adequate explanation. *Great. I've got another sphinx on my hands.*

"Help me connect the dots here. We're no longer married. We haven't lived together in forever. We don't speak—or communicate in any way for that matter—or ever see each other. *We have no ties*. How is *your* position a threat to *me*?"

His stare burns a hole straight through my face. "Because you're the only thing in my life that can be used against me. You're the only weakness I have. You're my Achilles' heel, and there are certain people who know that." He pauses. "People who wouldn't think twice about using it to their advantage. Using you to get to me."

My jaw is unhinged. My eyes are unblinking. An eerie sound echoes in my ears, like a thousand wolves howling at the moon.

I'm his weakness? His friggin' Achilles' heel? Since when?

Even during our courtship when we were falling in love, his work was always his priority. He never made it a secret that his career would come first—and boy, did it—but now he's telling me in a raw, emotional voice that I somehow still matter to him?

I matter enough that I'm blackmail bait?

Finally, I manage to ask, "What people?"

"Bad people," is his instant, clipped response. "I have

enemies, Livvie. Powerful ones. Ruthless ones. Which is why I need you to get your ass on a plane and get back to New York. Today. Right now. *This minute.*"

For a moment, I'm frozen with disbelief. I can't believe I'm hearing what I'm hearing.

Chris had a security detail when he was a member of the legislature before being appointed ambassador, but it was minimal, restricted to comings and goings at the Capitol and other affairs of state. There weren't any guys in black SUVs sitting outside our house at midnight. The Secret Service wasn't lurking around the bushes with drawn guns.

Then it hits me like a thunderbolt: if I'm blackmail bait…so was our daughter.

I go ice cold, then hot. Fury claws its way up my throat like a rabid animal. Adrenaline floods my veins, and my entire body starts to shake.

Leaning across the table, I grab Chris by the lapels of his suit jacket. "If you had anything to do with Emmie's death," I snarl into his face, "so help me God, I'll kill you."

Jean-Luc sails past our table on his way to another, saying, "Don't take it personally, monsieur. *Elle est folle.*"

Chris is on his feet and dragging me across the patio before I can lash out at Jean-Luc. He pulls me inside the restaurant and makes a hard right turn toward the restrooms down a hallway at the back. He kicks open the men's room door, slams it shut behind us, and pushes me against it with his hands gripped around my upper arms.

Leaning in so we're nose to nose, he says gruffly, "Of course I didn't. Emmie's death was a freak accident, you know that—"

"She was *murdered,*" I say loudly, my face hot. "A drive-by isn't an *accident*, Christopher. It's murder. She didn't fall into a pool and drown. That's an accident. She didn't slip and hit her head, or choke on a piece of food, or chase a ball into traffic. She was *shot*." My voice breaks. Tears swim in my eyes. "Our baby girl was shot to death, and that is fucking *murder*."

Exhaling a ragged breath, Chris nods and squeezes his eyes shut. He whispers, "I know. I'm sorry. I know. I only meant that it wasn't meant for her. It's like the police said…she was an innocent bystander. The gang wars…that bullet was meant for someone else."

He cuts off, his voice choked and his expression one of utter misery.

Then, to my total astonishment, my ex-husband starts to cry.

He pulls me into his arms, buries his face in my neck, and sobs like a child, his embrace so tight I'm left breathless.

Never, not once during all the years I've known him, has he ever shown anything approaching this level of emotion. If someone had told me before now that he was actually even *able* to cry, I would've laughed.

It would be more plausible that the rock of Gibraltar would shed tears.

All the fury drains out of me, leaving me filled with only a hollow ache.

"It's okay." I awkwardly pat his back. "Hey. Hey, now. C'mon. I didn't mean to upset you. I'm sorry I yelled—"

Before I can say another word, Chris takes my face in his hands and kisses me.

It's hard, sloppy, and full of desperation. His teeth clash with mine. Shocked, I suck in a breath through my nose and push against his chest, but he won't release me. Instead, he presses the length of his body against me and fists a hand into my hair.

All I can think is *James*.

I want James to be kissing me now, not this man I gave my heart to so long ago who casually tossed it into his Louis Vuitton briefcase and locked it up tight.

Gasping, I break away from Chris's mouth. We stand there chest to chest for what feels like an eternity, breathing hard, frozen in the unreality of the moment, until he steps back, holding his hands in the air like the victim of a robbery.

"I'm sorry."

A second apology within minutes of the first he's ever made. I have no idea who this stranger is.

Shaken, I drag the back of my hand across my bruised lips. I look at him with wide eyes and no idea on earth what to say.

He relieves me of the responsibility by going first.

"I love you," he says hoarsely, eyes shining. "I've always loved you. I'll never stop. I understand if you've moved on with your life, but I haven't. I can't. You're the only thing that has ever made my life worth living."

I blink, wondering if I've finally had that mental breakdown that's been nipping at my heels for years, but he's still talking.

"I know I fucked up in so many ways, and I wish to God I could make it up to you, but I'm telling you right now, Olivia, I'm willing to make you hate me if it means you'll be safe. I'd rather risk your hatred than your safety. So if you're not back in New York within twenty-four hours, I'll be forced to make that happen myself."

The laugh that breaks from my chest sounds crazy, bouncing sharply off the tiled bathroom walls. "What the hell is that supposed to mean? You'll kidnap me and smuggle me out of the country?"

Wild-eyed, he stares at me until I begin to feel frightened.

"It wouldn't be the first time I've made that kind of arrangement. And trust me when I say you don't want to meet the men who handle those things. You accused me of being heartless when we were married, but I'm a kitten compared to them. And sometimes the people in their care end up broken in ways that can't be fixed."

My heart pounds so fast I can't catch my breath. I gaze into his eyes—hazel eyes I've stared into so many times before—and realize with an icy tingle shooting down my spine that it's entirely possible everything I thought I knew about this man is a lie.

"Twenty-four hours, Olivia. Don't test me."

Before I can reply, he shoves me out of the way of the door and walks through it without looking back.

23

Back at the apartment, I'm a mess. I crave a drink, but am spooked that a team of masked men are about to burst through the front door and haul me off to the airport in an unmarked van. I need to keep my head clear.

So I wander from room to room, wringing my hands and fighting panic, going over everything Chris said to me at lunch and on his earlier phone call.

None of it computes. If he and I were characters in one of my novels, I'd have to give him an inoperable brain tumor the size of a grapefruit for his behavior to make sense.

When a phone rings somewhere in the apartment, I freeze and look around.

It's not the house phone. And my cell is still where it fell, busted up and silent on the floor. But the ringing persists despite those facts, so I head tentatively to the kitchen, following the muffled sound.

It's coming from a drawer next to the sink.

Feeling like I'm in a spy movie, I open the drawer and stare at the sleek black cell phone nestled in among a set of tea towels.

The phone the size of a credit card that looks exactly like the one James has.

It rings and rings, insisting that I pick it up.

When I do, I realize the thing doesn't have an *Answer* button. There aren't any buttons on it at all. When I turn it over, the back side is as blank as the front. The only way I can tell it's the back is because the surface is matte instead of shiny.

I shake it. When that doesn't make the screen light up, I tap my finger all over the screen, hoping that will have some effect. When that fails, too, I sigh and simply hold the phone to my ear, jokingly saying, "Yo," as if that will make it work.

In return, I hear James's velvety voice. "Hello, sweetheart."

I shout, "*James*!"

"Guilty. I see you found the phone."

"*What is happening right now*?"

His low chuckle sends a wave of relief through me. "I noticed your cell had some kind of accident that left it in pieces, so I got you a new one. Do you like it?"

He says "got" not "bought." For some strange reason, it feels as if that's an important distinction. "Where are the buttons on this thing? When did you put it in the drawer? Are you already in Germany?"

I'm still shouting. For a moment, I think that's the cause of James's odd pause, but then I realize I'm wrong when he answers.

"Yes," he says softly. "I'm in Germany."

I go cold with horror.

I'm not supposed to know where he was going.

I'm not supposed to know he's in clinical trials. Or that he has ALS.

Or that he's dying.

Oh fuck oh fuck oh fuck. Maybe he'll think he told me where he was headed. I stand frozen with the phone clamped to my ear, my heart up in my throat, and wait for him to say something. What he comes up with doesn't help matters much.

"Just breathe, Olivia. I can hear you panicking."

I exhale in a huge gust and hobble over to the kitchen table, where I collapse into a chair. "I…uh…I…" *I have no idea how I'm going to get myself out of this mess. Idiot!*

"Let me hear you take a breath. A big one. Go on."

I suck in a lungful like I've been drowning in the ocean and just broke through the surface. *Tell him the truth. When he asks how you knew about Germany, just spill the beans. Admit everything. Be honest.*

All my honking and wheezing makes him chuckle again. He drawls, "That asthmatic duck impression you're doing is cute. Have you missed me so much? I've only been gone a few hours."

"Yes, I've missed you." I think of Chris at lunch and shudder. "I can't wait until I see you again."

He must hear something off in my voice, because his sharpens. "What's happened?"

"Sweet Jesus, how can you read my mind *over the phone*?"

He growls my name. Bossy mode is now engaged. At least he's distracted from the Germany thing. I sigh heavily and slump lower in the chair. "My lunch with Chris happened."

The silence crackles. "I want to demand you tell me everything, but I don't want to be a nosy asshole. If you say we should change the subject, we will."

I love his straightforward way of saying what's on his mind while also respecting my wishes.

Debating how to answer, I decide that my messy personal life is the last thing he needs to be dealing with right now, away in another country trying to find a cure for the disease that's trying to kill him.

"We haven't spoken since we were divorced. He just wanted…" *To have thugs kidnap me.* I clear my throat before the lie, so hopefully it sounds more plausible. "To check in."

After another crackling silence, James says, "He's still in love with you. Seeing me at your apartment can't have been easy for him."

I smother the memory of Chris telling me he loved me in the men's room and ask too loudly, "What makes you think he's still in love with me?"

James's voice turns stroking, the softest, warmest caress. "How could he not be? You're the most perfect woman a man could wish for, Olivia. You're the brass ring."

My heart proceeds to do strange things. Weird, twisting gymnastic kinds of things. I swallow, breathing shallowly, letting myself sit with his beautiful words.

"You're not saying anything."

"Just enjoying the talents of your script writers. Boy, those guys are good."

I hear voices in the background. Male voices. Male voices that aren't speaking English…but they're not speaking German, either. I don't speak German, but it's very distinct, and that definitely isn't it.

In fact, it sounds much like the exotic language I heard—or imagined I heard—James murmur into my ear as I thrashed through an epic orgasm.

I listen to the sound of footsteps until the voices fade into the background and disappear. Either the men moved away from James, or he moved away from them.

His voice husky, he says, "I left something else for you in the apartment. Go check the left drawer of the dresser in the bedroom."

My curiosity piqued, I rise and go to the bedroom. In the dresser drawer I find a square black box tied with a red ribbon. "You bought me another gift?" I ask, touched. "When did you find time to hide all this stuff?"

"Open it."

"Let me put the phone down for a sec so I can use both hands." I set the phone on the dresser and eagerly untie the ribbon, then lift off the top of the box. When I see the beautiful gold and diamond earrings with a matching necklace sparkling on a bed of white silk, I gasp.

Holy shit. These must've cost a fortune.

I blow out a breath and pick up the phone again. "James, this necklace is incredible. And those butterflies…I've never seen such pretty earrings in my life."

He laughs, delighted by the awe in my voice. "That isn't a necklace and earrings, sweetheart. Take it out."

Not a necklace and earrings?

Confused, I pick up one of the diamond butterflies and discover that they're attached to the chain by delicate chains of their own. Small gold clamps decorate the backs. When I lift the butterfly higher, more of the delicate chain unwinds from the bed of silk, which is when I realize the end of the chain *also* has a butterfly with a small gold clamp.

The whole thing makes the shape of a Y, with a gold circle the size of a quarter in the center where the three chains are attached.

I hold it up and stare at it, trying to figure it out. "I don't get it."

"Think, love. Where might I like to use three small clamps on your body?"

My eyes go wide and my voice gets high. "I'm guessing… not on my toes?"

"Somewhere a little more sensitive," he murmurs, his voice warm.

Probably not my earlobes or fingertips, either. I gulp, starting to sweat.

"Put it on and send me pictures."

"I have no *idea* how to put this thing on. I might permanently damage something. Besides, I'm technology challenged. I don't even know how to use this phone."

If I thought that would get me off the hook, I was wrong. James has everything covered.

"The phone is voice activated, and my number's already programmed into it. Just point it at yourself and say, 'Take a picture and send to James.' Go ahead and try it."

I hold the phone a foot away from my face and repeat his direction. There's the smallest electronic ding, and that's it. The screen stays pitch black. I put the phone back to my ear. "How do I know it worked? I can't see anything on my end!"

"Because I have a picture of you scrunching up your nose at me, that's how. By the way, your hair looks great." He switches back into bossy mode, his voice going dark. "Now take off all your clothes, put on the butterflies, and send me my pictures."

"Um…yeah, I'm gonna have to take a pass on that, Romeo. If nudes of me ever leaked online, my publisher would drop me like a hot potato."

"You know I'd never share pictures of you with anyone else."

The hot possessiveness in his tone makes me smile. "Yes, I do. But phones have a nasty habit of getting hacked."

"That phone is unhackable. Anything you send to me is encrypted with ciphers that can't be broken."

When I pause for too long, wondering why he'd own an unhackable phone, he says lightly, "I've got a buddy who manufactures them for the government."

"Oh. Cool. Wait—does that mean the government can spy on me with this thing?"

He chuckles. "They don't need a phone to spy on you."

"That doesn't make me feel better."

"Don't worry about it too much. If you're not a bad guy, they're not interested in you. Back to my pictures. Send me some."

I scrunch up my face. "I mean, I want to? In theory? Because I know you'd like it? But honestly, it's not really my thing. I wasn't exaggerating when I said I'm technology challenged. I'd accidentally send a close up of my armpit. Which, in case you haven't noticed, is not the armpit of a supermodel. There's some serious random stuff going on in there. If armpit cellulite is a thing, I've got it. I'd rather rig myself up with this beautiful sex jewelry when you're here in person to help me."

His laugh is long, throaty, and beautiful. "Fuck. You're criminally adorable."

For some strange reason, that comment makes me think of Chris. Crying-in-the-men's-room Chris, who suddenly thinks he's in love with me.

"Yeah. I'm a real prize, all right."

Whatever James hears in my answer makes his voice turn sharp and demanding. "What does that mean?"

His acute perception is getting to be so commonplace, I'm hardly surprised by it anymore. But still, I don't want to dig into this particular dirt. "I was only being sarcastic. It doesn't mean anything."

"Are you aware, Olivia, that you're a terrible liar?"

My sigh is deep and resigned. "Okay, fine. But don't be mad when I tell you, because you asked." I wait until he growls his assent to continue. "Chris was acting really strange at lunch today. He said a lot of weird things."

James's voice turns deadly soft. "What things?"

Oh dear. "Really, it's nothing."

He insists, "Tell me."

I laugh nervously. "Like I should get back to New York right away."

"*Because*?"

Uh-oh. That sounded murderous. I should change the subject. "Ugh. Because he's an idiot. Forget I said anything."

There's a long, hard silence. "Did he threaten you?"

"No!" I pause. "I mean, not the way you mean it."

The sound of teeth grinding together comes over the phone. "I'm tearing out my fucking hair over here."

"That's why I didn't want to say anything. I don't want you to worry."

"Too late. If you don't tell me everything, I'm on the next plane back to Paris."

What's changed so much about me lately that I've now got men flying all over the world in a panic to fling themselves bodily onto my doorstep? "That's not necessary."

"It will be if you don't start talking."

I sit on the edge of the bed and pinch the bridge of my nose between my fingers, the golden chain dangling over my thighs. "He said if I wasn't back in New York in twenty-four hours, he'd arrange for someone to make sure that happened."

Without missing a beat, James snaps, "Get out of that apartment! Now!"

Opening my eyes, I frown at the wall. "Excuse me?"

"Go to my place. It's unit 912. There's a keypad on the wall next to the door. Type in your name backward and it will open."

Type in my name backward and his door will open. Like my mouth is open. Like the top of my head is open, because it just exploded. "*What?*"

"Do it. Pack your bags and get out. Don't tell anyone where you're going. Get over to my apartment—*right fucking now*—and wait for me there."

The line disconnects.

Stunned, I stare at the phone in my hand. My heart starts to pound. Anxiety sizzles through me. Looking at the blank screen, I say, "Call James!"

When I put the phone back to my ear, it's ringing. He picks up and growls, "Goddammit, woman—"

"You don't get to curse at me right now!" I holler, red-faced. "Tell me what the hell is happening or I'm not going anywhere!"

His breathing is ragged. His words come out sounding like he swallowed a handful of rocks. "You said you trusted me."

"James—"

"*Did* you or did you *not* say you trusted me?"

I look at the glittering diamond butterflies I'm holding, and curl my hand around them, wishing I'd never opened my big fat mouth. "Yes," I admit grudgingly.

His rough exhalation holds a tinge of relief. "And you were right to. I'll never let anything harm you, and that's a vow. But I'm not there right now, and in order for you to be safe, you have to listen to me."

I cry, "Why is everyone so worried about my safety now? How am I suddenly in danger?"

James's voice drops. "It isn't sudden, sweetheart. You've been in danger for years. You just didn't know it."

I start to shake. My armpits go damp. I can't control the tremor in my voice when I whisper, "How do *you* know?"

"I swear I'll tell you everything, just please, *please* go over to my apartment right now. Will you do that for me?"

It's the undercurrent of worry in his voice that finally makes me decide to obey him.

Probably the begging, too. He isn't a man who begs.

When I say yes, he mutters, "Thank fuck."

"But you better be prepared to answer a lot of questions, Romeo," I threaten. "And if I think you're not telling me the unvarnished truth, I *will* be on a plane back to New York within twenty-four hours."

This time, I'm the one who disconnects. At least I think I do. Who can tell with this stupid phone?

With a profound sense of disbelief that this is my life, I put the chain back in its pretty box, hustle over to the closet, pull out my suitcase, and drag it over to the dresser. I unzip it and start throwing things in. Jeans, T-shirts, panties, all the stuff I so carefully unpacked and folded now gets tossed in like garbage.

Danger. I'm in danger—and have been for years.

What the actual fuck?

I can't think straight. None of this makes any sense whatsoever. The only thing I can focus on is getting the hell out of this apartment, which now has the oppressive feeling of a prison cell.

Or a coffin.

Shoving the phone James gave me into the back pocket of my jeans, I hurry with the suitcase to Estelle's office, where I grab my manuscript off the desk and stuff it into the outside zippered pocket.

I don't even bother with my cosmetics or toiletries. I just hightail it out of there, grabbing my purse and slamming the door shut as I go. Panting and sweating, I jog down the hallway to the elevators.

When the doors slide open, I'm halfway expecting a pair of armed men to jump out and tackle me, but it's empty. The short ride down to James's floor feels like it takes a millennium. Then the doors open again, and I bound down the hall.

When I realize I'm going in the wrong direction, I turn and run the other way.

True to his word, there's a slick electronic keypad attached to the wall next to his front door. I use the keypad to type in the letters of my name backward, hoping that this is all a bad practical joke, but when the light on the keypad turns green and the door clicks open so I can see inside, hope turns rancid in my stomach.

You know that old saying, if something seems too good to be true, it is?

It's been around a long time for a reason.

The good news is that one entire wall of his elegantly furnished living room is lined with books. There's a glass-front bookcase with one of those cool rolling ladders libraries have that stretch all the way to the ceiling. A big brown leather armchair sits beside a window with a small table and reading lamp off to the side.

So he's a reader. At least he wasn't lying about that.

The *bad* news is that the window is blacked out with a thick panel of steel, and the wall opposite the bookcase houses another collection of items encased in glass…items designed with only one purpose in mind.

Killing.

"I'm dead. You've killed me."

I recall with horrible clarity how James's mood changed from light to dark in the blink of an eye when I said those words to him. Words meant as a compliment to his kissing, but that, for him, obviously signified something very different.

Like maybe I'd figured something out.

For a cold, breathless moment, I gape at the collection of pistols, rifles, and machine guns so neatly displayed on pegboard racks, cheerfully lit from above with pin spots and lined below with hundreds of boxes of various size ammunition.

Then I do the only thing that makes sense.

Run the fuck away.

24

The taxi driver thinks I'm a lunatic. I know because he shouts after me, "You lunatic!" as I claw my way out of his cab, flinging money over my shoulder and panting like a Labrador.

In and of itself, that little display of mental instability probably wouldn't have been quite so upsetting to him. But taken together with the way I hurled myself into the cab and screamed at him to *Go go go*! while pounding on the plastic divider between the front and back seats, then dove onto the floor and curled up there, babbling to myself as I hid underneath the safety of my suitcase, it was a bit too much.

I don't have a clue where he's dropped me.

It doesn't matter, however, because what I need is only half a block away. The cheerful sign of a hotel beckons me from the side of a tall brick building, promising safety and anonymity.

And a minibar. Arguably the most important of the three.

I hustle up the street, dragging my suitcase behind me, sweating and swearing and out of my mind with panic. At the front desk, a bearded young man with a tranquil smile greets me.

His name tag reveals him to be Christoph, which I take as an ominous sign, but at least it doesn't say James.

I'm not particularly superstitious, but there's a limit to what I can handle.

I shout, "I need a room! Whatever's available!"

"How many nights, madame?" He waits, hands poised over his keyboard.

Clutching the counter, I wheeze and gasp. "At least one. I'm not sure. Can I tell you later?"

He looks me up and down, his tranquil smile never faltering. Like Jean-Luc at Café Blanc, he probably thinks Americans are insane. "*Certainment*. Your credit card, please?"

I scrabble around in my handbag for my wallet, fumble through it with shaking fingers, then toss my Amex his way. It slides off the counter and onto his keyboard. He picks it up delicately with his index finger and thumb, as if maybe it's swimming with germs.

Why would James have so many guns? My brain flashes a set of wolfish teeth. *The better to shoot you with, my dear.*

"Ms. Olivia Rossi," Christoph reads from my card. "Welcome to the Saint Germaine. Any preferences on the type of room? Bed size? View?"

"No, no." I glance nervously over my shoulder. "Whatever's fastest."

His typing is quick and precise. He consults his computer screen. "I have a lovely room on the fourth floor, madame. King bed with a fireplace, overlooking—"

"I'll take it!"

He pauses to glance at me. In a lowered voice, he gently inquires, "Ms. Rossi…is everything all right?"

Oh God. Don't get thrown out. Act normal. Pushing my hair off my face and clearing my throat, I try my best to appear like a civilized human being and not a woman fleeing the devil.

"Actually, no. My boyfriend…" I glance with genuine fear at

the door. "We had a fight. I don't want him to know where I am."

"Say no more," Christoph says briskly, puffing out his chest. "I will check you in under a different name, madame." His typing is even faster now, bless him. He hits the *Enter* key with a flourish, then leans over the counter to whisper, "You are in room 402, Madame Pollitt."

"Pollitt. Thank you."

He informs me conspiratorially, "Maggie Pollit was the name of the character Elizabeth Taylor played in *Cat on a Hot Tin Roof*. Have you seen the film?"

"No."

"Best American film ever made. Of course, American movies do not have the same quality as French cinema, but that particular movie was perfect. And you, madame, bear a striking resemblance to its star."

Despite my panic, I have to laugh. I look like Elizabeth Taylor? Clearly, he's been drinking.

He insists, "It's true. No one has ever said this to you?" He waves a hand at my face. "It's the eyes. That incredible color—violet, *que c'est belle*! Haunting, one could say."

If I never hear that word for the rest of my life, it will be too soon.

I thank him weakly for the compliment. He beams at me, then turns to get a room key from a small cabinet hanging on the wall behind him. I sign the paper he offers me, take the key, then lurch away toward the elevators.

When the mirrored doors slide shut and I see my reflection, I'm surprised the nice front desk man didn't call the police. I look like I've just broken out of prison.

The room is well appointed with elegant furniture and is much larger than I expected. I suppose I should've asked the price, but when one is dealing with the discovery that her ex-husband has kidnappers on his payroll and her lover has a stock-pile of weapons in his apartment that could rival that of a small country's, commonplace things like money don't seem quite so important.

Maybe I'll send Chris the bill.

Leaving my suitcase inside the entryway, I throw my purse onto the bed, then yank the curtains shut over the windows. I could care less about the gorgeous view of the Eiffel Tower right now, and the suspicion that somehow James will discover where I am has lit a paranoia fire under my ass.

I raid the minibar under the TV cabinet and gulp down three tiny bottles of whiskey before drawing a breath. Then I sit on the edge of the bed and look around, wondering what the hell I'm going to do.

The obvious thing is hightail it back to New York. But waiting for me there is Chris's invisible surveillance team. The thought that I've been being watched for—how long?—makes me queasy. And, frankly, furious. Not only about the invasion of privacy, but also about everything I don't know that made Chris think a secret security detail was necessary in the first place.

"*I have enemies*," he said. Powerful enemies. Ruthless ones.

Enemies that might use me to get to him.

I reach for the phone on the bedside table to call Kelly for advice, but stop. If Chris had me under surveillance, might he have had *her* under surveillance, too? And what exactly does "surveillance" mean, anyway? People peering at me through binoculars? Listening to me through devices planted in my house?

Tapping my phone?

I feel sick to my stomach.

It's then that I remember James's unhackable phone in my back pocket. I pull it out and stare at its blank black face. "James Blackwood," I whisper. "Who are you?"

In a flat, computerized voice, the phone responds. "James Blackwood is an American-born artist specializing in portraiture."

I scream and hurl the phone across the room.

It lands on the carpet next to the door and lies there, smirking at me.

After a moment when I get the pandemonium in my body under control, I move warily toward the phone and pick it up again. Curse my damn overactive imagination, because I could swear the thing has a pulse that's beating against my palm.

I say to it, "Sure he is."

The blasted thing stays silent. Time for a different approach. "Who is Sir Elton John?"

The phone immediately provides me with the Wikipedia entry for the musician, including details about his birth, education, early career, and awards and accolades.

Okay, so it's got some advanced version of Siri onboard. Let's take this thing for a spin. "Show me a picture of James Blackwood."

The screen lights up. Photographs begin to fly past at warp speed. Young men, old men, babies, graduation photos, driver's licenses, birth announcements, obituaries, and finally a Wanted poster circa 1832 featuring a grinning, gap-toothed cowboy with a huge handlebar moustache.

This phone is a fucking smartass.

"Show me a picture of James Blackwood the American-born artist specializing in portraiture."

The screen goes dark. After a brief pause, the electronic voice speaks again. "No known photographs of James Blackwood the American-born artist specializing in portraiture exist."

The plot thickens.

"What's your name?"

"I am James Blackwood's phone."

"Hello, James Blackwood's phone. I'm Olivia."

"Greetings, Olivia."

I can't believe I'm having this conversation, but as my life is utterly insane lately, I'm going with it. "Phone, who is your manufacturer?" James said he had a friend who made it for the government, but I'm not inclined to believe a word from him anymore.

But the phone is playing coy. "That information is classified."

Shit. Not only is this thing a smartass, it's smart. "Is there anything you can tell me about yourself?"

"I am an Aquarius."

"Funny."

"And you are a Scorpio."

My breath catches. My heartbeat kicks up a notch. I have to swallow before I can speak. "How do you know that?"

"Your birthday is October twenty-seventh."

I try not to lose my shit. After all, I've got a Wikipedia page of my own. If this thing has some glorified version of Google in its operating system, it knows all about me.

But wait—I only told it my *first* name. There must be a million Olivias in the world. Ten million. More.

Gooseflesh rises on my arms. I whisper, "How do you know who I am?"

"Your voice matches the sample from the data file James Blackwood requested on 9 July, 2019 at 15:12."

July ninth was the day I met James at Café Blanc.

As for the time, 15:12 is military parlance for twelve minutes after three in the afternoon. I don't know what time it was when I first spotted him. Did he request the data file after I left the café…or before?

Oh God. Did he already know about me before I arrived? Did he know my face? Was he waiting for me?

Was he *sent* for me?

Is that the reason he owns all those guns?

My mind starts to fray around the edges like a piece of fabric unraveling. A fragile thread unwinding quickly from a spool. "What else is in the data file?"

I sit and listen in growing shock as the phone recites a detailed biography of me, including things not found on my Wikipedia page. Birth place, town where I grew up, parents' names, siblings' names, education, occupation, novel titles and dates of publication, hobbies, volunteer work, favorite foods, known allergies, list of current medications, marriage and divorce dates, and dozens of other specifics.

Last but not least—children.

"Emerson Luna Ridgewell, only child, born September ten, 2012. Deceased April eight, 2017. Cause of death: catastrophic injury to the heart from penetrating gunshot wound suffered at an outdoor political rally in Washington DC organized by her father, then a congressman from New York. Shots were fired into the crowd from a speeding vehicle, striking Emerson, the lone victim."

The electronic voice pauses for a beat. "Congressman Ridgewell was the assassin's intended target."

My breath whooshes out of my lungs as if I've been kicked in the gut.

I drop the phone in horror and clap my hands over my mouth, backing up until I bump into the wall. I stand there shaking until my knees give out, then I slide to the floor, blind and deaf to everything, drowning in terrible memories.

The most recent of which is from only hours ago when Chris was sobbing in the restroom at the café and telling me the bullet that killed our daughter was meant for someone else.

I think this phone and my ex-husband both know it was meant for him.

Here's another one plus one equals two moment: James also knows.

And if James and Chris *have* met before, as I suspected, not a single thing either one of them has told me is true.

I'm still sitting against the wall deep in shock sometime later when James bursts through the hotel room door.

25

He skids to a stop in the entryway, his blazing blue eyes fixed on me. He's beautiful and frightening, a vengeful god dressed all in black, gripping a Terminator-sized gun in his hand.

The door swings shut behind him with a *clunk* that seems final, like a lid closing over a crypt.

Flooded with adrenaline and pure terror, I jolt to my feet and grab the closest heavy object: a floor lamp. With a scream, I throw it like a javelin right at him.

Unfortunately, I'm as shitty at javelin throwing as I am at any other athletic endeavor, because the lamp lands with a thud on the carpet between us. The shade pops off and rolls to one side.

James looks at the lamp, then back at me.

I've never seen eyes glow that unholy shade of blue.

I bolt over to the small desk near the TV cabinet and rip the phone right out of the wall. I throw that at him, too, with slightly better results: the receiver grazes his hand as he bats it away, glowering.

The thick room service menu and hotel amenity binder follow the phone. One misses him by a mile, the other causes him to duck. After both are lying flat on the floor, he says, "You need to calm down."

His voice is even, but his expression could strike fear into the heart of the devil himself.

Which means I must've lost my marbles once and for all, because I shriek at him like a banshee. "*And you need to go fuck yourself!*"

Nostrils flaring, he says very softly, "Olivia."

It sounds like a threat. So I react the same way I've been reacting to threats since he walked in and start throwing things again.

"How did you find me?" I holler, hurling a desk lamp in his general direction. It crashes into an armchair instead of smashing his face.

"The phone I gave you has GPS."

Fuck. I hate his stupid talking phone with the burning heat of a thousand suns. "Get away from me! I'll scream!"

"You're already screaming," he says patiently. "And I'm not going to hurt you, so please *calm down*."

I don't know about you, but when someone tells me to calm down it has the exact opposite effect. Hysteria is injected into my bloodstream like a shot of heroin. Clenching my hands to fists, I let loose a scream of blood-curdling, biblical proportions, worse than a pestilence sent from God himself.

The only thing it does is make James look like he has indigestion.

He holds up a hand. "I get that you're upset, but let me explain."

I start to babble, backing up into the desk and scurrying toward the balcony windows like a frantic crab. "Yes, yes, please explain how you know my ex and why you're a liar and the reason you own a bazillion weapons and why you're pointing one of them at *me*!"

"I'm not pointing it at you, sweetheart. I'm simply holding it, which is a very different thing."

I can tell by his tone that I'm testing his patience. *I'm* testing *his* patience! "Don't you dare call me sweetheart! Get out! Leave me alone! I hate you!" I beseech the door. "Help! Someone please help me!"

He winces. "Don't say you hate me. I couldn't bear it if you hated me."

Panting and almost collapsing from hysteria, I stare at him for a moment, wondering if maybe both of us have lost our minds.

Then I grab the vase of flowers off a side table and send it flying across the room.

He easily sidesteps it, then sighs as it crashes against the wall behind him and shatters into a million pieces. "I can see you're not going to be reasonable about this."

He advances a step. I flatten myself against the sliding glass balcony doors.

"Stay right where you are! I'll throw myself off this balcony before I'll let you get your hands on me!"

To prove my point, I try to pull the slider open, but discover it's locked. I claw at the lock and yank at the door again, but it stays stubbornly shut.

James informs me in a matter-of-fact voice, "There's a security lock on the rail on the bottom."

I turn and glare at him. He shrugs. "Just saying."

The. Fucking. Nerve.

I pick up the wooden side table the vase of flowers was on and brandish it at him. And what does he do? The son of a bitch *rolls his eyes*!

"For God's sake, woman, you know I'm not going to hurt you."

"The feeling is *not* mutual! And stop calling me woman!"

I'm looking wildly around for another heavy object to throw

at him after I hit him with the table when something whizzes past my head at high velocity and pierces the patio door with a loud *crack.* The sound is followed by the snap of a sheet of glass shattering like ice underfoot.

The glass holds for a heartbeat, then the entire door falls to the floor with a deafening crash that leaves my ears ringing.

Then everything shifts into slow motion.

James dives at me, tackling me to the carpet. He rolls on top of my body, props himself up on his elbows, and points his gun at the hotel door. He fires a few rounds in quick succession right through it. There's a silencer on the end of the gun that spares my eardrums from destruction, so I can hear the heavy *thump* that follows the shots.

I understand on a cellular level that what I heard is the sound of a body hitting the floor.

My scream is the soundtrack to another volley of gunfire, but this time James isn't the source. He rolls us over and over on the carpet away from the balcony and toward the bed. Once we're between it and the wall, he pops up and fires three shots toward the entry using the mattress to steady his elbows. Then he drops back down to address me.

"I'm in love with you," he says. "We should get married."

Bullets whistle over our heads and embed themselves into the wall behind us, spraying chunks of plaster. The acrid stench of gunpowder burns my nose. I gape at him, holding my hands over my ears.

"You're probably thinking it's a little quick, but when you know, you know. We'll talk about it later. In the meantime, think about where you might want to honeymoon. Just my two cents, but I've always thought Bora Bora is incredibly romantic. There's a Four Seasons I've stayed at there that's amazing. But if you're not into the beach thing, I'm open to suggestions."

He hops up onto his knees and starts firing again. Whoever is trying to kill him—us?—fires back. Between shots, I hear the distant wail of sirens.

I truly regret not drinking more of those midget bottles of liquor from the minibar.

James jumps to his feet, grabs my wrist, and hauls me up so I'm standing.

The room is thick with smoke. The hotel room door is riddled with bullet holes and hanging off two of its hinges. The bleeding bodies of four large men in tactical gear litter the entryway floor.

My trusty scream shrivels up in my throat and refuses to make an appearance.

I teeter sideways, about to slither back down to the floor, but James grabs me by the waist.

"Woah! Hey. Look at me."

When I rip my horrified gaze from the corpses and train it on him, he's grinning at me. "You're doing great." He plants a firm kiss on my lips. "But we gotta go now. Just hang onto my hand and don't let go. Okay?"

Deep in shock, I nod like a bobblehead, planning on running away from him and finding a police station the second I get the chance.

James leads me by the hand out of the demolished hotel room, stopping only to sling my purse over his shoulder and grab my suitcase before we go.

PART III

…all stories, if continued far enough, end in death, and he is no true-story teller who would keep that from you.

~ Ernest Hemingway

26

A short journey by car takes us to a farm in the countryside, where we board a twin-engine plane, which James expertly pilots. Because hello, Dorothy, we're not in Kansas anymore. This guy is definitely not your average artist.

If he even *is* an artist. That's probably just a cover for whatever he really is. The murderer/gunslinger/hot psychopath thing.

And here I thought he was sensitive. I'd like to smack myself in the face.

After about an hour's flight in which we exchange exactly zero words, he lands on another miniscule strip of concrete in another country field. A sleek black Mercedes awaits, because hot psychopaths don't own Volkswagens.

We drive accompanied by more silence. He's probably thinking I'm musing over all our possible honeymoon spots, the delusional bastard.

In reality, I'm wondering what's stopping me from turning on him and clawing his pretty blue eyes right out of their sockets.

Curiosity gets some points. I honestly can't *wait* to hear what he has to say for himself. I doubt if even my own grandiose imagination could compete with whatever he's got up his sleeves.

Maybe I can use it in a novel.

Sheer disbelief is also in the race. My self-preservation and fight-or-flight instincts have been dumped into a Cuisinart and puréed. I don't know which way is up.

Then there's that idiotic impulse that has me rescuing sick kittens and runaway ostriches. That tender, warm-hearted, sentimental impulse that I'd like to cut out of my heart with a razor blade.

Unlike James, I can't shut off my emotions with the flick of a switch.

I still like the jerk.

I like him very much.

Okay, more than very much, but we've already established that he's a psychopath, so I'm not going there.

No, I decide, hardening my heart, the real reason I haven't clawed his eyes out yet is because I need to know what he knows about what happened to my daughter. Then I'm out of here.

Wherever here is.

Staring straight ahead, I ask him where we're going.

"Home."

His voice is soft and warm. I glance over and find him looking out the windshield, his hands relaxed around the steering wheel. The setting sun casts a golden sheen on his handsome face, making him look like an angel.

He's smiling.

"Where are we?"

"Southeastern France. Near the village of Sault, in Vaucluse." He meets my blank gaze, and his smile grows warmer. "Provence, sweetheart. We're in Provence."

We crest the low rise of a hill, and I gasp at the beautiful scene laid out before me.

Nestled on a ridge flanked by forest on one side and a rolling valley on the other, a medieval stone village glows warmest ochre in the dying rays of sun. Its tiled roofs are washed crimson. Its bell-topped church spire soars high into the cerulean sky.

Like a painting by an old master, the lush valley beckons the eye toward the distant horizon with a breathtaking view of mile beyond mile of lavender fields, glowing deepest purple and blue in the twilight. Their straight lines traverse the gentle rise and fall of earth as far as the eye can see, row upon row of luscious color and vibrant life interrupted once in a while by an olive tree spreading its gnarled, silvery branches over the teeming violet army of flowers bursting forth below.

It's a feast for the eyes. My vision is saturated with color. Everything is so vivid and bright.

Then James rolls down the windows, and I breathe in the scent of heaven.

Sweet and dusky, delicate and distinct, the heady aroma of the lavender fields overwhelms my senses. Inhaling deeply, I close my eyes and simply let it surround me, the most beautiful, relaxing cloud.

James murmurs, "There exists a field, beyond all notions of right and wrong. I will meet you there."

When I open my eyes, he's looking at me tenderly. "My script writers can't take credit for that. It's the poet Rumi. Are you familiar with him?"

"I watched you kill three men today. Don't you dare start quoting ancient Persian mystics to me."

He grins. "Four."

"Excuse me?"

"I killed four men at the hotel. And I should've known you'd recognize Rumi. You're one of the smartest people I know."

Laughing at my expression, he reaches over and squeezes my thigh. "I know you have questions and you're really fucking mad at me right now, but I have to tell you that I've honestly never felt this happy in my life."

I say flatly, "You're a psychopath."

"Nah."

My voice rises. "I hate to be the one to break it to you, pal, but a *normal* person who'd recently murdered four other human beings wouldn't be feeling quite so chipper."

He shrugs. "So I'm not normal. Doesn't mean I'm a psychopath."

"Fine. You're a serial killer."

He has the audacity to look insulted. "Now you're just being mean."

When I'm silent too long, glaring daggers at his profile, he sighs. "It's just my job, Olivia. I'm very good at it, but it's only a job. It's what I do for a living."

He kills people for a living. I know it isn't motion sickness that has bile rising up in the back of my throat.

With a profound sense that I've fallen through a crack in the universe and am now inhabiting another, unknown dimension, I say in a strangled voice, "You're…an assassin?"

He wrinkles his nose. "I prefer the term pest control engineer."

I stare at him. After a moment, I drop my head into my hands and groan.

James launches into an explanation of the situation that he obviously thinks will make everything rational and acceptable to me, evidenced by his confident, matter-of-fact tone.

"I freelance for governments, international corporations, and high net worth individuals who are in need of—as I prefer to call it—pest control. I'm very selective about the jobs I accept, and I have several iron-clad rules. The first is no women or children."

I mutter into my palms, "Such a hero."

He ignores my blistering sarcasm. "The second is that the target has to be a bag of shit."

I lift my head and squint at him. "I can't believe I'm going to ask you this, but what the hell is that supposed to mean?"

"I don't accept jobs where the motive is simply greed, hatred, or revenge. There are many others in my line of work who don't care about the reasons why someone would want another person dead—they only care about the paycheck. Not me. I have to know the intended target is someone who's caused a lot of pain and suffering to other people, and who the world would be better off without. My research into the mark's background is meticulous."

He glances over at me. His eyes are dark. "In other words, if I show up at your door, you deserve it."

I can't close my mouth. I try and try, but my lower jaw simply hangs uselessly open.

"The third and final rule," he continues, "is that I'm provided with pictures from the mark's funeral."

I manage to make my mouth work to form a single, horrified word. "*Why*?"

A series of strange emotions crosses his face. Distaste turns into pity which turns into something that looks like regret. His voice drops an octave. "So I can see the expressions of his family. Even the dirtiest dog has someone who loves him."

I'm glad I don't have anything in my stomach, because it would be making a reappearance right now. I say with contempt, "That's the most morbid, disgusting thing I've ever heard."

He shakes his head. "You misunderstand. The pictures aren't for me to gloat over. They're for me to draw."

When our eyes meet and I see the anguish there, I get it. "Your collection. Those portraits in *Perspectives of Grief*."

He nods slowly. "I'm not a monster, Olivia. I know the difference between right and wrong. No matter how noble I try to convince myself my first two rules might be, I realize that what I do is immoral. So drawing the grief of the people who are affected by my actions is my small way of paying penance.

"Maybe it's futile"—he laughs, a low, self-loathing sound —"no, it's *definitely* futile, but it's my small way of making amends. All the proceeds from the sale of my artwork go to charities that serve victims of violence."

"So you're a killer with a conscience," I say bitterly. "Congratulations. You're also a pathological liar—"

"I've never lied to you," he cuts in, his voice hard.

"I'd laugh at that if I weren't so sick to my stomach," I counter, turning to look out the window into the purple-blue dusk.

His voice turns urgent. "Name one thing I've lied to you about."

"Being an artist!"

"I *am* an artist. That's just not the only thing I am."

I mutter, "Please."

"What else do you think I've lied about?"

When I turn to look at him, he's leaning toward me, staring at me with his brows drawn together and a worried look in his eyes. Exasperated, I throw my hands in the air. "Everything!"

"Like what?"

Anger grabs hold of me, turning my face hot and making my hands shake. "Like that you knew who I was before we met."

"No, I didn't."

"Your phone told me different!"

He grips the steering wheel as if he's about to tear it off. Through a clenched jaw, he says, "When I saw you at the café, I had no idea who you were. All I knew is that you were beautiful and I wanted to meet you. I *needed* to meet you. I was drawn to you as I've never been drawn to a woman before. So after I sat at your table and you walked away from me, I did a little research."

"Bullshit. You targeted me. I'm just trying to figure out why. Are you one of the men Chris warned me about, the ruthless ones who want to use me against him?"

Pausing for a moment to get himself under better control, he says darkly, "It was fate that brought us together, Olivia. Nothing else. I kept an apartment in that building for *years* before you ever came to visit. Your friend Estelle could've had an apartment in any one of thousands of other places in the city, but she had one in mine. Fate threw us together at the café, and again at the party. We were destined to meet."

All this talk of fate and destiny is annoying me. I fold my arms over my chest and send him a challenging look. "I suppose next you're going to tell me you'd never met Chris before that night at my apartment."

"I *hadn't* met him." He pauses. "In person."

"I knew it!"

Unbelievably, he's frustrated by my outburst. His voice grows louder. "I knew *of* him. He knew of me. We'd never met."

When I make an impatient motion with my hand that he should continue, he does. Carefully. "Your ex-husband is…"

"Just spit it out. It can't be any worse than anything I've already had to deal with today."

His expression tells me I might be surprised.

I warn, "Tell me right now or I'll grab the steering wheel and send us into that ditch."

"Okay." He takes a breath. "Your ex-husband is an international arms dealer."

A quarter mile of winding country road passes before I speak again. "He's actually the US ambassador the UN."

"Yeah," he agrees, nodding. "And he's an international arms dealer. He uses his political position to facilitate his trade. You think it's a coincidence he spends so much time in the Middle East when he's the ambassador to the *United Nations*? He might as well be the ambassador to Oman."

I protest faintly, "That's ridiculous," but my brain swarms with memories.

Chris talking low on the phone in the middle of the night, getting up to close the door to his office when I called out for him to come to bed.

Chris taking meetings at home with darting-eyed men in

black suits and making excuses about avoiding the press when I asked why they weren't meeting him at the office.

Chris receiving documents at home via courier that he would never open in my presence.

Chris learning to speak Arabic, though it wasn't a requirement of his job, and he'd never shown an interest in Arab culture.

Chris learning to speak rudimentary Turkish…and Russian… and Czech.

Chris never, ever talking about his work, though he was consumed by it.

Chris's bizarre behavior at the café and his warnings that he couldn't keep me safe in Europe, that he had powerful enemies, and that if I didn't get on a plane to New York in twenty-four hours, he'd send someone to make that happen.

Chris's impotent fury when James said to him, "I think we both know she's safer with me than with you."

The only reason I'd be safer with a contract killer than my ex-husband is if my ex-husband is something much worse.

I stare in horror at James's chiseled profile. "How did you two know of each other?"

"There aren't that many people at my level who do what I do. And your ex has put out contracts that I've considered, but ultimately turned down."

My feeling of sickness intensifying, I cover my mouth with my hand.

Chris has hired contract killers. Which, by proxy, makes *him* a killer.

Then, with the sensation that my understanding is an onion with layers that are being peeled away swiftly one by one, I whisper, "You know what happened to my daughter, don't you?"

He nods grimly. "Yes. I'm so sorry. And I know it's not much consolation, but I'm going to kill him."

A high-pitched noise rings in my ears. I begin to shake. "Christopher?"

"No." James turns his head and meets my gaze. "The man who fired the shots into the crowd."

For a moment, my lungs freeze. I'm unable to breathe.

James knows who murdered Emmie.

Heat flashes over my body. I break out in a cold sweat, and my shaking grows worse. My voice comes out in a rasp. "Pull over!"

James's look sharpens. "Why?"

"Because if you don't, I'm going to throw up all over your dashboard."

He guides the car quickly to the side of the road. He doesn't have time to shut off the engine before I throw open the door, lean out, and retch violently into the lavender-scented twilight.

It isn't until the final heaves have subsided that I start to cry.

27

It's a full day before I speak again. A day I spend lost in thought, wandering aimlessly through the lavender fields that surround James's beautiful, centuries' old, cream-colored stone country mansion.

The low drone of thousands of worker bees harvesting their bounty of nectar from the fragrant purple blooms lulls me as I stroll between the uniform lines of flowering bushes, my arms wrapped around myself to quell the occasional chill brought on by the dark workings of my mind. My intellect struggles to adjust to this new reality, but it keeps stumbling and falling down.

I married a man who uses his powerful position to covertly sell weapons. I took a lover who kills people for money. And I suspected nothing of either of them.

I might be the worst judge of character who ever lived.

Beyond the obvious feelings of stupidity, betrayal, disgust, anger, depression, and guilt, there's a sneaky little bastard of an emotion I wrestle with that takes the longest time for me to accept. I keep strong-arming it away as I traverse the long, undulating rows of vivid violet, listening to the comforting crunch of gravel underfoot and breathing in the fine, perfumed clouds that fill the air.

Vengeance is bitter and burning within me. A poisonous snake flashing its fangs deep in my gut.

I don't want to admit I'm the kind of person who believes in an eye for an eye in the biblical sense. Justice is one thing… sheer bloodlust is another. I'm an educated woman, not some medieval peasant screaming for the accused town witch to burn, baby, burn.

It's hard to look my own savagery in the face. But, as twilight descends once again over the lavender fields, I finally accept the truth.

Not only do I want James to kill the man who shot my daughter, I want him to kill that son of a bitch in the slowest, ugliest, most painful way possible.

I want him to suffer.

I know it won't bring Emmie back. Of course it won't. Nothing can. But the pain I've been carrying since her death is a living, breathing beast inside me, and I didn't understand until now how pain can cut your legs out from under you one moment and the next grow you ferocious new sets of sharp claws and teeth.

Looking at the graceful stone estate set back against a stand of ancient pines that James calls his home, I wonder how I'll recover from this. How can I keep putting one foot in front of the other in this world when everything I thought I knew about life —and about myself—has been proven wrong?

A peregrine falcon turns lazy circles in the deepening blue bowl of the sky overhead. I track her progress for a moment, admiring the elegant spread of her wings, feeling her piercing cry in a lonely corner of my heart. When she banks hard and dives like a rocket between two bushy rows of lavender then emerges moments later to climb back into the heavens with a small, wriggling bundle caught in her talons, it seems like an omen.

A dark sense of purpose fills me.

First things first: I'll decide what I'm going to do about James, Christopher, and the rest of my ruined life once my thirst for revenge is slaked.

Dorothy, you're a long way from home, indeed.

Feeling oddly calm after that decision, I make my way slowly back to the house. My hair and clothing are saturated with the sweet scent of the lavender fields. A fine, pale gray dust clings to my shoes. I slip the shoes off inside the front door, then pad barefoot over the cool, smooth travertine pavers to the place where I know James will be waiting.

When I enter the library, he looks up from his book. Our eyes meet. Whatever he sees in mine makes him close the book and set it aside.

I can read the title from where I stand: *A Moveable Feast.*

Hemingway again. I'm starting to sense a theme.

James asks, "Did you sleep at all?"

"Enough."

We gaze at each other across the room. Dressed in a navy sweater and jeans so worn they've faded almost to white, he sits barefoot with one long leg crossed over the other in a battered brown leather chair. A matching sofa sits opposite him. Between the two is a wooden coffee table laden with a cut-crystal decanter filled with amber liquid and two glasses on a square silver tray.

He carried me into the house last night, as I found my legs unable to when we arrived. Shock has a way of undoing the normal workings of the body. He tucked me into bed fully clothed except my shoes, arranged the covers around me, and kissed me on the forehead before turning out the light.

He knew somehow that I wouldn't run away or call the authorities or do any one of the million other things I could've done. I suppose it's the same way he seems to know everything else about me. All my secret needs and longings, all the tucked-away thoughts in my head.

I say, "I'd like to talk now."

Inclining his head, he gestures to the sofa opposite him. "Of course." When I sit, perching on the edge, he inquires, "Whiskey?"

His tone is polite. His face is exquisite. His sweater is made of the finest cashmere. The killer with beautiful manners, a beautiful face, and a beautiful home in the French countryside who worships my body like a religious fanatic and is going to do for me what no one else has been able to do. The awful thing that must be done if I'm ever to crawl out of this hellish pit I've been living in for the past two years.

My dark knight in black, bloody armor, taking up his sword for my cause.

He couldn't be more perfect if I'd conjured him from a dream.

"Whiskey would be good, thanks."

He pours me a measure, pauses to glance at my face, then pours more. He hands me the glass across the table then settles back into his chair and waits for me to begin.

I sip the whiskey, savoring its smoky burn. Then I lift my eyes and look at him.

"This man, the one you said fired the shot that killed my daughter. How do you know it's him?"

"He's a colleague of sorts."

My upper lip curls like a wolf's.

"No—not like that," James says quickly, leaning forward to rest his elbows on his knees. His tone is low and urgent. "We don't work together. I don't work with anyone. But as I told you before, there are only a few people who do what I do at my level. It's a small, elite group, and everyone knows who everyone else is. And if someone fucks up, everyone knows that, too."

He pauses to assess my expression.

"Go on."

"The bullet that hit your daughter was intended for your ex."

So the phone told the truth. "Why would someone want to kill Chris?"

"A deal he was brokering went south. Chemical weapons were set to be transferred from one group to another—"

"What groups?"

James pauses for a beat. "Does it matter if I say the US to Israel? Or Russia to China? Or rebel factions to freedom fighters in any country? All over the world, every day, people are trying to kill each other because of differing ideologies. Religious, political, or otherwise. The names change, the methods of mass destruction change, but the goal remains the same: death."

Swirling the whiskey in my glass, I say absently, "No, the goal is power. Death is just a means to an end."

After a moment, he replies. "And those means are what your ex-husband specializes in."

"As do you. Apparently, I have a type."

Hearing my dry tone, he frowns. "There's a million miles between what I do and mass murder."

Settling back against the comfortable sofa cushions, I kick my feet up on the coffee table and swallow another swig of whiskey, my strange feeling of calm intensifying. "It's only a matter of degree, James. You can tart it up however you like, but you're a killer, just like him."

"Not like him," he counters, his voice hard. "I'll never be like him. He doesn't care who he hurts. Men, women, children, the elderly, animals, anything. He sells weapons that destroy everything they touch, and he does it without a second thought to the consequences."

"And what is it you think you're doing? Culling the herd? Separating the wheat from the chaff? A service to society?"

A faint smile plays over his full lips. "In a word…yes."

"Nice to see a man take pride in his job. Let's get back to why Chris was targeted."

After another pause to examine my expression, he turns all business. "To put it simply, he got greedy. The shipment was delayed, the people who were expecting it got antsy, and Chris decided it was an opportunity to make more money. He told his clients the deal was off unless they ponied up more cash—for bribes to customs officials to get the gears moving more quickly, or so he said—but they found out what he was doing and didn't appreciate being blackmailed.

"They ordered a hit to make an example of him. Only the hitter they hired got sloppy."

"Sloppy," I repeat, needing more.

James restlessly adjusts his weight in his chair, uncrossing his legs and sighing.

"Shooting accurately from a moving vehicle is extremely difficult under the best of circumstances, but attempting it while the mark is surrounded by a crowd is just dumb. Professional protocol dictates the hitter should've set up in a building across the street and taken aim from an elevated, hidden spot with an easy exit. But for some unknown reason, he decided to go cowboy and make a mess.

"It was total amateur hour. A complete fucking disaster. It's a miracle the license plate of the car wasn't caught on camera. The only reason that idiot isn't in federal prison right now is sheer luck."

Luck. That's not a word I'd use to describe anything about the situation.

Suddenly, I'm back in that moment, in the dizzying panic of the screaming, fleeing crowd, kneeling in shock on the cold ground over the still, silent form of my baby girl, pressing my palms over the small hole between the second and third button of her favorite pink velvet coat while a dark red stain bloomed around my hands like a flower.

Emmie's eyes were wide open when she died. They were hazel, like her father's. A gorgeous, deep green-brown flecked with gold.

I close my eyes and rest my head against the back of the sofa, awash in terrible memories but somehow more peaceful than I've felt in years. Perhaps it's the sedative effect of the lavender fields, calming my mind and easing my nerves with their famously mesmerizing scent.

Or perhaps I no longer have a grip on my sanity.

James murmurs, "I'm sorry. I can't imagine how hard this must be for you to hear."

"I want to hear it," I say, keeping my eyes closed. "I need to hear everything. It's better this way. At least I'm no longer living in the dark."

After a moment wherein the only sound I hear is the faraway, gentle tinkling of the bells around the necks of the goats grazing in the spelt fields on the other side of the valley, a few things realign themselves in my head.

"I've always loved you. You're the only weakness I have. I'm willing to make you hate me if it means you'll be safe."

It makes an awful kind of sense. When you love someone, you'll sacrifice anything to protect them. Anything…including your relationship.

I open my eyes and gaze at James. "Chris thought divorcing me would keep me safe from the people who wanted him dead."

He nods slowly, his gaze never leaving mine. "And he was right."

"Those men at the hotel…who were they?"

His beautiful blue eyes harden. "Not the kind of men you'd enjoy spending time with as they smuggled you back to the States."

So they were Chris's hired hands. Mercenaries. He made good on his threat. "How did they find me? The hotel clerk checked me in under an assumed name."

"Did you use a credit card?"

Shit. Note to self: next time you're running for your life, use cash. "Why would he hire them if he couldn't trust them to treat me well?"

"Desperate times call for desperate measures."

"I don't understand."

He pauses for a moment to gaze at me, his expression unreadable. "It doesn't matter now. They'll never find you here. No one will ever find you here. This is the only place on earth you're truly safe."

I take another swallow of whiskey, watching him over the rim of the glass. When I lick my lips, he follows the motion of my tongue with burning eyes. I inquire calmly, "Am I your prisoner?"

His tone turns suggestive. "Only if you want to be."

"So I could walk out of here right now and you wouldn't stop me?"

"Of course. But you won't."

His confidence sends a flare of irritation through my stomach. "I might."

He huffs out a small, amused laugh, then rises from his chair to go stand at the windows. Dusk paints him in a palette of purple and gold. Looking out over the lavender fields, he says quietly, "You might…if you weren't in love with me."

He turns his head and stares at me. There's a challenge in his look.

When I don't respond, he strolls back toward me, his sharp gaze never leaving mine. Then he sits beside me on the sofa, takes the glass from my hand and sets it on the coffee table, and drags me onto his lap.

I don't fight him. There's no use in denying I'd rather be here than anywhere else, even if he is what he is.

The killer that he is. The man who takes money to end lives

and makes himself feel better about it by drawing portraits and giving the proceeds to charity.

I close my eyes and rest my head on his shoulder. His arms come around me and cradle me tight. I whisper, "This is madness."

"It's the opposite of madness. This"—he squeezes me—"is the only thing that makes any sense."

As I listen to the steady thump of his heart, I wonder if he's right. Has the world gone so insane that I'm safer in this killer's arms than anywhere or with anyone else?

"Tell me about that night, when I walked in on you and Chris in my apartment."

"He didn't know who I was when he opened the door, because he'd never seen a picture of me, but I recognized him instantly."

"You talked about me with him?"

"I informed him who I was. He assumed I'd been hired to finish the job the other hitter failed at. When he discovered that wasn't the case, it didn't take him long to figure out what was really going on. And to freak out about it."

I recall how enraged Chris was when he asked if I was fucking James. Sadness pierces my heart like the tip of a spear. All those years I believed my marriage ended because my husband didn't care enough, all the pain I suffered believing I wasn't loved, and the truth is that he cared so much he walked away instead of selfishly staying.

He left me to save my life.

But he wouldn't have had to if he wasn't facilitating the trade of chemical weapons from one bunch of savages to another. If he hadn't been doing that, there would have been no need to walk away.

And our daughter would still be alive.

No matter if his motives for leaving me were good, I can never forgive him for what happened to Emmie. For all the terrible choices he made that led directly to that.

After a long time where we just sit quietly, twilight deepening to gloom around us as shadows creep farther and farther up the walls, James says, "Tell me what you're thinking."

"I was just wondering how one gets into your line of work."

His laugh is a pleasing bass rumble passing through his chest. I close my eyes, letting myself be lulled by it. "Through a long series of strange occurrences. It started when I was in the Army. I won't bore you with the details."

"The Army? Was that before art school?"

A smile creeps into his voice. "I never went to art school. That's just part of a carefully crafted bio in case anyone takes too close a look at who I am."

I don't realize my mistake until several moments later: there's no way I'd know about his phony art school education unless *I* took too close a look.

He whispers into my ear, "I get a notification whenever someone investigates my background. Someone, for instance, named Mike Hanes who works for the FBI."

Fear for Mike and Kelly makes my entire body turns cold. "It wasn't his fault," I say quickly. "I asked him to do it as a favor. He's the husband of my best friend, and I was only trying to protect myself—"

"It's all right," he reassures me, tipping my head up with his fingers under my chin so we're gazing into each others' eyes. "I know why you did it, and they're not in any danger from me. They didn't discover anything I didn't want them to know."

He pauses briefly to run his thumb over my lower lip. "What I'm really interested in is why you chose to keep seeing me after you discovered what's in my medical file."

I'm about to answer him truthfully when all of a sudden it feels as if the floor has dropped out from under me. Because if his education was manufactured…

"Oh my God. You're not dying of ALS, are you?"

He chuckles. "I'm as healthy as a horse. But every five years or so, I kill myself."

I stare at him, not understanding the words he's speaking.

"As a change of cover," he explains, as if this is a commonplace thing. "It's a normal precaution in my line of work. It's much harder to track a dead man. I shed identities like a snake sheds its skin."

I can't decide if I'm furious or relieved. My brain throws its hands in the air and gives up, leaving me to fend for myself in this mosh pit of craziness that is my life.

I climb out of James's lap and stand staring down at his handsome face.

Then I slap him across it as hard as I can.

His head snaps to the side, but otherwise, he doesn't move. After a moment, he rubs his jaw. "Ouch."

Eerily calm, I say, "If you ever lie to me again, about anything, no matter how inconsequential, that won't be the only ouch I give you. Understood?"

"Understood. Oh, wait—does this mean I should tell you my real name?"

Now I'm absolutely certain of the emotion blowing through me like wildfire. It's fury, plain and simple.

I slap him again.

When he looks up at me, cheek glowing red with my handprint, he's grinning. There's a wicked gleam in his eyes. "Just admit it, sweetheart. You're in love with me."

"If this is love, I'd rather have dysentery. At least then there'd be a good reason for all the shit I'm dealing with."

He stands and pulls me into his arms. His eyes hot and his voice rough, he says, "You promised me a freebie. I'm calling it in."

When I only stare at him with thinned lips, he tries to give my memory a nudge. "One free pass in Touchy Subject land in exchange for telling you about my water competency. Remember?"

I shake my head in disbelief. "We're so far beyond Touchy Subject land now, I can't even see the shoreline from the water."

He presses, "Why didn't you walk away from me when you had the chance, Olivia? You had the perfect out. We had an argument. I said if you didn't call me in two days, I'd understand. You never would've had to see me again. It could've been simple. Clean. Instead you doubled down. Believing I was terminally ill, believing our time together would be limited by either the end of your time in Paris or the end of my life, why would you keep seeing me?"

"Because I'm a masochistic fool."

"Try again," he whispers, brushing his lips along my jaw. "And this time tell me the truth."

My hands are flattened over his chest. Under my palms, his heart beats like a wild thing.

"Don't you think it's a tad ironic, you insisting on the truth?"

"*Tell me.*"

I know what he wants me to say. I probably would have, too, if I were the same woman I was only twenty-four hours ago. But now the world has turned upside down and my priority is no longer my love life, or my happiness, or trying to maintain anything that might resemble mental health.

All my priorities have been whittled down to a bare-boned need to see the man who killed my daughter pay the price for what he did.

I push James away. He allows it, dropping his arms to his sides and gazing at me in silence. His eyes are filled with urgency. The pulse in his neck thrums like mad.

"Bring me that bastard's head on a platter," I say quietly. "Do that for me and I'll tell you anything you want."

His smile is dark and dangerous. He steps closer, takes my

face in his hands, and presses a soft kiss to my lips. "If I leave right now, I can be back before sunrise."

"Back?"

"From Germany, where he's been lying low." When he sees the shock register on my face, James's small smile grows wider. "I tracked him down with the help of a few of my associates. We don't normally work together, but nobody wants that baby killer alive."

So now I know the truth about his mysterious trips to Germany. He didn't travel there to participate in clinical trials… he went to find a rat hiding in its nest.

If I wasn't already in love with him, I definitely am now.

My emotions must show on my face, because from one moment to the next, James's smile vanishes, and his eyes start to burn.

He sweeps me up in his arms and carries me into the bedroom.

28

That night, our lovemaking has a desperate edge to it. The frenzy of unleashed wild animals that leaves my body sore and bruised in the morning.

My mind it leaves scraped clean. A pumpkin hollowed out by knives, awaiting its Halloween candle.

James left in the dark with a whispered word of farewell, kissing me as I laid nude under the sheets, my skin still slicked with sweat from our passion. I didn't sleep a wink after that. I simply listened to the song of crickets and the lonely calls of night birds, the heady scent of the lavender fields drifting in through the open windows like the most comforting balm.

I told him I wanted to go with him on his lethal errand, but his *no* was unequivocal. It was too dangerous. He wouldn't take the risk. But he *would* honor my other request.

He found the idea of bringing me a head on a platter pleasingly biblical.

Yes, we're quite the pair, we two. A modern day Salome and Herod, happily lopping off their enemies' noggins. I should start looking for competent couples counselors the moment the sun crests the flanks of the mountains.

But when that moment comes, I'm no longer in bed. I'm dressing in a hurry, pulling on my jeans and yanking my T-shirt impatiently over my head, because I've heard the sound of a car pulling up the long gravel driveway outside.

The throaty purr of the Mercedes's engine is unmistakable.

With my heart in my throat, I run barefoot through the darkened house. The heavy wooden front door I fling open as if it weighs nothing. Then I watch breathlessly as James parks the Mercedes by the low stone wall that surrounds the circular drive court and cuts the engine.

When our gazes meet through the windshield, my heart stops dead in my chest.

A purple bruise darkens the hollow under his left eye. His lower lip is split and swollen.

He exits the car, closes the driver's door, and walks around to the hatch in the back. Gravel crunches under his feet. The hatch lifts silently with a push of a button. Then James reaches inside the car and removes a leather satchel.

It's black and rounded on either end with two short curved handles and a zipper that runs between them, front to back. It's something you could carry over your shoulder, about the size of a big purse. It looks like a bag that might be used to store a bowling ball.

James shuts the rear hatch and turns to look at me. Carried on the sweet-smelling dawn air, his voice floats across the driveway. "Honey, I'm home."

He lifts the bag like a trophy.

I press my shaking hands over my pounding heart.

Then my legs give out and I sink to my knees on the floor.

In the end, I couldn't look at what the bag contained. I told James to bury it somewhere far out in the lavender fields, then I went inside and made coffee and omelets and waited for him to come back.

When he did, we didn't talk about it. We never spoke of it again.

I stayed in Provence for the rest of the summer, telling Kelly that I'd broken it off with James and needed a change of scenery, and informing Estelle that I found Paris far too crowded and hot. I said I'd gone instead to a small fishing village on the coast that I loved and might want to relocate to.

Being good friends, they were both supportive. They didn't ask too many questions. They just wanted me to be happy and could tell by my voice that I was.

James dealt with Christopher via a single phone call. I don't know what was said, but Chris later sent me an email letting me know my name and face had been removed from the computers and security cameras at the hotel Saint Germaine, so I'd never be associated with the "incident" there. He told me he loved me and always would, and to contact him if I needed anything.

I never wrote back.

It's September now. I'm almost finished with my novel. The lavender fields have been harvested. The briefly blooming rows of purple and blue have returned to their normal earthen shades of brown and green. They'll lie fallow through winter and spring until bursting forth again in one glorious, short-lived riot of color next summer.

But not every field around here lies fallow. One small plot has proven itself surprisingly fertile. In one miniscule acre, a tiny bud of life grows.

"A baby?" whispers James, eyes wide as I show him the little plastic stick.

"A baby." I laugh when he bursts into tears. It's always the big tough guys who're the mushiest inside.

"When?" he demands, excitedly pulling me into his arms. "We have to get ready!"

We're outside in the garden. It's a glorious fall day: the sky blue, the air crisp, the potted geraniums blooming in a burst of crimson around the burbling fountain. I've never been happier.

"It's early," I murmur, winding my arms around the solid mass of his shoulders. I press a kiss to his strong neck. "I don't know exactly how far along I am, but I'll make an appointment at the doctor's."

He pulls away and grins at me. His eyes are shining. His cheeks are wet. He's so handsome it hurts my chest.

"Let's look at a calendar and try to figure it out!"

"I'm glad you're so happy about this."

He pretends to be outraged. "Did you think I'd be a total asshole and ask who the father was?"

"No. But…I wasn't sure…"

All his laughter and teasing vanish. He says urgently, "You weren't sure about *what*?"

Avoiding his eyes, I pick at the top button on his shirt. "Well, to be totally honest…" I glance up to find him staring down at me in blistering intensity. My voice drops. "I wasn't sure how a baby would fit into your lifestyle."

He slowly exhales a breath, then pulls me closer, cupping a hand around the back of my head and tucking it into his shoulder. "In case you hadn't noticed, sweetheart, I've been here with you every day."

I frown. "Um…and?"

"I haven't been working."

He says it as if there's some deeper meaning to his words. If there is, I'm not grasping it. "Yes," I say carefully, "having you here has been nice."

He throws his head back and laughs, startling me. "What's so funny?"

"You are." Still chuckling, he takes my face into his hands. "All those big words you know, and 'nice' is what you come up with nine times out of ten."

I grouse, "Nice is a nice word." When he grins, I smack him on the shoulder. "Quit it!"

"I have." He kisses me gently, rubbing his thumbs over my cheeks.

"Have what?"

"Quit."

"Quit what?" When he just stands there smiling at me with tender eyes, I gasp in understanding. "You *quit*?"

"God, you're slow. Are you sure you have a college degree?"

Gazing at him in disbelief, I say, "My grandmother used to tell me I was so clueless I'd starve with a loaf of bread under my arm."

He makes a face. "She sounds like a charming woman."

"Sicilians don't fuck around. Back to this quitting thing."

He kisses me again, this time a little deeper. "Hmm?"

"When did it happen?"

"As soon as I realized I wanted to spend the rest of my life with you. After that, my line of work didn't make sense anymore. If I was going to be responsible for taking care of you, I couldn't be flying around the world killing bad guys who sometimes tried to kill me back."

I think of his bruised face and split lip when he returned that night from Germany with the leather bag and shiver. "So you can just walk away? I mean, with no consequences?"

His face darkens. For a moment, he simply gazes at me in silence.

I say quickly, "Just tell me if me or the baby will be in danger."

"No," he says instantly, shaking his head. "But remember I told you I'd break rules to make you mine? Well, I broke them. All of them. And there's a price to be paid for everything in life. Someday that marker will be called in, and I can't refuse it."

Holy shit that sounds bad.

He stands waiting for me to grill him with questions, and I

know he'll answer them if I do. But I've gotten very good at handling ambiguities. I'm an expert now at navigating the dark, dangerous waters of life, and I know that whenever this "marker" of his is called in, I'll handle it.

We'll handle it together.

Adopting a lighter tone, I say, "Well, I hope you're not expecting me to support you, Romeo. You're still going to have to pull your weight around here, contract killer or not."

Slowly, his face breaks into a smile. "And here I thought you were a feminist."

"What does me being a feminist have to do with you not being a slacker?"

"I thought feminism was all about equality."

"*And*?"

"And what if I wanted to stay home and take care of the baby while *you* worked?"

This man is so good at saying things that make me stare at him with my mouth open. Seriously, it's a Jedi-level skill.

He laughs and gives me a hard squeeze. "I'm going to find a calendar so we can figure out when James, Jr. is coming." He turns and heads back toward the house, leaving me shouting after him, "What if the baby is a girl, you chauvinist?"

As he disappears through the open French doors, I hear his chuckle. "Then we'll name her Jamie."

Laughing weakly, I sit in one of the cushioned wrought iron chairs that surround the square wooden table where we love to eat supper in the evenings. The olive trees are alive with birdsong. The sun is warm on my head. I toy with the plastic pregnancy test stick, smiling like a crazy person and shaking my head at how the universe conspired to bring me here, to this moment.

To drag me through the sewer and test my mettle before rewarding me with such beautiful gifts.

When James returns, holding a wall calendar, I scoff. "What happened to your super spy phone?"

He rolls his eyes. "Your grandmother was right. Didn't you notice? I haven't used that phone in weeks."

"Side with my nana again and this child will be the last you'll ever be able to produce, my friend."

He drops the calendar on the table in front of me, kisses me on top of the head, then ambles toward the raised beds of vegetables growing rampant along the wall on one side of the patio. I watch his ass—the eighth wonder of the world—as he goes.

When I turn my attention back to the calendar, I notice its theme is fall foliage on the East Coast. "Pretty pictures," I call out to James. "Have you ever seen the leaves change in Central Park in September? It's magical."

He says something I can't quite catch over the chirping of the birds, which has grown louder. They're fighting over the last of the wild plums in the hedgerows, no doubt. There's a faraway buzzing sound in my ears, too, a mechanical noise, something distant and slightly irritating. Idly wondering if a farmer is plowing one of the spelt fields nearby, I flip open the calendar to September's page.

The photo for the month is of an apple orchard outside a quaint village in New England. The trees are brilliant shades of scarlet, yellow, and gold. Beneath the photo is a description of the trees and location it was taken, along with the name of the group who sponsored the calendar.

Rockland Psychiatric Center in Orangeburg, New York.

My breath is knocked from my lungs. The skin all over my body prickles with gooseflesh. The strange mechanical noise intensifies until it's all I can hear.

I whisper in horror, "*No*."

When I look up in panic, my eyes desperately seeking James, he's no longer bending over the vegetable beds, picking tomatoes for dinner.

He's gone.

When I look back at the wooden table, it's gone, too. So is

the chair I was sitting in, and the house, and the patio, and the garden, and the rolling fields of harvested lavender bushes, and all the beauty and tranquility of Provence. Everything has vanished.

The only thing left is the calendar in my hand—the calendar with a big red circle around Monday the 23rd.

The first day of fall.

The day I was supposed to return to New York from my summer vacation in Paris.

White light surrounds me, growing brighter and brighter until I'm blinded. I can no longer see, but I can still feel my blood pounding hot through my veins, and I can still hear the strange, irritating mechanical noise, though it's quickly drowned out by something much louder.

The high, wavering sound of my scream.

29

"... But if you ask me, babe, he was one sad individual. All the obsession with war and death? Blech. And don't get me started on the whole bullfighting thing. That's just toxic masculinity, right there. You can keep your beloved Ernest Hemingway—I'm sticking with Nicholas Sparks. At least he knows how to write a happy ending."

Dressed in a pretty floral summer dress, her dark hair gathered into a low bun at the base of her neck, Kelly snaps shut the book in her hand and sighs.

She's sitting across from me in an uncomfortable looking metal chair. The room is cold, white, and smells sharply of antiseptic. The door to the room is open. Outside in the hall, a bald man dressed in a starched white uniform pushes a mechanical buffer over the yellow linoleum floor.

The sound it makes is loud and irritating.

"Anyway, I gotta get going. I'll be back again tomorrow, same time as usual. Hopefully we can get through this story so I can read you something more cheerful." Under her breath, she says, "The friggin' obituaries would be more cheerful."

Reaching for a bulky striped handbag on the small plastic table next to her chair, Kelly stuffs the book into it.

I catch sight of the title—*For Whom the Bell Tolls*—and make a small sound of grief.

Jerking her head up, Kelly stares at me with long-lashed brown eyes. Eyes quickly growing huge in disbelief.

In a raspy, reed-thin voice that sounds as if it hasn't been used in a while, I whisper, "I am thee and thou art me and all of one is the other. And feel now. Thou hast no heart but mine."

I start to sob. Deep, chest-wracking sobs that are unstoppable.

Kelly leaps to her feet, frantically shouting, "Doctor! Help! Nurse—somebody get in here!" She bolts to the door, grabs the orderly in the hall by the arm, and points at me with a shaking finger. "*We need help in here right now*!" she hollers into his startled face.

In my lap is an afghan I somehow know was knitted for me by Estelle. I look at my hands, thin and white, curled atop the afghan into ugly, bent shapes. Distorted shapes, like claws.

I try to move my legs, but can't.

And the chair I'm sitting in has large rubber wheels on either side.

Through my sobs, I start to scream again.

The drug I'm administered through a shot in the arm works quickly. The tall African-American nurse who gives it to me speaks to me in dulcet tones, gently stroking my damp hair off my forehead and promising me everything is going to be okay as the room begins to spin, then darken.

"You're safe, sweetheart," he murmurs. "Don't worry, you're safe here."

When I awaken sometime later, my room is full of people

in white lab coats. They all stare at me with bated breath and an air of heightened expectation, as if I've returned from the dead.

Which apparently I have.

"Olivia," says one of them. "Hello. How are you feeling?"

He's short, elderly, and seems to be in charge. His bowtie is slightly askew. His French accent is pronounced.

"Let me guess," I say dully. "You're Edmond."

His smile looks delighted. I must be doing well. "Yes, I'm Dr. Chevalier! Very good. *Very* good."

Everyone nods and murmurs to each other how very good it is, indeed.

I think I'm going to be sick. I want to cover my mouth with my hand, but can't. The will to do it and the effect it's supposed to have are disconnected.

"Why can't I move my arms or legs?"

That shuts everyone up for a good thirty seconds. Edmond makes a motion that the others should leave, which they do, whispering amongst themselves. When the room is emptied, Edmond approaches my bedside—apparently I was transferred to a bed while unconscious—and rests his hand on the metal safety rail alongside it.

"We don't have to talk now, Olivia. Why don't you rest for a while? We can speak later."

I gaze at him, willing his head to explode. "Don't fucking patronize me, Edmond. I'm in no mood to be treated like a child."

If he's insulted or surprised by my words, he doesn't show it. He merely looks at me with fatherly concern, his cotton lab coat so white it's almost blinding.

When he asks, "Can you tell me where you are?" I understand it's a test. He's worried I'm too fragile to deal with the reason I'm paralyzed. He's thinks starting with a little light incarceration will get the conversation flowing.

"All signs point to the Rockland Psychiatric Center in Orangeburg, New York."

He takes a moment to assess my expression. Whatever he finds there must satisfy him, because he smiles. "Correct. And do you know why you're here?"

I search my memory. It's fuzzy, at best. "Because…I'm unwell?"

Another pause to examine my face. Then, his French accent flowing gently over the words, he says, "You've had some mental health challenges that we're helping you with."

Feeling sick again, I close my eyes. "I had a mental breakdown."

"A single, isolated episode of catatonic psychosis," he replies in a soothing tone. Like it's really not so bad since it only happened once. "You've been with us for some time now."

"How long?"

"Three months."

Since the start of summer. I never took a trip to Paris. That trip was all inside my head.

The pain that forms around my heart is so huge and burning it leaves me breathless.

James.

I want to kill myself, but without a working set of arms or legs, I doubt that will be possible.

"Your husband is coming to visit you tonight."

My eyes snap open. I stare at Edmond in horror. "Husband?"

He says warily, "Yes. Christopher. Do you remember him?"

Oh my God. I'm still married to Chris. I know if I start screaming again, I'll get another shot in the arm, so I simply bite my tongue and nod, focusing on the poster someone tacked up on the wall opposite my bed.

Glowing an unearthly shade of violet and blue, the lavender fields of Provence carpet a lush valley, stretching far into the distance until they disappear into mist.

~

"Hey, Olivia."

With an expression like he's attending his best friend's funeral, Chris stands in the doorway to my room. His blond hair is greasy and disheveled. There's a food stain on the front of his T-shirt, just below the Budweiser logo. He's wearing threadbare jeans and a pair of ratty Converse sneakers that look as if he's had them since college.

He's also short and paunchy, with the red nose and sallow skin tone one acquires through years of hard drinking.

When I smile, thinking how funny it is that I'd made him so much more handsome and sophisticated in my hallucination, his eyes narrow.

He doesn't like me smiling at him. Interesting.

"Can I come in?"

I try to gesture toward the ugly metal chair Kelly sat in earlier, but can't. So far, no one at the hospital has been willing to tell me what's wrong with my body. I'm guessing they think it would be too much for me to handle, considering I've only just returned from my trip to La La Land.

But I'll bet I'm about to find out from dear hubby, here.

"Have a seat."

Chris glances at the chair, but apparently decides he won't be staying that long, because he remains standing. He edges a few feet closer to my bed. "So you're awake."

And you're not the US ambassador to the UN. A hysterical laugh threatens to break from my lips, but I fight it back. I can't have the natives thinking I'm a total whack job, or I'll never get out of this place.

"I'm awake." I watch him shift his weight from foot to foot. His gaze darts all around the room but refuses to stay on me for more than a second.

I wonder why he's so unsettled. Obviously, having your

spouse wake up unexpectedly from a catatonic episode would be a tad startling for anyone, but there are no hugs or tears, no *I've missed you so much, darling.* He's bothered by something else.

My memories surrounding our relationship are murky, almost as if my brain is willfully trying to block them out.

The memories or him.

He says, "You still…?" With his index finger, he makes a loopy motion next to one of his ears.

Charming. Biting back a smartass reply, I try to be polite. "I'm feeling good, thank you."

"Huh. Well, that's great. That's just great."

He's got the best-friend-funeral expression again. Apparently my unexpected return from comaville isn't exactly cause for a party.

"How are *you*, Chris?"

He'd been staring at my claw-shaped hands resting in my lap with faint distaste, but now his gaze flashes up to mine. He snaps, "That supposed to be fuckin' funny or something?"

Ah. So the baggage between us is hefty and full of dismembered bodies.

"No. I'm sorry. I'm having trouble with my memory. Are we…" *There's no delicate way to say it. And you've literally got nothing left to lose. Full steam ahead.* "Are we estranged?"

He snorts as if I've said something extremely funny. "*Estranged*? More like strangers. After what happened to Emmie, you totally checked out."

What happened to Emmie.

Suddenly, my head is flooded with images—images too horrible to bear.

I'm in the car, backing out of our driveway. It's a big car, *Chris's* car, an older model SUV. I never liked it, but my sporty little Honda had been rear-ended the week before and was in the shop. So it was the loud, hulking Bronco I was taking to the grocery store that day.

The Bronco that didn't have a back up camera.

Or back up sensors.

Or good brakes.

At first, I think that bump is the recycle can. It was trash day, and for some unknown reason, the garbage collectors always left the garbage cans in the middle of the driveway when they were emptied. I hadn't looked when I'd opened the garage door, and the Bronco sat so high I probably wouldn't have been able to see the cans, anyway.

But when I heard our next door neighbor Beth's scream and looked over to see her white-faced and horrified at the edge of her yard as she stared at the ground behind the car, I knew what I'd hit wasn't a garbage can.

Then, when I threw the car into park and jumped out, I discovered the worst. The impossible.

I ran over a child.

My child.

I thought she was taking a nap inside. Chris was home, it was a Saturday afternoon, he was supposed to be watching her. But he was drinking beer in front of the television and didn't notice when she wandered out.

Her small body was crushed under the Bronco's big rear wheel. She was dead long before the ambulance arrived. She was cold by the time they loaded her onto the gurney and closed the doors.

Emmie's eyes were wide open when she died. They were hazel, like her father's. A gorgeous, deep green-brown flecked with gold.

This time when I start to scream, the nice African-American orderly has to give me three shots before he can get me to stop.

30

Five weeks later

It's amazing how fast I grow accustomed to the humiliation that accompanies having a useless body. For instance, right now I'm watching in disinterest as the nice orderly changes my diapers.

His name is Ernest. Ah, the irony.

He's quick and efficient, whistling as he does his work. My pale, scrawny form is just another widget to him, one of dozens he cares for daily in this facility. His large hands protected by blue latex gloves, he cheerfully cleans my ass with a baby wipe as I lay on my side in the hospital bed.

"We gotta watch this pressure sore," he says, tapping a spot on my butt. "Gettin' bigger. I'll need to start shifting your weight around more during the night."

"Hmm." I turn my attention to the poster of Frank Sinatra tacked on the wall by the closet door. Ol' Blue Eyes grins at me from beneath the brim of a fedora, those famous peepers of his the color of a tropical summer sky.

Or, you know, an artist/contract killer's.

Apparently, Ernest put up the Sinatra poster, though it was Kelly who brought the one of the lavender fields of Provence. I understand the urge to decorate: this place is so sterile it would instantly kill any bug who accidentally wandered in.

"Do I have to go to the lounge today? That place is totally depressing."

Ernest chuckles. "Ha ha. Depressing. I get it." Removing a fresh adult diaper from a box underneath the bed, he snaps it open and starts the tedious process of getting me into it, one wasted leg at a time.

"Is that a yes?"

"I don't make the rules around here, sweetheart. Doc says it's good for you to socialize with others."

Others. Thinking of the variety of human misery that word encompasses, I shudder.

"But if it makes you feel better, I'll take you for a spin around the garden before community group. Deal?"

"If either of us doesn't want to get into the details of something, we'll just say, 'touchy subject.' It'll be our safe word. Safe phrase, technically. Deal?"

Remembering James's words, I have to squeeze my eyes shut and breathe deeply for a moment. His imaginary words live on like beautiful ghosts inside my head.

Every moment with him, in fact, still lives in my head. All our conversations are so vivid. I still feel the warmth of his kisses on my lips. The time I spent with him seems so much more real than this, actual reality.

Cold, horrible, actual reality, in which not only did I accidentally kill my child and I'm married to a man who likes beer *way* more than me, but also—wait for it—I'm dying.

From what, you ask?

Can't you guess?

Finished pulling the diapers up around my hips, Ernest drags me upright and props me against his chest as he reaches for the fresh set of pale blue scrubs he laid on the bedside table. I rest my head against his shoulder, marveling that this disease that's robbed all my muscles of their power has the audacity to leave all my senses intact.

I still see, hear, taste, smell, and feel touch, like the warmth of Ernest's shoulder against my cheek and his tap on my bottom. And aside from some leftover fuzziness around long-term memories caused by my catatonia that I'm told will go away, my mind is working perfectly.

Which means that when the muscles that control my lungs become paralyzed in the final stages of this disease, I'll be completely aware that I'm suffocating to death.

With practiced ease, Ernest arranges my limbs and moves me this way and that so I'm quickly dressed in the soft cotton scrubs that have no pesky buttons, zippers, or strings on which the patients might hurt themselves. Then he lifts me from the bed and carefully places me into my waiting wheelchair, propping my feet up on the metal footrests and arranging my hands in my lap. He covers me with the knitted patchwork afghan, tucks it around my thighs, then assesses his work.

When he purses his lips in dissatisfaction, I say, "Don't tell me—my lipstick's all over my teeth, isn't it?"

I'm not wearing makeup, but he plays along, nodding somberly. "You look like you ate a crayon."

"A crayon would taste better than what they served for dinner last night. Do you think the chef knows that green beans are called *green* beans for a reason? I've never seen that shade of gray in a vegetable before."

Ernest guffaws. "*Chef?* That's generous." He grabs a wide-toothed comb from the nightstand and begins to run it through my hair, gently working out the tangles.

He's the one who showers me, too. Soaps me up and rinses

me off with brisk impersonality, like I'm a car going through a car wash at the strip mall down the street.

There's a different wheelchair for the showers. A special waterproof one, with a hole in the middle of the seat so Ernest can reach all the nitty-gritty places that need to be cleaned.

Yeah, good times. I keep praying for another psychotic break to come and save me, but so far I'm shit outta luck.

Once he's satisfied my hair looks presentable, Ernest wheels me to the main congregating area for the patients, a dayroom ironically called the "lounge" in an effort to make it sound relaxing. The noise level is anything but relaxing, however. People in the throes of mental illness are not a quiet bunch. And whoever decorated it obviously watched the movie *One Flew Over the Cuckoo's Nest* for inspiration, because it looks exactly like a room of which the evil Nurse Ratched would approve.

It's amazing how a space so bare can also manage to be so ugly.

First up, it's medication time. Ernest wheels me to the dispensary window. It's reminiscent of a bank teller's window, complete with a person in uniform sitting behind a thick plexiglass safety shield trying too hard to smile.

"Mornin', Bernadette." Ernest salutes the lady with the bad perm behind the plexiglass.

"Howdee*doo*, Ernest!" Smiling like mad, she turns her sparkling green eyes to me. "And a grand good morning to you, *too*, Miss Olivia!"

The woman is always as chipper as a fucking chipmunk. I'd like to reach through the small opening in the window where the medicine is placed and grab her around her throat.

"Your hair looks nice today," I tell her. "Did you just have it done?"

Patting her hideous helmet of curls that resemble a poodle's coat—if the poodle dyed itself a screaming shade of orange that doesn't occur anywhere in nature—she beams at me. "Why, yes! How sweet of you to notice!"

"Your curls look especially tight. And the color is very…fresh."

When she thanks me, turning away to get a paper cup of water to go with my medicine, Ernest chuckles quietly. He says under his breath, "You're so bad."

I play the innocent. "What? I'm giving her a compliment."

"Mm-hmm. And I'm Taylor Swift."

"Really? You're bigger in person that I would've thought, Tay."

Ernest clucks his tongue, trying to be disapproving, but I know he gets a kick out of my smart mouth.

Imaginary or otherwise, men seem to enjoy a smartass.

When Ernest holds out my anti-psychotics, I open up obediently for the pills. He places them on my tongue, then helps me swallow water from the paper cup, watching carefully to make sure I don't choke.

My throat muscles have been getting progressively weaker. Swallowing is one of those things we take for granted until we can't do it anymore.

Like walking. Like wiping your own ass. Like everything else in life.

Then Ernest rolls me to my favorite spot in the room, a window that overlooks the lush green lawn outside. It's my favorite because it's as far away from everyone else as possible.

Especially the young blond woman who screams like she's having an orgasm—except it's pretty much all the time—and the tall thin man who only communicates through grunting.

Gigi suffers from paranoid schizophrenia. The voices in her head tell her everyone wants to kill her. Gaspard has severe bipolar disorder and clinical depression. He tried to commit suicide six times before he was committed.

Today he's simply staring at the wall, interjecting a grunt here and there in between Gigi's lusty screams.

Daily routines at the Rockland Psychiatric Center are managed through an inflexible schedule. After breakfast and an hour of "free" lounge time, I'm scheduled for community group. This is when all the patients get together to discuss such fascinating topics as the rigorously enforced no-touching policy, who stole (insert item) from someone else's room, why *Forrest Gump* is an overrated movie, and the quality of the food, which everyone agrees stinks.

After that excitement, it's lunch. Then one-on-one time with my psychiatrist for an assessment of how I'm feeling, sleeping, pooping, etcetera, and if I currently want to kill myself. If necessary, adjustments to meds are made. Then my vital signs are taken, and I'm off to process group with my social workers, where I usually nap in my chair while everyone else talks about how to combat negative thoughts. Someone always cries.

Then it's recreational therapy, education group, visitation hour, dinner, quiet time, and lights out. The routine never varies.

So imagine my surprise when, after only ten minutes of window gazing, Ernest shows up again to take me to see Dr. Chevalier.

"Why does he want to see me?"

"You think anyone tells me anything? I just work here, sweetheart."

We pass a group of men playing chess. One of them screams "Beetlejuice!" at me. I smile, because I liked that movie.

When we arrive at Edmond's office, he's ensconced behind his big oak desk, examining papers from an open manila file. He looks up and says, "Ah."

I don't know why, but that feels ominous.

Ernest parks my chair in front of Edmond's desk, then leaves, closing the office door behind him. Folding his hands together over the papers he's been contemplating, Edmond gazes at me in silence. After a full minute, I can't take it anymore.

"What's up, Doc?"

He smiles. "I'll miss your sense of humor, Olivia."

I arch my brows. "Are you planning my funeral already?"

"You're going home."

It feels like an atom bomb just exploded atop my head. I can't breathe. I can't see. My organs are shriveling up and dying. "*Home*?"

"To live with your husband. Now, don't look so shocked. You knew this day was coming."

"No, I can honestly say I had no idea this day was coming!"

Edmond looks like he's trying to resist rolling his eyes. "We've talked about your re-entry into society extensively in our sessions."

"I meant I didn't know this day was coming *today*!"

He gathers the papers and taps them on end on his desk to straighten them, then places them neatly back into the file. He closes the file and rests his folded hands on top of it, which is his passive-aggressive way of telling me the matter is settled.

Not everyone is as direct as my imaginary James. If I had use of my hands, I'd rip that file to shreds and toss it like confetti around the room.

Edmond says, "Let's talk about why you're upset."

"For starters, you know Chris has only visited me once. And you know how well that went. Now I'm supposed to go live with him?"

"I've spoken with him many times, including today. He's very eager to have you return to your home."

Everyone has a tell when they lie: shifty eyes, restless hands, toying with their hair. Edmond's is fiddling with his bowtie.

I watch him nervously adjust it for a while before I look at my crooked hands resting like dead doves in my lap. "Who's going to care for me there? I know it won't be him."

"We've assisted him in finding twenty-four hour daily home care from an excellent company that specializes in patients with ALS."

"Round-the-clock care? That sounds expensive."

"It's covered by a combination of Medicare and a policy included in his work insurance."

Chris is a mechanic, as I remembered after his first visit. It's honest work, and the pay is decent, but he doesn't own the shop, and he has no ambition to move up.

I also remembered that he'd been having an affair with the busty twenty-something receptionist at the shop and was planning to leave me.

But that was before I was diagnosed with ALS—the diagnosis that came a few months after Emmie died.

I'd been ignoring the persistent twitching in my right thigh muscle, the numbness in my feet that would come and go, how I'd occasionally drop a pen or stumble. But during the investigation after the accident, while the police were ruling out intoxication as a possible reason I didn't brake fast enough, I happened to mention that my foot had been bothering me that day. It had tingled then gone numb.

I hadn't quite hit the brakes in time.

The bump I felt was the big metal rear bumper hitting Emmie. She was thrown a few feet back into the driveway from the initial impact. If I'd stopped right then, she would've been safe, but I fumbled with the brake just long enough to roll over her…

And stop right on top.

Edmond says gently, "Olivia."

I glance up. He looks pained, so sorrowful and compassionate. I feel bad for him. He tries so hard. He really does want to help me. But what help can anyone offer a mother who killed her own child?

There's a special place in hell for people like me. And I'm right here in it.

"You can still have quality of life," he says softly. "You might have years left yet—"

My laugh is sharp and bitter. "God forbid."

"You could reconnect with your husband."

I scoff. "The husband who only didn't leave me because he didn't want people to think he was a total asshole for abandoning his dying wife? Yeah, that's doubtful."

"You could be an inspiration to others in your situation."

I sigh, closing my eyes. "I'm a cautionary tale, Edmond. Not an inspiration."

"You could write a book."

A book? I've always wanted to write a book. I open my eyes and stare at him.

Encouraged by my attention, he warms to the idea, nodding and leaning forward. "Yes, you could write about your experiences. Here at Rockland, and with your disease, and as a mother coping with losing her child—it would be a riveting story. Simply *riveting*. Imagine what people dealing with hardships in their own lives could get out of it!"

"Major depression?"

"Inspiration," he counters. "*Hope*."

I suppose it makes a certain kind of sense. Even the worst tragedies have their lessons. And if my story could save even one parent from losing a child because they ignored strange medical symptoms…if even a single accident could be prevented…

"I wouldn't know the first thing about writing a novel. Before I was a stay-at-home mom, I was a secretary."

Edmond brightens. "So you have experience writing for business!"

"Only correspondence," I argue, hoping he won't give up too easily because if I'm going to do this, I'm gonna need *tons* of moral support.

I mean, I can't use my hands! How the hell am I going to write a novel?

But Edmond is reading my mind. "You could dictate the whole story into a recorder. I'm sure there are many freelance editors you could hire to polish the final draft. And if you can't find a publisher, you can publish it yourself. More to the point, it would be excellent therapy for you."

My tone turns dry. "No matter how many books I might write, I think we both know I'll never be mentally stable again."

He waves a hand in disagreement. "The mind is an incredibly powerful thing. Just as it has, say, the potential to remain in a psychotic state forever, so too does it have an unlimited potential to heal itself."

In reaction to Edmond's words, I stop breathing. My blood stops circulating. Everything inside me screeches to a stop.

A person can remain in a psychotic state forever?

Forever?

Talk about hope.

For the first time, I'm grateful for my paralysis. Otherwise, I'd shake so violently the good doctor would call for enough tranquilizers to sedate a horse.

I say slowly, "You know, I just realized we never talked about the nuts and bolts of what happened to me. The logistics of how a psychotic break actually works."

Surprised by the change in subject, Edmond blinks.

"I mean, I've told you how it all seemed so real to me. As real as it seems to me now, sitting here across from you. Maybe if I understood the process better, it would help me be prepared. Perhaps if I'm aware of what the mind goes through before a psychotic break, I could catch the signs. Like there were signs with my ALS that I ignored…are there any indications of imminent psychosis?"

After a moment, he nods. "Yes, there are. And to be frank,

Olivia, I'm pleased you want to know. Facing your challenges directly is a significant step in your recovery."

So get talking already! I gaze at him, outwardly composed. Inside I'm a rave party with screaming crowds, flashing lights, and deafening music, with riot police closing in.

Because if I can discover how I found James the first time…

Maybe I could do it again.

31

I listen carefully as Edmond begins to describe the multi-dimensional state referred to as psychosis. He goes on for several minutes about the variety of personality disorders that can lead to the diagnosis—including schizophrenia, delusional disorder, and the like—and the various things that can exacerbate it, such as misuse of illegal drugs. He follows that up with a clinical description of what happens to a person experiencing psychosis: hallucinations, disordered thinking, delusions, and sometimes catatonia, where the individual is completely lost in their fantasy world and non-responsive to outside stimuli.

Which of course I'm already familiar with.

"But I didn't have any of those personality disorders you mentioned," I interrupt, agitated. "I never abused drugs. I'd never been diagnosed with any medical problems, mental or otherwise. How could someone like me, specifically, become psychotic? What would be the trigger?"

In the following silence, I can tell that he's carefully choosing his words.

"You may not have had a formal diagnosis of depression, but you were undoubtedly depressed."

When I don't say anything, he continues. "Your relationship with your husband was strained. You'd discovered he was having an affair…with someone much younger than you. Even before that, the two of you had been drifting apart, and you felt extremely lonely. You told me you were having trouble with the idea of turning forty in a few years, and you longed for another child, but didn't want one with your husband because of what a poor father you found him to be. *Inattentive* and *cold* were your exact words."

Two things he had in common with his alter-ego in my hallucination. "Go on."

"Then…the accident happened."

He lets it hang there for a moment in all its monstrosity.

"Shortly after the accident, you were diagnosed with a terminal illness." His voice gentles. "And when you were eventually confined to a wheelchair as the disease progressed, you experienced what we refer to as a psychotic break. Simply put, your mind could no longer handle the stress and pain of reality, so it kicked into self-defense mode and took you on a beautiful vacation."

Anguished, I close my eyes. An image of James appears behind my lids. He's heartbreakingly handsome. His beautiful blue eyes burn as brightly as they always did.

I whisper, "It felt more real to me than this does, talking with you right now." A thought occurs to me, and I open my eyes. "How do I know *this* is real? How can I be sure I'm not hallucinating *you*?"

Edmond shrugs. "It's a legitimate question. I've never experienced a hallucination, but every patient I've worked with gives the same account: there was no discernible difference between their hallucinations and 'real' life."

Hope surges inside me again. My heart pounding, I say eagerly, "So maybe this is all a dream? Maybe one day I'll wake up and be back in France with James?"

Edmond leans back in his chair. He exhales heavily, then rubs a hand over his eyes. When he speaks again, he sounds weary. "I know it's tempting to believe. But if there's anything I've learned in my time on Earth, it's this: if it seems too good to be true, it is."

Yeah, I've heard that one before. "That's not proof of anything."

"No one can offer you *proof* of reality, not even Einstein himself. But just because it can't be proven doesn't mean the sun won't rise tomorrow. It will."

When I only stare at him with a challenging look, unsatisfied by his answers, he takes a different approach.

"Let's talk about the man you call James."

The way he says James's name makes me feel defensive. "What about him?"

"He's beautiful. By your own description, an Adonis. He's soulful. Artistic. Attentive. Accomplished. Intelligent." Edmond pauses. "He's also ruggedly masculine and strong, incredibly virile and sexually experienced, but also conveniently single… and has been celibate for years. But the moment he sees you, he falls in love. Forgive me for saying so, but that only ever happens in a romance novel. That's not real life."

Miserable, I mutter, "I never said he fell in love the minute he saw me."

On a roll now, Edmond ignores me. "This beautiful man pursues you relentlessly. You have an intense sexual and emotional connection with him, despite knowing him a very short time. He makes you feel desired, needed, and happy for the first time in many years."

I groan. "Okay, you've made your point! I created the perfect man!"

"So perfect he becomes the dark knight who slays the dragon of your guilt. The thing your conscious mind cannot bear to face: you were the cause of your child's death. Instead, Emmie's death came from an assassin's bullet—a bullet meant for your husband. Thereby excusing you of wrongdoing and shifting the blame to him."

Edmond's voice lowers. "And when your James killed the killer, the circle was complete. Justice was served. You lived happily-ever-after in a beautiful place untouched by the outside world and even conceived a child with the man who set everything right. The man who, ironically, brought death only to those deserving of it. The killer with a code of honor."

After another pause, Edmond adds, "The only killers who have a moral code, my dear, are fictional." His voice grows pityingly tender. "Or figments of our imagination."

I don't realize I'm crying until the room begins to blur.

Edmond presses a button on the intercom on his desk. "Catherine, would you have Ernest come to my office, please?"

Standing, Edmond grabs tissues from a box next to his phone and comes around his desk to blot my cheeks with them. "I'm sorry, Olivia," he murmurs. "I know this is difficult. What you're feeling is normal. You've experienced a loss, and you're grieving. Allow yourself to grieve the loss of James and your time together, then turn all your focus and energy on healing. And I meant what I said about writing a book: not only could it be of value to others, I believe it would be good therapy for you to get it all out."

Ernest arrives, looking alarmed to find me in tears. He sends an accusing glare toward Edmond, then grabs the handles of my chair and guides me to the door.

"Wait."

Ernest leans over to cock an inquisitive brow at me.

"I need to ask him something before we go."

Looking as if he doesn't agree at all with this decision, Ernest swings my chair around so I'm facing Edmond. He's behind his big oak desk again, hands folded over the manila file that I assume contains all the dirt on me there is to dig.

I say, "You didn't tell me about the warning signs of psychosis."

"Ah. Yes. Well, typically patients report things like unusual sensitivity to light and noise, memory problems, withdrawal from social relationships, increased suspiciousness or aggression, inappropriate laughter or crying…"

He goes on. I don't recall any of the symptoms he's listing happening to me.

Irritated, I interrupt him. "What if there weren't any of those signs? Could there be something else? Like…like a main cause? A single event that would be the straw that breaks the camel's back?"

Edmond gazes at me with deep sympathy shining in his eyes. "I know it would be reassuring to have a sole trigger we could point to, but the reality is that the onset of psychosis is typically a slow downward slide, not an abrupt snap. I'll send a list of symptoms home with you today so your husband can be on the lookout for any unusual behavior. Keep on top of your meds and let your psychiatrist know immediately if you start to feel anything odd."

He picks up his pen and begins to write on a pad of paper, and just like that, I'm dismissed.

As Ernest wheels me out of the office and back to the dayroom, he starts to sing softly to himself. He has a beautiful smooth bass voice that goes perfectly with the soulful tune of the song.

Still distracted by my meeting with Edmond, I ask, "What is that you're singing? It's pretty."

"Old gospel song. You recognize it?"

It sounds vaguely familiar, but I can't place it. "Should I?"

He chuckles. "They been playin' the album it's from in the lounge every Sunday since you got here, sweetheart."

So that's why it sounds familiar. "Who's the artist?"

"Legendary gospel singer who died about twenty years ago. Name was James Blackwood."

I close my eyes and let the pain burn through me until I'm nothing inside but ashes.

~

It's getting dark by the time Chris picks me up in a wheelchair-accessible van on loan from the body shop where he works. It doesn't belong to the shop: a client left it for repair.

We exchange a muted greeting without meeting each other's eyes.

The other patients watch from the lounge windows on the third floor as Ernest loads me into the van in the parking lot while a reluctant Chris stands nearby, watching, looking like he needs an airsickness bag.

When I'm securely buckled into the back, my wheelchair strapped down so it can't roll around during the ride, Ernest leans in and kisses me on the cheek. "Gonna miss you, Miss Olivia. You take care now, you hear?"

"You, too, Ernest," I say, fighting tears. I wish like hell I could hug him.

Then the back doors are closing. I watch through the third-story windows as a thrashing and screaming Gigi is dragged off by an orderly. A few feet away, Gaspard raises a thin hand in farewell. It's the first time he's ever acknowledged me.

He turns and shuffles out of sight of the windows. Chris guns the engine and we pull away.

I don't break down until later, much later, after Chris is snoring on the sofa in the living room and I'm alone in the dark in the master bedroom, lying on the dirty sheets where he left me, in a soiled diaper that's starting to smell.

~

The next day begins the routine that passes for what I call "life."

The caregiver arrives promptly at 8am, startling Chris from a sound sleep. He'd forgotten she was coming.

"Good thing you got here when you did, or I'd be late for work," he says, scratching his belly as he leads her into the master bedroom. He sends me an irritated glance. "With all the excitement yesterday, I forgot to set my alarm."

The caregiver, a robust German woman named Maria after Julie Andrews' singing nanny character in *The Sound of Music*—I swear I couldn't make this shit up—has what I call a forceful personality. Meaning that she intimidates the holy hell out of Chris, who starts avoiding her the second after she gives him a vicious scolding for leaving me alone all night in my "state."

I like her immediately.

When she asks me how I got on before she came, I tell her my husband cared for me. She darkly mutters a few things in German that sound frightening, possibly because they're in German. Then, in English, she tells me not to worry because Maria is in charge now—as I'll come to discover, she enjoys referring to herself in the third person—and everything is going to be swell from here on out.

I think that's an exaggeration, but I don't call her on it. Right now, I need all the friends I can get.

Maria changes my diaper, bathes me, feeds me, and cleans the house, all with the masterful efficiency for which the Germans are famous. By the time Kelly comes to visit at noon, my home is sparkling, my stomach is full, and I'm—dare I say it?—in a good mood.

Or at least a non-suicidal one.

Kelly takes one look at me sitting propped up in bed and promptly bursts into tears.

"You're welcome to some of my anti-depressants," I tell her. "Now please come over here and give me a hug before I start crying, too."

She drops the bag she's carrying on the floor and runs to me. I'm engulfed in a hug and a cloud of her floral perfume.

"I'm sorry," she says, her voice choked. "I don't mean to be such a wuss. It's just so good to see you."

I know she means it's good to see me here at home and not in the awful mental institution where she'd been visiting me daily to read me books. Hemingway's books, because my real life is Opposite Land from my delusional one.

In this life, I love the macho old goat. Go figure.

"It's good to see you, too. Did you bring it?"

Sniffling, she withdraws, nods, and wipes her wet cheeks with her fingers. "Yup. Do you want me to turn it on and leave you alone, or should I stay?"

I think about that for a minute. "Will it be too weird for you to listen to? Because if you think you can handle all the gory details of my delusions, I'd like you here. Moral support and whatnot."

She says softly, "Sure, babe. I'd love to stay." After a beat, she adds, "Are you allowed to drink alcohol? Because I brought snacks and a bottle of rosé. I figured if you wanted me around while you did your recording thing, we'd probably both need some booze."

I beam at her. She's such a good fucking friend. "Nope, I'm not supposed to drink. Now crack open that bottle, pour me a big ol' glass, and settle in, because I'm gonna tell you a story that will blow. Your. *Mind.* By the way, you're in it."

"Oh God. Did I have bad hair?"

She's always had this weird insecurity about her hair, which is thick, shiny, and glorious. For some reason, she lives in fear of it all falling out.

I smile blandly at her. "I couldn't tell, because you shaved it all off in an act of radical feminism. You also grew out your armpit and leg hair and stopped wearing deodorant."

When she stares balefully at me, I sigh and give up. "I only talked to you on the phone, but you sounded like you had fabulous hair. Happy?"

She claps, then hops up from the edge of the bed to retrieve the bag she came with. From it, she produces a small tape recorder, which she sets on my lap. Then she brings out a cheese plate complete with crackers and salami, a bunch of green grapes, and the bottle of rosé.

"Wow. We're picnicking. This is awesome, Kell."

"Twist off wine caps are a genius invention," she says, cheerfully tossing the metal cap aside. It lands on the floor and rolls under the bed. I smile, imagining Maria on her hands and knees later, muttering German curses as she retrieves it.

Then Kelly stops short. Looking around, she says, "Oh fuck."

"What's wrong?"

"I didn't bring any straws!"

It takes me a second before I understand. Then I start laughing. "Then you'll just have to hold my glass for me and give me little sips whenever I demand them, won't you, nurse?"

Kelly's expression sours. "I think you're enjoying that idea a little too much, princess." She pours some of the wine into two plastic cups, then sets the bottle on my bedside table.

"Cheers," she says, tapping the cups together.

"Cheers, bitch. I love you."

"I love you, too, babe." Trying to quickly blink away the moisture in her eyes, she lifts one of the cups to my lips so I can drink.

It's cold, tart, and delicious. I swallow, smacking my lips. "Yummy. Thank you."

"You're welcome." She throws her head back and downs her entire cup of wine.

Laughing, I say, "Some things never change."

Shrugging, she pours herself another cupful. "You have to

drink rosé before it gets warm. There's nothing more depressing than room temperature pink wine."

"Except maybe the dayroom at the Rockland Psychiatric Center."

Kelly freezes in horror, looking at me with wide eyes.

"Oh stop," I say wearily. "If I can't joke about it, it'll be way worse."

After a moment, she sends me a tentative smile. "Does this mean I can still call you a nutjob like I used to before you were *technically* a nutjob?"

"I'd be offended if you didn't. Now give me another sip of my wine and turn this recorder thingy on. Let's get started."

And that's how the dictation of my memoir of catatonic psychosis began.

When it was finished five weeks later, I titled it *Until September.*

Because fate isn't the only one with a dark sense of humor.

32

ne year later

When the phone call comes, it's raining outside.

I'm in the hospital bed Chris installed in the living room because the mechanical whirr of my ventilator disturbs his sleep. As I watch through the patio doors, the rain slides down the glass in meandering silver streams, like tears. Twilight is falling, but hasn't quite engulfed the yard yet: the grass reflects glints of the setting sun. The mulberry trees shimmer and gleam.

It's a gentle rain. Soft and melancholy, blue and misty, the perfect backdrop against which to die.

At least I hope it will happen tonight. I can't bear the thought of another day of living.

Another day of living without James.

I was never able to crack the code, you see. Whatever trigger pushed me off the cliff into insanity and my visit to Rockland, I haven't been able to reproduce it.

With Kelly's help, I've spent twelve months researching the

known causes of psychosis, poring over thousands of individuals' cases in medical journals, reading everything I could find online on the subject.

But all that I discovered agreed with what Edmond told me: psychosis is a slow slide, not an abrupt snap. Almost always, a psychotic episode is preceded by gradual, progressive changes in a person's thoughts and functioning that can take anywhere from several months to several years.

And in the few cases where psychosis did seem to occur without any outward signs or triggers, the cause remained a mystery.

It's a terrible thing, living without hope. It's the worst thing imaginable. A person can survive even the most brutal physical or emotional trauma if they believe—somehow, some way—there will be an end to it. But when there's no light at the end of the tunnel, when every day is a cold, black, unending road of misery and hope is only a faint memory you once had, the only thing that can help is death.

For people in my position, death is a friend we wait for. The merciful friend whose face we long to see.

I've been waiting for quite some time now. I don't remember if it was after my throat muscles stopped working and the feeding tube was inserted into my stomach or after my lungs stopped working and the breathing tube went into my neck. Either way, I'm waiting for death to come and set me free from this wasted body and release me into the sweet relief of nothingness.

Maria answers the phone somewhere in the house. Her murmuring mingles with the patter of the rain. Then she's walking toward me with the cordless phone in her hand.

"There's a call for you," she says softly, bending over the bed. "Do you want to take it?"

I can't nod or shake my head because the muscles that

control those motions are paralyzed, but I can still blink. Our system is simple: one blink for yes, two for no.

I blink once. What the hell, let's see who wants me so late in the game.

Maria presses the speaker button on the phone. "I'm here with Olivia now, Ms. Perkins. You're on speaker. Go ahead."

Andrea Perkins is the literary agent Kelly found to represent my book. She knew a guy who knew a guy who worked at a literary agency, and she asked him if someone at his company might be interested in taking a look at my story. As it turns out, one of their agents—Andrea—had recently sold the true account of a woman who had an inflammation of the brain so severe her doctors thought she was suffering from schizophrenia and committed her to a psychiatric ward.

The book was an instant bestseller. The acquiring editor at the publishing house Andrea sold it to was in the market for a follow-up hit.

As I was a complete unknown with no publishing cred, I didn't get an advance. Chris bitched and moaned about that, but I didn't care. The money never mattered to me.

Having other people meet James did.

I wanted them to love James, too, so he could live on in their memories the way he lives on so vividly in mine. That's the only way we can ever achieve immortality. Love is what binds us together eternally, the only thing that survives after death…or the end of a psychotic episode.

And if you laugh that I think my love for James is as real as your love for your spouse or partner, just remember where love truly exists—in the mind.

"Hi, Olivia! I hope I'm not calling too late."

This evening, Ms. Perkins sounds happy. I don't read anything into her bright tone, because she's always like that. She has the personality of a terrier: smart, loyal, and easily excitable. I like her a lot.

"I just wanted to share some incredible news with you. You'll find out formally tomorrow when the lists are published, but…" She squeals in excitement. "*Until September* is a New York Times bestseller! In its first week out! Isn't that amazing?"

It is. I wish I could jump up and down and start screaming, but my heart is doing it for me, so that will have to be enough.

Maria exclaims loudly in German. Either she's happy or she just spotted a stain on the carpet. Sometimes it's hard to tell.

Andrea says, "I'll let you go, I just wanted to be the first to share the great news. Fantastic job, Olivia! We're so proud of you."

It's ironic that she's proud of me for being a head case and inventing a grand love affair, but she's getting fifteen percent of the proceeds, so I suppose it makes sense.

"We'll be in touch. Thank you, Maria. Talk to you both soon."

She clicks off. Maria hits the *End* button on the portable. Then we stare at each other in amazement as night creeps into the room.

Chris wanders in from the garage. He's talking on his cell phone, his head bent, his voice low. "Yeah, I know, honey. I love you, too. Just a little longer. No, I told you, I'll sell the house after she's—"

Dead.

He doesn't say it because he just realized Maria and I are within earshot. He freezes in guilt, but the word still hangs there in the air.

He tiptoes down the hall toward the master bedroom, closing the door quietly behind him.

Maria glares in the direction he went. "If you want, Maria will smother him in his sleep with a pillow." She looks back at me, her eyes blazing hellfire. "He is very puny. It won't be much trouble at all."

God, I love this woman.

But I don't want her getting arrested for homicide, so, very deliberately, I blink twice.

She sighs. "Psh. Anyway, Maria is also very proud of you for your accomplishment." She pats my arm. "Next you will write a murder mystery about a paralyzed woman who uses mind control to convince her caregiver to bludgeon her worthless philandering husband to death, eh? Yes. This will be another bestseller."

She turns to leave, but turns back. "Oh—Maria bought something for you today at the nursery. You're always looking at that poster, so hopefully you'll like it. It's in the car." She heads out the front door, leaving the phone on the kitchen counter.

The poster in question is the one of the lavender fields of Provence that Kelly brought to my room in the psych ward. I took it home with me and made her put it up where I could look at it every day. It's taped to the wall across from my hospital bed. The long purple rows of lavender glimmer mysteriously in the gathering gloom.

"There exists a field, beyond all notions of right and wrong. I will meet you there."

I've remembered those words so many times. Remembered the tender look in James's eyes when he spoke them, remembered the sound of his voice, so rich and full of love.

But until this moment, I've never thought of the words as a clue.

"There exists a field, beyond all notions of right and wrong. I will meet you there."

I will meet you there.

I will meet you…*there*.

In the lavender fields of Provence.

I know it's not a malfunction of my ventilator that's suddenly making it difficult to breathe.

Maria returns from outside with a large bundle in her arms. She kicks the front door closed with her foot then marches to my bedside with a wide grin on her face. "Tada! A lavender bush. What do you think of that?"

It's a large plant with a profusion of showy purple buds, their stems long and silvery, the plastic container wrapped in hideous neon green cellophane. The unmistakable scent of lavender envelops me in the most beautiful, sensual cloud.

I close my eyes and let the delicate aroma fill my lungs, my heart bursting with joy because it knows, oh it knows that finally finally *finally* the waiting is over.

"There exists a field, beyond all notions of right and wrong. I will meet you there."

I've been looking in all the wrong places. I've been searching for a trigger, when what I should've been trying to find is a much simpler thing.

The only thing that can open a locked door.

A key.

Scent is the key that unlocks our deepest memories. A single whiff of a certain perfume or freshly baked bread or even the type of mold that grew in the basement in our childhood home can transport us through time and space so we return there, to the secret place in our memory, inaccessible except through the magic of smell.

Sweet, dusky, and distinct, the fragrance of the lavender buds overwhelms me.

My nerve endings tingle. My blood rushes hot through my veins.

"There exists a field, beyond all notions of right and wrong. I will meet you there."

Maria places the bush on the table beside my bed, admires the extravagance of the flowers for a moment, their petals arranged in perfect spirals along the thin bud, then props her hands on her hips.

"Almost as good as edelweiss." Smiling, she turns to look at me. "Do you like it?"

I blink, once, long and slow.

"Good," she says, drawing the bedsheets up my thin chest. "Now I will get my dinner, and then I'll finish reading you that book Kelly left. I love that author, what's his name? Nicholas Parks. Barks? Yes, he's a very romantical writer. My favorite is the one where the old lady has Alzheimer's, the husband reads to her the story of their life, and then they die together on her bed in the old folks' home. Ah, my heart!"

She clutches her ample bosom, sighs dramatically, then waves a hand at her own silliness. "Too bad these things don't happen in real life."

I wish I had a voice, because I'd tell her *Oh, but they do, Maria. They absolutely do.*

Out in the yard in the glimmering rain, beneath the spreading branches of the mulberry tree, James stands waiting.

He's smiling. Even through the gentle evening mist, I see how brightly his eyes burn for me. That beautiful, blazing true blue.

Maria bustles off to the kitchen to start her dinner. I hear the hum of the microwave, the gentle drum of the rain on the roof.

My gaze locked with James's, I rise from the bed.

I walk to the patio doors, slide them open, and step outside. The cement is rough and cool under my bare feet. The fragrant evening air clings to my skin and hair. The edges of my gown drag over the wet grass as I walk, the beads of moisture gathering into a circle of deep blue at the hem, a blue darker than the fabric itself.

I stop an arm's reach from James and gaze at him in love and wonder. Raindrops crown his dark hair, sprinkle his wide shoulders, slide in leisurely paths down the gorgeous planes of his bare chest.

I say drily, "I should've known you wouldn't be wearing a shirt."

His beautiful smile deepens. He reaches out and gathers me

into the circle of his warm, strong arms. "And I should've known you'd be wearing this dress that almost gave me a heart attack the first time I saw you in it, sweetheart."

Gazing up into his eyes, I wind my arms around the breadth of his shoulders and smile.

The rain tapers off. Overhead, the sun breaks through the clouds. I hear the low drone of worker bees busily gathering nectar and smell the heady scent of the lavender fields rising up from the fertile earth all around.

Behind James, their military-straight rows stretch off into the distance, glowing unearthly purple and blue in the slanting sunlight until swallowed by mist.

He whispers, "I am thee and thou art me and all of one is the other. And feel now. Thou hast no heart but mine."

Euphoric, I laugh softly. "You need to come up with some original lines, pal. Are your script writers on vacation? You can't rely on Hemingway forever."

He chuckles. "Oh, yes I can." His smile fades, and his blue eyes start to burn. In a voice thick with emotion, he says, "Forever and ever, sweetheart."

He cradles my head in his hands and kisses me.

I don't look over to see myself lying frail and motionless in my hospital bed in the living room, staring out into the falling rain. I simply close my eyes and lose myself in my lover's kiss, whispering the words I know he's waiting to hear against the smiling curve of his mouth.

"I love you."

James whispers back, "I love you, too. Until the end of time."

It's a vow, a solemn promise, and the fulfillment of every dream I dared to dream.

Hand in hand, we turn our backs on the melancholy rain and walk into the waiting warmth of the lavender fields.

PART IV

"There's no one thing that's true. It's all true."
~ Ernest Hemingway

EPILOGUE

When Olivia walks into Estelle's big corner office, Estelle is sitting behind her desk, dabbing at her eyes with a hankie and sniffling.

On the desk's blotter, the manuscript is open to the final page.

Filled with sudden dread, Olivia stops short. In all the years they've known each other, she's never seen her agent cry. "Please tell me you loved the book and those are tears of happiness. I'd hate to think I took the train all the way to Manhattan just so you could fire me in person."

Blowing her nose into an embroidered handkerchief, Estelle waves her in. The motion makes her gray beehive wobble. "Sit down. Oy. Let me get myself together." She blows her nose again, honking like a goose. Then she tosses the handkerchief into the top drawer of her desk, removes a mirrored compact, flips it open, and heaves a sigh at her reflection.

"You've wrecked my face. Look at me. I'm a raccoon."

Settling into the comfortable leather chair opposite Estelle's, Olivia smiles. "Could be worse. You could look like Alice Cooper. At least raccoons are cute."

"*Cute*?" Estelle scoffs, swiping at her cheeks. "Don't they carry the plague?"

"You're thinking of squirrels."

Estelle shudders, closing the compact and placing it back inside the drawer. "I can't stand squirrels. They scare me. Those beady eyes and stumpy arms. They look like furry little T-Rexes."

"Are we going to talk about the manuscript or your fear of cute rodents?"

With a dramatic exhalation, Estelle flops back into her captain's chair, dangles her arms over the sides, and looks at Olivia with watery red eyes. "Yes, we're going to talk about the manuscript. And I'm going to start by saying this: you're evil! *Evil*, you hear me?"

Olivia knows this is good news. The more Estelle carries on about what an awful person she is, the more she loved the book.

"Oh, gawd, what am I doing?" Estelle cries, jumping up from her chair. "I didn't even give you a hug yet!"

She rounds the desk, teetering in sky-high heels. She's wearing vintage Chanel—a pink suit today—three ropes of pearls, and her glasses on a chain around her neck. Even with the heels and beehive, she doesn't reach five feet tall.

Olivia rises. They hug. Then Estelle pulls away, holds her at arms' length, and pronounces, "You're a terrible human being. How could you *do* that to me?"

"Don't take it personally. I'm doing it to everyone else, too."

Estelle throws her hands in the air. "When I got to the part where they're in the garden in Provence and the heroine looks at the calendar, I thought I'd die!"

Laughing, Olivia, shakes her head. "I think you exaggerate more than I do."

"I'm not exaggerating, you awful person. I literally gasped out loud. Then when she woke up in the psychiatric hospital, I screamed. Scared the crap out of my secretary. I almost peed my pants, and that would've been a real tragedy."

She points at her beautifully tailored Chanel slacks. "If I had, I would've sent you the dry cleaning bill. You *monster*! And don't get me started on the final chapter. That scene at the end where they're reunited in the rain—Christ on a crutch, Olivia, if you hadn't walked in when you did, I'd be lying facedown on the floor at this very moment, sobbing into the carpeting."

Thrilled by her agent's reaction, Olivia grins. "You're really earning your commission right now, you know that?"

Estelle gives her a friendly push. "I should get a raise for the trauma you just put me through. Now sit down and let's talk about. I've got a few things I think we should address before I send it out."

While Olivia sits, Estelle closes her office door then crosses to an elegant antique breakfront on the other side of the room. She swings open a cabinet on the bottom half and removes a bottle of Blanton's and two crystal glasses. Closing the cabinet with a bump of her hip, she crosses back to her desk, sits, and pours two fingers of bourbon into each glass.

As she pours, she muses, "Do you know why I love you?"

Olivia thinks about it for a moment. "Because I make you so much money?"

"Ha. Yes, of course. Other than that."

"I'm stumped."

Estelle caps the bottle, sets it aside, and pushes one of the glasses across her desk toward Olivia. "Because you're the only other person I know who thinks it's reasonable to drink bourbon at eleven o'clock on a Tuesday morning." She lifts her glass in a toast. "Here's to day drinking."

Olivia picks up her glass and smiles. "Drinking bourbon during the day doesn't make you an alcoholic. It makes you a pirate."

Estelle makes a squinty face and says, "*Arrrggh*!"

Olivia lifts her brows. "Is that supposed to be a pirate impression? Because it was awful."

"What am I, starring in a Broadway production of *Pirates of the Caribbean*? Obviously not. Acting isn't my strong suit."

She gazes lovingly at the manuscript, resting a hand atop. "Books are my strong suit, doll, and this one's a gem."

They spend a while catching up on their personal lives, then move onto business. They discuss the various editors Estelle is thinking of sending the manuscript to, how much of an advance she's planning to ask for when they get an offer to publish it, and other details. After more than a decade long partnership, Estelle has successfully sold all of Olivia's books. She knows this one will get an offer fast.

Setting her bourbon aside and turning to the beginning of the manuscript, Estelle puts her readers on her nose and references some notes she's made in the margins.

"Let's get to the important stuff first." She peers accusingly at Olivia over the rims of her glasses. "When I gave you permission to put me into this book, I had no idea you were going to make me a seventy-year-old Jewish woman."

Smiling, Olivia sips her bourbon. "You are a seventy-year-old Jewish woman."

"Exactly!" says Estelle, exasperated. "Let's take some literary license here and make me more like, say…Sharon Stone."

Olivia laughs. "Oh, you want to be hot."

"Extremely hot. In fact, Stone might be too old. A Charlize Theron lookalike's better. No—who's that youngest Kardashian, the billionaire? Make me look more like her."

"It would be really stretching the bounds of credulity to make my agent be a twenty-something reality TV star, don't you think?"

Estelle purses her lips. "I said *look* like her, not be her. And obviously we have to change my name. I've always wished I were named Seraphina. Let's go with that."

"Yeah, Seraphina's a hard no, but I'll think of another one. I just always use everyone's real names as placeholders when I'm writing characters based on people I know. It makes the characters more real to me if their names match. I was going to change all the names after you'd had a look."

"I realize that's your process," says Estelle, her expression sour. "But while we're on the subject, you have to start naming your heroes something other than James. Do you have any idea how uncomfortable it is for me to read your first drafts knowing you're writing about *your* James?"

"Why is that uncomfortable for you?"

"Hello? The sex scenes?"

"You can rest easy, because those are made up. I was simply using my imagination."

Estelle looks unconvinced. "Oh yeah? Tell me that incident in the book store in Paris was made up."

With a straight face, Olivia says, "The sex scene at Shakespeare and Company never happened."

When Estelle narrows her eyes, Olivia smiles. "That actually happened at an indie bookstore in Queens."

"I rest my case. And then there's all the dirty talk. How am I supposed to look the man in the eye next time we have dinner knowing the kinds of things he says to you in bed?"

"I never should've told you I base all my heroes on my husband."

"You don't think I would've gotten a clue, considering all your heroes start out with dark hair, blue eyes, a cleft chin, and an Energizer Bunny dick? *And they're all named James*? Be real."

Olivia laughs. "Fine. I'll change his eyes to green and give him a British accent. How's that?"

"The British accent I like. Fits in nicely with the whole assassin thing. Very 007. What about his name?"

"How about…Edward?"

Estelle crinkles her nose. "Too *Twilight.* What do you think of Brock?"

Olivia nearly spits out her sip of bourbon. "*Brock*? Dear God. Where'd you come up with that?"

"I follow this hunky model on Instagram named Brock. The man has the most magnificent breasts."

Olivia snorts. "I believe they're called pecs, Estelle."

"Whatever, they're glorious."

"Tell you what. I'll write a Regency romance just for you with main characters named Brock and Seraphina. But I'm not putting either one in this book."

Estelle waves a hand, ending that part of the discussion. "I know you'll come up with something."

She consults her notes again, flipping forward several pages until she stops and taps a manicured nail on a highlighted sentence. "Did you ever explain that tattoo on the hero's shoulder? I'm assuming the black marks under the Latin phrase were a body count of all the people he killed, but I don't think that was stated outright."

"Hmm. I'm not sure. I definitely translated the Latin, but I don't remember specifically clarifying about the marks. I'll take another look." Olivia sets her bourbon on the edge of Estelle's desk, pulls her cell phone from her handbag, and makes a note about the marks.

Nodding, Estelle flips forward another few pages. "And the foreign language he spoke—once when they were having sex, and another time she overheard it in the background when they were on the phone—what was that?"

Olivia shrugs, setting her cell on the desk and picking up her bourbon. "I don't know. Do you think it's important? I was just thinking it was part of his whole mysterious vibe."

"A sentence or two somewhere to explain it would suffice, just so readers know you didn't forget about it. Maybe his assassin's group only speaks Latin to one other, something like that."

"Noted."

They go back and forth like that for a few more minutes, until Estelle chuckles. "I noticed you made *Until September* a New York Times bestseller. Love the ambition, doll." Then she sobers, looking up. "Oh, I almost forgot—your ex-husband can't be the US Ambassador to the UN."

"Why not?"

"Because he *is* the US Ambassador to the UN—and you turned him into an arms dealer. And then into a fat, cheating auto mechanic with an alcohol problem. He'll sue you for defamation."

"Are you kidding? He loves it when I put him in my books. This is first time I've used his real job, but he'll still love it. The man can't get enough of himself in print."

Estelle wags a finger at her. "No can do. I know you and Chris are on good terms, but any publisher will insist you change it. The potential liability is too big."

Olivia sighs. She knows this isn't a fight she can win.

Scanning over more of her notes, Estelle continues. "The red pill/blue pill *Matrix* reference won't need permission because you're not directly quoting the film, and neither will the lines from Dostoevsky because they're in the public domain, or the Rumi meet-me-in-the-field thing because he's been dead for centuries. But you'll have to get in touch with Simon and Schuster for permission to use the Hemingway quotes."

"Already got it. They were really nice, too."

Estelle nods, pleased. "Good to know. Okay, that's all I've got."

She closes the manuscript, picks up her bourbon, and smiles. "A book within a book. I love how you continue to stretch your own narrative conventions."

"I was going to go full *Inception* and make it a book within a book within a book and have another ending after the lovers meet again in the rain."

Estelle looks intrigued. "Really? What would've been the additional ending?"

"Us, doing exactly what we're doing now."

Estelle is confused for a moment, then her eyes widen and her mouth forms the shape of an O. "*Yes*. Do it! Margaret Atwood had three books going on at once in *The Blind Assassin* and it won the Man Booker Prize."

"You think so?"

Estelle nods vigorously, her beehive bobbing. "Definitely. How long do you think it will take to write it?"

"Not long, considering it will basically be me transcribing this meeting and whatever happens for the rest of today."

Estelle says, "Transcribing this meeting? I guess I'd better figure out something interesting to do then, hadn't I?" She looks around her office, as if for ideas, but immediately gives up. "Nah. I've got nothing." When she looks back at Olivia, a knowing smile creeps over her face. "Guess you and that hot hubby of yours will have to make up for it."

"I thought you said reading about my sex life makes you uncomfortable?"

"It does, doll." She laughs. "But what a way to end a book."

They toast to happy endings and finish the rest of their drinks.

After lunch at Estelle's favorite Asian-whatever fusion restaurant near her office, the two women part ways with a hug. Estelle returns to work, Olivia to the commuter train that will carry her home to the suburbs.

She works during the ride, reading her manuscript again on

her Kindle. She makes a note to ask Estelle her opinion about how she addresses the audience directly as "you" several times, breaking the fourth wall and risking making the reader aware of the narration, and makes a few other notes to change this word or that.

Every time Olivia rereads a manuscript, something new jumps out that she feels needs to be changed. It's a never-ending process. Every book she's written has been published with something she's still not satisfied with, but she's learned over the years that the perfect book doesn't exist.

Unlike the perfect man, who definitely *does* exist, despite what her character Edmond would have to say on the subject.

Olivia doesn't know if it's coincidence that she happened to be having brunch at that particular restaurant on that particular day with her girlfriends or if fate intervened on her behalf. All she knows is that she glanced up from her eggs benedict and found a gorgeous stranger staring at her from across a room full of people…staring at her with the most beautiful blue eyes she'd ever seen.

Her heart beating painfully hard, she stared right back.

It wasn't until her girlfriend nudged her with a laugh that Olivia realized she and the handsome stranger had been gazing at each other, mesmerized, for quite some time.

Every love story has a beginning. That was theirs. One look, one locked gaze, and they were both done for.

Until that magical moment, she didn't believe love at first sight existed. She didn't believe in soul mates, or happily-ever-afters, or something as idealistic as true love.

Because it's childish to believe in a fairytale…until suddenly you're starring in one.

With a wink and a chuckle, her husband would later tell people who asked how they'd met that Olivia had thrown herself at him. The reality was the opposite. After the end of brunch when she and her girlfriends were leaving, the handsome stranger followed her out to the valet stand where she was waiting for her car. As Olivia's astonished girlfriends looked on, he boldly asked her on a date—before even asking her name or introducing himself.

Actually, he didn't ask. He demanded. "Go on a date with me," were his exact words.

Because…bossy.

When she replied that she didn't date strange men, he had a quick answer. "I'm not strange. Unless you like that, in which case I definitely am."

He grinned. She laughed.

They moved in together two weeks later.

In all the years since, they haven't spent a single night apart.

"Honey, I'm home!"

Olivia's voice echoes in the empty foyer of their 1920s Craftsman, which they've been renovating since they moved in. It's an endless project: as soon as one thing is fixed, another falls apart. But she loves it in the way one loves an old friend, all its eccentricities only adding to its charm.

"In here!"

She follows the faint sound of James's voice past the living room and kitchen toward the back of the house. She should've known he'd still be in his studio. He usually doesn't emerge until it's time for dinner. Pausing outside the closed door of attached garage they converted to a work space, she lightly knocks then pops her head in.

James has his back to the door. In paint-splattered jeans, bare feet, and no shirt, he stands gazing at his work in progress, a canvas that stretches the entire length of the room and nearly to the ceiling. It's a gorgeous abstract splash of colors, but in terms of sheer beauty, it's no match for him.

His bare back is a masterpiece. And his ass…

James turns his head and looks at his wife over his shoulder. "That was a big sigh. Your meeting with Estelle go okay?"

She smiles. "The meeting went great. And I won't tell you what the sigh was about, because I don't need your ego getting any bigger than it already is."

He grins, flashing a dimple in his cheek. "Yeah, I know. I'm irresistible. Get your butt over here and give me my kiss."

Pretending to be stern, Olivia walks a few feet into the room and crosses her arms over her chest. "Excuse me, Romeo, but I'm not a dog. I don't obey on command."

James turns, sets his paintbrush on his messy work table, wipes his hands on a rag, and strolls toward her. His grin grows wider. His blue eyes sparkle with mischief. Reaching her, he takes her into his arms.

"No, you're definitely not a dog, sweetheart," he says, pressing a soft kiss to her lips. His voice drops and his eyes start to burn. "But we both know you *do* obey on command."

She winds her arms around his shoulders and tries hard to keep the smile off her face. "Only in bed. Which we're not currently in. So quit bossing me around and use your manners."

He acts confused. "Manners? Not familiar with the word."

He kisses her again, deeper this time, threading his fingers into the mass of her dark hair. When he breaks away several moments later, they're both breathing harder. He murmurs, "And anything can be a bed. That couch, for instance. The armchair in the corner. The floor."

Though they've made love on every piece of furniture in the room, the floor is a brand new suggestion. Her laugh is husky. "I'm way too old to be having sex on a floor, thank you very much. I could hurt myself. Break a hip. Bruise the peach."

James takes a big handful of her ass and squeezes. "Guess we'll have to find you a mattress, then, you geezer."

In a swift, practiced movement, he bends and lifts her into his arms.

Laughing, Olivia clings to his shoulders as he strides out of the garage and into the house. "Wow, somebody ate their Wheaties this morning!"

"I missed you," he says, heading for the bedroom.

"Missed me? I was gone for four hours! By the way, Estelle thinks I should name your character Brock."

James sends her a horrified look. "*Brock*? Jesus. Is this new book of yours about a gay porn star?"

"No. Guess what I made you."

On mutual agreement, James doesn't read any of her books. If she'd write a novel that didn't feature some version of him as the main character, he might, but unlike her ex-husband, he finds the idea of reading about himself too weird.

Gargantuan ego notwithstanding, he's actually quite modest.

He says, "A rock star?"

"No, silly. I already did that."

"Oh. Right. Okay, um…a race car driver?"

"Something hotter!"

"Hotter than a race car driver?" He sounds impressed. "I must be keeping my woman satisfied if she's turning me into a fictional guy who's hotter than a race car driver."

Olivia rolls her eyes. "Just because you're obsessed with Formula One racing doesn't mean everyone else is, honey."

He turns sideways to carry her through the bedroom door. "So you've already made me a rock star, a bodyguard, a Special-Ops badass, an Italian fashion tycoon, the head of a bourbon empire—"

"Oh, look who's keeping track!"

He grins at her teasing tone. Stopping at the edge of the mattress, he sets her down on the bed, then stretches out on top of her. Smiling into her eyes, he says, "How 'bout an astronaut? I've always wanted to be an astronaut. That'd be so cool."

"Astronauts were cool in the fifties."

"Brad Pitt's gonna be an astronaut in his new movie."

"Oh." She can't find fault in that logic. "Okay, maybe astronauts *are* cool. But what I made you this time is even cooler than that."

He kisses her deeply, settling his weight between her spread thighs. She twines her fingers into his hair and melts into the mattress, sighing in pleasure.

"Tell me," he commands, biting her lower lip.

She closes her eyes, reveling in the feeling of his warm mouth moving over her jaw and down her neck. He nuzzles her cleavage, inhaling her scent.

As he licks the upper curve of her breast, she whispers, "An assassin."

James stills for a moment. "You made me a guy who kills people?"

She hurries to explain. "Only bad ones who deserve it. And no women or children. You have an iron-clad rule about that. And you're also an artist who gives money to charities for victims of violence."

That seems to satisfy him, because he unbuttons the top few buttons of her blouse and eases her bra aside so he can access her hardening nipple. "I'm so complex. Did I have any awesome tattoos?"

She gasps when he draws her nipple into the wet heat of his mouth, then giggles. In real life, he'd love to get a tattoo, but the man is deathly afraid of needles.

A nurse once told her that it's always the biggest, baddest guys who get queasy at the sight of needles. Olivia finds the pairing of swaggering machismo and boyish vulnerability utterly irresistible.

It's probably why she loves Hemingway so much.

"Yes, I gave you an awesome tattoo, honey." She groans at the feel of his teeth scraping over her sensitive skin. "And a twelve-inch dick."

Against her breasts, he bursts into laughter. "*Twelve inches*?"

"What? You're almost that big."

Incredulous, he looks up at her. "Uh, *no*. Thank you very much, I'm truly flattered, but I don't have a foot-long cock."

"Really?" Olivia frowns. "It feels like you do."

He dissolves into laughter, resting his forehead against her chest and giving himself over to it for so long that Olivia starts to get irritated. "It's not that funny!"

"Yes, it actually is."

"Why?"

"Because you're always griping about my huge ego, and then you go and say something like that."

She says prissily, "Fine. From now on, I'm only giving you a tiny little Vienna sausage of a dick. Three inches at most. Satisfied?"

Alarmed, he raises his head. "Let's not get carried away, now. A regular-sized dick will work fine."

"If you think my audience is interested in reading about a hero's 'regular-sized' dick, you've got another thing coming."

"Think."

When Olivia only smiles at him, James says, "The correct phrase is, 'you've got another think coming.'"

"So you've told me, honey," she murmurs, her chest expanding with love.

He examines her expression. "Why do you have little red confetti hearts for eyes right now?"

She doesn't tell him it's because her real life is even better than fiction. His ego is already too big. She decides to distract him instead. "I was just wondering if we were going to try that beautiful sex jewelry you got me for our anniversary that we haven't broken out yet."

James's smile comes on slow and heated. "The butterfly clamps? I thought you were worried they'd cut off circulation to your delicate lady parts."

Drawing his head down, she whispers against his mouth, "I know you'll take care of me."

Their kiss is long and passionate. She writhes underneath him, rocking her hips into his erection, making small noises of need in the back of her throat. When they come up for air, James rasps, "Slow and sweet?"

"No," replies his wife, reaching between them for his zipper. "Hard and fast first. We'll save slow and sweet for the jewelry."

His cock is hard and hot in her hand. She's too eager to waste time removing her panties, so she simply pushes them aside and guides him inside her.

They share a groan then another kiss. Then, with his hands framing her face and his hips thrusting, James whispers into her ear, "Did you decide on a title for this new novel of yours?"

Olivia arches her back and closes her eyes. "*Perfect Strangers*."

It's a long time before either of them can form coherent words again.

When she arrives home from school several hours later, Emmie isn't at all surprised to hear the sound of her mother and stepfather's lovemaking coming from behind their closed bedroom door.

AFTERWORD

Thank you for reading! For notifications of new releases, please sign up for my newsletter.

ACKNOWLEDGMENTS

This novel was inspired by the cover photo. I was browsing a stock photo site, took one look at it, and was floored. There's something so ethereal about the light—like maybe he's a ghost? An angel? A dream?—and the intensity of their emotions just leapt out and grabbed me. I asked my cover designer to add some rain, and voilà. The cover is the scene at the end of act three when James and Olivia are reunited and head back to the lavender fields in Provence.

Originally, James was really going to have ALS, but then in the middle of chapter ten Olivia asked him about his tattoo and I went—wait. WAIT JUST A MINUTE NOW. What if the secret he's hiding isn't that he's sick...*but that he's an assassin*? I have no idea why, that's just how my brain works. So off we went. I hope you enjoyed their very twisty journey.

And yes, because truth *is* stranger than fiction, the very first words my husband ever spoke to me were, "Go on a date with me." The story about how Olivia and James stared at each other across the restaurant, he followed her out to her car and demanded a date, and they moved in together a few weeks later is true, only it happened to me.

My girlfriends thought I'd totally lost my mind, but when you know, you know. We've been married nearly twenty years now and have never spent a night apart. He's the reason I write romance.

Thank you, Jay, for everything. I promise I'll never name you Brock.

Thank you to Letitia Hasser for your wonderful work and professionalism. I appreciate you accommodating all my changes.

Thanks to my wonderful readers for your support! It truly means the world to me.

Big thanks also to my Facebook reader group, Geissinger's Gang, for being so much fun to hang out with and showing so much enthusiasm for these people I create in my head.

During the writing of this book, I used many different sources in researching ALS and psychosis, but two of the most helpful were the ALS Association (www.alsa.org) and the National Alliance on Mental Illness (www.nami.org). However, this is a novel—hence fiction—and I'm not a physician. Creative license was taken.

ABOUT THE AUTHOR

J.T. Geissinger is a #1 international and Amazon Charts best-selling author of emotionally charged romance and women's fiction. Ranging from funny, feisty romcoms to intense erotic thrillers, her books have sold over ten million copies worldwide and been translated into more than twenty languages.

She is a three-time finalist in both contemporary and paranormal romance for the RITA® Award, the highest distinction in romance fiction from the Romance Writers of America®. She is also the recipient of the Prism Award for Best First Book, the Golden Quill Award for Best Paranormal/Urban Fantasy, and the HOLT Medallion for best Erotic Romance.

Find a full book list and reading order at www.jtgeissinger.com

Made in United States
North Haven, CT
23 September 2023